CROSSING THE FORD

CROSSING THE FORD

A NOVEL

GAIL HERTZOG

Printed in the United States of America
ISBN: 978-1-7370858-0-5 (softcover)
ISBN: 978-1-7370858-1-2 (e-book)

Long-Legged Something Press
Winnemucca, Nevada
https://www.longleggedsomething.com
10 9 8 7 6 5 4 3 2

Book Designer: Vicky Vaughn Shea, Ponderosa Pine Design
Publishing Consultant: Jacelyn Rye
Illustrator: Theodocia Swecker
Cover Art: Brian Hertzog
Author Photo: Jerry Hirsch
Address permission request to: gail@longleggedsomething.com

To purchase multiple copies of this book:
gail@longleggedsomething.com

Library of Congress Registration Number: TXu 2-244-053

To my dear sisters,

Devona Hertzog Brannan
&
Sharon Hertzog Yeager

Remember what it was to be me.

—Joan Didion

Prologue

Dear Ruby,   May 21, 1894

Reno

I hope you are doing all right. I am fine here. I been working pretty steady and making a go of it here. My work is the
same every day and my days are long, but the boss is fair. I load
cattle on the train cars all day long. It is hot and dusty work.
Ruby, you would never believe how many head of cattle we ship
every day.

I am renting a room right now, but I have my eye on a little
house down the way. It's down close to the Truckee. It has a
good well and a couple little sheds and corrals. I am saving all
my money and trying to get enough gathered up to buy the
place. Hopefully it will still be for sale by the time I am ready.
Don't think I am writing to ask for money. I will make my own
way. I just wanted to let you know I am still kicking.

I don't have any bad feelings toward you, Ruby. I wish I
could hear from you. We all want to hear from you. I will come
visit one of these days if you say it is all right. I could come there
for Christmas.

Your son,
Tom

CHAPTER 1

Now, who sent you here, Miss? Miss Ramsey? And why did she do that?

I never heard of the National Association of Army Nurses of the Civil War. Maybe someone ought to tell them that the war is over.

I am sick, but I didn't ask for anyone to come sit with me. What will you do all day, sitting here? Surely, you don't really plan to come every day! When will I sleep?

Well, whatever it is, it doesn't hurt. I just can't breathe good, and I don't have any strength. I'm weak, Miss, and can't do anything. Makes me furious, too! I hate being like this. No, I don't want a doctor. I just want to let go of my earthly frame and go on, you know? I just want to go on. I'm ready to go on.

Well, I wish these do-gooders would check in with a person before they send in the saviors. That Jessie Ramsey thinks she knows what's best for everyone in town! What a relief to know that I don't have to worry about my business since Jessie is doing it for me.

Fine, you can come sit here, but don't expect me to do any

talking. I'm not the talkative sort. I keep to myself. We'll just sit here in silence.

Yes, tea would be nice. You'll have to go put the kettle on downstairs.

No, I'm not hungry. I only eat once a day these days. Just any old thing. I'm sure Jessie thinks I'm starving to death. There's not much to cook down there anyway. There are some canned goods in the larder. You could warm something up for me, I guess.

I've lived here for years and years, Miss. Came here from Kansas as a young, married woman some thirty years ago now. Oh, times were much harder then. Nothing like these days.

I'll tell you a little, Miss, but I'm not going to lay here and prattle all day.

CHAPTER 2

"James! James, get in here and watch these babies! Come on! Right now!" I yelled at James like that, though he never listened much.

"James, right now! I'm going down to watch the train come in. Come keep an eye on these babies."

"Do it yourself, Ruby. They're your babies. I'm not coming in," he said. He turned his scrawny frame away from me. He had taken his shirt off to chop some kindling, and his ribs and collar bones stuck out like anything. He was a scarecrow of a boy, not as big as most fifteen-year-olds; scary skinny, but that wasn't my fault.

"You get in here right now, or I'm going to kick a slat out of you! Right now. If the babies start to fuss, give them each a syrup rag to suck on. We got no milk."

Sometimes it seemed like the walls closed in on me, the babies toddling after me and yammering for something to eat; always tugging on my skirts, plus taking care of Frank's boys;

cooking for them or tending to them when they were sick. I just
had to get out! So, I took to leaving the babies with James, or
sometimes Tom, though looking back on it, Tom was really too
young to be left with the babies. He was only six or seven, and
stunted in growth to boot. So, I took to walking down to the
Post Office of an afternoon—watch a train roll in. I would sit
on the bench there, just to see who was about. Not that I mind
after my neighbors, but just to see what was going on in town
that day.

Early spring, it was. I sat waiting to see the 2:17 come in.
There was not much going on in the Ford then, and it was a
common practice to watch a train roll in. Lots of times folks
were expecting freight off the train and what all.

Anyway, it was hot that day, even for spring. We were in
dust up to our elbows. Railroad Street was always some kind of
mess then—either too dry or too wet. That day the dust hung in
the air until it settled to coat shoes and faces and everything in
between; it lay in the wheel ruts like mounds of flour.

The train chuffed, heat waves boiling up to the sky and
making the cottonwoods seem to wobble. Every person who
stepped off that train looked near dead, for the heat was
miserable indeed; cattlemen in sweat-stained shirts; women
dragging children and lugging bags as they left the platform.
Just regular people, that is, until that little lady lighted off the
car. I first saw her coming out of the fancy passenger car—the
Pullman. The conductor helped her down, bowing and scraping like she was the Queen of Sheba. She held her skirt with
one hand and grasped his hand with the other, her black gloves
reaching just to her slender wrist. She kept her gaze down at

the car steps, so I couldn't see her face right off, but she was a sight just the same.

She was a doll of a lady, petite, as they say. A little bird of a thing, dressed in a travel suit of what we called bottle green; rich, Merino wool with a bustle. A man could span her waist with his hands. The jacket had a wide lapel, and her shining, white shirt-waist was made of cambric, with little pintucks all up the front. Her black, felt hat with its flouncy feathers swept up above her eyes, and the whole creation was finished off with flowing, black netting going down her back to her shoulder blades.

Well, yes, Miss, it was bottle green, deep and rich, and she was as neat as a bandbox; nary a spot on her. Nothing like the rest of the passengers that day. She was different all right.

And Miss, she wore her hair tucked under her hat and tied up off her neck so that it just peeked out here and there and under the hat netting. It was deep red, and it wound and twisted, with a bit of it escaping behind her ear and curling along her neck.

She looked all around the platform, acting like she owned the place. You could tell she had traveled some and had landed on strange ground before, for she was not afraid. Right then Mr. Ferris came running up to her. He said something, and she put her hand out so he could shake it. He took just the tips of her fingers in his hand and began bobbing his head at her every word. I could not hear what she said, but she was pointing at the train and then pointing up across the tracks. Mr. Ferris continued bobbing his head like anything.

Next thing you know, the Ferris boys jumped into a freight car and started unloading dusty crates and brass-bound trunks and heavy furniture and I don't know what all. I had never seen such a collection of household goods. Quite fine and rich, they were, from what I could see! Ferris ran for his freight wagon over by the Martin Hotel. I had not even noticed it parked over there in the shade of the old cottonwoods, and Miss, I notice everything.

Then you know what she did? She kind of pinched her skirt with her fingers and just picked it up off the floor *one* inch, walking down from the platform to the street. She crossed over and headed for the Lafayette. Do you know the Lafayette? It was a decent hotel in its day. It's a might run down now, but back then it was a fine place to stay with private guest rooms and a dining hall with good food and service.

Right then, just as she crossed the road to the Lafayette, Valentine came walking out of the dry goods on the other side of the road. He meandered over, minding his own business, heading who knows where. Valentine always kept to himself, and no one knew much about him anyway. Now, from where I sat, I could see them both. As long as I live, I will never forget what happened next.

Here comes lanky old Valentine, wearing that blank look on his face that folks get when they aren't thinking of anything in particular. I remember looking at his hands. Valentine had masculine hands that had seen their share of hard work. Yes, worn hands.

He looked up and spotted that little gal and at the same time she turned her head and looked at him. The feathers on top of her hat quivered, she holding on to her skirt. Their eyes locked onto each other, and then the strangest thing happened. Now,

I'm not crazy, but I do see things—notice things that other people might miss, so I have seen plenty. But nothing like this.

When those two people saw each other, everyone and everything just froze up. You couldn't hear a thing—no train, no harness jingling, no voice, no sound. Valentine was paralyzed in the street, midstride; one foot stuck out in front of him, so he was kind of perched in the air.

The only thing I could move was my eyes, for I was frozen, too! I watched them two people. The lady looked at Valentine with an irritated frown on her face. Valentine stood there with his big paws hanging at his sides, kind of helpless. His fingers were half-curled and I swear, they exposed his very soul.

My heart knocked against my ribs at the sight! Somehow, Valentine unfroze enough to put his foot down hard, like someone who had missed a step. He raised one arm toward the lady, those curved fingers still the same. He bent forward a little from the waist, and I thought, "*That Valentine must have been a fine gentleman once.*"

Valentine opened his mouth to say something, a big bubble of spit growing there. There he stood, like a statue. Even though Valentine could move a little, the magic spell continued, because when that bubble of spit broke, it went into all pointed little pieces of crystal that made tinkling bell sounds when they hit the road, like glass breaking.

The gal was too far away to see or hear all that spit, I believe, but she seemed to come out of her trance at that same moment. She moved on to the Lafayette, turning back to look at Valentine once. He still posed in the street like a jackass. He liked to got run over.

Valentine stayed just like that until that lady had walked up onto the boardwalk in front of the Lafayette, pushed the door open, walked in, and shut the door behind her. With the click of that door latch, seemed like the world started spinning again; everything picked up where it left off. The sounds came back, people moved on down the road, the train hissed. Valentine wandered off, a man in a fog. He staggered a few paces, turned in a circle, and headed back the way he had come. He was lost from that moment; he was forever lost.

Ferris brought his wagon around to the side of the freight car and his two boys began loading it up. Not long, and they had the thing full and still plenty more freight setting on the platform for the next trip. The boys hopped on the tailgate, their brogan boots dangling down. The wagon rattled across the tracks and headed up the hill toward the Sonomas.

I wondered how on Earth one person could have so many things to care for, and where would a person possibly keep all those things? I certainly would not want to be saddled with all those carved tables and fancy trifles. The houses here in the Ford didn't accommodate so many things.

Well, just except for the one fancy house up the hill. It had been built a few years earlier by some tenderfoot from Boston. It stood alone, well up the hill from town. The front of that house looked real nice, the porch trimmed with fancy woodwork around the eaves. The windows were pretty too, with colored leaded shapes of glass put together in interesting designs. It even had a stained-glass window above the front door. It seemed special indeed, and did not fit with any of the houses round here.

Yes, it was rich, but anyone with any sense would have known better than to build up there. Not a drop of water on the place. You would have to haul it up from the river. You would have to be crazy to build up there, and I guess the fellow was crazy, because he up and killed himself shortly after the house was built. No one knows why. Killed himself in the barn, I heard.

Well, you know, that house is exactly where Ferris headed with that first load of crates and all. Cross the railroad tracks and up the little road that gets you to the Sonomas; right up to the big house on the hill. All that truck would fit in there after all.

I guess Ferris finally got all those goods hauled up the hill and shoved in that big house. I hear tell he stacked empty crates and pallets in the yard, and it left quite a stack of wood to burn all winter. That's what I heard. I know there was plenty of freight. I saw it with my own eyes that day out by the Post Office.

Soon after she moved here, I heard tell that she went looking for some help. She needed a well dug, it seemed. I just shook my head when I heard that. Of course, she needed a well dug, and she was going to be digging for a long time, too. We all knew that place was dry.

Well, nothing for it, but she up and hired Valentine. I don't know the details, but I did see him slinking up that hill not long after she arrived here. I saw him stop a couple of times, and once he even turned around and headed back to town. But then, no, he headed back to the house again. It seemed like the house frowned down on him; telling him to turn around and go back to the Ford. I guess Valentine didn't listen though, because I followed a ways. Well, not followed exactly, but I was looking for Indian camp remains out in the sagebrush. Once in a while I found an arrowhead or a grinding stone or something. I liked to collect them to study them close; it kept my mind occupied. So, I hunted around in the brush and I watched him go.

Straight to the front door he went, and rapped right sharp. Then he waited, and I swear if he didn't look like a schoolboy waiting for a whipping. He took off his hat and sort of paced around the porch, waiting. His hat had made a ring round his head, and his black hair curled behind his ear. Durn if my heart didn't skip a little to see him like that, like anything could have brought him to the ground right then; like he was weak and afraid, and I thought, *Well Valentine, you are something amazing to see. Like a great, tall schoolboy.*

We waited and waited. I mean, he waited. Seemed like that door never would open, but then here she came around the side of the house. She was not so fine now, let me tell you. No ma'am, she was about a mess. Her hair flew all wild, her eyes snapped, and she was fit to be tied. She came stomping around the corner, and I don't know what she was saying, but it may have been curse words. Yes, cursing. I think she was. Valentine, he turned white and he started working his hat into a rag, and then it happened again. They saw each other, they sucked in some air, and they froze. They just stared at each other like they were so surprised to run into each other; like no other human could have showed up, but here was one.

Oh, right then I felt so sorry to be out there. I did not know what was going on, but I did not feel it was fit for my eyes. No, but I could not move. If I had, they surely would have spotted me out there in the brush, and then they would have got the wrong idea. They surely would have thought that I was spying after them, so I stayed quiet. Luck was with me because I hunkered down behind the brush looking for arrowheads.

As soon as Valentine got his wits about him a bit, here appeared right in front of my eyes the same gentlemanly person I had seen on the street. His shoulders straightened, and Valentine was a big shouldered man. He stood up tall and sort of bowed from the waist, saying something to her. I could not hear exactly what he said, but I could hear his deep rumbling voice carrying on the air. Valentine was a fine man, Miss, as handsome as paint, even with his hat ring round his head.

The woman seemed to gather her wits about her as well. She brushed her hair out of her face, took a big breath, and straightened her skirts. She moved right up on the porch and shook hands with Valentine. His big paw swallowed her dainty hand, and then he did something odd. He grabbed hold of her arm with his other hand. I had never seen the like. It did not seem right to me; over the line of kind manners to familiarity if you ask me.

I believe that it is not right to be jealous of people, and I don't think I felt truly jealous, but there was a pang. I saw something happening when those two strangers met, and it made me feel so low, and right fast too. All of a sudden, I felt so lonely and so crestfallen, you might say. I swayed on my feet, near about sick with it. Thank the good Lord, she opened the front door and motioned him to follow her inside. He followed, and the door snapped shut.

I don't know what in the world grew out in that brush, but I was seized with an affliction right then that made my eyes sting like anything. I could barely find my way down the hill and back to the Ford, and the whole time I wound through the sage-brush, I wondered what those two were saying to each other up there in that big house.

CHAPTER 3

Well, to hear tell, Valentine woke up one day, and he had gone dead blind in his left eye, just like that. No accident or anything, but just up and went blind. I did not see this myself, of course. I only heard about it from the folks down at the mercantile. It was Ferris who first said about Valentine waking up half-blind. Ferris made quite a career of standing around the merc, discussing the people of the Ford. Lots of times when I walked in there, everyone got quiet real sudden, and I knew they had been talking about me and Frank. We provided quite a lot of entertainment, I am sure.

"Yes," he says. "Valentine has lost his sight in one eye. He can't work at all."

"What? What do you mean, lost his sight?" I had a sick feeling in my gut, for right away I connected his trouble to him laying eyes on the little gal lighting off the train, and how funny everything turned when he did. "Which eye? Completely blind?" I asked, and I sat down quick on the stool by the wood stove.

"Yes, stone blind. He went to see Dr. Brock about it. I guess the doctor said there's nothing for it. Says the path between Valentine's eye and his brain is damaged. I don't know what'll become of Valentine now." I swear, Ferris was so pleased with the news! Some folks revel in other folks troubles, Miss, though he did allow, "It's a good thing his other eye is holding up, at least for now."

Now, any fool knows that a man needs two eyes to make a go of it in this country. I felt right sorry for Valentine, big fellow like that. What on Earth would he do? I knew he worked up on the hill for the lady, but how long could that last? Why, he was apt to walk right out of the hayloft with no eyes!

I walked clear up there to check on him. Clear up to the house, I mean, and I did it out of care for other folks. But you know what? When I got close to that house, I stopped in my tracks, I did. The strangest feeling came over me. I could not get closer. I felt as if I might drop on the spot.

So, I just stood there for a bit, looking the place over. What a place, too! I could not understand that house; not in a town like this. Why, there was fine furniture for out of doors on the porch; a fine chair and settee with pillows, and a glass-topped tea table. There were delicate lace curtains hanging in the open windows, billowing out with the breeze. All the sagebrush had long ago been cleaned out all around the house, and a pretty whitewashed picket fence surrounded the dooryard. The dirt in the yard was smooth and mostly free of weeds.

Not a sound though. I thought the house must be empty, for sure. That's why I didn't bother to knock. Why, no one was home, I was sure of it. I had already walked so far, and I was so very hot. After I caught my breath, I managed to wander up on the porch, just to get out of the sun for a minute. Once I was close to the house, I listened careful, just to make sure, don't you know. And no, not a sound from within. It was an accident really, but just then those lace curtains blew open, and that's when I saw them. As familiar as you please, and him a hired hand! She sat on her velvet settee in the front room, and that big old Valentine sprawled across it, his long legs half hanging off the settee. Why, he slept with his head in her lap. Yes, I tell you, his head in her lap.

That wasn't even the worst of it. She held her hand above his forehead, but not touching it; she with such a set expression on her face, fierce and determined; he sleeping like the dead. Her hand just hovered there. It struck me very strange, and frightening at the same time.

I could not help but stare. There they were, she looking so grave and him looking like an old sheepdog napping under the porch. His feet even jumped a couple of times. I guess Valentine chased rabbits in his dreams, too. Then, Valentine turned on his side and cupped her thigh with his paw. It was so natural for him to do. She did not budge.

Now Miss, far be it from me to judge folks, but there was something unnatural about that whole picture I saw through the lace curtains. But you know the thing that always puzzled me? Why, Valentine got his sight back right soon after that. Yes, ma'am, his sight was restored. To hear tell, he woke up one morning, and he could see as clear as you and me.

CHAPTER 4

Back in those days, the Ford was a busier place than it is now. The Ford's almost dead now, but it used to be growing and thriving on the cattle business and mining and what all. We had a lot of people traipsing round the country after the war. Lots of folks were just trying to find a place to light—a place to belong again and forget those hardships. When the railroad came through here, it just looked like nothing could stop the Ford from growing into a nice town. Seemed like a good thing then.

Our little town sets in between the Sonoma Mountains to the east there, and the river to the west, and then Frenchman's Mountain beyond. It was much like you see it now, Miss. There wasn't much more than Railroad Street and Coffey Street and the railroad siding back then. The Chinamen lived on the north edge of town, and had their own little town there. Most the Paiutes had been run off, and the Shoshone were mostly gone too, but a few camped out south of town and wandered in every once in a while.

Well, I didn't really know where Valentine came from. He just showed up one time, like so many other people here. I don't rightly remember what year he even got here. Let's see. When would that have been? I was well settled here, and the babies were real little. They were born in '68, so I guess that was right around then when Valentine come to the Ford. I'd say he was about thirty years old or so; not much gray to his hair or many lines to his face.

I kept busy with young ones, and didn't get around much, but I saw him for the first time at the mill. He leaned against the wall, looking for all the world like he ran the place, and maybe he did. He was a man of few words, but his crooked smile could disarm even the most somber. He had a look about him then; sort of a haunted look around his eyes, like he had things needed forgetting.

When people moved here to the Ford in those days, it was best not to ask too many questions. Most people were looking for a fresh start. I think that is how it was with Valentine. He didn't have much to say and folks didn't have much to ask. He did have a bit of a southern sound to him though, and that is why I thought he came from Georgia or somewheres down there. I figured he had fought with the Rebs, not that I cared. I was way past caring about politics and bloodshed by then. I just wanted to live and let live. I just wanted to find my place here, too.

I, myself, am from Kansas, Miss. Just like everyone else, I wanted to forget the war and live in peace. I lost about everyone and everything in the war. I was done with it. I didn't care about politics anymore.

Well, as I was saying, the lady up the hill, she needed a well dug. And Valentine, he had wandered up there and got himself a job digging. Now, he got Ferris and a few young boys to help him, and that's how I heard about the dowsing. You understand dowsing? Witching?

I don't hold with it; it's nonsense really, but it is mentioned in the Good Book, so there is that. Anyhow, the interesting thing I heard is that the little gal herself did the witching. I guess she tied up her red-black hair, rolled up her sleeves, and went right out there with the men and dowsed around for quite some time. There was a little, low place out back of the house with a couple green sprigs of grass growing there, and that's where she said they should dig, and the dowsing rods said so, too.

Well, you know, they hit water within a few days. Lots of folks walked up there to see about it because it just looked like a waste of sweat to us. I went along, just to see. Valentine dredged and hoisted buckets of mud. What a sight; a mess, coated in black mud up to his knees, black mud on his shoulders and chest, black mud on his face. But they found plenty of water, much to the surprise of the whole town.

Now, that little lady paraded around like the Queen of the May, and talked to folks and allowed as how she planned to grow some vegetables and some trees and I don't know what all.

"And I want to have bees! Bees and honey!" she sang out. "As soon as the well proves, I'll plant flowers everywhere!" And on and on she went. Very serious, she was, acting like she lived in Kansas City or somewhere, instead of the Ford. I kept from laughing, but just barely.

I leaned over to someone and said, "Maybe she ought to

think about growing some corn and beans instead of all those flowers. Flowers aren't much for eating." I often spoke unkindly like that.

I guess that is the day I found out her name. Kenna, named after her father, she was; a Scot. Kenna Fletcher, a water witch from Boston, but her people were Scots. That explained the black-red hair and the white skin, just as Scotch as she could be. She reached her twenty-sixth year that summer, only a year older than me. So, here I am twenty-five years later—twenty-five long years since she came here! Twenty-five years that turned me into an old woman before my time.

Those two working together on that place up there, and Valentine looking so pleased with himself under all that mud; him glancing across the way to her every few minutes; and her, acting like she didn't even notice.

Well, I must say, I am feeling poorly. I think I have told enough for today.

CHAPTER 5

Now, where was I? Oh, yes, the well digging. Well, as I said, a bunch of folks went up there to see what was going on. Valentine and those few boys had been digging for three or four days, I guess. Then Ferris, he hauled a bunch of river rock up the hill on his wagon, and that set people to talking. No need for river rock unless you got water. So, me and a few other people visiting at the merc headed up there.

That afternoon, Valentine and his crew set the rocks in the well, and durn if it didn't start filling up. Then, late in the day, Valentine brought up a half-filled bucket, and offered a cup to Kenna. She took a sip and then handed the cup right back to him. He took a sip, and they were staring and blinking and blushing, all at the same time. I felt kind of sorry for them, making a picture like that for all the Ford to see. How some ever, they determined that the water tasted sweet and good, and for some reason, we all busted out cheering, crazy like.

Then, right out, she shouted out to us all, "Now, I've a big stew cooked and a bit of bread and some pie and a good Scotch whisky. Celebrate with me, all of you!"

Her voice, her air, did not match how she looked. All prim and proper, she looked, but right then I saw that she was not. She was a wild one, that. I must say though, the idea of some food with neighbors and some music sounded very appealing to me, so we all decided to stay. A few of us women allowed as how we would run down to the Ford and get some more victuals. Ferris loaded us up, and off we went. I looked back as we were bumping down the hill. The sun slipped down toward the mountains, bathing that big house in yellow, glowing light. It looked like a dream; high pillow clouds hanging up there; it looked like heaven.

Frank had magically appeared here at the house when I got home, so I invited him up there, too.

"We're gathering at the Hill House to celebrate the new well. Come on up with us. We'll have some dinner."

Frank grumbled and glared, but when it was time to go, he came along. We brought the food back up straight away, thanks to Ferris. By then, they had set a table outside by the barn. Some of the boys laid wood for a little fire, and folks milled around, visiting; very happy, everyone was. We all ate our fill, and then some. Lots of the women had brought canned goods from their larders, so apples and applesauce and apple butter abounded. I had baked just the day before, so I brought bread and pie; apple pie. There were lots of apples there that day. Guess that's about all that we grew in the Ford in those days; apples.

It surprised me how accommodating Kenna was. Why, when we were done eating, all us women went into her house through the back door and washed up all together. And no wonder she had so many crates from all that shipping! She had stacks and stacks of plates and bowls and platters; fancy ones with tiny roses all round the edges, and plain, white ones for every day.

Her kitchen astounded us all; a dry sink and a worktable and an icebox, with no ice. Lots of shelves for her goods and dried herbs hanging on the wall; lavender and sage and thyme. She had fine linens for drying dishes and pots and skillets. Her cookstove had shining designs on the front, and it had a nice big oven for baking; a water reservoir too, soon to be filled with her own well water. Fancy paper lined the walls with tiny, pink roses and green scrollwork on it, and white boards edged the floor and the ceiling. And the ceiling! It captured us with its design of lines and circles dented in tin. I saw right away how very rich she was, and not just rich with money. Why, that woman had space and peace and her own oven. No one to tell her when or where; she ran her own life.

"Now that the well is established, I'll get water into the house," Kenna told us as we cleaned up. "I'll have Valentine put a hand pump right here!" Kenna drew her hand across the dry sink.

"You sure have nice things here in your kitchen!" said Mary Craig. "I wouldn't know what to do with all these nice dishes!"

"Well, it's funny you would say that," said Kenna. "I hardly know how to cook at all!" And she laughed a sparkly laugh and put her hand to her heart. "I have all these things, but no idea what to do with them!"

We all laughed with her, but we were looking at each other sideways. "*What in the world?*" That's what I wondered.

Once we finished clearing, we all went back outside. The men leaned around, talking men talk; cattle prices and weather. Big talk that wasn't going nowhere. Tom was running here and there, squealing and chasing other young ones. Even James was running wild, chasing some girl with long, blond braids. The babies were near filthy, toddling around in the yard. The night had turned dark and cool, and the desert air smelled sweet with sagebrush and greasewood, while a crescent moon hung over Kenna's place. It seemed like she owned that, too.

One of the boys stoked the fire, and it lighted the party. Next thing you know, Bradford and Ferris and Wade struck up some music. Wade played the mandolin and the fiddle, so he was considered an asset to the Ford. Bradford had a guitar, and Ferris borrowed Wade's mandolin, so they made a good little band.

Well, they began playing a little, and folks were talking a little louder and laughing and all. Kenna put some Scotch and little cups on the table, and most people tried a sip or two. About an hour in, a few couples commenced to dancing. Not me and Frank. Frank didn't hold with dancing, and by then he was pretty drunk, for he took a nip here and there from other folks' bottles.

"Why don't you go dance with Valentine? Or who is it you're after today?" Frank growled at me.

That was my clue to stay clear of him. I was having a good time, it is true, but I felt a little sick in my stomach. Just the same old thing; a drunk man over yonder.

Late into the night we went, more and more folks dancing on the flat, dirt place by the little barn; firelight dancing, too. Valentine leaned around like he always did, looking for all the world like he didn't care about nothing. He had washed up before dinner though, his black hair slicked back. Kenna, she wandered around with a bucket of water for all to test. We all allowed as how it was real good, and it was real good, Miss.

I don't know what song they played, but the boys were whaling away on their music, and it sounded like mountain music or foreign music or what all, and here came Kenna. She had tied up her bustle so her skirts were out of the way, but she picked them up even more so that all could see her boots and stockings, but not her garters. She began dancing a foreign dance—a dance from her lands, I guess. Her heels pounded, and she pointed her toes out in the air and she looked right pretty. She put her hands at her waist, and her hair escaped her pins like always, and she commenced to dancing and spinning, and sometimes she would put her hands up in a circle over her head. Sometimes when she pointed her toes out, I thought the whole Ford would get a glimpse of her altogether, but she somehow danced past it.

Folks were clapping in time and hollering and whooping, already falling under Kenna's spell. And she called out, "Come on! Come on!" And durn if she didn't dance over this way and that and grab people to the dance, but only women. Why, she grabbed me too, and she taught us how to do the dance. We laughed and carried on, and I felt like a girl again. Well, I was a girl, only twenty-five, but an old girl, since all my troubles weighed me down.

Anyhow, when the song ended, we were all wheezing and gulping air and laughing. Her face shined in the firelight, and she looked like she didn't belong in the Ford. She spun magic that night in the moonlight.

Well, Valentine, he walked over to Wade and said something, and Wade struck up another song a lot like the other one, and no one could believe it, but Valentine took to dancing. He showed us a dance a lot like Kenna's, but different. It seemed like a dance for men only. I don't know why I thought that, but that's what I thought. But then, no, because Kenna joined him in the dance. Next thing you know, they were flying around each other and linking arms, and a couple of times Valentine jumped clear up in the air. Who could know a man like Valentine could dance like that! But he did. He sure did. And one time when he jumped so high, Kenna let out a screech. She gave a high-pitched call—a woman-call from her lands, I guess. Then we all began screeching like wild animals; like a bunch of coyotes.

It seemed like then that Valentine quit trying to hide the way he gazed at Kenna. He stared at her in front of everybody, and seemed like he didn't care who saw him; she was flushed of face, her wild curls sticking out all different ways, and looked like she didn't care either. Seemed like folks either had to start dancing too or get the Sam Hill out of there. So, mostly we all started dancing again, but not the far lands' dance; just our folks' dancing.

On and on we danced into the wee hours, most of the young ones sleeping in wagons or even on the ground. Finally, Ferris put the mandolin in Wade's beat-up case and allowed as how he was heading down to the Ford. That was about it for everybody. Frank reeked, so drunk he could barely walk, so Ferris and Valentine flung him in the back of Ferris' wagon, and Frank was out like a light. I felt disgusted, as you can imagine. I knew what the next day would bring; a stinking drunk snoring away the day, or yelling at the young ones to make themselves scarce. I wanted to disappear right then.

So, the boys kicked dirt on the fire and all the folks wandered down the hill, or wandered off somewheres else to be alone, or I don't know. I saw Valentine head down. He was bunking in a little shack down by the river. I rode in Ferris' wagon with my drunkard, the babies lolling on my lap and the boys drowsing nearby. Kenna stood on her porch and watched us go. She looked a little forlorn then, waving goodbye to us all, her skirts still tied up a little in back, and her hair flying around.

I waved from the wagon and shouted out my appreciation, and she waved right back and called me by name. "Goodbye, Ruby! Goodbye!" she said. "Goodbye, goodbye, goodbye!" And then we were out of earshot.

CHAPTER 6

The ride down to the Ford that night seemed to last for hours, though really it passed in just a short while. We all were worn out and quiet. It was still nice and warm for so late in the night, and the moon hung low in the sky. So, down to the houses we rode, and then the wagon stopped in front of my house, this very house here. Ferris got down and sort of drug Frank in the house. Frank woke up then, and began the drunk talk. Ferris pushed him down on the bed and threw a pillow over his face, smiled crooked at me and then he strode out.

I will tell you that my heart became so heavy after that. I looked around at my sad, little house with my rag rugs and poor kitchen wares; my husband sleeping with his boots on. All size of children all around the house like a box full of puppies. It was as if I saw my whole life stretched out in front of me, and it would always be just like this. I got to where I couldn't breathe almost and I had to have some air, so I left the house right then.

At first, I didn't know where to go, but then I found myself headed back up to Kenna's. It wasn't a hard walk in that cool predawn. I crossed the tracks and wound my way through the waist-high sagebrush. It just took a short time, seeings as how it's only about a mile up there. I could see the outline of the beautiful porch and the dark house beyond; no lights at all, so I thought Kenna must already be in bed.

I walked around the side of the house to go look at the well one more time, walking very quietlike, so as not to bother Kenna. I thought a quick look at the well and the yard and all would be fine—wouldn't hurt anything, but when I came around the corner, there she stood in the night. I could see her faint outline even though it was as dark as all get out. Seem like the clouds had stacked up and blocked all the light. She stood well away from the house, her head tipped back, her hair cascading down to her waist.

I could not let on that I was there! She had already said goodbye to me in such a pleasant and kindly way. I could not show myself, so I just watched her for a minute. I just wanted to see how Kenna lived when she was alone. I wanted to see who she was.

Now Miss, you must think so many bad thoughts about me when I tell you the things I did. It is true that I did plenty wrong. I know I did. But don't think too harsh of me until you are older and have some life in your satchel. Wait and see what you do when your heart turns wild on you whilst you aren't looking.

Well, there I was, hidden in the dark like a sneak thief, skulking beside that big house with its smooth, wood siding and fancy trim circling the porch and eaves and all; with its tall windows and stories up high like in a big city mansion. There I was, hiding and watching, peeking round the corner of the house, dreaming of being someone besides who I was.

So, Kenna stood in the dark, and she looked awful serious. I could not see her face, but the set of her shoulders and the width of her step, I could tell she thought deep thoughts somewhere else. Then I saw that she wept, her shoulders shaking as she pondered very serious heartache. Now, us women know how it is, and how sometimes we cry for not much of any reason, but sometimes we cry because we know too much about life and the world and the dark hearts of us all. And mostly when you see a woman crying, you can tell which one it is. That night, when I saw her like that, I knew straight away that her heart was breaking, or maybe already broken.

Just as I turned to slink off, Kenna surprised me good, just like she always did. She tipped her head back even more and reached her arms out and said, (and I'll never forget what she said, for I didn't know if she prayed to the good Lord or some pagan god or the devil himself), but she said, "Give me then my water and my bees! Give me every good thing to grow! Give it to me!" And she bawled and carried on.

Well, that about hung the cat for me. Who runs out of doors and puts up such a fuss? It scared me, it did; scared me real good. I figured maybe she was drunk, though I had not seen her do much drinking.

Right then, what do you think? It came a rain. Oh, not a big gully washer or something, but a little, fine rain; pretty as you please, just showering down on the house and Kenna and me.

She laughed like a little girl and spun around in her rain and her heart lifted. I just watched like a simpleton. I could not blink my eyes, for she looked so beautiful. Her hair streamed down her back, dripping rain as she laughed and cried at the same time. From far away I heard the water hitting the roof.

The next day I began my own prayers, and I don't know who I prayed to any more than I know who Kenna prayed to, but I prayed so fervently and so deeply and so long and so many times that I became right tired of praying, and do you know what I prayed for, Miss? I prayed for my husband to die. God forgive me, Miss, I prayed that he would fall over dead and set me free. Yes, every day when I dug weeds, I prayed and wept. Every time I washed a shirt or swept a floor or stirred a pot, I prayed. Every time a child screamed or laughed or slept or waked up, I begged, "Give me then my dead husband."

CHAPTER 7

Well, for one thing, Miss, I was an old maid by the time I met Frank. He showed up in Lawrence about a year after the raid, and there I was, almost 20 years old and no husband or family of my own. He came snooping around, and Mama pretty much sent me off with him. My papa and my brother were dead and gone, and Mama was sickly. We lost everything after the raid. There was nowhere else for me to go, so I up and married Frank, and there he was with two young boys; James about eight, and little Tommy just toddling around. All of a sudden, I was a wife and a mother, thinking I was going to live happily ever after. Frank didn't drink so much back then, though he did have a mean streak all the same.

It is hard to even remember those times. Everything I did just seemed so hard; nothing was easy. Then I met Kenna, and it seemed like everything Kenna wanted or needed fell right into her lap.

Her well turned out to be real good, and the more she planted and watered, seemed like the more water it made. Bit by bit, her place started turning green; a willow here and a piece of grass there; a flower; a tree that Valentine dug up and brought down from Water Canyon. She planted and worked and next thing you know, she had flowers growing round her porch.

Valentine planted her a fine, big garden out back, with straight rows so that it had an organized beauty to it. Not like my little mess of a garden. No, Kenna had a beautiful garden with all manner of vegetables; different kinds of beans and beets and carrots; tomatoes and peas and cucumbers; potatoes; onions of course. And pieplant; beautiful, big-leafed pieplant.

Her corn patch was real special. They call it a Three Sisters Garden. Have you heard of that, Miss? One section of her garden was all planted up with corn, but then right in the corn grew beans—string beans with gigantic, clinging leaves and clumps of velvety beans. The bean vines liked to climb up the corn stalks, so no need to stake them—corn staked them for you. And then right in the middle of that lived all manner of squash plants, and they covered all the ground under there and kept it shaded and helped keep the weeds down, and the tall corn plants shaded the squash in turn.

It seemed like those sister plants helped each other grow in all different ways, and that corner of her garden grew more lush and full than the rest by the end of summer. You couldn't tell which plant helped which the most, but they did right good together.

Kenna had a different little garden, too, for herbs and all; spearmint and chamomile, sage, thyme and rosemary; plenty of dill and mustard. That little circle garden had rock paths between the plants, so each plant had its own little corner, of sorts. She had sweet-smelling chives and garlic, and basil for soups. She grew lots of lavender—different kinds with all pretty purple blossoms, but the lavender grew over to the side of the yard along the picket fence, and some of her lavender plants were so huge they spilled out across the sandy path.

She had her gardens and her flowers and her trees and all manner of growing things, just like her prayer, and she used her good well to keep it all watered. So, yes, Kenna's prayer was answered, but you can't catch a bee. Any fool knows that. I had never seen a bee in the Ford. Wasps, yes; yellow jackets, yes; but not just some old honey bee. They didn't live here. We all allowed as how Kenna would have to give up on that idea, or maybe she could order them in on the train and pay a fortune while she was at it. That would make for some expensive honey.

But she was set on it. Valentine took to building a bee hive out of a piece of a log, well a stump really. He worked on it while her baby garden just started to come out of the ground. He hollowed the stump out with a hatchet and made a right nice little bee house in there. He built a little pointed roof for the house, some frames inside, and Valentine had himself a hive. A hive with no bees, and not going to be no bees either.

How some ever, next thing we know, Valentine is at the Post Office picking up a package from the "Farmer's Friend Mail Order Catalog", and it's beekeeping goods. Now, you don't need those big gloves and all unless you got bees, and I straight out said so. I happened to be sitting outside the Post Office on the little bench. That Valentine, he was right cagey about it though, and wouldn't say a word; just hustled up the hill with his wares, acting like the cat that ate the canary.

There was quite a spring in his step, and I could not help admiring him. Seem like Valentine's looks improved with every passing day. Seem like he outshone every man in the Ford. I hung my head when I realized I mused like that, right out on the street for all the Ford to see, for it must have been all over my face that I loved Valentine. Dreaming of a man I could never have; hating another man I had and couldn't get rid of. It was real bad.

Well anyhow, pretty soon, a bunch of us gathered up and went up the hill to see what was what. And you know what? Kenna had bees. They buzzed and zipped and spun round Valentine's hive like Highland dancers so that we were all flabbergasted. Turns out that Valentine found a bunch of them clumped up on a fence post somewheres and smoked them into a box and brought them to the Hill House for Kenna. Who ever heard of such a thing? We didn't really believe that story. Seemed a bit farfetched, if you know what I mean.

And they were regular bees! Bees from somewheres else, and they sure didn't belong in the Ford or anywhere near the Ford. Folks looked at each other sideways and felt funny in the gut then, and wrinkled up their noses and foreheads. Very consternating, it was. Not to me though. I knew what she was.

The whole rest of that summer it went on like that. Kenna would dream something up and next thing you know, she would have it. Valentine worked the place real good, and built a corral by the barn and a wood shed by the back door and what all. He still lived in the shack down by the river, and you can bet we all watched mighty close when the sun was getting to go down; watched to see if Valentine would come down the hill and head to his shack. Every evening, here he came, walking like a man with a purpose to his life. And if he saw me, he would tip his hat and say, "Evening, Miss Ruby." And I would say back, "Valentine, good evening." And he would stride past and on down to his place.

Just about every time he built something for Kenna, we would have a gathering up there and play some music and dance some. It got to be a regular thing. Someone would say, "There's a gathering at Kenna's tonight. Bring that good cake you make." Or, "You got any of that rot-gut left? Bring that up to Kenna's tonight."

Just about every time, we would have the same good time. Seemed like I was getting to be friends with Kenna. We would talk a bit and visit and she would ask after my young ones. I guess one of the biggest times was after Valentine put up the corral. We had a big party then. We all gave them a pretty bad time because there wasn't a piece of stock on the place. What they need with a corral? But there it was, built out of poles Valentine bought off of Ferris.

I heard a couple boys joking about Kenna and her sly ways, saying, "I guess there'll be some stock in this corral come morning. I guess Kenna will conjure it up!"

CHAPTER 8

It was my habit to observe folks and see what was what, and I had been doing plenty of observing. Look like Valentine was about ready to start courting Kenna right out. Look like he had it pretty bad for her. I guess everyone in the Ford thought the same thing. I guess we all knew they were to be together.

Once I realized that, I got this panic feeling in my gut about every time I thought of Valentine. I felt like something was wrong all the time, but I couldn't quite figure out what it was. Seemed like the days kept going by, and I kept seeing Valentine picking up this or that in the Ford for Kenna, and we gather again, and there he goes. And Kenna's place looked better and better, and more like someone really lives there; still dirt in the yard and all, but it looked different. More green around there as summer wore on, more wood box, more clothesline, a root cellar, a shed, a chicken coop with no chickens. Right homey, it was. Seemed like every time Kenna wanted something, it showed up, and all the time I had less and less; like there was getting to be less and less of *me*.

Well, one night, way down in the summer, I perched on the step to my house, this house right here, Miss, and it come on me like a fit. I had to act. I had to do something to save myself, and if I didn't do it fast, Valentine would be gone to another woman, if he wasn't already. I began crying like anything. Tom, he came up to me and said, "What's the matter, Mama? You got a belly ache?" And that just made me feel worse, like I could die. I straight jumped up, dried my face with a rag, and cleaned myself up a little; tried to smooth my hair and all. Then I headed down to the river; headed to find Valentine.

I had seen Valentine around town many times. He was a bit of a fixture around the Ford, I guess you would say. We had only spoken in passing while at the merc or Post Office, but he was always nice to me, asking how I was doing and all. Whenever he talked to me, he always looked me right in the eye. Seemed like he really cared about what happened to me. Truly, I did not know him much at all. I only dreamed about the man I thought he must be. It was very wild of me to go after Valentine like I did.

Now, you know the river and the crossing is what started the Ford; just a gravel bar happened to be in the right place, or none of us would be here. But God saw fit to make a little crossing here, and that's how we got the Ford. Well, Valentine's place was not far from the actual crossing. It consisted of a little adobe box with sagging roof and crooked stovepipe sticking out; one window and a broke-down door hanging on a leather hinge. But lamp light streaked through the crack around the door that night, and a little smoke puffed from the stovepipe, so I knew Valentine was in there.

God help me, Miss, my heart about jumped out my chest. I about fainted, but I could not turn around. I thought I might just wait a minute and see what I see, like I did other times; like I did when I wanted to see Kenna. So, I stopped and stood there, and anyone could have seen me, but no one did. And I waited a bit.

I did not even know what I was going to say, Miss. I had no reason to be there, no story I could tell. I just stood there and waited.

Then Valentine opened the door and came outside. He looked quick and said, "What is it, Miss Ruby? What is the trouble?" Real nice like that. And my heart just broke open then and I began squalling again. Then Valentine took my arm and he says, "Why, Miss Ruby, whatever is the matter? Is it one of the children? What is it? Please, sit here. Let me help you." He guided me with such tenderness that I could not see nothing for the tears in my eyes. He helped me walk to his little front step and sit down, and he listened close, as attentive as any man could ever have been. I could smell his smell; clean and salty at the same time, and I could see his whiskers on his neck, his pulse beating there. My heart rolled in my chest.

He handed me his hanky, so I covered my face with it. Valentine, he sat down beside me and he says, "Now, Miss Ruby, it can't be all that bad. Nothing can be that bad."

I uncovered my face and I looked at his eyes, and straight away he knew why I was throwing such a fuss. He knew! He swallowed hard and turned red in the face.

I got right brave then, and I said straight out, "Valentine, let's us run away somewheres. Let's leave the Ford and start a new life for ourselves somewheres. I got to get out of here! What do you say, Valentine? What do you think?" I struggled for air and I felt like my eyes were shining in the moon light. I felt pretty and womanly, and I wanted Valentine right then. I leaned toward him and kissed him right on the mouth.

I will say that Valentine kissed me back. He did. My whole body shook. When he stopped kissing me, I looked up into his eyes. We locked eyes, just like him and Kenna, but the world didn't stop spinning, for Valentine did not love me.

He saw into my secret heart, yes, but he did not have the same feelings for me. He tried to look nice at me and he patted my arm and he said, "I'm sorry, Ruby. I'm so sorry, but I have feelings for another."

I said, "I know that, but you will forget her if you get away from her."

"I don't want to get away, Ruby," he said, and I saw how he loved her real bad.

"I don't care then. You can have us both. I'll share you with your precious Kenna." I hated myself for showing Valentine this ugly side of me, but the words were already out. The thought of letting him go made me sick. The thought of them together forever with me on the outside was too much for me, Miss!

Valentine kind of snorted then. "Share me, huh? What if I don't want shared? I'm not a loaf of bread, Ruby. No, I don't think so. It wouldn't be right. Not for any of us, and I would never do that to you or to Kenna. And what about Frank? What about your young ones?"

I didn't say anything then, for it seemed like I had forgot all about my babies; like they slipped my mind, and that seemed terrible. So, I just didn't say anything for a minute.

Then Valentine said, "Your offer is very tempting, believe me. You are a very handsome woman, but I count myself a gentleman, Ruby. At least I once did. I'm sorry. I'm sorry, Ruby."

"Well, that's fine," I said with my big broken heart. "That's just fine. I'll just go on with my way. But you will always know how I feel about you, Valentine DeRoo. Just remember that I loved you and would have done right by you. I will go on my way, and no one will know how I dream of you and wait for you to wander by my dooryard, but you will know. You will know."

Then I said, "I'm sorry I came here. I don't know what got into me, Valentine. I just went crazy, I guess. Sometimes my heart goes wild on me."

"I'm sorry, Ruby," he said, all sweet to me. "I'm sorry. I think you are a fine woman. It's just that I love Kenna."

"Oh, is that all? Well, I loved you long before she came here. I loved you before she ever saw you. But, that's fine. Kiss me goodbye and show me how much you love your Kenna. Or are you afraid of me, Valentine?" I asked him, and I jumped up. He jumped up too, and grabbed me by my arms. Oh, I remember how the air snapped. And I thought, *"Yes, Valentine. You love Kenna for sure, don't you!"*

Then Valentine kissed me the way a man kisses a woman when he means business. He bent my head back and liked to broke my neck. He put his hands round my waist, and I could hear him make a groan noise down in his throat, and I about floated up to the sky. I put my arms round his neck and leaned right into him. It was like a dream, Miss.

Just when I thought Valentine was going to carry me off to his little shack, he broke away from me and sort of set me away from him. I could tell he was feeling the passion and was weak in the knees and what all, but he set me from him, and he said, "Ruby, I'm sorry. I can't do this. I'm sorry."

"Are you sure? Seem to me like you want to do it!" I said back, real tart.

"Go home, Ruby. Please. Go home."

"You're a fool, Valentine. And you're going to get just what you got coming. You're going to be sorry one day. Go ahead and go to your precious Kenna," I said. "But one day you are going to be sorry!" And I said like that for a while. But Valentine would not be moved, seem like.

Finally, I turned and headed back to the house. I just turned and walked away. By then I was so fiercely angry with myself! What was I doing, going to some man's house in the night? Making a durn fool of myself, that's what. And I did not look back. My rag-thin dress hung on me and my run-down heels showed with every step. I had brown hair back then, instead of all this gray, but it lay limp and dry and it flew around my face like a bird's nest. My shoulders curved like an old lady, and my whole being burned with shame. I saw how ugly I was. I saw myself for me, and it wasn't nothing pretty, Miss. And Valentine did not offer to accompany me.

Why am I telling you this story, Miss? I don't want to tell it no more. I'm done with this story. There's no sense in going over all this again and again. I've gone over it enough. For twenty-five years, I've lived this, over and over. What's it good for? Reliving this won't change anything that happened, won't undo anything, won't free me from my guilt.

I wish that confessing all to you would help me. I really do. For I'm bound to meet my maker soon, and I carry plenty of sins on my back. But confessing to you won't bring me forgiveness. It's like those times I waited for Valentine. I torture myself, only this been a longer wait. This been a good long wait, and I'm about full up of waiting.

Oh, Miss, I am not crying for Valentine. I gave up crying after Valentine a long time ago. No, these tears are for that young woman I was! It's much better to be alone than to be lonely, and Miss, and I was lonely. There was nothing for me, and not going to be nothing. Back then, I got real mad when I finally faced that. I was hateful, and everyone around me suffered. Sometimes I wish I had done different, and sometimes I think I did just right, and sometimes I don't think about it at all.

CHAPTER 9

*W*ell, shock of all, I had a visitor this morning, and guess who it was! It was Jessie Ramsey. Yes, she was here to offer me a nurse from her fancy Nurse Association of the Civil War, or whatever she calls it. Turns out she's a nice lady! Yes, and was she surprised when I told her I already have a nurse. She's never heard of you, Miss; doesn't know you from Adam. You been lying to me this whole time. I hate a liar, Miss. Only good thing about it was the look on Jessie's face. I guess she doesn't know everything after all.

I been thinking, Miss, and I'm just wondering who you are. Who are you, really? I hear tell how you showed up here and started talking around and looking for folks with stories and folks who been in the Ford a long time. So, who are you, Miss? When are you going to tell me your story?

You think I'm a fool, Miss? You think I'm going to lay here dying and tell you all my deep, dark secrets? Now, why would I do that, Miss? What you doing here?

Well, I guess it don't matter anyway. What they going to do to *me now? Put me in jail? Ha. And it is true that telling you this old story helps me a little; lightens my load, you might say. I had reasons for doing what I done. I was forced to do what I done.*

What do you mean, 'How did it end?' Why, they got married and had babies and lived happily ever after, of course. They grew old together and died together, and their children laid them in the ground, side by side. And the children had children, and they still live up the hill, and the house rings with laughing and music.

Nah, that isn't true. That's not what happened. So, I will tell you the story, Miss, and I will tell it all, and maybe you will leave the Ford a little wiser for your trouble. Maybe you will choose your path with more care if you listen close.

See that trunk over there, Miss? Open it up. Help me sit up. Help me get over there. Let me catch my breath a minute.

Now, Miss, this trunk has all the rest of the story. Look here. These here? These are Kenna's diaries; all her deep, dark secrets. And this velvet box? The garnet necklace. These papers? Deeds to the land and the house and freight office and what all. This photograph? Their wedding picture. And this bundle tied with string here? All me and Kenna's recipes. This here? Kenna's tartan she wore on her wedding day. Let's see what else. This here? Valentine's pistol; Valentine's outlaw pistol. He had deep dark secrets too, Miss.

Back in them days, no one knew about Valentine or his past. No one knew about Kenna or what she kept hidden. They got a fresh start here in the Ford, and all that long, first summer after Kenna showed up here, we had a right nice time together, singing and dancing and all. Kenna and me, we started visiting at the gatherings, and she befriended me; treated me like a real person, talked nice to me, and I started to like her too—liked the person I was getting to know.

Of course, Valentine never told Kenna about that night down by the river. How could he? Kissing like that don't leave much room for telling! No, we kept that to ourselves. Far as I know, Kenna never knew about that.

Oh Miss, help me back to bed. I'm worn out.

CHAPTER 10

Well, anyhow, it got to be fall of that first year when Kenna moved here to the Ford, and a beautiful fall Mother Nature gave us too, with mild nights and warm days and all. The leaves turned on the cottonwoods, and the gardens finished up. I always love the Ford in the fall. It is my favorite time here; my favorite season.

Things had settled down at my house for a bit. Frank pretty much disappeared, and that suited me just fine. I made it my business to save up food for my young ones, and I made it my business to gather what I could to keep clothes on their backs and what all. I don't even remember being that worried about us. I just kept going, day after day. I put up apples. I put up beans and beets out of my garden. I dried some meat; rabbit, and Miss, I hate rabbit, but I did it anyway. I had my sourdough starter for bread and pancakes and all. I had a tab at the merc, and sometimes I would put my mainstays on my tab and worry about it later; just flour and sugar is about all. We made do.

Thank the Lord for that mean old Mrs. Ricker giving me some milk and cream now and then. And thank the Lord for them few sad, little chickens I kept out back. We made do.

So, time passed and I tried to forget the night down at the river; tried to forget what a fool I made out of myself. When I saw Valentine, we both acted like nothing ever happened. We both acted like normal neighbors, but inside, I harbored such strong attractions to Valentine, remembering how he kissed me that night and how he made that sound like a man about to give in, and sometimes I thought about that and felt better.

One day, I saw Valentine down at the lumber yard he had a little paper in his paw, as he talked to Braginton about an order. When he come walking through the Ford though, he kept to himself about it all, and wouldn't tell us a thing. He just walked on up to the hill house and left us all wondering what he was up to.

Well, next thing you know, Ferris gathered a load of rough-cut beams and boards and hauled it up the hill to Kenna's place. When I asked Ferris about his load, he said he don't know nothing. So, then there we were just wondering what Valentine was doing.

Come to find out, Kenna didn't know what he was up to either, because he was making her a special gift for her birthday. So, he shut up the empty barn and worked day after day. Curiosity got the best of me, and I wandered up that way to see what was the goings on. Kenna met me at the porch and invited me in, real nice. I said as how I would be pleased to come in there and take a rest for a minute, so we went in.

Finally, I entered that house, and not just the kitchen, and how fine it was! The floors were a rich, dark wood, just as smooth as the back of your hand, and the bottom half of all the walls covered with dark and gleaming wainscoting. The tables and lamps set here and there, just so. Right when you come in, you could see up the stairs, and how they turned a corner half-way up. A pretty rug draped the stairs with swirly reds and greens all along it going right up to the top, the stair rails turned and carved and shining with oil. In fact, every piece of wood in the place gleamed. My neck twisted this way and that, I was look-ing so fast.

Then Kenna said, real nice like she always did, "Would you like to see the house, Ruby? Would you like to look around?"

I didn't know what to say. I didn't know would it be right to go snooping around somebody's house, but then I saw that Kenna would show me, so I said, "Why, that would be real nice, Miss Kenna. I have always admired this house."

So, she started showing me around, and she showed me every room. She led me here and there, explaining everything to me, like she said, "Here's the front room, my parlor. This is my favorite room in the entire house." That's how she talked, Miss, and she smiled very sweet.

Well, Miss, lace hung in every window and lace lay on every side table and fancy kerosene lamps were dotted all round. There were leather books in tall cases and mirrors on the walls and a great family portrait of her people over the fireplace. Wood was laid for a fire, even in that mild weather, and a thick Persian rug covered the floor. Green velvet, lush and deep, covered the settee and the dainty side chair. A pretty china tea set was displayed on the middle table; the teapot tiptoeing on its curved feet, its round sides sprinkled with dainty, pink and red roses, the spout the same, only rimmed with gold. Even the air smelled sweet in that room, like furniture oil and old books and wild flowers. I could have stayed in that room forever, and it was only just the first room I saw!

Room to room we went, as Kenna showed me her things and told me about each. "This chest belonged to my mother," or "My grandmother made this quilt," or "That's a portrait of my father." It was overwhelming, but no matter how beautiful the place was, Kenna acted so humble and worked to make me at ease. She was like that. She was kind.

She had one room that resembled her parlor, but not quite so fine, and in there Kenna had her music! I did not know you could have a room just for music, but yes! She had a flat drum from her lands, a drum the size you could hold in your hand, and it had a hammer that went with it. She had another instrument, a harp, also from her far lands.

"Oh, this harp has been in my family for a long time, Ruby. I learned to play when I was a little girl. One day I will take it to a gathering! I will play a song just for you, Ruby! I'm not quite ready to play in front of everyone yet. I have to build up my nerve!" she said, and then she laughed real pretty and reached out and touched my arm. And I laughed too, as if I understood the joke.

Right next to the kitchen she had a room just for eating, or dining as Kenna would say, the table in there carved of gorgeous wood, dark and gleaming so that you could see your reflection in it. Fine chairs were pulled up all around and tucked under the table, made of the same wood, beautiful designs cut in the wood of the chair backs. To the side stood a great cabinet of the same shining wood, all filled with sparkling glassware and big platters and bowls and what all. Each dish fascinated me, and I couldn't imagine using such fine things for every day, but Kenna said yes, they were used all the time.

Then she took me up the big staircase, and I loved going up that staircase. When I turned around and looked down, why, I felt so high it made my stomach roll, but I could see the parlor and the other room and the door to the kitchen, and I thought that was the best house anyone had ever made. Every color in it shone with a special brilliance, and the light coming through the stained glass up above the front door cast magical shadows. I looked close and I could see that there was all manner of birds in that window, and it wasn't just shapes after all, and it had purple flowers and green leaves, too.

I said, "Miss Kenna, your house is so beautiful. I can't believe how beautiful it is!"

"Thank you, Ruby," she said. "I like it here, very much." We looked at each other and nodded our heads at each other, and a tie passed between us, for we were both women looking at a good place and seeing it the same and appreciating it the same.

"Now, come look at my room and see these windows!" She grabbed my arm and led me on to her room. She had a nice bed with a big mattress all stuffed with feathers and that bed stood so tall she had a little ladder to climb up. The headboard and footboard of the bed were carved wood just like everything else, with woodland images and leaves and vines. She had a dressing table with a mirror and a hair brush and a bowl for her hair pins. A fireplace laid for a fire covered one wall, its high mantel and river rock surround standing like a guard over Kenna's bed. I never seen the like. Her fine blankets draped over the edge of the mattress and her pillows leaned up against the headboard.

"Now, what do you think of these windows, Ruby? I have my own private view of the Sonomas from here! Every morning I watch the sun rise right here. It is so beautiful and so peaceful! I like to sit right here and have a cup of tea and watch the world wake up." She pointed out an oaken round table with a chair right by it. I could see how that would be so wonderful.

I looked out at the craggy Sonomas far above the Ford, with their sharp ridges and hidden green valleys, and I could just imagine watching them every morning. I pictured the sparse grass growing there, turned sere and brown by the hot sun. I could see the junipers lined along different ridges, with the sweet-smelling sagebrush covering the slopes.

"I can see how that would be so wonderful," I told her. "Yes, indeed."

Then she showed me the other rooms up there—other rooms for sleeping, but they didn't have such pretty things as her room. Nice though, with wooden beds and dressers and chests and all, and they had tall windows too, some looking out at the Sonomas and some looking down to the Ford.

When we got all finished looking, Kenna said, "Ruby, come down and let's have some tea now!" We clattered down the stairs, and went to the kitchen so Kenna could put the pot to boil. Sure enough, there stood her pretty stove in her cozy kitchen, lavender and thyme drying on the wall, her great, wooden bread bowl glinting in the light. She put some water on and got out some cups and what all. She made us a tray with cups and spoons and a plate of tiny ginger cookies with the dearest, scalloped edges you ever saw.

"Let's go to the parlor, shall we?" she said, all beautiful. I couldn't think of anything to say, so I just followed along.

We finally got settled in the parlor and to a spot where I could ask about Valentine and his load of lumber and she says, "Oh, I don't know what he's doing! It's a surprise for my birthday!" She leaned toward me, laughing all nice, like a lady.

"Oh, my!" says I, all nice, like a lady. "That will be so nice! I wonder what he's doing."

"I don't know, but he spends every spare moment out there, hammering and sawing. Valentine loves to make things."

"Well, when is your birthday, Miss Kenna?" I asked, all nice, like a lady.

"On the tenth. Coming right up!"

"Well, I guess that Valentine had better hurry up!" I said. She laughed and said yes, he had. Then we sipped our tea and it tasted right good. I watched Kenna and everything she did, and I tried to do like her. I tried to sit like her, and sip my tea like her, and hold my head like her, and I wished I *was* her.

CHAPTER 11

I got the most serious feeling in me, and I knew that come Kenna's birthday, things would change for good and all. Then here came the tenth, and word came around that there is a birthday gathering at the Hill House and we should all come, like always. So, I got the young ones washed and cleaned up a little, giving Tom an extra scrub round his filthy neck, and I grabbed a loaf of my crusty, brown bread and some preserves. We were just about to leave the house when who should show up, but Frank.

"Where you going, woman?" he asks.

My heart sank when I heard the hard edge of Frank's voice, for when he sounded like that, you could count on trouble. I tried to keep my voice light and said, "There's a gathering at Kenna's tonight. Come on and go up the hill with us."

Frank grumbled about some folks acting like they own the whole town, but then he allowed as how he would come along even though he hated everyone. So, him and me and the young ones went up past the railroad tracks and then out on to the trail through the brush. I remember that night exactly, I guess because that was the last night I lived that way and the first night I lived a new way, but I did not know that then. I just wandered up the hill, round this brush and that, heading to Kenna's.

Well, we got up there and folks were starting to visit and laugh and all, just like always. The table sagged under the food laid out, the best dishes covered with tea towels to keep the flies out. I added in my bread and preserves and looked over the rest of the food. Back then, gatherings were a good way for me to get a few extra bites for my young ones.

Before long, the boys struck up some music. The sky lit up with the sunset, the sun sinking behind Frenchman's Mountain; behind Winnemucca Mountain they call it nowadays. The colors flared across the sky, purple and lavender and pink and red, the few little lights of the Ford shining down below us. We were all a town then. We belonged to something then, small though it was. We shared food and talked nice and asked after one another. Yes, we were a town then, but that was a long time ago.

Finally, here came Valentine. He looked mighty handsome, his hair slicked back and his face freshly shaved, plus he wore a clean shirt. It was tucked in at his slim waist, his gray suspenders spanning his broad shoulders; looked like even his work boots had been cleaned up. I saw that his black hair curled up just behind his ears and along his neck. I could not stop looking at him. He looked happy too, his cheeks a little red. I couldn't take my eyes off him, but only stared until Frank jabbed me good in the ribs with his elbow.

"Good God, woman, go take him out back right now," he growled at me, trembling with fury. I cowered down, turning red to the roots of my hair.

Right then Valentine called out in his rumbling voice, "Now listen, folks! I have an announcement! You all know that it's Kenna's birthday! Kenna, girl, where are you? Come over here!" and he waved his arm to Kenna to come over to him. Kenna blushed like a girl, but here she came. He took her hand and held it to his heart, and he said, "Listen, now, all you people! This Kenna girl, she's only been needing for one thing, so I built it for her!"

That brought on plenty of hooting and hollering then, and someone yelled, "Yeah, with Kenna's money!"

Valentine shamed them all to silence. "That you, Branson? You are a scoundrel! And, for your information, I bought all this lumber you are about to behold. Now, quit trying to spoil our fun. Right now, I want to show Kenna her birthday present!"

Then he led us over to the barn and unlatched the doors. One swung open on its own and Valentine pushed the other one back as if he were the ringmaster at the circus.

"Come look, Kenna!" Kenna stepped up to the door and looked in, and we all followed. Then we knew what he had done with all that lumber, for Valentine had made a dance floor in one corner of the barn! It rested just a few inches up out of the dirt, a raised platform for the boys to play their music connected to one end. Flat benches circled all around the edge for folks to sit on. The rough and yellow wood looked beautiful in the kerosene lamplight, and it smelled heavenly. Half a dozen shaded lanterns hung by fence wire from the barn gables, and the light turned the barn into a sparkling dancehall. The spicy smell of fresh lumber and the sawdust in the dirt finished it all off.

Then Valentine took Kenna's hand, and said, "What do you think of this? Will this suit you?"

Kenna beamed. I have never seen a face shining so! Her hands and her voice shook a little when she said, "It suits me perfectly," and then she laughed. "Thank you. Thank you so much."

Well, the boys hurried up and moved right on to the stage, and we all allowed as how we should have some food. Folks began milling around the table, eating and visiting.

"You want a plate of food?" I asked Frank. "You want I should get you something to eat?"

"I'm too sick to eat," he said, real meanlike, and then he wandered off to find some whiskey. I felt sick too, for regardless of all the terrible times I had with Frank, I knew better than to pine after another man in front of the whole town. I knew Frank's evil temperament, and him knowing how I felt about Valentine meant more trouble for me.

I struggled to stay there and watch all the people be so happy with each other; seemed like I was the only one in a big mess. After we ate our fill, I gathered the little ones and started them toward the front of the house. I figured we might as well just go home and wait out the storm.

Just as I came round the house, Kenna caught up with me. "Why, Ruby, where are you going?" she asked. "We haven't even had any dancing yet!"

"I'm heading down to the Ford, Kenna," I said to her. "I'm feeling poorly."

It seemed like Kenna saw right through me then. "Is your husband giving you trouble, Ruby? Are you all right?"

"Oh, no more trouble than usual," I said to her, and sort of snorted. "He's a trial, Miss Kenna."

"Don't go, Ruby. Stay for a while at least. Let's have a dance or two!"

I could not resist. Who could say no to Kenna, with her sweet smile and kind manners? So, we turned around and went back to the gathering. We cleaned up the dinner then, and I sort of knew where what dish went in Kenna's kitchen. We had hot water all ready to go from her water reservoir on her woodstove. All us women talked a lot while we washed up, and we laughed some and compared men and what all. I did not tell much about Frank, as I did not want folks to know about our problems. It seems silly now, since every person in the Ford had to know all about his low ways.

By the time we got back outside, the boys had struck up some music. I felt worse and worse with every passing minute, and there was no sign of my drunkard. So, there I waited in the most beautiful place I had ever seen, feeling so low and scared I wanted to die. I tried to hide my fear, but my eyes were stinging like anything.

The boys were going to town on their little stand, and folks were starting to dance. Sometimes the boys would play a nice waltz, and all the folks would pair up and you could see who loved who; all the old married couples cozied up, the women smiling up at husbands and the husbands' heads bent down to meet eyes. I tell you, Miss, that seemed the worst of it; to see old folks who loved each other and to know that I would never have that. My heart broke, Miss, right in front of the whole town. It felt like everyone could see into my very soul, whispering softly to each other about how sorry they felt for me as they waltzed across the sawdust floor.

Then, to top it off, here came Valentine, toting Kenna's harp. He carried it up to the stage, and called out to Kenna. "Where I come from, birthday girls give gifts to their guests, not the other way around!" He looked at her with sparks in his eyes, giving her a wide smile under his mustache, his face a sight to behold. "Come on, Kenna girl!" he called. "Come give us a tune!"

Do you know a harp, Miss? A harp is pretty big, but plays the most beautiful notes. And it looks like a woman should play a harp, and not a man. It looks like a woman's instrument, I guess. And when a woman plays a harp, Miss, she looks right feminine and heavenly. The music is so pretty and light and the notes can get so sweet, it puts you under a spell. So that's how it felt that night. Kenna worked her magic on all of us, and we all fell under her spell.

Kenna had finally built up her nerve, or Valentine had forced her into playing. Either way, she decided to play. She sat on the edge of a chair on the music platform, her skirts flowing around her feet, the harp standing guard in front of her. She leaned forward a little, and with shaking hands, gently pulled the harp to her shoulder; the whole place went dead silent. She began just plucking on the strings so gentlelike at first, as if checking to see the harp was properly tuned, her brow furrowed as she listened. Then she played in all seriousness, her head tilted prettily, her hair piled high, every movement of hand and wrist and finger perfect. The line of her movement, the curve of her wrist, the whisp of hair at her cheek made us all love her. How could we not, for she was beauty and innocence and everything womanly. Kenna looked at no one, but looked inside instead, playing without trying, without concentrating—just playing like it was so easy. The most beautiful music came floating out of that barn; it floated up above the Hill House and the Ford and the Sonomas and then above the whole world, and Kenna didn't even notice it. She just played on for us all.

My throat grew thick with sadness and my cheeks burned red as I listened, so carried away was I. I stood stock still, suddenly understanding everything about life and beauty and having and wanting. With each bend of her wrist, I saw what it is to be a woman; to be judged by your appearance, to forever lack something; to always wish to fulfill something for someone else. Seemed like Kenna and I had that in common—both women in a world full of dirt and sawdust and longing.

When I thought I couldn't stand there any longer; when I looked around for a way out, the music changed. It slowed and became like me—longing, pining. It was the most beautiful and heartbroken song I had ever heard, nor have I heard a finer one since, in all these years. It came a mournful tune, so Kenna just plucked gently on the strings. Then, the shock of us all, Kenna began to sing with the sweetest voice, warbling when her voice shook, a cry in her voice when the notes came high. She said the words in a strange accent the way people from her far lands must talk, and I could not stop tears from gathering in my eyes. She sang like an angel, Miss, like a being from some other existence; and she didn't look at anybody. Seemed like she went to her own world too, her cheeks flushed pink, her face a sad countenance, and I thought, *"Well, look like Miss Kenna still has her heartache, too."*

Oh, no Miss, I can't sing a song like that! I know the words, though. I sung them in my head a thousand times. No, I can't sing. I will tell you. It went like this.

Black is the color of my true love's hair.
His lips are like some roses fair,

Oh, Miss, I wish I could sing it to you! Well, I will try, but my voice is so shaky. I will try. It's a very old song, from Kenna's far lands. I will try.

Black is the color of my true love's hair.
His lips are like some roses fair.
He has the sweetest smile and the gentlest hands.
I love the ground whereon he stands.

I love my love, and well he knows.
I love the ground whereon he goes.
And I wish the day, it soon will come
When he and I will be as one.

Black is the color of my true love's hair.
His lips are like some roses fair.
He has the sweetest smile and the gentlest hands
And I love the ground whereon he stands.

I go to the Clyde for to mourn and weep
For satisfied I ne'er will be
And I write him a letter, just a few short lines
And suffer death ten thousand times.

Black is the color of my true love's hair.
His lips are like some roses fair.
He has the sweetest smile and the gentlest hands
And I love the ground whereon he stands.

Black is the color of my true love's hair.
His lips are like some roses fair.
He has the sweetest smile and the gentlest hands.
I love the ground whereon he stands.

Never a sound made me so very sad then, for I saw as how women been crying after men all the centuries, and how they been going from ford to ford looking for the right man, and how it only added up to heartache. I knew right away that the Clyde is a river in Kenna's far lands where the sun doesn't set in the summer until way into the night, and I saw in my mind how the calm waters of the Clyde glided by in the moonlight.

So, there sat Kenna, singing to us all, and I guess the whole town fell in love with her that night. Well, all except Frank. He was nowheres to be seen. When she finished the last verse, seemed like the final note hung in the eaves of the barn, every person completely silent. We all stood there when the song ended. Kenna looked up and came back to herself, blushing like anything.

No doubt about it, Valentine was a goner. He stared at Kenna without blinking, his hands limp by his sides again, not even knowing the rest of us were there. I had not thought to look at him during Kenna's Black Hair song, but when I looked at him after the song, it seemed his hair was blacker than ever;

blacker than stove black; blacker than raven black, blacker than moonless black. While Valentine stared at Kenna and I stared at Valentine, both of us hypnotized, the folks round about came out of their trances and started up clapping and begging for more, so then Kenna played a couple more songs; not quite so mournful though, and folks started to feel more like their old selves.

"That's enough of that!" Kenna said after a bit, and she set the harp away from her. She stood then, and I caught a glimpse of the old woman living inside Kenna. I saw that for all her fancy tables and dishes and all, Kenna carried a heavy load. She wiped her hands on the front of her skirts like she had harp dirt on them, and I could see that there was plenty we didn't know about that little woman from Boston.

CHAPTER 12

Oh my, Miss, that was quite a night. When I remember back, seems like we were all so young! Seems like our faces were rounder and our backs were straighter and our eyes were brighter. Even with all my man troubles, I was so young! Many a time I've thought it over, and I never figured out why I let myself get into such straits. I don't even remember making a decision to go off with Frank, or knowing if I loved him at first, or what; just seemed to glide downstream into destruction.

Well, the party finally wound down, and as usual, we piled into Ferris' wagon and bumped down to the Ford. Frank had disappeared, so that was fine with me. All the way down to the house, I prayed he was gone for good. If I couldn't have the happiness I saw that Kenna and Valentine and some of the other folks around the Ford had, at least I could have peace. All my folks were dead and gone, my father killed in the raid on Lawrence, and my mother died of a broken heart. So, I had to find my own way, but I felt I could make a go of it. That's what

I dreamed of that night; just going on my way and making the best of things and watching Kenna live a good life. I felt heart-sick with it, but I thought that might be as good as I could get.

That black hair song rang in my head. I remembered how Valentine kissed me, and how that had to be enough for me. I felt so lonely, Miss, knowing that Valentine loved Kenna, and would never love me. I recognized that they loved each other so powerful, not like normal folks, but like legendary lovers from an ancient poem! I tried to set him free in my heart, and not harbor any bad feelings toward him. He didn't love me, and that was all there was to it. You can't make someone love you; it ain't like catching bees, Miss.

So, I laid my children around my sad, little house here and there, tucking them in where I could. I think that is the first time I really looked at my children. My little girls, with rosy cheeks and curly hair and pudgy baby hands, sleeping like angels. My dear, little Minnie and sweet, tiny Elsie. I kissed them goodnight, and I had never done that! They smelled sweet, like brand new babies, and my heart swelled up. I walked into the kitchen and looked around, and it was a good and sensible kitchen I saw! It was warm and neat, and though I had no fancy dishes or drying herbs like Kenna had, I had my good wood stove and my mother's old pie safe.

I leaned there against the wall a moment, thinking that I could have a new start with my babies, and find other ways to be happy in this life. I felt a little lift to my heart, and tears began streaming down my face, and I felt strong and hopeful for a minute. I felt my power raising up. I felt strong instead of weak, and I saw that my babies and the boys were part of my strength.

Seemed like the light dawned on me right then, like seeing Kenna and her ways made me want better ways for myself.

I tried to fix my hair a little then. I looked at my dress and shoes and all, and I saw that I looked all right. I was not an ugly monster that no man could ever want or love. I had a small waist, though not a tiny one like little bird Kenna. My teeth were good then, and I was healthy of body; just normal aches and pains, but no real ailments. And I was smart and feisty. I could make my own way. Why, I had a solid house and a few chickens, didn't I? And I could find my way.

I straightened up and took a deep breath, and I felt real hope, Miss. That is when I saw Frank glaring at me from the doorway. The hatred fairly beamed out of his face, his lumpish fists balled up at his sides like clubs, and I knew I was in for it.

"Get out of here right now, Frank Holt!" I screamed at him. My fury overflowed too, and I had a quick vision of killing him with a hatchet or a piece of firewood or what all. I was so disheartened to see him show up and come after me right when I was lifting myself out of the muck. I was ready for a fight, Miss, and this time I might just win.

So, here he came, and started whaling on me, but good. The babies woke up and started screaming, and it was right terrible. I fought as hard as I could, banging him across the face with a wooden spoon, but that just made him madder. He came at me but good, Miss, and liked to kick a slat out of me. I lay balled up on the kitchen floor while he kicked and stomped with his nasty old boots, and I thought I was going to be free of all my troubles soon.

Have you ever taken a beating, Miss? I guess unless you have, you can't understand it. Seems like it turns into a business deal, and one is handing out and the other is taking, and it don't seem personal; just beating business. And when you're getting a beating, don't nobody look nobody in the eye. I don't know what would happen if you looked each other in the eye. Guess you'd end up dead for sure.

Funny thing is, the whole time Frank beat on me, I knew Kenna and Valentine were up the hill, loving on each other in Kenna's big, tall bed. I knew they whispered each other's names and touched each other's faces. Surely, the moonlight glided across the gleaming wood floor in Kenna's room, and the curtains at the open windows bellowed out with the night breeze. I even heard a bird call in the night; I heard the crickets sing.

I dreamed of them while I lay on the floor, and I saw another me standing over to the side with her arms crossed, watching the whole thing. She wore my same frayed dress, my same worn shoes, her hair loose around her face. She was thinking how odd it was to think of another man loving another woman while getting nearly killed by yet another man.

You would think it would have scared me to see another Ruby looking on, but it didn't, Miss, for I had seen her all my life. She used to pop up at any time to surprise me. She mostly came and watched when I had trouble, but sometimes she came for good times, too. Why, she came when I gave birth to the babies, and she whispered so sweet to me and promised me that I would live if I held on just a little longer. I thought I was dying for sure, but Watching Ruby kept her word, and I survived after all.

So, she came here for the beating, and stood looking on. No whispers of comfort then, but only scowled at Frank, looked daggers at him like to stop his heart from beating. Maybe that's why he stopped. I don't know for sure, but he stopped before he killed me; just one kick more, and he stopped.

"Damn you, Ruby. Damn you to hell. You're no good for nothing. A waste. You are a disgusting excuse for a woman. I never felt nothing for you. You hear me? I never cared about you, at any time, ever."

Then he left.

I laid on the floor while the babies carried on like anything. James came in from the back room, rubbing sleep from his eyes as he tried to hush the babies. He didn't offer any help to me, but quieted the babies.

"What you do now, Ruby?" he asked me, and I thought I might kill him with a hatchet too, only I couldn't get up off the floor. He took the babies to the back room, and that's what saved them from seeing what happened next.

What you looking like that for, Miss? You never heard about beatings before? You never heard about kicks and stomps? You look like you could kill someone with a hatchet, too. Ha! Go on, Miss. This happened long time ago, way in the past now.

I laid there and cried quiet, trying to figure out if I could crawl to bed when Frank came back. He grabbed me by my hair and yanked me up on my knees, bending back my head so I had to look at his face. I screamed then, for my insides were hurt mighty bad. Watching Ruby clenched her fists at her sides, a most worried look on her face. That scared me as much as being held there by Frank. If Watching Ruby felt afraid, it was very bad news indeed. Frank jerked my head to the side, leaning close to me so that I could smell his foul breath and see his crooked, yellow teeth. He put his pistol to my temple and cocked it. Time slowed way down then, leaving the three of us trapped there together, him breathing hard and raspy in his fury, me clutching his wrist for all I was worth, and Watching Ruby covering her face with her hands.

Even though I felt terrified, a kind of peace settled over me and I said, "Go ahead. Go ahead and do it, Frank, you bastard." I never swore, Miss, all my life, but I did then. I wanted him to kill me; I wanted him to free me from this torment.

"You are no damn good, Ruby. Not worth my bullet," he said, and he clenched his teeth together the way people do when they are beyond furious. "Not worth my damn bullet!" Then he flung

me back down on the floor, and I guess I fainted, because when I waked up the babies were playing on the kitchen floor in pee pants, and daylight streamed across the room.

CHAPTER 13

I stayed in bed quite a few days; no walking to the Post Office bench or any of that. I was in sad shape. I didn't know what all was broken, but all my insides and my ribs were hurt, and I had bruises all on my legs and arms. My face swelled up and my mouth was cut up inside so that I couldn't eat or drink really. I was filthy, laying in bed in my torn and bloody dress.

James and Tom helped with the babies a little; mostly gave them a cup of milk or a bite of a biscuit or what all. The diapers ran out, so the babies went naked. They spent plenty of time crying and whining them days, but I couldn't help them at all. Just couldn't hardly move. I laid on that rickety bed with my wrinkled rag quilt, sleeping and waking and sleeping again.

James kept the water bucket full most times, thank the Lord. But it was a big chore for me to get water or get out to the outhouse too; just about had to crawl out there. If Tommy stayed nearby, which he did most of the time now that I think about it, I made him walk out there with me so I could lean on his skinny shoulders. That helped a little. He waited so patiently outside for me, and then helped me hobble back to bed.

Tommy would say, "Almost there, Ruby, almost there." And once he said, "I bet you are sorry for making Pa mad, ain't you, Ruby? Ain't you sorry?"

"Yes, Tom. I'm more sorry than you can know. Sorry through and through." I didn't explain to him what I really regretted—ever laying eyes on his sorry pa. I didn't try to teach him anything. I saw what a bad picture this showed the boys, and I couldn't keep from crying. I didn't want those boys to be like their pa; drinking every day, caring only for themselves, relying on someone else to take the blame for everything that went wrong. I didn't want them to be like that, but it didn't seem like I could stop it.

Then to top it all off, I lost a baby right in the middle of all that ache. Didn't even know I had a baby in me, but I know I lost one because of all the blood and all. And what a job to keep the blood rounded up and not all over everything! It did get all over everything so that my quilt stank of it, my yellowed sheets were stiff with it, and the back of my dress was soaked with it. The more blood I saw, the more shame I felt, for no woman wants her blood showing all over.

We all hide in shame, don't we, Miss?

That beating baby was my last; no more babies for me. Frank beat that out of me. I didn't mourn that baby for many years, not until I was old and alone. Then it came to me how I had lost that baby, and I mourned for ages. I'm not the only woman ever mourned for a baby no one even knew about, for it's part of our trial, Miss, to bear these feminine ordeals alone and in silence. Best keep quiet about it or else you might never stop crying.

You can't guess how I felt during those days, Miss, for I was so down and low. I wished that Frank would have finished the job and killed me. That would have been a lot easier for me, I will tell you. But that wasn't the way it was to be, because I just kept on living; kept on crawling around and feeling that the world held no place for me. I kept a wet rag on my face and other old blankets between my legs for the blood, trying to doze off when I could and sobbing when I couldn't keep from it.

A few days into that terrible time I lay in bed, neither sleeping nor bawling, but listening to the house settle. The babies slept for once, their hands and faces grimy from lack of care, their chubby thighs red and chapped from peeing on themselves. It was a warm afternoon, birds chirping outside my open window. Tommy came into my room like a whirlwind; filthy, grime on his brown hands and dirt on his neck. His white hair stuck up here and there as if he had just crawled out of bed.

"Can I take a spoon outside, Ruby?" he asked. "I'm digging a tunnel!"

I didn't answer him but only nodded, and he shot out of the room. Soon I could hear him humming to himself as he squatted by the kitchen step, digging with one of my few spoons. The day dragged by, and I held still as much as I could, for my insides hurt like anything.

Then, out of the side of my ear, I heard Valentine's rumbly voice say, "Hello there, Tom. Where's your mama? Is she here?"

At first, I thought I only dreamed that Valentine had come,

but then I realized it was no dream. He stood right outside my kitchen door.

"She's in the house in bed," said Tom. "She's real sick."

"Go in there and tell her Valentine is here," I heard him say. "Ask her if she will see me."

Even in my sickness, my heart hammered in my chest. I could not let Valentine see me like that! By then my face was black with bruises. I was filthy, and the blood! I was not fit to be seen.

Tom appeared by my bed and said, "Valentine is here, Ruby. He says for you to come out."

I whispered, "Make him go away, Tommy. Tell him I am fine, but too sick. Make him go away. You hear me, Tom? Make him go away!"

Tom scooted back outside and I heard him say, "Mama says for you to go away. She says she's too sick for you."

"What's wrong with her, Tom? What kind of sickness does she have? Has the doctor been here?" Valentine asked, his voice heavy with worry.

"She made papa right mad, and he liked to killed her," said Tom, as if explaining a simple idea to an idiot. Then I heard Valentine's big boots stomping across my step and through my kitchen.

"Ruby!" he shouted out. "Ruby, where are you? Ruby!" His voice was thunder so that I wanted to hide under the bed, for it sounded like Valentine cared about me, but the idea of him seeing me half dead, filthy, and bloody was more than I could bear. I was so ashamed, Miss. But there was no stopping him, for there he stood by my bed, looking down at my sorry face.

"Jesus Christ!" he roared. "Where is he? Where is that bastard?" Then he looked closely at me, maybe to see my wounds. He rubbed his face with shaking hands and whispered, "Ruby, I'm going to kill him. I should have killed him the first time I laid eyes on him." His fury outshone anything Frank expressed, for this was a quiet, deadly rage, and even in my state I saw that Valentine had a dark side to him.

I tried to talk, though it was almost impossible. I finally whispered, "Please get out of here! Go now! I don't want Frank to see you here. It will only cause more trouble."

Valentine wore a horrible look in his eye, fury and grief at the same time, and then he said again, "I should have killed him already. Long time ago." He called out, "Tom! Tom, come in here!" When Tommy appeared, spoon clutched in a grubby fist, Valentine said, "Tom, listen to me very carefully. Run get Dr. Brock. Run all the way. You know where he is? You know?"

Valentine's big paws clutched Tom's scrawny shoulders and gave him a quick shake. "You know, Tom?"

Eyes as big as plates, Tom nodded without a word.

"Now, Tom!" said Valentine. "Run now!" Tommy tore out of the house as if the devil himself was on his heels.

I so desperately wanted Valentine to leave. He paced back and forth in my room, muttering under his breath, practically tearing at his hair.

"Go get Kenna. Kenna will know what to do. Go get her," I whispered to Valentine. I was frantic to get him out of there before he saw the shape I was in. I would rather have died than have him stay there another second.

He seemed to come to himself then, because he said, "I'll

go get Kenna. We will be right back. And the doctor is coming. Hang on, Ruby. We'll be right back,"

I sort of smiled at him through my cut-up lips, because he thought I was dying, and I knew I was not that lucky. But off he tore through the house and out the dooryard. I wanted to get cleaned up a little or something before they all came back, but there was no way to do it. I could not really get around, and the bucket held no water anyway. Those no-account boys of Frank's! I was going to be shut of them soon.

After a bit, I opened my eyes, and there stood Dr. Brock, looking gravely down at me, asking me questions. I just looked at him and didn't answer since I didn't want to talk about pain and blood and what all; I just stared like a simpleton. Then here came Kenna, and she touched my arm and said, "Oh my God, Ruby! Oh my God!" and she was like to cry.

They both left for a time, but I could hear them out in the yard, their voices mixing together and coming apart again. I began thinking in a funny way, like everything was happening to someone else and not me. It seemed like I had turned a corner with my beating, like maybe I would die after all. Finally, the doctor and Kenna came back in, taking turns talking to me very slowly and quietly as if I really was simple.

Kenna said, "Ruby, I'm taking you up to the Hill House until you are better, and I won't take no for an answer. You're coming up to the house, and so are the children."

"I think that's for the best, Ruby. You need help in order to heal. You need proper food and care. And you need something to take the edge off the pain. I'm going to give you some lauda-num, and I want you to take it every few hours until you feel better. Mrs. Fletcher will see to it for you, so don't trouble about it, but I do want you to take it. I guess I don't need to tell you to stay off your feet as much as possible," said Dr. Brock.

I motioned for Kenna to come close, and when she leaned near, I said, "Please leave, Kenna. Take Valentine with you. Take the doctor with you. Even take the babies if you want, but you got to leave right now. No more trouble. Please."

"There isn't going to be any trouble, Ruby. We are taking you up to the house. We're taking the babies too, and the boys. You can stay there until you are back on your feet," she said. Then I saw that Kenna understood my straits, and was trying to help me over it. Her bow mouth was drawn tight, her face as pale as milk.

So, I said, "Well, get Valentine out of here. I don't want him to see me like this."

"All right, Ruby," she lied. "Whatever you want. Now go to sleep until we are ready to move you. Valentine is going to get a wagon."

I don't know much about how it all came to be, but I do remember them putting me on a pallet in back of a wagon later that day. Kenna had a clean blanket from her house, and she wrapped me in it to hide my troubles. They waited until the doc's medicine went to work, I guess, because things became very puzzling for me, and I didn't know what was going on. I didn't really care who saw me, or how, or why; not much mattered to me once that medicine got to going. I remember looking up and seeing Valentine's broad shoulders and his back, him sitting on the buckboard with reins in his hands.

When we finally got to Kenna's, I do remember this. Here

came Valentine, stomping around the side of the wagon. He grabbed hold of the pallet and pulled me to the edge of the buckboard, and scooped me up in his arms, blankets and all, like I weighed nothing. I lay my head on his shoulder as he carried me from the front gate, across Kenna's dooryard, and up the wide porch steps. I could hear his footfalls, tromping up the stairs, for he was still furious.

Kenna opened the front door for us, standing to one side as she said, "Take her to my room."

"You know her room?" I whispered against Valentine's neck. "You know her room?"

Valentine did not answer me.

CHAPTER 14

The first thing Kenna did was make me a nice bath in the room next to her room, a small and cozy space with a tiny window and a smooth plank floor. Right there in the middle stood a great, copper tub with soft linens and scents and soaps and all. Valentine carried bucket after bucket of hot water to the tub, even though I begged Kenna to send him away.

I lay there in bed, listening to the water pour into that tub. Kenna and Valentine whispered to each other and then one or the other would say something sweet to me about hanging on and things going to get better. Seemed like the nicer they were to me, the worse I felt, hot tears stinging my eyes every minute.

Once the tub was full enough, Kenna said, "Just one bucket more, Valentine, and please leave it beside the tub. Then we won't need any more of your help, only just lift the big tub off the stove on your way out."

"All right, Kenna," said Valentine, "Only won't you need me to carry water back down?"

I looked at Kenna, pleading with my eyes to send Valentine away. She must have understood because she said, "No, thank you, Valentine. James and I will manage. I'll walk you downstairs. I'll be right back, Ruby. Stay there." I heard them talking softly as they went downstairs together.

When Kenna came back, she said, "Now, let's get this dress off of you."

Shock of all, she straight cut that dress off me while I lay on her bed. My dress was ruined for sure, but I'll never forget her cutting it off. She cursed and swore the whole time, calling Frank all manner of names, some I had never heard before. She cut it off in parts—a sleeve here and the piece of skirt there; a collar; the bodice.

I whispered, "Miss Kenna, are you putting a spell on Frank? Because if you are, I feel right sorry for him." She gave me no answer. She did stop swearing; only snip, snip, snip.

Finally, she said, "All right Ruby, let's get you into that tub, nice and easy." She helped me climb down off the bed, limped me to the tub, and held my arm as I climbed in. When that warm water washed around me, turning pink with blood, I cringed in shame.

"Oh, Kenna," I lisped, "I'm so sorry. I'll clean this up. Let me out and I'll clean it up."

"You'll do no such thing," she said, matter-of-factly. "You're going to lie there and soak and rest. Don't worry about a thing. Now, is the water hot enough? Are you doing all right?" Then Kenna helped me get cleaned up. She washed my hair with lavender soap and rinsed it with water from the bucket, using a small pitcher to pour water over me. She sponged my back and took up swearing again when she saw more bruises.

"Oh my God, Ruby! I can see Frank's bootprint!" she hissed, swearing some more.

"Well, I can feel it," I said.

"I imagine you can," she said. "He's going to get his, Ruby, just you wait and see. I think Valentine is going to wring his neck."

Then later, "All right, I think you're all clean. Now rest a few minutes. I'm going to go turn down your bed, and I'm going to burn your dress in the stove. No more thinking about that!" Kenna hustled out.

Soon Kenna was back with a big sheet for me to dry off. She helped me back to her room where she gave me a soft flannel gown to wear, pulling it over my head and buttoning the wee buttons at the neck. I felt so grateful! Kenna helped me into bed, and last of all gave me clean rags for my blood, turning away a little while I put them on. Then it was constant attention, with Kenna running downstairs to get something or to take care of the babies and then running upstairs to take care of me.

"Sit up a little, Ruby, and let me fix your pillow," she would say, or "What can I get for you, Ruby?" or "It's time to take some medicine, Ruby. Just a sip." until I felt like a queen. Each day she combed out my hair and then rebraided it, leaving my braid to hang down my back. She put soothing unguents on my face, made mouth wash for me out of spearmint, and rubbed fragrant lanolin on my legs and feet. She brought me sweet teas to drink and savory soup to sip, and every night she brought me fresh lavender to lay on my pillow for sleep. She made me an amulet bag to wear that she called a crane bag. Lord knows what was in there—rabbit teeth and arrowheads, for all I know. It was made of the softest leather, and Kenna embroidered a beautiful knotted design on the front.

"Wear this all the time, Ruby. It will help you heal," she whispered as she draped the leather strap around my neck.

"What is it, Kenna?" I asked.

"It's your crane bag. I made it just for you."

Every day she made sure I had it on. Sometimes she took me to the table and chair there in her room to sit a bit and watch the sun wake up the Sonomas, its first light barely peeking over the peaks, and then suddenly pouring out across the whole mountain range. Dear, sweet Kenna; she got to be my friend.

Most afternoons as I napped, Kenna sat on the edge of the bed and put healings on me. She held her hands over my ribs and my chest, but not touching me. She said nary a word, but only stared and frowned and glided her hands through the air, just as I had seen her do with Valentine that day that now seemed so long ago. Usually I fell sound asleep, and when I waked up, she was gone.

Kenna took to telling me poems, too. She knew lots of them by heart, and she could tell them for ages. I loved to listen to her soothing voice every afternoon. Some of those poems I understood right away and other ones I had to think about. I was very ignorant in those days, before Kenna educated me. Though I could read, of course, I didn't know any literature, nor did I have any sense of history. Kenna taught me so much! During those dark days after my beating, she would recite so many different poems, but my favorite was a great, long poem by Lord Byron. Kenna knew it all, and I know lots of it, but the very best part was this:

> From the wreck of the past, which hath perished,
> Thus much I at least may recall;
> It hath taught me that which I most cherished
> Deserved to be dearest of all.
> In the desert a fountain is springing,
> In the wide waste there still is a tree,
> And a bird in the solitude singing,
> Which speaks to my spirit of *thee*.

I can almost hear her voice saying that poem to me, Miss. She recited it in the sweetest voice, very quietly, but not quite a whisper. Most days I would ask her to say just that part again and again, and Kenna would just keep on saying it. Every time she said it, my heart would swell up with new hope for my life. That part about "from the wreck of the past," and "there still is a tree," Miss, would get me the most. Most times while Kenna told me that beautiful poem, I would just lay there with my eyes closed, tears running into my ears.

The babies and the boys stayed there at Kenna's too, though I never saw them for days. Kenna took care of the babies and she told me that Valentine was keeping the boys busy doing chores around the place. I did not know it, but Kenna had got a cow and calf, so they had milking to do. She had a batch of chickens too, so the boys helped gather eggs and such as that.

All those first days, Kenna could not have been kinder to me. I did not see Valentine up close, but sometimes I saw him out the bedroom window. As far as I could tell, he had not killed Frank.

I guess the folks around the Ford had plenty to talk about on my account, and Frank was nowhere to be seen. It got deeper into fall then; a snap in the air, you know, chilly mornings and chillier evenings. Kenna took to lighting the fire in the bedroom fireplace in the evening, and I sure enjoyed that. I lay there listening to the fire snapping and the wind sighing around that house, taking in the clean smell of that house, and Kenna's cooking aromas floating up the stairs to my room; all the elements of Kenna's beautiful home comforting me as I healed. Sometimes all that comfort just up and sent me to bellering like anything. Kenna said that was all right, and I should cry all I wanted, even if I was crying about fried chicken.

CHAPTER 15

My ribs were right sore, and it hurt to do much of anything. The bleeding finally stopped altogether, and Dr. Brock allowed as how I was going to live. No more babies for me though. That's what he said.

Finally, came the day I could be up and about again. That day would have come much faster if I had been on my own, but Kenna wouldn't hear of it. She made me stay in bed until I healed some, so I did. When it was time to get up, Kenna gave me a real nice dress made of the prettiest blue, calico fabric; so blue it was almost black, and what's more, just like new. It had fine white lace around the cuffs and the neck, and it had tiny seams going all down the bodice. I had never owned such a fine piece of clothing.

"This is so beautiful, Kenna, but it's much too fine for a house dress. Don't you have something old I can wear? Something more simple?" I asked as I held the amazing thing up to me. "I better have something else."

"What? Nonsense," said Kenna. "This will work perfectly until we get you a dress of your own. It's yours, Ruby." She smiled at me so sweetly, Kenna being her generous self. Possessions weren't that dear to her since she could always buy something more if she wanted it, so why not give it away? Not like me; I saved everything I laid hands on. I guess the trunk proves that.

Anyhow, I must have been under a dress spell, for when I went to put it on, I could see right away that it was way too small. My heart sank when I felt the gap at my back.

Kenna saw the look on my face and said, "Don't worry, Ruby. I can fix that so easily! I'll let a few seams out and it will fit just fine!" But when we got to looking, we see she would just about have to make the whole dress over.

So, I wore it without buttoning the back, and we tied it shut with a string. I just put a shawl on. The dress only came to the top of my ankles, leaving my black stockings and worn shoes to show, but Kenna said it would do for now.

It seemed like life started turning good for me even though I was living in another woman's house, eating another woman's food, loving another woman's man; for Valentine belonged to Kenna, and there was no way around it. He came to the house for supper each night, while I stayed upstairs to avoid him. I could hear their quiet talk though, as they ate, making plans and discussing problems and what all; forks scraping and cups clinking and chairs sliding away from the table when they were done.

Sometimes in the afternoon, I would sit downstairs in the parlor and rest. Then Kenna would bring me my babies, and I started to see that I loved them terrible.

"Come give your mommy a kiss, girls," she would say to

them, and they would shyly hug my neck, each by turn, eyeing me suspiciously since I had never hugged them much. Kenna kept them shining like new dimes, with ringlets in their hair and clean pinafores. She found them some little dresses too, and durn if they weren't beautiful little girls! They were starting to talk some and I heard them call Kenna by name.

"Kenna, soup. Soup, Kenna."

"Yes, darling. Kenna will get you some soup. Come sit in your chair. Come here, my sweet," she would say. Then I would get stinging eyes again.

The boys slinked around the place, and it looked like they were ashamed of their old man and what he had done. Kenna and Valentine were nice to them though, and acted like folks move in with folks every day. Especially Tom had a hard time; sometimes when I saw the curve of his little, skinny neck and how his white hair needed cut, how he cast his eyes down all the time, my heart cried out for him and I thought how bad he needed a mama.

Finally, I told Kenna that I ought to be getting back to my house. "It's time for me to get back to my place, Kenna. I'm sure it's a mess and my chickens all dead. I need to see what is going on down there. Like it or not, winter is going to get here, and I got to get ready as much as I can."

"It's too soon for you to be on your own! You're not ready! You're not healed. You can't take care of yourself, let alone the boys and the babies. You don't have anything there. We'll ask Valentine to get some wood for you and whatever else you need. After things are better prepared, you can all move back home. That's an end to it, Ruby, and I won't hear any more of this.

Now." She nodded her head once at me, like a queen giving her commands.

My secret heart sang out when she said that, for I hated the idea of leaving that house. I didn't see how I could live without my sunny mornings and my shining parlor and my pretty kitchen. So, I stayed on.

Valentine worked like a mad man, building this and that. Seem like a few days would go by, and here is something new. He made Kenna a nice quilt frame that hung from the ceiling in the music parlor, and Kenna could pull it down when she wanted to quilt and then reel it back up to get it out of the way. It was nice and light, but big enough for both of us to sit by and work. It was right handy, and like nothing I had ever seen.

Then one night at dinner, Valentine allowed as how him and Ferris and a couple other boys were going up to the Summit to get some firewood and they would be gone for a few weeks.

"This is a good chance to get enough wood for all of us for the winter. It's a lot of work to cut firewood, but since it'll be a bunch of us, the work will go easier. There's pinyon up on the Summit. Nothing like pinyon for keeping a house warm," he smiled at Kenna. "I'm going to get some coal too. We'll keep Jack Frost out this winter, boys!"

"Who's Jack Frost?" Tommy asked. "Is Jack Frost mean?" My poor, little Tommy!

"Who's Jack Frost?" Valentine's voice boomed. "He's the fellow that nips your nose in the winter, Tom. We got to do everything to keep him out!"

Tommy stared so solemn at Valentine that we all laughed together.

There was that old winter again, leaning in on me. As I thought about laying in wood at my house for the winter, my face burned red, for I knew I had no way to pay for anything. I guess Valentine saw me because he said, "Now, Ruby, I am getting your wood and coal this year, and you can square up with me later. Don't worry about it right now." I couldn't answer him, since I knew I would never be able to square up, even if I saved every penny I ever came by the rest of my life, even if I magically got rich, even if I wasn't me at all. I could never repay my debt to Valentine and Kenna.

Well, Kenna made up a big grub box for those boys, with some bread and boiled eggs and what all. I sat in the kitchen and watched her, still not worth a hill of beans. She put in some starter so they could make a pancake up there and she put in coffee, of course, a bit of sugar, and lots of jerky. Just whatever was around the house so they could have some food up on the Summit.

You see the Summit up there, Miss? Look way out there, way up high. You see that? That's where they always went for firewood. It took a couple days just to get there and more days to get home, plus all those days chopping and dragging, and on and on. That gnarled pinyon and all that effort made those cozy fires right special, it did.

So, came the day they all headed up to the Summit. Once Ferris' big freight wagon was loaded with provisions, all the men climbed up the sides and settled in the bed of the wagon, voices layering on top of one another. Ferris flicked the reins at his mule string, and the wagon lurched into motion. Kenna and I waved goodbye from the porch, the babies and Tom standing by. James went along with the men, refusing to wave goodbye as he was still giving us all the silent treatment. He was starting to see life in a different way, realizing his pa behaved like an animal, and that he, James, had gone along with it. He was just a boy, after all, and it wasn't his fault he got Frank for a daddy.

Kenna said we should start a quilt then, so we did. It was a "Sunshine and Shadows" pattern. Have you seen that one, Miss? It's a scrap quilt, and you lay the pieces together by color so you got rows of light and rows of dark and then you turn it sideways to make a diamond shape.

"This is a good pattern for us to do this fall, Ruby, for it will help us remember both good times and bad. Sometimes our lives are bathed in light," she said, "and sometimes we fall under a shadow." Her voice became right serious and quiet. I didn't know if she was talking about me and Frank or about herself, but she looked very forlorn. It made me think about that night I had watched Kenna do her rain prayer, and I wondered if she would ever tell me about her shadows. She sure knew plenty about mine.

Sometimes we would both sit at the quilt frame and work a little and if the babies were sleeping, the house became so quiet you could hear the ticking of the clock. I loved those days. I came down the stairs every day then. We decided which piece of fabric needed to go where like our own lives depended on it; sewing perfect, little stitches. Sometimes Kenna would say, "Let's have some tea, Ruby." She would fix us a cup of hot tea. We sat for hours that way, quilting with the afternoon sun streaming in through the colored glass, dust motes floating in the air.

It was one such afternoon as we were quilting away, I got to feeling worse and worse about living off Kenna and taking her room; it weighed on me terrible.

"Kenna, I think it's time for you to have your room back," I said. "I will move to the other room. Besides, your bed is too tall for me," and right away I felt ashamed and ungrateful for saying that. I loved Kenna's tall bed, but somehow I just had to say cruel things, Miss. It was my way.

"Well, I guess that will be all right," she said. "We'll trade things around after we quilt this row of patches."

And so, I lost my little table and chair for my mornings, but my new room seemed real nice. The tall windows faced straight west, so I could look down to the flat and see the whole of the Ford, or I could look way across and see Frenchman's Mountain. I could see the tiny wagons in the Ford; people looking like miniature toys, and Chinatown fenced off from the Ford to the north. I got used to being up tall in a house like that, and not just looking out at the level.

It seemed so wonderful that just Kenna and me and the young ones lived in the house. It seemed like we had anything and everything we wanted, and we got to where we had a kind of routine every day. Breakfast, then cooking or gardening, then lunch, then quilting and hot tea, then supper, then get the little ones in bed, and finally sit in the parlor by the fire so Kenna could tell me poetry. Sometimes we just sat without talking at all, or Kenna would play some music. Each day was perfect, but Kenna did all the work, and I just watched or gave ideas about the food or did easy jobs from my chair.

One day, we stood in the kitchen talking about how we should fill the larder up good so that there would be plenty of food for winter. In my mind, I was thinking, *"Ruby, that's not your food. Don't start thinking that's your food."* I felt sick inside when I thought about the coming winter and not knowing what was to become of me and my young ones.

But then Kenna came up with a plan that surprised me plenty. She said, "Now Ruby, I have an idea. What if you help me put by the garden and make some quilts and organize the larder? I don't really know all the things I need to get through the winter. What if I hire you to help me, and then I pay you with a share of the food? You could teach me the recipes I'm missing. What do you think?"

Well, I saw right then that she was trying to think of a way to keep me alive without making me a charity case. But I didn't see no way out of my troubles, so I took her up on her deal. It was fun then, because right away we started planning and scheming to see what we would do, and I felt a little less worried about my winter supplies. Kenna had money running out of her satchel and her garden flowed over like Eden, so we could do about anything.

"Even before the food though, Ruby, we have to get you a dress. Let's sew a dress for you, and that can be part of your pay too."

"Oh, Miss Kenna, I can't do that. I can never work all that off. If I can just lay in some food, I would be beholding to you. I can't repay you for all you done for me already."

"Oh Ruby, don't worry about that," she said. "And it's partly my fault that you don't have a dress. I was the one who cut it off of you, if you remember. I was so furious!"

"Oh, I remember," I said, "and you had some choice words

that day, too!" Kenna put her hand over her mouth and her eyes got big, and then we both laughed like anything, and Kenna reminded me of some of the names she said to Frank, and then we roll laughing again, and my ribs were like to kill me.

"I used all my good ones on him. Dirty, son of a bitch!" she said, and we screamed with laughing.

"Piece of shit, waste of skin!" Screaming!

"Miniscule brain and a pecker to match!" More screaming.

"Backward, yellow peckerwood!" Clutching my ribs.

"Don't make me laugh no more, Kenna!" I gasped out. "Please, don't tell me no more!"

"Numb fuck!" she called out, and off we go again. We leaned on each other with our arms around each other, and we were fit to be tied, we laughed so hard. Tears ran down my face, but happy tears. Then we stopped laughing for a minute, but I hear Kenna laughing real high voice, and off I go again, laughing and clutching my ribs.

When I could catch my breath, I said "How about this one?" And I tried calling Frank a name, but used one of my mama's cuss words. "Dog dirt!" I said, and I tried to say it mean like Kenna did, but didn't know quite the right way to do it, and my voice squeaked high, and that made Kenna scream with laughing. Then Kenna couldn't talk, but she waved her arm at me like she needed help from laughing.

Oh, Miss, it makes me smile now to remember that day. I guess that was the first time I laughed so free with someone and no one hushed me or said I was stupid. Kenna said she might have some broke ribs after that day, just like me, but hers broke from laughing.

Valentine's Missouri Cookies

  2 cups sugar

  ½ cup butter

  ½ cup milk

  4 tablespoons baker's chocolate

  2 cups porridge, well cooked and completely cooled

  ½ cup nut butter

Combine all ingredients except oats and nut butter. Bring to full rolling boil, stirring constantly. Boil 2 minutes. Remove from stove. Add
oats and nut butter. Stir to combine. Spoon onto cold griddle or
cookie sheet. Allow to set.

CHAPTER 16

Kenna was real clever with a needle and thread, and she had a good eye for fabric and style and color, as well. She went down to the merc and chose the piece goods without me, since I wasn't quite up to the walk yet. I waited for her on the porch, expecting to see her trudging up the hill with all manner of parcels, but when she came home, she was empty-handed.

"I couldn't walk all the way up here with all those packages," said Kenna when she saw my questioning look. "Ferris is bringing them up this evening," she said, like having Ferris deliver packages was an everyday event.

"How many packages?" I asked, feeling sick inside. "We are only making one dress."

Kenna saw right away that I was worried about money, because she said, "Now, don't worry, Ruby. I'm going to make some clothes for myself too, so this isn't all for you. I'm in the mood to sew!"

"We going to have time to sew and work on food before I

go back down to my place? Seems like an awful lot to get done."

"Oh, Ruby, I didn't show you! Come on upstairs. Come look at the machine that is going to save our lives!" she said, laughing like a girl. She took my arm, led me inside, and up we went to one of the spare bedrooms.

"Look at this! It's a sewing machine!" Kenna said, pulling me over to a little table. But then, she just lifted the top of the table up and I see the top is hinged, opening to show a beautiful, black machine inside the table, a black contraption all covered with golden scrollwork and designs and all, and it said, "New Home". It smelled of oil and dust, and I could see the bright wheel on the side, shining silver like anything.

"Why they call it a New Home?" I asked in my ignorance, for I knew little of modern machines and household goods then.

But Kenna was always right nice to me. "New Home is the name of the company that made the sewing machine, Ruby. This machine will do the sewing for us! And look down here. You see this foot pedal? That's how we will make it run! Just wait and see. Our clothes are going to fly together!"

Knowing Kenna the way I did, I got a picture in my head right then of our skirts jumping together on their own while we slept. Seemed like Kenna read my mind, because she took hold my arm and laughed and said, "Not like that, Ruby! No conjuring! Now, come downstairs. It's time for our tea." Down we went.

Ferris finally brought up Kenna's goods late in the afternoon. I was about on pins and needles, waiting to see what she had gone and done. She had package after package wrapped in brown paper and tied with string, and I couldn't believe what all she had! Why, she had soft cotton for underclothes; velvety, black bombazine for skirts; bleached, white cambric for shirt-waists; hooks and buttons for finishing; just everything you can think of. She even had dear, gold buckles and soft leather strips for belts.

Besides the sewing goods, Kenna had bought all manner of jars and lids and pots for canning. I was amazed. I had a few jars at my house, but nothing like that. She bought gallons of vine-gar for pickling and a handsome, wooden box filled with neat rows of spices; cinnamon and nutmeg, sage and cloves, thyme and ginger.

Ferris toted in box after box, stacking them here and there on the kitchen floor. We tore into them, creating one big mess, flying from one crate to the next, praising each new thing we found. Finally, Ferris put down the last crate with a groan.

"That's about it, Mrs. Fletcher," he said, wiping his brow.

"Thank you so much, Ferris!" she said, handing him a coin of some kind or other.

When it seemed we had gone through everything at least twice, Kenna showed me one last package. "This is a gift for you, Ruby, because I love having you here and sharing my day with you, and because you have been so generous in sharing your children with me. So, please accept this gift." She looked like she was about to cry.

"Please, Kenna. No more. I can't take any more handouts. I'm feeling right low and poisonous," I wailed, and I was about to bust out bawling, too.

"Ruby, listen to me. I want to do this for you. Please, don't say no. It's a gift. Please, take it in the spirit it is given," she said, rubbing my arm right nice. "Come on in the parlor and open it."

We walked into the parlor; my hands trembled and my throat ached as I carried the package. We sat down, side by side on the settee, and I pulled the string off the parcel. My air jumped out of me and I could only stare, for there in that paper wrap was the richest, blue Merino fabric with matching trim, blue silk for a shirtwaist, and delicate mother of pearl buttons nested on top. The color made me think of the sky over the Ford right when the sun sets behind Frenchman's Mountain, not the red and orange near the center, but the deep blue right next to the fire in the sky; the blue that like to break your heart. That's what it was, and when I touched it with my fingers, it was the softest thing I had ever touched; angel wings.

"To match your blue eyes, Ruby," Kenna smiled at me. "It's called delphinium blue. We'll make a nice skirt and coat for you. I have a pattern that will work perfectly. And look at this delicate, black fringe! Won't that be beautiful around the edge of the jacket? And this is for the necktie," she said, rubbing some black satin. "Oh, Ruby, I don't know what to start sewing first!"

Well, it turned out that we used the batiste first, to make new drawers for each of us, mine a little longer than hers, so that they really were just for me, and a new chemise for each of us, with dainty shoulder straps and a tiny bow at the neckline; and then, a petticoat for each of us, and Kenna put a pretty ruffle around the bottom. That was all nice and easy to make, and Kenna had them done in one day. She cut out the pieces and then sewed them up so fast on her machine that it did seem like magic! There she was, hunched over that machine with her feet on the treadle, and them working back and forth as fast as she could go. Pins held in her pursed lips and her scissors lost in the mess, but she was right fast with that sewing!

As soon as she finished each piece, she handed it to me, and I sewed on the lace and buttons and made buttonholes. That was easy for me to do at my chair. We kept the babies up there with us, and they played on the floor with their dollies that Kenna made out of rags and string. They talked pretty to each other, and sometimes one of them would give the other one a kiss or say something in their baby talk that would cause the other one to look right serious. I guess they were in their baby world.

Kenna said next we would make my blue traveling dress, as she called it.

"You know my green dress, Ruby? The one I use to travel? Have I showed it to you?"

"Yes, I've seen that dress, Kenna," I said, my heart hammering again.

"Well, this one will be like that; the same pattern. Do you like that idea, Ruby?"

Right then I was swept back to that first day; the first time I saw Kenna light off the train in her bottle green suit to steal Valentine away from me without even trying, and my fun flew out the window.

"Yes, that will be fine," I said. "I love that dress. It's so pretty, Kenna."

"What's wrong, Ruby? Are you all right? You don't look well," she said. "I've worn you out with all this work. Let me help you to your bed. You need some rest," and Kenna tried to help me.

"No, Kenna. I'm fine. Let's keep going," I said, trying to change my face to hide those dark feelings that snuck up on me every once in a while. So, Kenna got out her paper pattern, and it had a picture of a fine lady on the wrapper, and she was wearing the outfit just like Kenna's green one, only it was pictured in black. Again, I felt that I could never own such a dress, but looked like I was going to.

But then I said, "Kenna, maybe we should make my everyday dress first so I can get out of this little, tiny dress."

She laughed and said, "I guess that does make more sense. I'm just so anxious to see you in this blue!"

Our skirts were easy for Kenna to make since they only had long panels all round and no ruffles or what all; just plain. They flared a little at the bottom, and the back panels had more to them. Kenna explained that was to accommodate our bustles.

"I don't have a bustle, Kenna. What am I going to do with all that skirt back there?"

"We're going to make you a bustle. It's easy. You are going to look beautiful!"

So, Kenna made skirts and when she was done with one, I did the handwork and hemmed the skirts; sewed shiny, brass buttons and made buttonholes *again*. Then, while I was still working on the skirts, Kenna started on our shirtwaists; spanking white cotton, I swear. I didn't even want to touch it, and surely not wear it for every day!

But, before long, one shirtwaist was finished and then the next, and again I helped with the handwork. The sleeves were generous with big puffs at the top, but they ended in long cuffs that buttoned up too, so I sewed buttons and buttonholes aplenty. Kenna made pintuck down the front of each shirtwaist so that they looked beautiful, with a flowing tie at the neck.

What a relief it was to get out of Kenna's dress! I was tired of tight arms and shoulders and my ankles sticking out. We looked right fancy when we wore those white shirtwaists, and we pinned up our hair but let a few curls sneak out. The tips of our boots just peeked out of the bottom of our skirts.

The first time I wore my beautiful, bombazine skirt and my shining, white shirtwaist, Kenna brought me yet another gift.

"I have something for you, Ruby. These amber beads belonged to my grandmother. Look, I have a string of them, too. They are perfect with black bombazine and white shirt-waists!" she said. Kenna fairly glowed when she placed that string of warm, amber beads around my neck. How beautiful they were, Miss; one, long string of slim beads hanging almost to my waist.

Well, I guess I left out the part about the blue traveling suit. I loved and hated that dress at the same time, but I still have it. It's down in the trunk, Miss. I'll let you dig it out later.

I remember the day we finally started in sewing that dress. We were still in our sewing frenzy, night and day it seemed like. The babies were used to being locked in that room with us every day, and Tom pretty much ran wild. He left every morning and came home at sundown, starving to death, having survived his boyish adventures down at the Ford with the other town boys. Who knows what he got up to.

Anyhow, Kenna laid out the blue fabric and put the pattern on it and started to work, turning the pattern pieces this way and that, and I could not tell what the deuce she was doing. I could see that sewing was not for me. It looked very complicated to me. Sometimes she would say something about a sewing idea she was having, but I couldn't make heads or tails out of it, so I just agreed.

Kenna got the dress cut out, measuring me a couple of times. She held the pieces up to me and pinned them together and what all. She allowed as how I had a tiny waist and how she wished she was tall, like me. I could not believe my ears, for I thought Kenna so pretty and tiny, and I wanted to be like her. She made sure the skirt was long enough, and it had extra fabric in the back for a bustle, just like my day skirt.

Seemed like all we did for days was cut and sew, cut and sew, hardly stopping to eat. Finally, I said to Kenna, "We haven't done hardly one bit of work on our food, Kenna. When will we get that job started? There's got to be plenty to gather out of the garden. We haven't picked anything for days, and it's going be time for me to move back down to the Ford before we know it."

"We are on our last project, Ruby. I think I can have this suit done and ready for handwork in a couple more days. But let's stop for today and go sit on the porch. We need some air! Some light!"

So, down we went to her pretty out of doors furniture. The dust from the desert hills had settled pretty bad on the settee, so Kenna got a broom and gave it a few good licks. Then we sat down to sun and watch the babies in the yard. I remember sitting there, sighing and thinking how I was feeling so much better and how my life was turning around; thinking that maybe I could make a go of it after all.

Kenna and I were in our matching skirts and shirtwaists. We didn't really mean to dress the same, but we did it lots of times because I only had one thing, and Kenna liked her new skirt. So, there we were in our same outfits, just sitting there enjoying the end of the day. The babies played in the dooryard, their little baby voices singing to us from the dirt. My face was getting better; most of my bruises were a yellow-green and my lips were pretty much healed up. Of course, my ribs still had a long way to go to healed, but I felt pretty good.

I guess you know what happened next. Like always, when my life took an upturn, Frank would show up and ruin everything. Well, here he came then, sidling up the hill, looking like he felt bad about what he had done to me. But I knew by then that Frank never felt bad about what he did. No, he was feeling sorry for himself instead.

CHAPTER 17

My stomach rolled over to see him striding up the hill like a horrible monster. Frank wasn't a very big man, but wiry and mean, with a sharp weasel face—sharp nose, sharp ears, sharp chin. It seemed like he noticed when I felt happy and he would come squish it, if he could. He wore dusty, faded pants and a wrinkled shirt that I had not seen before; no hat, and his forehead looked sunburned. Anything like that would really set Frank on edge. He could find a way to blame someone else for everything that came his way. He could blame you for a cloud in the sky or if someone else was standoffish. Then it was my fault. So, right away I thought he came explain to me how I had burned his head.

He didn't have a gun or anything, but Frank didn't need a gun to get his point across. I tell you, I felt right scared then. I didn't want to be with Frank ever again, but there was bound to be a fight. I tried to muster up some courage, looking for some fight in me. It burned low, like dying embers in my stove.

"Get the babies in the house, Kenna. Right now. Hide them," I whispered to Kenna, even though Frank was still way down the hill and could not have heard me anyway. "Lock them up and don't give them to him, no matter what he does. Hurry, Kenna. Hurry!"

Kenna got a look about her then, and I saw her hands shaking, but she did what I said. Down the steps she went, scooping up first one baby and then the other, carrying one under each arm, like two little sacks of potatoes. The babies set up hollering, but Kenna paid no mind. Into the house she stomped with nary a word, her skirts flying behind her. I heard the sounds of baby crying growing distant as she carried them upstairs. I thought that would probably be the last I heard of my babies, and I got to crying.

Minutes dragged by and I became right sick. I stood clutching the porch railing, watching Frank get closer and closer. No sound came from the house by then, so I thought that was good. I don't know why I just stood there or what I thought would happen. I had plenty of time to go in the house and get a knife or something, but I didn't move; I stood frozen.

So, finally, here came Frank through the gate and into the dooryard, and he looked up at me on the porch. I saw how desperately he hated me, but also how desperately he didn't want me to get away. It was all over his skinny, red face. His cheek trembled with fury, and his hands shook a bit until he stuffed them in his pockets.

"Get down here, Ruby. You get the babies, and you get down here, and you get home. Right now." He didn't yell or curse, but looked deadly furious. "And I want Tom and James, too. Right damn now." He took one hand out of his pocket and stabbed toward the ground with his finger, one stab for every word. "Right. Damn. Now."

Then what should come out of my mouth, but big threats I could not back up. I surprised myself. I said, "Valentine be here any minute, and he's going to kill you. He told me himself. 'Ruby, I'm going to kill Frank.' That's what he said. You better get out of here."

Frank snorted, "I know where Valentine is, and he ain't going to save you, so you can quit that idea." Then he acted nice for a minute, and said, "Ruby, come home now. It ain't right of you to ruin everything like this. It ain't right of you to take away my babies. And the whole town is talking about what a fool you are, thinking you can live up here, all high and mighty." But when he saw that wasn't working, he said, "I swear to God, Ruby, get down off there right now. Don't make me come up there and get you." He spit the words at me. Frank's face turned purple, he was so mad, and he was clenching his teeth together again. He was on the verge of an apoplexy.

"You don't care about the babies. You never even look at them, Frank. What you think happens to us when you run off like this? You left us to starve, Frank! You left the babies with nothing! Nothing!"

The depth of Frank's deeds came so clear to me, it like to broke me; my tears betrayed me, for they showed how very hurt I was. They streamed from my eyes so that I covered my face with my apron for a minute. At that moment, I no longer cared if Frank saw my pain. In fact, I wanted him to understand what he had done to us, over and over, every time he went on a tear and disappeared.

I gathered myself finally and dropped my apron. I said, "You think the boys don't know it's you that left us with nothing? Have you ever really looked at James or Tom? They are skin and bones, Frank, because of you!" I pointed a sharp finger at him. "Because of you! You only look out for yourself, Frank. You're a selfish pig!"

"See here, Ruby! Don't you dare talk to me like that! Don't you say another word! Shut your damn mouth or I'll shut it for you, but good!" he shouted as he neared the porch.

"Everyone knows you are worthless. You too busy worrying about yourself to even feed your own family. Your own flesh and blood, Frank! Well, I set you free then! Go do what you want!" I flung my arm at him. "Go chase after whatever it is you chase, but let us go. Leave us be. Get out of here before it's too late for you. Get!" I said, like I was running off a stray dog.

"Is that a threat, Ruby? You think you can talk to me like that? You will never be free of me. You understand? You will never be free. Now get down here and let's go!"

"Where you get that shirt, Frank? Where that come from? You got another wife somewhere? Is that it? And did you forget your hat on her bed?" I shook with righteous fury.

Frank drew his lips back, grinning at me like a coyote does when you catch it in the hen house. He rubbed his sunburned forehead and changed his tune for a minute. He said, "Why you got to be like this, Ruby? Why you got to ruin everything? Why you...?" I remember how he stopped right in the middle of his tirade and started up the steps, so furious he couldn't stop himself.

I could see that I was in for it again, but I just stood there; Frank moving toward me in great, long strides, very puffed up. Somehow through the haze of his rage, something caught his eye, and he looked toward the door for just a second, and then, once again, I watched Kenna paralyze a man. For he froze right there, but not like Valentine that first day. No. Frank was looking at Kenna in the doorway, and Kenna was standing behind a sleek, gleaming Winchester that I had never seen before. All of a sudden, Frank was not so mad. No sir.

Then, just as sweet as you please, she said, "No need to wait for Valentine, Ruby. I'll kill him where he stands and we'll bury him under the porch here." She tilted her head toward the floor. Speaking like a regular outlaw, she was, and then she cocked the rifle and beaded in on Frank's chest. She looked right gorgeous; her hair escaping her pins, her lips smiling a little lady smile, one hip leaning forward real pretty like.

"Now, lady," Frank stammered, holding his hands out in front of him, and I saw he was a coward. He was afraid, and when I looked at Kenna, I thought he was right on track, for she was not afraid at all, and she was not shaking anymore. She was not even mad.

I could barely breathe, but I said, "Kenna! What you doing? Kenna!"

I will never forget what she said then, Miss; makes me laugh. Our little outlaw from Boston said, "Why, Ruby, I've ruined a man before. Haven't I told you? Oh yes, and I'm sure I will do it again. This is no trouble to me." She changed her aim a little from Frank's chest to down lower, if you understand my meaning, Miss.

"Now, Frank, shall we end all your woman troubles here and now, or are you going to run down the hill like the lowdown, sack of dog dirt that you are? You decide." Her aim stayed true, with nary a waver at all.

My heart sang! I wanted her to kill Frank! I did! But it was not to be. Frank started walking backwards, and he got out of there. Out the dooryard he went, and it was so funny because he closed the wooden gate behind him, right nice like. Kenna kept her aim on him the whole time. He started to say something, and Kenna stopped him short. "No thank you, Frank. Keep going."

Frank hot-footed it down the hill while Kenna and I stood at the gate and watched. She held the little rifle in the crook of her arm like threatening to kill someone did not bother her at all. When Frank was way down the hill, he turned around and sent us some threaten talk, but we couldn't make out what he was saying. Looked like he was right mad again, though.

"Well, I would say that our troubles with Frank Holt are not over. Come inside now," Kenna said, like we were deciding how much lace to put on a petticoat.

CHAPTER 18

Kenna took to locking the doors then, and she kept the little rifle within reach all the time.

"Let's get extra wood in the house for the stove, Ruby. We'll feed the chickens a little early. I don't want anyone outside after dark. Not until Valentine gets home." Kenna was determined that Frank would not win.

We watched the babies constantly and we made Tom stay home, too. He was plenty mad about that, but we kept him close anyhow. We didn't want Frank to grab him. Even though I was not Tom's mama, I hated the idea of Tom ending up living with Frank all his life, for I didn't see how any good could come of that. Frank would only turn Tom into a poor excuse for a man.

"Valentine will be home any day now," Kenna said over and over, even though Valentine did not really live there. "Things will get better when Valentine gets here." Each evening, I watched Kenna stand at the front porch railing, looking off toward the Summit, hoping to see approaching wagons. I would say, Miss, longing was drawn in every line of her body and in every turn of her expression, for she missed Valentine terrible.

We went back to our sewing though, and we went back to work on the blue traveling suit. It was coming together beautiful, but when Kenna asked me to try it on, I put her off. I felt like if I put that dress on, I would never be the same. How could I go back to my old life with a dress like that? How could I make a new life with a dress like that? It didn't fit, Miss.

But finally came the afternoon when Kenna said, "Ruby, it's time. Put this dress on, now. It's going to be fine." And so, I did.

We went in Kenna's room, and she helped me put on the blue skirt that flowed like water. She helped me button my blue shirtwaist with a hundred tiny, pearl buttons, adjusting my crane bag like it was fine jewelry. She helped me put on my perfect coat. Though a tall mirror hung on her wardrobe, she wouldn't let me look.

"Don't look yet, Ruby. I want you to see how pretty you are!" She laughed and gave me a hug, like we were family. "Wait a minute!" Then she got out her beautiful hat with its feathers on top and netting down the back, putting it on my head with the brim tipped sideways a little. She handed me a little satchel with embroidered flowers and a little gold clasp. "Hang this on your wrist." She acted like I was a doll she was dressing. Then she led me to the mirror.

"Here you are, Ruby. Here *you* are. Here you *really* are."

I looked at the woman in the mirror, and I did not know myself. I did not know myself at all, for I saw a nice lady looking back at me. She looked like she had a chance and a plan and prospects; pretty even, under yellow bruises. She looked smart, like she could do plenty.

"Oh, Ruby," Kenna whispered. "You look gorgeous!"

I looked sharp at Kenna, thinking she was making fun of me, but no, she looked very serious.

"Don't you know you are beautiful, Ruby? Did no one ever tell you? Did no one show you?"

"Stop it, Kenna. I don't care if I'm plain. I'm used to the idea. You don't need to try to make me feel better about it. I'm fine."

"I'm not saying anything to make you feel better. I'm telling you the truth. Look at yourself."

She stood behind me there at the mirror, and showed me each feature, explaining what made me pretty. I had never heard of such a thing, and Frank had told me plenty of times how ugly I was.

"Look at your eyes, Ruby! Beautiful, blue eyes! Your pretty lips, just full enough! Your pert nose, high forehead, feminine line of chin and cheek. You are beautiful! Truly!"

That's what she said, Miss. On and on she went until my eyes stung like anything!

"You know what I wish, Ruby?" she asked. "I wish there was a way you could wear this suit in front of the whole town! I'd love to see the looks on their faces! I'm of a mind to put you on the train to Reno for no reason other than to parade you in front of every single person in the Ford!"

The idea of that scared me to death, but at the same time I wanted to wear that dress somewhere! Anywhere, Miss!

I wanted to stand there and act like Kenna, turn this way and that in the mirror and say, "Why, the bustle is just right, but these old shoes! What am I to do?" I could not be Kenna, no matter how hard I tried or how much I wanted to be. So, instead I busted out bellering like usual, squalling like a squished cat. But you know what, Miss? Kenna just stood by and let me have at it. She never shushed me or what all; just stood and waited for me to finish.

Finally, I started to take off the jacket so I could change back to my other skirt, but Kenna said, "No, Ruby. Don't take it off yet. Let's have a tea party! And we will pretend that we are fine ladies. We will sit in the front parlor, rifle at hand, of course!" Kenna laughed like anything.

"Kenna, you are a fine lady already," I said with all earnestness whilst blowing my nose. Kenna gave me a very serious look then.

"Ruby, there's plenty you don't know about me. I came here for a new start and to forget my past. I've made more than my share of mistakes, and I'm no fine lady. I'm just a person, Ruby, just trying to make my way."

Why, yes, Miss, that's what she said. That's what I remember her saying. I could tell she was trying to be happy again, and that she had not been happy in Boston. Didn't seem like it anyway.

We went downstairs for our tea party, but I gave Kenna back her hat first. When I walked down those stairs in that fine dress, I felt like a queen, my glorious skirts flowing behind me making magical, swishing noises. Very fine, it was, with purple and green light shining through the stained glass above the door and falling on us in rainbows. I pinched my skirt and picked it up a little, like Kenna, and I squared my shoulders.

Like always, Kenna made us a tea tray with sugar and cream and gingersnaps, and we used the fancy cups and the teapot with the gold spout. We sat in the pretty parlor and sipped and nibbled and smiled nice, talking about our food plans and what we needed to get. We allowed as how we should work more serious on the quilt and how busy we would be every day.

You want to see that dress, Miss? Get it out of the trunk there. It's down in the bottom. Bring it here.

Oh, it's a little faded, isn't it? It was the most beautiful blue, Miss. Look here in the fold of the skirt. That's the right color. See how beautiful it was? The fringe on the jacket is a little worn, but you can see it was so fine. You see? And the lapel? You see? Do you see, Miss?

I guess this dress saved my life as much as anything. I kept it hidden away and dreamed of it every day; dreamed of where I would go and how it would flow round my feet; dreamed of how people would see me. Most of all, I dreamed of how Valentine would spy me in that dress and suck in his breath and freeze up; how he would kiss me again, my hat slipping back a little and the netting reaching down to the small of my back. Dreamed of that plenty.

It's a hard thing to be an old woman and look back on dreams like this and face the fact that my dreams didn't come to fullness. It's sad and heartbreaking, Miss. Makes me wish I had another go at it; makes me wish I had done different.

But that can never be. This is the only chance we get, Miss, leastwise, as far as I know. So, my day went by, and all I got left is this old dress and this old story, and old friends that I miss real bad, wishing that I had done better by them.

CHAPTER 19

So, let's see. We finished off our sewing for that time, and we worked on the quilt when it suited us. The garden was real good that first year, even if it only had that sandy soil of our pretty, little desert valley. We gathered food out of there most every day. Mostly Kenna did, but I helped some. The backs of her hands were brown by the end of that fall, and her cheeks had color to them too, even with her fair complexion.

I loved going out to that garden spot. It did me good to see those things growing there, so green and healthy. Kenna's garden was not like other folks' gardens, but lush and green and rich, every plant screaming bounty, her bees buzzing here and there. Never failed, but a little breeze blew by, rustling up the leaves. I loved to smell the dirt—the good clean, perfume of the Earth. It made me want to just lay down in the rows, and so one day I did; I just laid right down in the dirt and rested the side of my face on the sweet soil.

"What on Earth are you doing, Ruby? Get up from there!"

Kenna said.

"I love the smell of the dirt, Kenna. It's so sweet. Makes me sure that I'm not afraid to die and get buried up in it, for how could something so sweet be anything bad?"

"What the deuce are you talking about? No one wants buried in the dirt! Death is a horrible, frightful thing!"

"Not to me. Not when I smell this sweet earth!" I said, breathing it in.

"You are crazy, Ruby. I'll hear no more of this!" Off she stomped to the house.

Why, when I lay in that garden, I wasn't afraid of anything; not afraid of dying and being buried, for the dirt smelled so sweet to me that it took all the fear out. I felt a little sorry for Kenna for being afraid like that.

We watered with buckets, so we toiled every day, but it felt so worthwhile. Any time something would come ripe, we harvested it right away and hauled it into the kitchen. There was bounty, Miss; abundance. We didn't know it then, but it was a good thing, for one of the hardest winters the Ford has ever seen was coming our way; hard in many ways, Miss.

Well, soon as we finished with our sewing, we knew we had to get to work on our canning. I learned how to can foods when I was just a girl, so it wasn't new to me, but Kenna didn't know much about it, so I showed her best I could, and we wrote down our recipes so we could remember them for next time. How I longed for my mother's cookbook that fall, Miss! Even the idea of canning set me to remembering days with my mother, putting up food for the winter. Dear Mama!

That's what we did while we waited on Valentine. It seemed

like he'd been gone forever, and it was right lonely without him around, not to mention we had to do all the chores he usually did for us. Just knowing Frank could turn up at any minute put a shadow on our days. We put our minds to our work, and kept at it all day.

Every morning we started out with a vegetable to put up. That meant keeping the kitchen stove cooking hot so we could ready the vegetables for the jars. Once they were cooked and put in the jars and sealed, we lined them up on the work table to admire what we had done.

"I feel so good, Ruby!" Kenna said, wiping her hands on a towel. "Look at our beautiful jars!" We stood there, arms around each other's waists, admiring them together. I had never looked at kitchen work that way before. It had always been just one more thing to get done for me, but with Kenna it seemed special. It was worth something.

There was the pieplant. Have you done any canning, Miss? You know what I'm talking about? Well, for pieplant, you have to cook it up first with some sugar, and then put it in jars. Not too much sugar, but some. The color of pieplant; pink and purple and green tones so pleasing to the eye! Soft colors, but when you look at them, your mouth waters because you know how tart that rhubarb is going to taste!

Kenna was very particular about her canning, filling every jar perfect. I outworked her without half trying. To Kenna it was play, but to me it was life and death; it was winter for my children. To this day, I don't think Kenna realized how hard life was for me. There she was, dallying around in the kitchen, when I was desperate to get the beans and peas done up. She never saw our hunger.

Lots of times when we were doing that work, we did it without talking much; just side by side; chopping, peeling, blanching, boiling. But other times we would talk and talk about what we wanted to make next or how much we thought we would put up. We planned each day, and lots of times we said the same plan over and over, even though we both knew it real good. Then every afternoon while our jars cooked, we sat at the table to drink tea and eat cookies or bread and butter.

We used the crates the jars came in for my share. Each crate had twelve little nests for the jars; wooden dividers that made boxes just the right size. Every time I put a jar in a safe little compartment, I felt comfort. Day by day, over in the corner of the kitchen, my stash of food grew; green beans, peas, beets, corn, pieplant. Wonderful!

Now, of course, we didn't can the winter squash. Why, squash is already canned for us, isn't it, Miss, in its own shell? So, we had stacks of that too. Kenna put her squash on the floor of the larder, and we stacked my share by my case goods. Those shining sugar pumpkins and little round acorn squash with their green and yellow coats winking at me from the corner. Oh, how I loved that! How safe I felt, Miss! I had a nice pile of butternut squash too, tall and skinny, their shells like wood; tough, like me.

At night, before I fell asleep, I counted my jars and my winter squash in my head, and figured out how long my food would last if I watched it close, and I could see that I would probably winter all right. I planned how I would use first one kind of squash and then another in my sad, little kitchen down in the Ford; my canned goods lined up on my high shelf, jar after jar after jar. Kenna played at filling her jars endlessly, every bean placed just so. I, all the while, poured and sealed as fast as I could; it was my business to stave off starvation.

But the smells, Miss, in that kitchen! The hot stove and the steaming vegetables, a gentle little breeze in through the window, a curtain bellowing out. When we made dill pickles, the aroma was so spicy and tart, it made me want to eat them all right then. When we made bread and butter pickles, the onions and cucumbers together with a little mustard seed and cider vinegar was even better! Sometimes the aroma of onions and vinegar was so strong in that kitchen we were right thankful for a little breeze.

We always made sure to test all our foods and taste them very carefully, and then we would look at each other and allow as how they were real good, and sometimes we would test them twice, just to make sure.

Now, pickled beets were my specialty, and I had a real good recipe I learned from Mama, with cinnamon and cloves. The beets dyed our hands purple, and all the tea towels were stained purple too, by the time we got done. Once the beets were in the jars, how beautiful they looked! They stood out from the other jars with their rich, scarlet color. Redder than red, Miss, jars lined up like Roman columns, each filled to the brim with glistening beets and bobbing cloves.

Kenna dug the potatoes that fall, not me. She got her shovel and had at it. I watched from the side and let her do all the work, for a change. Right soon, she got the hang of it and dug those potatoes like anything. She turned the soil while I sat with my legs stretched out in front of me, searching through the dirt for those potatoes and stacking them over to the side. Each one was a treasure when I came on it, still smelling like the blessed Earth. Same as all the food, Kenna gave me a share. We put my potatoes in a gunny sack and put the rest down in the cellar for Kenna.

Our work was finally done for that time. We tucked the babies in bed, shooed Tom to bed, and took us our baths. With our braids hanging down our backs, we called it a day. I settled in, feeling like I had enough food to survive the winter with my young ones, and drifted off to sleep like the innocent.

Next thing I know, I hear a voice calling to me from far down the hill.

"Ruby! Ruby! Come out, Ruby! Come on out, now!"

Lord God, it was Frank, hooting and hollering in the night. I could hear him getting closer to the house, calling my name all the way. I sat up in bed, but didn't light a lamp. Kenna was in my room in a flash, and we stood looking out my window down toward the Ford. Though we could hear Frank plain, we could not see him, for there was no moon.

By then, I could tell Frank was at the dooryard gate, though he still only looked a shadow. Here he came, though, through the gate and disappeared under the porch roof below my window. Kenna and I clutched at each other, holding hands for dear life. It was so scary, Miss, for it was the middle of the night, and no one to help us.

"Gather Tom," said Kenna. "Make sure we have him. Meet me on the stairs."

I quick did what Kenna said, rousting Tom from his bed

and dragging him down the stairs in the dark, him grumbling and rubbing his eyes all the way. By then, Frank was pounding on the door, calling for me to come out. He was drunk for sure.

"Ruby!" he yelled. "Ruby, come on! It's me, Ruby. It's Frank." As if I didn't know.

"Pretty Ruby, come home with me! Let's go home, now." He was carrying on like that. Kenna perched on the stairs with her Winchester laid across her lap. Tom and I sat down behind her. We said nary a word, but only waited in the dark for Frank to go away. A couple times he rattled the doorknob, and he sounded like he was near crying, the old sot. Thank the Lord, Kenna was still keeping everything locked up.

"Ruby, I love you! You know I love you! Let's go home and go back to how we used to be. Do you remember, my Ruby? Remember how we were in Kansas? We were so happy, my Ruby. I know you're in there. Come on out, now."

Frank had not called me 'My Ruby' for a long time. I had forgotten that's what he called me, and it was embarrassing for me to have Kenna and Tom hear that. I did not really want Kenna to know there had ever been anything good between me and Frank. How else could I keep her hating him?

Frank howled around out there for quite a while, mumbling to himself from time to time. Finally, like a drunkard will do, he gave up and staggered off the porch and back into the night. We sat on the stairs for a long time, and every once in a while, Kenna crept back to the kitchen to check that door. He came back no more that night, but I durn well knew he wasn't going to stay away. Frank always turned up, like a bad penny.

Kansas Pickled Beets

INGREDIENTS

20 pounds of beets

5 cups water

7 cups white vinegar

4 cups sugar

10 teaspoons cinnamon

5 teaspoons ground cloves

5 teaspoons salt

2 tablespoons whole cloves

Cut off tops of beets. Boil beets until skins are easily pulled off. Peel and quarter beets. Combine all ingredients except whole cloves and beets in a large pot and simmer. Add beets. Simmer until beets just start to become tender. Fill canning jars with beets and juice, leaving headspace. Add a few whole cloves to each jar. Seal and can. Makes 20 pints.

CHAPTER 20

Valentine finally showed up. We had our backs to the door, working on something, corn, I think it was. Valentine snuck up on us, leaning against the doorjamb, watching us. He was lean and tall and brown as a berry, slouching sideways and smiling out the side of his mouth, looking right pleased with himself.

"Well, what have we here? What have you ladies been up to?" he asked, just as cool as a cucumber. We both about jumped out of our skins, screamed, and threw corn in the air and what all.

"Good God, Valentine!" I said. "You liked to scare me to death!"

Kenna didn't say a word, staring at him and holding a tea towel in one hand. Valentine looked a little perplexed since he wasn't receiving the welcome he expected.

"Where have you been? I've been waiting for you," Kenna said. Then she dashed across the kitchen and sort of jumped on Valentine, hugging him on the neck and kissing him on the cheek. He let out a big laugh, picking Kenna up and spinning around so her skirts flew out and I could see the bottoms of her shoes. Kenna laughed and threw her head back, having a grand old time, and they stared in each other's eyes again, like anything.

You can imagine how I felt. I wanted to sink through the floor for starters, I wanted to disappear, I wanted to vanish. They looked so happy and in love, Valentine broader of shoulder than ever, and healthy, his shirt sleeves rolled up to his forearm, muscles rippling under his brown skin. He looked full of life, like something growing in Kenna's garden; nigh about perfect.

After a minute, seemed like they woke up and remembered I was even in the house. They turned to me and smiled with their arms round each other's waists, he grinning like a jackanapes and she swinging one foot back and forth, leaning into him. I could see that they had loved on each other before, for there is a certain way men and women touch each other after they have been lovers. They are more at ease with touching, and they hold onto each other longer. So, that's how it was; I could see it plain.

"Well, just look at you, Ruby," Valentine smiled at me. "You are looking so well! Are you well? How are you doing?"

"Oh, I'm near about healed up," I answered him, hoping he wouldn't notice that my cheeks were on fire. "I'm much better than I was."

"And the babies? How are the babies, and Tom? How's Tom?" he asked. Valentine was always kind toward my children, forever making sure they were doing all right.

"Good," I said. "Real good. Tom is outside somewhere, digging in the dirt. Babies are sleeping, but they are all good.

Thank you, Valentine."

"Well, that's good to hear," he said, looking around the kitchen. I tried not to stare at him; tried to behave myself as best I could.

"Look at all this!" Kenna beamed. "Look at what Ruby and I have done! We are just about finished with the garden. Just about!"

She showed Valentine all our work, and he admired every bit of it, and sometimes he picked up a jar, turning it this way and that, holding it up to the light. Seemed like he really did care about what we were doing, and not just listening to us rattle.

"We've kept ourselves occupied all these days you've been out scouring the countryside," Kenna said. "We've cooked and sewn and gardened and quilted until we are almost out of our minds! Come look!"

She grabbed Valentine by the hand and led him out of the kitchen and into the music parlor. She pulled down the quilt frame, Valentine standing there waiting for her every word.

He admired the quilt and looked close at our stitches, which about floored me. I had never seen a man do such a thing, but Valentine did. He stood back a little and looked at our colors and allowed as how the quilt was so pretty and going to be fine when it was done.

"Are you hungry? Where's James? Why didn't we hear the wagon come up here to the house?" Kenna started firing questions off one after another.

"The wagon is out by the barn, and James is putting the horses in the corral, watering and feeding, I expect. He's turned into a good hand. And, yes, we are hungry. I'll go help him finish up and then we'll be in. I want to find Tom. Where is that rapscallion? Tom! Where are you, boy? Tom!" His voice boomed out as he headed to the kitchen and out the back door. Just like that, he was gone again.

Kenna and I looked at each other for only a second and then headed to the kitchen ourselves. We started fixing something for them to eat right away; fried potatoes, fried bread, eggs, and a rasher of bacon for Valentine and each of the boys, for we figured Tom would want to eat with James and Valentine even though he had had a good breakfast a couple of hours before. We could hear their voices nearing the house, Tommy talking excitedly all the way. He had missed them pretty bad.

So, in they came, James looking very good. Not too skinny, but his hair was pretty scraggly. They sat down and started in to eating, telling stories of the trip and how much wood they got, how the freight wagon was loaded to the gills, and how they had brought us some presents too.

"What is it? What did you bring?" Kenna asked.

"Guess you'll have to wait a minute to find out, Kenna girl," Valentine teased. He was always teasing her. "Just wait and see. Boys, don't say a word. Don't let her wheedle it out of you! She's a charmer, and will get it out of you! Don't look her in the eyes, men. Don't look!" Tom and James covered their eyes, acting like she might turn them into stone. Kenna pretended like she was irritated with them all, but then they all set up laughing.

I laughed too, but my laughing wasn't as happy as theirs. I felt so lonely, like I didn't belong there, but the rest of them did. It made me mad at myself too, for I was tired of feeling sorry for myself. I didn't want to feel so funny all the time. Seemed like I couldn't bust out of it, though.

Well, finally we went out to see the wood and our presents, and there, tied on top of the wood stack, were two buckskin. Tom stood nearby, staring like anything.

"That's my present? A dead deer?" Kenna put her hands on her hips and looked very peevish. "That's my present? More work to be done?" She half-smiled too, pleased with Valentine for bringing home such a good winter provision.

"One for us and one for Ruby," Valentine said with a happy shrug of his shoulders. "I'll tell you what. James got this one." Valentine pointed to the biggest deer. "James got it for Ruby, and for the babies."

I looked at James so fast I about broke my neck. He turned scarlet, stuffing his hands in his pockets and looking suddenly very interested in the toes of his worn boots. My heart changed for him then, and I saw that he would grow up to be a good man after all, even if he had a man like Frank Holt for a father.

"This deer for me? And for the babies, and Tom?" I asked him. "Why, James, that's so good! That's going to save us!" I said, my voice shaking.

"He used my rifle, but he shot it, and he took care of it. He said right away it would be for you and the babies. That's what he said. Pulled his own weight the whole time we were up there too, with not one complaint. Just worked and helped and made a big difference. Yes, he's a good hand, and welcome to come with me again next year. Besides, who else is going to work for us like that, if James doesn't come along?" Valentine's eyes sparkled.

"Yeah, who else?" James asked. "I'm the camp slave and

hardly anybody else did any work at all." He smiled at Valentine, and Valentine put up his fists and acted like he was going to box with James. James hunkered down a little and put his fists up too, and they sparred around for a minute, so fierce and manly. Then Valentine pushed James on his shoulder, and James leaned forward into the push, and they tussled around like puppies.

"Well, I see that you two have become fast friends," Kenna said.

"He's no friend of mine," Valentine said right away. "He's a scoundrel, and will steal your coffee right out of your hand. We have to keep a close eye on this one." James looked right pleased with the teasing and smiled sweet. Then, surprise of us all, Valentine scooped Tom up high in the air and threw him over his shoulder.

"Come on, James," he says. "Come help me put this little sheep in the barn." Tom wiggled and kicked his bare feet like all get out, and those three walked off round the barn, just like they had been together forever; just like family.

CHAPTER 21

Kenna and I went back in the house to clean up the dishes, and we had a mess of corn right in the middle of canning and drying, so we needed to finish. It all felt different though, because we weren't on our own anymore; not with Valentine and James back.

They started unloading the wood right off. Lots of it was in big pieces of trunks and well-trimmed logs. They drug it off the wagon and piled it best they could by the barn. There was still lots of work to be done with cutting and splitting and stacking. Valentine allowed as how they would leave some on the wagon and haul it down to the Ford the next day, saying it would be better to cut and split my share down there instead of unloading and reloading, so that made sense.

James and Valentine hung the deer up in the barn to age the meat a little before we cut it up and salted it. James and Valentine skinned the deer that day, throwing the hides off to the side of the barn to be salted and tanned later, and they wrapped the deer in canvas to keep it clear of bugs. So, that first day they got back, it was just work, work, work.

While Kenna and I worked in the kitchen, we got to thinking about how we needed to tell Valentine that Frank had come to the house those times while he was at the Summit.

"I'll tell him about it at the dinner table, Ruby. Leave it to me. I think if we have the boys there, it will help," she said. "I'm worried that Valentine will be so furious. I don't know what he will do. I don't want him to kill Frank and end up dead himself."

I had not thought of that. I guess you can't go around killing folks for bad manners, even if you want to. The thought of Valentine getting in a scrape like that made my blood run cold; it scared me to death.

"Let's don't even tell him. Just let it go, Kenna," I said. "I'm moving back to the Ford tomorrow, and you won't talk me out of it this time. I have to go back home and get things going there again. Frank won't bother you once I'm gone from here."

"No, Ruby! Don't go yet! We aren't ready! We aren't finished! I don't want you and the babies to leave. You can stay here."

I stopped working and turned right to Kenna and took hold of her hands, and I said, "Listen to me now, Kenna. I cannot stay here no more. It's time for me to go. I can never repay you for all you have done for me. You have been better to me than any person I have known in my whole life, and I thank you." I was like to cry, my eyes stinging good. "But I'm going, and you won't stop me."

Kenna hugged me so tight and said, "Oh, Ruby! You may not realize it, but you have been good to me, too. You have been a friend to me."

I straightened up and said, "Well heavens, Kenna, I'm not moving to California, but only just down the hill."

She wiped her eyes a little on the corner of her apron and said, "Well, yes, that is true, and you can come here every day. We still need to finish the quilt! And the food! And now we have deer meat to handle. I have no idea how to do that! I don't think I can do it!"

"I will keep coming here and working, Kenna," I said. "We still have a deal, and I haven't worked off my share of the food, not by a long shot. So, I will come and help every day. We can still have our visits and work, but I will stay at my place. Besides, you need your own place, Kenna. You don't need me hanging round here all the time."

I saw that Kenna got my meaning, realizing that she wanted her own house back so she could be alone with Valentine. She nodded, and said, "All right, Ruby, but you must come every day that you can."

"I'll come until we get snowed up," I promised. "Every day, and we'll finish all our grand plans!" She hugged me again, and we turned back to our work, still holding the tie between us.

Part of me was real anxious to get back down the hill and try to fix up my little house. In Kenna's kitchen, there was a special place for every single thing; a special way to hang the towel on the hook, a special shelf in the larder for flour and sugar, while my kitchen was a disaster. I longed to go home and work there, bringing order now that I saw how things could be.

In my mind's eye, I could see my stock of food setting on the shelves, bread just out of the oven, and my rag rugs shaken and straightened on the plank floor. I dreamed of fresh curtains at the window, instead of the faded and ragged ones that hung there. I looked forward to winter at that moment, excited to return to my own place.

By sundown, Valentine and the boys showed up, having washed up for dinner out at the pump. They all came tromping into the kitchen to sit and wait until we were done cooking. The babies were on the floor over to the side of the kitchen, sweetly babbling to each other while they played with their ragdollies. I put plates on the dinner table while Kenna finished her brown gravy. The house was warm and lighted by shining lamps of coal oil, the floors swept and the chairs in place. It was so beautiful; so peaceful; a dream.

As soon as we all sat down to dinner and began passing dishes around, Kenna said, "Well, we have something to tell you all, something that happened while you were gone."

Kenna held one baby while I held the other. She looked at me, and I nodded my head.

"Listen, Frank showed up here at the house while you were gone. He came here to get Ruby and the boys and the babies. Now, I ran him off, so don't get so excited," she said, reaching a hand out to hold Valentine's clenched fist. "He left quickly enough. We just wanted you to know what happened so you can keep an eye out for him."

"Just so you know, he hasn't changed his spots. He was anything but nice, and threatened Ruby. She held her ground, though," she said, smiling at me. I noticed Kenna didn't mention Frank's midnight visit. I figured that was for the best, judging by the stern look on Valentine's face.

"You should have seen Kenna with that little rifle," I said

real quick when Kenna was done telling. "Why, she near about scared Frank to death!"

Tom already knew what had happened that day, of course, and he put his fork down and hung his head. James didn't move a tick, but Valentine pushed his chair back from the table and sort of turned sideways like he was about to jump up. He laid his fist on the edge of the table, and I was right worried then. It was plain to see that Frank was in a bunch of trouble this time.

Valentine looked funny at Kenna, and said, "How do you know about rifles, and who taught you?"

"Is that really important right now?" she asked, raising a raven brow at Valentine.

"It's important to me. That's enough reason," he said back, his face flushed a little.

"My father taught me, if you must know. I don't know why that is important right now. Surely, you knew I had an existence before I stepped off the train, didn't you? You know I didn't just materialize here for your benefit?" Kenna's voice was quiet and dangerous.

"Well, I don't like it! I mean it, Kenna!" His voice was quiet and dangerous, too.

"What? What has gotten into you, Valentine? What is the matter with you?"

"I'll tell you what. You won't be acting like that again. I'll see to it. And Frank won't be around to cause you to do so."

"You have lost your mind. Perhaps the water up on the Summit is tainted." She gave me her baby real sharp and stomped off to the kitchen.

"Come on, Tom. Let's go check the barn quick before it gets

dark," James said, and he and Tom disappeared like wraiths. That just left Valentine, me, and the babies, sitting round a spoiled supper.

"Well, that's just perfect," I said to Valentine. "Come home from days and days out who knows where, running with the boys, and try to throw your weight around here. You been in the hills too long, and Kenna don't belong to you. Kenna's her own person. You better figure that out, or else you'll be gone, just like Frank."

I stomped into the kitchen too, packing my two babies. Valentine stalked through the house and out the front door, slamming it soundly behind him.

It seemed like we made a pretty funny family. None of us blood except for me and my babies, and we all practically living together. We all knew each other real good and cared about each other enough to have a family fuss. Even James and Tom and me were different with each other, like I was their real mama and not some stranger living with them.

When I went in the kitchen, Kenna was cleaning like a house afire, her cheeks flaming red. She was right furious, grumbling to herself, but not loud enough for me to hear. We both jumped when the door slammed, rattling the whole house.

"Don't be so mad, Kenna," I said, putting the babies on the floor. "He's just fired up because he wasn't here to protect you from Frank. He's scared and it made him go bossy," I said. "Listen to me, now."

"You listen to me, Ruby," she answered back. "No man will ever again tell me what to do, not in any circumstance. Not Valentine DeRoo, nor any other man on this green Earth. The sooner Valentine comes to that realization, the better. He will either reach that understanding or he will lose my company for good."

"All right, Kenna," I said, understanding there was no arguing with her on this. I knew the lovers would get over their spat, but I sure was jumpy as a cat wanting to get out of there.

Then the boys came back in, walking with us from the kitchen to the parlor.

James said, "We saw Valentine on his way down to the Ford. He said he'll be back in the morning to take the rest of the wood down to our house."

"He'll have to return the wagon to Mr. Ferris," said Kenna, "and the team."

"Oh, no," said James. "Valentine made a deal with Ferris when we were up on the Summit, and he bought the wagon and team off him. Valentine's going into the freight business. Going to have his own business now. He's real excited about it, too. Going to get an office down in the Ford, and a place for the team. Going to get some deals with some of the mines around here, and the ranches out at Paradise and Novado, maybe Unionville. I guess Valentine's going to get rich! And I'm going to work for him soon's he gets going. Valentine says the Ford is just going to keep growing, and more and more folks going to be moving here and needing goods hauled here and there. The mines going to be needing timbers and spikes and dynamite and whatnot; all kinds of provisions." It was easy to see that James was very excited about the whole prospect.

Kenna kept her eyes on James the whole time he prattled on, shocked by this news. It seemed like she couldn't believe her ears.

"What about his work here? Here, on my place?" she asked, her eyes wide.

"I don't know. He didn't say nothing about that," said James, suddenly looking nervous. "I better turn in," he said, and he got the Sam Hill out of there again.

"Well, I guess he can do whatever he wants. He's not required to discuss his business dealings with me," Kenna said in a huff.

All at once, Tom set up squalling, saying he bit his tongue. Off he went to bed.

"Valentine is his own boss, Kenna," I said, "just like you are your own boss."

"Oh, is that so! Well, thank you for reminding me of that, Ruby! Thank you very much!" Kenna stomped off to bed, her skirts flying behind her as she fled up the stairs. That set the babies to crying like anything and calling for Kenna, and they looked right broken hearted.

I went back in the dining room and sat down, the babies toddling after me, squalling all the way. So, there I was in that fighting house that had just been paradise a while ago. I sat all by myself in the glowing light of the lamps while Kenna's tasty gravy turned to stone in the bowl. A little part of me wondered if maybe Kenna and Valentine wouldn't stay together after all; I even kind of hoped they would go separate ways. Maybe I had a chance to win Valentine after all. I gave the babies a crust of bread to hush them, and a little smile came on my lips, and I hummed a little hum, and then I cleaned up.

CHAPTER 22

Valentine was there bright and early, hitching the team to the towering freight wagon. He headed back down to the Ford, James and Tom tagging along with him. I think Valentine got some other men to help him too, because some of those logs and tree pieces were real big and heavy.

Kenna drank her tea up in her room, and I took the babies downstairs to clean them up and get them something to eat, so our day was started off. All the squash and pumpkins were still shining over to the side of the kitchen, and my case goods were stacked there too.

Finally, Kenna came downstairs, and we said good morning to each other. Seem like she was over being mad. She kind of looked at me sideways, and then she said, "I'm sorry, Ruby. I was very short with you last night. I'm sorry."

"Don't worry about that!" I said. "Goodness sakes, Kenna, everybody says a cross word now and then." So, our friendship was mended and we began our work for my moving day.

Kenna opened the back door, starting to head out, but she stopped dead in her tracks. There, on the back step, sat the grub box she had sent with Valentine, empty of grub but plumb full of sarviceberries and sarviceberry boughs; overflowing. Beautiful and fragrant, purple and red berries on top of berries, waiting for us, the sun shining on their dew drops in the fall morning air. It was like seeing a box of treasure there on the stoop.

"What the deuce?" Kenna swore. "What on Earth? What has he done now?"

"Why, they're sarviceberries," I said. "They grow up high places like the Summit, and come ripe in the fall. They make up real good into jelly! Look at them, Kenna! Look how beautiful! Enough for pints and pints of jelly! And we can make pies! They are good with pieplant, for sure! You can mix them in with your pancake batter, or make some delicious breads! I forgot sarviceberries! I forgot how wonderful they can be!" I felt the gift to the soles of my feet, as if the berries were for me too. "I guess this is what they call a peace offering," I said, and gave a little laugh.

"I guess so!" said Kenna as we lugged the box into the kitchen. "The leaves must be good, too. Valentine wouldn't have brought all these boughs unless they were important."

"Yes, that must be true. I bet we could dry them and make tea and medicines. Don't you think?"

"Yes," said Kenna, putting some leaves to her nose. She got a look about her then, her brain working hard a special way, and then she said, "Yes, for medicines."

"Well, we have to take care of these berries. They are ripe and we need to put them up! Let's dry some of them, too." She was bright and happy to be working again, and she stopped thinking quite so much about Valentine, but sometimes she would take a deep breath, and her air would catch in her throat like she was about to cry.

After we washed the berries, we added some of them to the drying place up on the woodshed, but mostly we kept them for canning. As we dug down into the box, we found other treasure besides berries and leaves. Down in the bottom lay a smaller box Valentine had filled with all kinds of plants from the Summit, their roots and dirt carefully wrapped in chunks of wet gunny sack. Kenna gasped at the sight.

"Look at this, Ruby! This is amazing! How did he do this? How did he know to do this?" she asked, her face shining.

"Guess he knows what you like," I said. "But these won't grow here, Kenna. They don't belong in the Ford. These are mountain plants."

"We'll see," she said, treating the plants like little babies, lifting them carefully from the box and moving them to the work table. "If I keep the hot sun off them, they might live. And it's down into fall, so they might get a start before the summer comes again," she schemed.

Well, we had to plant those little baby plants right then, before we did any more canning or other work. Kenna chose a special place for each one, planting each with loving care, whispering to herself while she did it—maybe even praying for all I know. I stood back mostly, for it seemed like Kenna cast a spell on those little stems and roots and leaves, and I didn't want to bother her.

"I wish Valentine and the boys would get back. They've been gone all morning." Kenna looked sad round her eyes, and

I knew she was wearying for Valentine.

"Well, let's cook up the berries that we're going to use for jelly at least, while we are waiting, and then we'll just save the juice for a while."

Even though we still had tomatoes to go, we put all that aside to take care of those berries before they went too far. We took to stemming and cooking berries, straining and sweetening juice, and washing jars and lids. If you think that kitchen smelled good before, you can believe that it was nothing like what it smelled when we got to cooking sarviceberries. I would just stand over by the pot and breathe it in, it was so sweet! Made me glad to be alive just so I could smell cooking sarviceberries.

The juice was ruby red, as they say; rich in clarity and deep in color, right pretty. We strained it through yards of cheesecloth, so it was a good thing Kenna was rich. It was a sight when we got done, for we had a huge pot of perfect juice waiting to be made into jelly.

By the time we ate lunch I was already worn out for the day. I trudged upstairs to pack up my belongings and get ready to move down to the Ford. I thought about my little house and how I had so much to do when I got down there, how all my quilts would be filled with dirt and dust; how I had to get things cleaned up. I was excited to go though, and I looked forward to being in my own place again. Yes, I would miss Kenna's beautiful house, but I would be back in my own place.

That's when I happened to look out the window and down into the dooryard. Who do I see but Kenna and Valentine, talking down there, maybe arguing again. I couldn't take my eyes off them, Miss, even though I felt like a sneak, spying on them like that.

You know, Miss, how when you see someone far away and you can't hear what they are saying, but yet you know exactly what they are saying anyway just by how they hold their heads or move their hands? It was like that. I watched and I saw Kenna was pretty mad at first, and when she talked, she held her hand to her heart, shaking her head back and forth. Valentine stood with his hands in his pockets, listening to her right close, and sometimes he nodded his head, and sometimes he spoke to Kenna, she tipping her head back to look him in the eye. Then once, while Kenna spoke, Valentine reached out and tucked an escaped curl behind her ear, touching her with such tenderness that Kenna stopped talking and just looked at him.

Valentine grabbed her then and kissed her very fiercely, and I could see the nape of his neck and his black curls just at his collar so that my heart twisted in a knot. He looked so sweet to me, standing there kissing another woman. A gust of wind came by and stirred up a spinning dust devil out in the brush, but they didn't even notice, just kissing and holding on out in the dooryard; holding on for dear life.

When they finally stopped kissing, Valentine took Kenna's hand and held it to his heart like I had seen him do before. He said more words to her, and Kenna said some words back, and he nodded his head. Then Kenna spoke again, smiling a glorious smile, hugging Valentine's neck, and I knew they were to marry. Valentine had asked her and she had agreed, and they would be happy. They would build a life together and work together. I saw it all laid out before me. I didn't shed a tear then, but only held the curtain to the side and watched from my used-to-be window in my used-to-be room.

Valentine walked off to the side of the house, Kenna standing and watching him go. Then he did a funny thing. He didn't turn around, but he reached his hand out behind him and beckoned at her, like saying, "Come on, come on." Kenna ran to catch up with him, taking his hand, and they were gone round the corner.

CHAPTER 23

I felt sick to see them after that, so I took a good long time gathering my things. I heard them come in the kitchen, laughing and talking about the plans for the afternoon. They were their old selves again and not fighting at all.

Kenna finally came to the foot of the stairs and called up to me. "Ruby," she said, "where are you? Come down, Ruby." So, I walked out to the top of the stairs.

"I'm just packing up everything," I said, keeping my voice light. "Just about done."

"Ruby, when you are ready, will you come have a talk with Valentine and me? We need to talk to you."

The last thing I wanted was for them to tell me about their wedding plans and all, but I came down and walked into the kitchen. The two of them sat there, very deep in their talk, stopping when I walked in. I felt I might fall through the floor; I just wanted out of there.

"Ruby, Kenna and I have been talking about your situation

with Frank. We just don't think you will be safe at your house. Not with Frank wandering around out there."

"Don't worry about me," I told them. "I managed Frank this far. I will be fine."

"I'm not so sure about that," said Valentine. "I'm going to make sure he leaves you alone, once and for all."

My heart skittered in my chest. I sure didn't want Valentine in a scrape on my account.

"What you talking about, Valentine? You're starting to scare me now. I don't want trouble. I just want to go home with my babies and live in peace. That's all I want." That lie made my eyes sting with tears so that I had to squint and look down at the floor. Lucky for me, they thought I was crying about Frank, so they were none the wiser.

"Hold on now, Ruby. I have a plan for Frank. I'm going to go hide out down by your place and wait for him to show up, and then I'm going to run him off for good. He won't be back. You can have your peace. Wait and see, Ruby. You won't even know I'm around. Neither will Frank, until it's too late." I had not heard Valentine sound so deadly since the day he got me out of my house. He sounded especially serious, and I knew Frank was in for it this time. I didn't see a way to get out of it, and I sure didn't want to be on the receiving end of any more of Frank's punches or kicks.

"All right, Valentine. I guess there's no other way unless I pack up and flee from the Ford, and I don't know how I could do that. I have nowhere to go and no way to get there." I felt very low indeed. It seemed like I would never dig out of the mess I was in.

"We're going to haul your food down in the wagon and help you get settled in. Then we'll leave and I will sneak back down after dark. You'll have to keep a good eye out until then, in case Frank shows up faster than I think he will," Valentine said.

"And we need to figure out what to do about James and Tommy. How are you feeling about them, Ruby?" he asked. I thought he was right nice to ask me instead of deciding for me. "It will be hard to keep Frank from taking them, but I'm going to try, if you are agreeable. I'm ready to hire James on, and Tom needs to go to school."

"I want the boys to stay on with me," I said, even though I had not thought it out before. "I think we will do all right together. We were doing all right before. I guess we better ask the boys, though. Maybe they won't want to live with me anymore."

Valentine allowed as how he thought talking to them would be good, and he hollered out the kitchen door for the boys; they came running. Then, we all sat down at the dining room table. The boys looked scared as could be, and I don't know what they thought was going to happen. I had never talked to them about Frank before. I guess Valentine could see I was about to set to howling again, because he did all the talking, and when he told the boys I wanted them to keep living with me, my throat closed up completely, I was so afraid they didn't want me.

But no. Both boys said straight out they wanted to move down to the Ford with me. I looked sharp at James to see if he really meant it, but he was looking serious at Valentine, and they were talking like men.

"I can help take care of Ruby, Valentine," James said, like a grown man. "Especially if you still got a job for me with the freight. Then we will be fine."

"You still have a job, James. Of course, you do," said Valentine. "Of course, you do. But boys, I have to say this to you now, and I'm sorry to say it. Your pa is going to come looking for you, sooner or later. You have to decide what you will do when that happens. It's bound to happen soon, because I'm going to run him out of the Ford as soon as he shows his face. He'll most likely want to take you boys with him. What do you think of that?"

"I'm not going anywhere with him, and neither is Tom," James said, his eyes fierce. "I hate him and his low ways. I want no part of him."

"Are you sure? If you are sure, I will stop him from taking you, but you have to be sure."

"I'm sure. I'm real sure," James answered, and he looked like he had never been so sure of anything in his young life.

"Well, Tom, what about you? Where do you want to go?" Valentine asked.

Poor, little Tom, his chin quivered like anything. "I want to stay with Ruby and James." He squeaked the words out.

"All right, then. That settles it." I could tell that Valentine meant it. I thought there was yet another side to Valentine that I had not seen before. "Now boys, how about we get this food loaded on the wagon and hauled down to your house? Can you help me out?" Both boys jumped right to work.

"I'll keep the babies for today, Ruby. Then you can get your work done without having to mind after them."

"That will be a big help, Kenna. Thank you."

Kenna and I helped load the wagon, too. It didn't take long

to get the case goods loaded and the batch of squash and potatoes, plus my few clothes. Kenna gave us milk and cream and
butter and some bread too, and wouldn't take no for an answer.
She had been saving her extra eggs in her water glass all summer,
and she gave us some of those, also. Soon we were all loaded and
bumping down to the Ford one more time.

CHAPTER 24

The house was about in the exact shape I thought it was going to be; one big mess. Dust and dirt lay everywhere, thanks to our beloved high desert wind; it formed rivulets by the door and tiny dunes on the shelves. It looked like I had some mouse problems. The beds were filthy, the dishes and pans needed washed, and there was hardly anything in the house; a half used-up can of baking powder and a bit of spices and such, but no food. Good thing I brought some of my own with me.

Valentine and the boys unloaded my case goods right quick and then went to work. James and Valentine moved the team over to Ferris' place and then came back to work on the wood. I started right off by building a fire in the stove and hauling water from the hand pump for house cleaning and laundry and what all. I was thankful that the babies were up the hill so I could get something done.

Before you know it, I was cleaning and washing and getting things in place. It felt good, too. I was happy to put my beautiful jars on the shelf and stack my squash in the corner, and one pretty pumpkin I put in the middle of the kitchen table for looks. I saw my little house differently then. It was to be mine alone, and I would make it the best I could.

The house was about the same as you see it now, but without the front room or upstairs. James built those on later. And my porch—he added that on. So, back then you walked right into the kitchen to get in, and then the two little rooms were off to the side of the kitchen. The kitchen stove was the only heat in the house. The little windows haven't changed. They are just enough to give a little light, but not let all the winter in. Back then I had pretty raggedy curtains on the windows, but later on I made pretty yellow curtains all round.

I had no cupboards really, but a sideboard and a couple shelves on the wall. I had a little stand for my water bucket. Just like now, I hung my skillets on the wall by the stove. It was and is a simple, little house, as you can see, but it has been a good house. It has been my house. Somewhere along the way I hung some paper in the kitchen, trying to be like Kenna again, I guess, but that was long after I moved back down the hill.

Well, that day. Hours seemed to jump past me, and all of a sudden, I realized it was late in the day and I was starving, so I quick heated up some beets and fried up some potatoes and eggs, sliced some bread, and then went outside to find Valentine and the boys so they could come eat. There they were, shirtless, splitting and stacking wood. Valentine was a sight, for he was skinny enough so that his ribs showed a little. His chest was furred with black hair, and I noticed a puckered scar high up on his chest, by his shoulder really. It looked like a star with points going out all around. It looked like Valentine had taken a bullet somewhere along his history, probably during the war.

"Come in and get something to eat," I called to them, and for a minute it seemed like they were mine, like Valentine was mine and he was going to come sit at my table and have some food. I blushed a little, turning quick into the house so he would not see me.

They washed up and in they came and sat down to eat, hungry as wolves.

"I'm sorry that I waited so long to cook for you fellows," I said by way of apologizing. "I guess I got carried away with my work in here and the time plumb got away from me."

"Not to worry, Ruby," said Valentine. "This is good food! Thank you! Are these the beets you made up at the house? They are delicious!" He kept on eating, and it made me happy to see him eat that way; eating like the big healthy man that he was.

Next thing you know, they were back outside working on that woodpile, even though the afternoon sun cast long shadows. I went out once to get more wood for the stove, and there was my shining row of firewood, stacked up by the back door. It smelled clean and sweet, like fresh-split wood does, and it made my heart sing to see how rich I was!

I remembered how I felt when I first saw Kenna's kitchen and figured out she was the captain of her own ship. I felt that same way about my place then! I felt free; my own boss. It was a fine feeling, I will tell you, and almost made me not even want Valentine around. It made me want to be on my own.

You know what it was, Miss? I wasn't lonely anymore, but just alone. Not the same thing, Miss.

By the end of the day, I had quilts and sheets drying on the fence and the dishes washed and back on the sideboard, the floor swept and mopped. I used the wooden crate from my jars to make storage in my room for my few unmentionables. I hung my crane bag on my bedpost so Kenna's magic could watch over me when I slept. My traveling suit hung from a peg on the wall; my beautiful traveling suit, hanging in that little, empty room. Ha.

Anyhow, those fellows worked until they couldn't see good enough to split wood anymore. Valentine came in to say good-bye, and James and Tom headed back to the food, scarfing it down like they were about to die. I offered Valentine some more food too, but he allowed as how he was heading up to the Hill House to see Kenna.

"I can't thank you enough, Valentine, for everything," I said, even though it was hard to talk. I couldn't bring myself to look at him right then, so I wiped off the table for the hundredth time that day.

"I'm happy to help you and the children any way I can. Don't forget that, Ruby. I mean it."

Then I did look at him, and I didn't care if the boys were right there, eating like there was no more food to be had, ever.

"You best head up the hill, Valentine. You best get out of here. Go away, now." And I meant it. I didn't want to see him anymore. It was too hard to see him around. "I don't think you should come back down here tonight. Frank won't come around, and James is here if he does. I would feel better if you don't come around here." I felt that it was much worse to see Valentine when Kenna wasn't around. It made all my heartache come back with a vengeance.

Valentine looked at me funny, but he didn't say much. "All right, Ruby. Whatever you say. Take care. I guess I'll see you up at Kenna's then."

"Yes, I'll see you up there. I will be working up there every day until the snow flies."

Then Valentine kind of bowed his head to me. "Good night, then. Good night, Ruby, boys."

"Night, Valentine," James called out around a mouthful of bread. "See you tomorrow!"

And Valentine was gone. I felt miserable and happy at the same time, for when I watched Valentine walk out my door, my heart liked to break. It seemed like something had really changed between us; the tiny thread between us was broken and not to be tied together ever again, and that made me sad indeed.

But when I looked round my little kitchen, it didn't seem so sad. It seemed like the house knew right then that I loved it and prized it; like it wrapped its arms round me, and it looked bright and cheery. It smelled clean and looked like good folks lived there, like the jars were lined up straight for a reason. Even though the boards on the floor were apt to give off plenty of splinters, the boards were clean. It was my home. Mine.

We were all plumb worn out, so we allowed as how we would call it a day. James sort of staggered off to the back room, and I saw how he would work himself to death if Valentine said so, trying so hard to show Valentine he could keep up and pull his own weight and all. I felt proud of him and made plans to fix him a big breakfast in the morning before he took off for his day.

The house was as silent as a shadow. I poured myself a cup of coffee, and sat down at my own table. I just had the one lamp then, but the room was aglow and nice and cozy. It was just like my dream, with my jars and squash and my tidy rugs.

I took my hair down, letting it hang down my back. I was pretty worn out. I took my shoes and stockings off, sitting barefoot, like a girl.

I thought then of my garden spot and how good the dirt would feel on my bare feet; the elm growing tall and broad in the very back of the yard, casting a black shadow across the ground; how I might hear a nightbird or a quail call to me. I picked up my coffee and wandered out there to look around for a minute. I didn't expect Frank to show up, and he didn't. Not then.

What a beautiful night it was! I remember it clear. The moon shone down on the Ford, but seemed like all the folks were in for the night. I have close neighbors now, but back then there weren't so many houses; just a couple on this block here. But anyway, I could see that no one was out. It was just me and my little place. I surveyed the low fence all around my place, noticing how it sagged a little on one side. I could see my stable out back, and I thought I ought to look in there tomorrow and see what was what. And there was the giant elm, just like I had dreamed of it; its shadow looked like a secret laying across the dirt.

I must have been a sight to see. I had been working hard all day, my hair was a loose mop, I wore no shoes, and I still had on my apron and oversleeves to save on my shirtwaist. I didn't care; I felt wild and free. I put my cup down on the step and headed for the garden spot. Most everything was way past dead; husks of forgotten bean plants, yellow carrot tops, scraggly corn stalks. Dead, dead, dead. But that seemed right to me. I needed to let the dead be dead; let the dead bury the dead. I needed to go forward.

And the moon! She shone down on that little patch of Earth, and all was forgiven. I sat right down in the dirt; plopped down and dug my toes in, Miss, like a child; dug my fingers in, too, like I used to do in Mama's garden back home. I wished I had one of Kenna's pagan prayers to say, but I didn't know those secrets, so I just opened my heart and soaked up the moon; just let her wash over me and heal my sadness a little.

I don't know how long I sat there, but I finally decided to head back in and go to bed. But, surprise of all, when I stood up and turned around, there was Valentine, standing there watching me. I saw that the moon was soaking into him, too. It was funny, because when I saw him, I didn't jump or yell or what all. I just looked at him and sucked in my air, and he looked at me, and I thought he might come kiss me again.

He didn't, though he did take a step closer to me. Finally, I said, "What are you doing here, Valentine? I told you not to come back here. Why are you here?" I felt pretty irritated with him. It is beyond me why men act like they do. Valentine didn't want me; didn't love me, but as soon as I started moving off on my own, here he is, wandering around in the moonlight like he loves me terrible.

I became right furious.

"Answer me. What you doing here?"

"I'm waiting for Frank. Guarding against Frank," he said,

but it didn't ring true to me.

"It's one thing to make ideas like this when we are sitting and talking to Kenna, but when it's just you and me, it's different. I don't need you here. I don't want you here. Not like this. I can take care of myself. I want you to go away. Take your big ideas of protecting me and get out of here." I shooed him away with my hands. "I don't want you to come around here like this."

"I can't do that. I can't countenance the thought of him laying his hands on you again. I won't abide it." Valentine looked so handsome, standing there in the night. It seemed like he didn't know what to do with himself; like he cared about me, but didn't know how to go about being with me.

"So, let me be sure I understand what you are saying. You don't want Frank to touch me ever again, bad enough so you slink around my yard all night, but you don't want anything to do with me either. You just want me alone, pining after you night and day. Is that right? Am I catching the drift?"

"I been breaking my heart for you, Valentine, wearying for you every day, watching for you every day." I was like to cry. "Why you got to come around here? Why you got to make me wonder about you? Don't be coming here! Go away!" I sort of flipped my apron skirt at him, like when I'm scaring off a stray cat.

"Ruby, please. Listen to me."

"Listen? Listen to what? You going to save me? You going to make everything all right now? You slinking around here for a reason, Valentine? What on Earth?"

He put one hand on top of his head, and I saw his throat

work as he swallowed. He turned his eyes away from me, looking down at the garden dirt, shaking his head.

"Please, Ruby. Give me a chance to explain."

"No, Valentine. You get now. I won't have this ruined thing. I said no."

He said no more, but turned and disappeared into the shade of the elm, melted back to the black from where he came. Right sneaky he was. I could see that. I thought about that funny scar on his shoulder, and I knew Valentine had a dark history for sure. And I thought, *Well, I guess I'm a little fey too, just like Kenna, and I know things when most folks don't. I can see things for the way they are, if I give myself a chance. And I see you, Valentine DeRoo.*

Then I turned sharp and headed inside, but I almost went back out to find him. I was sorely tempted. Here I really had a chance to be with Valentine, and instead I ran him off like a stray dog. I wanted to go back out and find him. I stayed in though, and I left my coffee cup on the step all night.

CHAPTER 25

I did not get much sleep that night, and it wasn't because of worrying about Frank. I knew Valentine lurked out there most all night. I was so tired from all my work on my house and from all my pining after Valentine. Even still, I could barely sleep.

But come morning, I had to be up and at it again. James and Tom were up early too, and ready to head up the hill. I fixed them some breakfast first, though it wasn't all I wished it could be. I made them some milk toast with pepper and a little butter and fried some eggs, and they seemed pretty happy with that. Those boys were so skinny, all corners and angles; no meat on them.

"I'm heading up the hill to help Valentine, Ruby," James told me when he was done eating. "Me and Tom, heading up."

"All right, James. You two behave yourselves. Don't make a pest out of yourself, Tom," I said as they slammed out of the house.

Off they went, winding up the hill, and there went Valentine too, so the boys hurried to catch up with him. James walked like a grown man then, but little Tom hopped and skipped about. I watched them go and thought how good they were doing.

As soon as I cleaned up, I headed up the hill, too. Kenna and I still had work to do, starting with jelly and ending with deer meat. I walked across the tracks and headed up through the brush. The road was pretty beat down and passable, but I still cut through the brush anyway.

By the time I got up there, the babies were up and running around the dooryard playing and chattering away like anything. They squealed when they saw me and came running, and that made my heart sing. I swept them up in turn and gave them big kisses on their sweet, baby cheeks. I loved them so, Miss.

It seemed like I wasn't a natural mother. I didn't love my babies the right way when I was all broiled up with Frank and life was so hard. I guess I didn't let myself look at them close, maybe for fear of more heartbreak. But then when things got better, I fell in love with my darling ones; my sweet little babies!

Anyhow, Valentine and the boys spent the morning working out in the barn, quartering the deer and what all. Kenna and I drank a cup of coffee in the kitchen while we made our plan for the day. That kitchen was sure busy all day! We boiled apples and sliced deer meat off the bone until we were blue around the gills. Valentine and the boys did most the deer meat, and Kenna and I layered it in the barrels with rock salt in between. It was a job, but just like our case goods, it was sure a good feeling to see that meat stacking up in those little barrels. When each barrel was full, we finished it off with brine to keep the meat from spoiling. It would last all winter.

Seemed like everything in our lives was like that then. We had a way of making things work. We stored our foods in our neat kitchens and stitched our quilts beside our snapping fires, and our lives were very rich, Miss; very good. I felt like a real mother then, and when I looked around my kitchen, I felt pride in my work, my house, and my family, knowing they would eat all winter. I had a true sense of accomplishment instead of just seeing it all as woman's work that somehow didn't measure up to what men do. In those moments of comfort and security, I knew that no matter how long I lived, it wouldn't be long enough, for I loved that feeling and wanted to feel it over and over. I just wanted to live my simple life, and find my joy in everyday things, Miss, for that is where the best happiness is, I believe.

Well, I guess you didn't know I was a philosopher!

We brined both deer, and that took a couple days altogether. We made the sweetest, sarviceberry jelly you've ever seen. It set up right pretty too, and we tried it on some of Kenna's good, crusty bread. It seemed like we had captured the Summit and put it in a jar, for the mountain colors were there if you looked close; red and purple and orange. The sweet fragrance of sarviceberries, it was fine; heavenly!

We all ate dinner together, and we fried up some tenderloin steaks, and if that deer meat wasn't tender and good! It was a luxury to me! I showed Kenna how to dip the steaks in flour and fry them up in some lard with salt and pepper. We fried those little steaks up until they were good and done, and then made some gravy with the drippings. Oh, Miss, that Kenna could make some good gravy! We cooked up potatoes from the cellar and fixed some string beans. It was a feast; a regular feast, with bread and butter and jelly, and the boys and babies drinking milk like rich folk.

Once again, the lamps glowed from the sideboard, the chair-backs gleamed with oil. It was paradise again, this time with no fighting at all. We visited and laughed and passed the food round again and again. Those boys were getting used to eating plenty, and they were growing like bad weeds. For the first time in a long time, I felt happy. I could sit at that table and feel peace instead of pining.

After dinner, Kenna and I went to the kitchen to wash dishes while the boys did evening chores. The house grew still and calm, except for the babies running back and forth. Finally, I said, "Well, we better round up and get down to the house. It's past dark."

Kenna said, "You can leave the babies here, Ruby. It's no trouble to me. I love the babies!" and she smiled sweet, for she really did love my Minnie and Elsie.

"No, Kenna. It's time the babies came home, too. The house is all ready for them. I'm taking them home with me tonight, but thanks for all your help."

"All right, Ruby," she said, looking like she could cry. It was hard for her to let them go.

"I'll haul your meat down next time I bring the wagon up here," Valentine said, real nice like always. "And your share of the jelly, too."

"Much obliged," I said. "Much obliged to both of you. Thank you." It felt like a real change had come to the three of us, for they stayed there, and my little family and I did not.

So, I took one baby and James took the other, and we all headed home. Kenna and Valentine stood on the porch and watched us go, and they called good night to us as we closed the little gate. Then James and Tom and me visited a little all the way down, with little Tom's voice piping high on the night air. Down to the Ford we went.

Kenna's Gravy

Fry meat in big cast iron skillet. Save drippings.

Add a few tablespoons flour and a small amount of lard. Stir until flour is browned, scraping skillet often. Add 2 cups milk or one cup milk and one cup water, depending on supplies on hand. Heat to boiling, stirring frequently. Once gravy thickens, salt and pepper to taste.

CHAPTER 26

Oh, Miss, look at this day! This is the kind of day I love here in the Ford; lowering clouds and rain far off, hanging in the air like a curtain. And see the sun shining on the other side of the valley, the yellow hillside glowing in the light! One mountain in shadow, all purple and blue, and the next one bathed in light and shining for all to see with yellow and gold and green! See how the junipers dot the Sonomas, and how the snow is just dusted way up on the peak, like fancy skirts for the mountain. It is my favorite, Miss.

Well, we were about done with all our work that fall, all except the quilt. We finished up the tomatoes and the garden was all done in. The garden spot looked a little sad and deserted then, empty of all Kenna's beautiful plants, her sister garden, her herbs. All done; all put up for the winter to come.

Kenna decided it was time for a gathering since we hadn't had one for an age.

"We'll invite the whole Ford," she said. "We'll show all those women what great work we have done!"

The idea of giving away stacks of our food turned my stomach; my heart was gripped with such greed!

"We are too tired for any such thing!" I said. "Let's just celebrate with us, and leave the Ford out of it."

"Nonsense!" said Kenna. "What's gotten into you, Ruby? We need to have some music and fun for once! We've nearly worked ourselves to death!"

There was no way to talk Kenna out of something once her mind was made up, so I eventually gave in, though I brought very little food to the gathering. I couldn't bear to, Miss. It just wasn't in me.

Valentine brought the wagon down to the Ford to load us all up, just like Ferris always had done. He was so proud of his wagon and mules and all, only he didn't use the freight wagon and whole team for little jobs like that, but just a small team and buckboard. So, we all climbed up in the box and up the hill we went.

The barn was lit with lanterns and the little fire was going in the fire pit outside. The big table was soon weighed down with lots of food; breads and cakes and pies, savory dishes and stews and beans. Mrs. Braginton brought baked root vegetables; turnips, beets, carrots, and two kinds of potatoes, all swimming in herbs and butter. That table was nothing to be ashamed of; it was a picture of bounty.

Before long, the boys struck up some tunes. The moon set over the Ford, and folks danced and laughed. Kenna and Valentine danced together plenty, almost every tune. They stared at each other the whole time, like they always did. They didn't care who knew they were in love, who talked about them, who thought it was good or bad. Kenna's skirts swayed and swirled across the dance floor when they waltzed, and Valentine kept his big paw on the small of her back.

Come late into the night and Valentine called to the boys in the band to play some of the good Highland music, the far lands' music Kenna loved and knew from her childhood. The boys played so that the fiddle fairly sang with Highland airs, so sweet were the notes.

"Kenna girl, get your drum. It's time you showed us what that drum is all about!" Valentine said after a while. "Play that drum for us!"

Kenna looked like she wanted to kill Valentine for that, but then all the folks started in saying, "Yes, yes, play for us!" Finally, Kenna agreed. Then, there stood Tom behind her with the flat drum and hammer in his hands, a bodhran it's called, holding it out to Kenna. She gave Tom one of her beautiful smiles, and took the drum like it was a big honor, kissing Tom on the cheek. Tommy blushed and ran for the hills.

Kenna walked up to the top of the dance floor and joined the boys there. She whispered to Wade for a while, and then he struck up a reel that we had heard before. Kenna only stared at him for a minute, and seemed like she went somewhere else, and none of us were there anymore. Then she started pounding on that drum in time with the fiddle. We were all consumed, swept up by the wild sound of that drum and the fiddle crying in the night.

Kenna became right free with her body, moving her head

in time to the music, tapping her toe, and sometimes she would right out stomp her foot in time with the drum. A little smile played round her lips, her cheeks shone, and her hair floated around her face in a very becoming way. She looked gorgeous; alive and young and free.

Then the music came and claimed me, and my heart set to pounding. The drum made me feel like a wild woman, and I wanted to dance and spin and hold my hands over my head like I had seen Kenna do, but I scarcely moved. I barely tapped my toe, for I was afraid to let folks see that I was moved. But inside, in my heart, my spirit sang! My blood gushed through my veins, and I knew I was alive, too! I watched Kenna move her head to the music as she played on, sometimes with closed eyes. Wade was working mighty hard to stay caught up. It seemed like when they first started, Kenna was chasing the fiddle, but by the time they finished, the fiddle was chasing her. When they finally quit, the last beat echoed off to the hills and over the Ford, and I wanted it back right then. I wanted more of that far lands' drum!

We all clapped and yelled for more, but Kenna said that was enough for now. She asked Wade to play some more mountain songs so we could dance, and that's what we did. Just like the first gathering, all the women danced Kenna's far lands' dance as best we could, and we laughed like anything each time the music stopped. Sometimes the boys would play a waltz, and most of the folks would pair up and waltz around the floor. I can still hear their feet shuffling in the sawdust, Miss, like it was yesterday.

Finally, it came time to head back down to the Ford. It was

awful late and all the Ford was about done in. Valentine hauled us down the dusty trail back to town, dropping folks from house to house. He dropped us here, Miss, just like always, watched for a minute to make sure we all got inside, and then off he went down to his little shack. I could hear the wagon rattling as he drove down through the Ford.

James helped put the babies to bed, and then him and Tom were off to bed, too. There I sat in my little house, so tired but not able to sleep. I guess all the folks were worn out after that big gathering, even all the dogs in town were quiet. No owls hooted nor coyote howled, just quiet; a sleeping little town.

As I sat there that night, I saw how time had changed things; how the turning of fall to winter was upon us, and we were all done with fall anyhow. All the jobs done, and me all moved home for good. I felt very sad then, for season change is always a sad time for me. I don't know why.

I grieve a little for the season going away and dread the season coming, even though I fall in love with it before it's over. Doesn't make sense, does it, Miss? Always pining for something I can't have. Just my mournful nature.

I can see by your face that you're wondering if Frank didn't show up that night, if he didn't come and spoil the last gathering of the year for me. Well, you can rest your mind. He didn't come that night, nor for many more nights. Little did I know, Valentine hid out under the black, old elm all those nights, waiting and standing guard. I didn't know, Miss.

CHAPTER 27

You know, it's funny how folks act sometimes. For example, my old neighbor, Mrs. Ricker, she was so mean to us all for so long. Why, she used to throw her wash water over the fence onto my clean laundry. Yes! Can you imagine? While I wasn't looking! Just as mean as a sack full of snakes, she was. But then, you know what? When I got rid of Frank, she started being so nice to me, even giving me milk for the young ones now and then.

And, after that last gathering of the fall, she talked to me over the fence about how I was doing. She had a tiny wagon. More of a cart really; a sulky, but she offered to loan it to me so I could haul the babies up and down the hill to Kenna's house. No mule, but a cart. So, I talked to Valentine and Kenna about it, and Valentine loaned me a molly mule from his string. Tommy named her Ginger, for she was a roan. Anyway, then I had an easy way to get the babies up the hill, for they were getting way too big to carry, but were too little to walk up there. I kept the mule in my lean-to at night. Valentine said he had too many mules right then anyway, so not to worry about it, but I did. It was just one more debt I owed them.

My days took on a nice routine again. Tom started school, though he tried real hard to get out of it. Valentine had a talk with him, and I don't know what he said, but Tom pure changed his mind about skipping school and got himself there every day. James went to work early with Valentine each morning. They either walked up the hill or went on down to the Ford to feed the string. Then the babies and I headed up the hill to work with Kenna.

Valentine rented a place down by the river for his freight business, down where First Street is now. It had a sturdy barn and corral with a little office in the front, glass windows and all. Valentine was about beside himself over that. He was right proud of that property and hired the fellow from the newspaper to paint a sign on the window; DeRoo Freight Company. Valentine was his own man, I guess.

He had a nice string of mules, and sometimes he harnessed up twenty mules to pull a heavy load. Then he would have the string and big wagon in the road for all to see, and once a fellow even took his picture with the mules. Valentine got to where he hauled freight all over the country, sometimes to Golconda, sometimes to Unionville the other way, and sometimes out to Andorno, which was real far. It took days to get to any of those places from the Ford. Lots of times, Valentine hauled supplies one way and hauled goods from the ranches back this way to put on the train to ship to further destinations. It was a good business he had there.

Kenna and I spent some nice days together working in the house. We quilted a bit each day, but we did a little other work too. We sewed shirts for Valentine and the boys for Christmas, and dresses and aprons for the babies, so we worked on those. Mostly quilting though. We finished the Sunshine and Shadows early that winter and set to work on our next one. I can't remember if it was a Texas Star or a Pinwheel, but we used up lots of our scraps on those, even cutting up some old clothes and aprons and what not to make it.

How some ever, I didn't get to have that many days up there like we planned. It wasn't that we snowed up; it was that it turned so devilishly cold that winter; too cold to haul the babies up there, even if I did have a cart for them. Before long the babies and I settled in for a long winter.

It was way lonelier then, for I had gotten used to being with Kenna every day, talking and planning and what all. Now, it was just the babies and me during the day, with Tom and James home at night. They were good company too, but just not as good as Kenna.

That was the first time little Tom got a job helping to cut ice out the river. Some fellows had built an ice house down by Valentine's old shack, so then when the river froze up good, they started storing ice in there. Tom somehow got a job as a helper, though he wasn't ten years old. Still, every day he ran down there to see if anyone was cutting, and then he'd check the ice house and make sure the ice was good and covered with slaked coal. That kept it from melting when the weather turned warm again.

I spent quite a bit of time trying to block up the holes in my little house. It's better now than it was then. Back then, the winter would just walk right through the walls, and you could see daylight under the door frame. A rolled-up rag rug laid across the door sill helped a little to keep out the cold air. I stuffed a few cracks here and there with newspaper, though James allowed as how I was building a firetrap.

"Well, at least if the house burns down, we'll be warm," I told him, and that made him laugh. Then he helped me out by gluing newspaper all over the walls as much as we could. It helped keep the cold out.

James brought home a little money that winter since he worked for Valentine. He had to feed and water every day that the string was in town, and that meant going out in the bitter cold with no gloves and a skinny coat that didn't amount to anything. Then he went on trips with Valentine when they had freight to deliver. When they had a job like that, they would be gone for days on end, and I worried terrible about James being out in the elements like that.

He gave me his money though, and was happy to do so, as far as I could tell. It seemed like he felt good to be taking care of us like that. The first time he got paid, I made James go get a coat and some gloves. He didn't argue, so I know he had suffered in the cold. I spent next to nothing, since I wasn't used to having money anyway. I did buy a little book for writing and some ink and a quill. I was so excited to buy that! I used it to make a recipe book for Kenna.

It's the very one in the trunk, Miss; all our recipes.

I bought some coal to help heat and cook for the winter. I

know this house was like an icebox that winter, but you know what? I don't remember it that way. No, I remember my little stove with a nice fire burning, and the babies warm in the kitchen. We ate good that winter because I had all that food put up. Why, we ate meat most every day! The babies grew good! They were about to quit being babies and turn into big girls!

That cold spell lasted for weeks. Just as cold as it could be. And then the pogonip came. You know pogonip, Miss? That's a Paiute word. Here in the Ford and here abouts we get heavy frost on everything sometimes, and it can linger for days. The whole world turns into a white, frosty landscape, and the fog sets down on the floor of the valley and won't budge. That frost coats everything too; windows and fences, trees, roofs, everything. It's beautiful really, but it can get tiresome. And all the noises change. Seem like you're listening with a blanket wrapped around your head. Everything gets muffled, and sound won't carry. You can call out to someone across the street, and they won't hear you.

So, we were just biding our time, and I hardly saw Kenna for days. Valentine sent word with James that he was checking on us, and did I need anything, but I hardly saw hide nor hair of Valentine. He was very busy with his new business, I guess, trying to make a living and all. James said Valentine was right determined to be successful with his business so he could provide for Kenna someday.

"Looks like Kenna does all right providing for herself," I said to him. "Looks like Kenna has plenty of her own money." I couldn't quite figure Valentine out.

"Valentine says he has to take care of her and he doesn't

want her money. Says it wouldn't be right to live off Kenna. Says he has to make his own way. He says Kenna's pretty mad at him too, because his business makes him leave town too much. Kenna don't like it when Valentine and me have to go out of town."

"I don't imagine she does," I said, thinking of Kenna up there in that house all by herself, all those days. At least I had babies and the boys to keep me company. So, then I sent word with James that Kenna should bundle up sometime and come visit us for the day. I said we would bake bread and gingersnaps together and tell some stories and what all. So, James said he would ask.

Kenna did come down a few times, sometimes riding down with Valentine, and sometimes walking if it wasn't too bitter. Those days were wonderful, too. Kenna enjoyed the babies so much, and she raved about how big they were getting, how beautiful they were, and what good girls they were. Of course, Minnie and Elsie loved Kenna, too.

Most times when Kenna came, we gave the girls a little bath in front of the stove, just a sponge bath. It was too cold for much more than a quick wash, but Kenna loved to slick up the babies and put ringlets in their hair, and so on.

She always told them a funny story when she bathed them. She would say, "Now girls, when a lady washes, this is what she does. She starts with her face," and then Kenna would wash a face. "And then she washes as far down as possible. Then she starts at her feet, and she washes as far up as possible." And she would be washing away on a baby. Then she would say, "Then, she washes possible!"

At first the babies didn't understand the joke, but then the light dawned, and we all laughed like anything, every time. Then Minnie or Elsie would say, "Kenna, don't say possible!" and we all screamed with laughing, and then we would scoop them up and dry them by the stove.

That little kitchen was safe and clean; smelled of baking bread. The wood floor creaked when you walked, just like now. It didn't seem like the same place where I had my run-in with Frank. I didn't seem like the same woman who took that beating in there. Seemed like I was changing into a whole different person, even though I was long grown up.

CHAPTER 28

That cold snap lasted for days and days, weeks I guess, and when it finally broke, we were all so relieved. I was so tired of the bitter cold days and nights. It was almost too cold to run outside for wood for the house. It was terrible.

Well, we were all so happy when things warmed up a little, but not for long, for when the cold broke, the snow came. Now, Miss, this is high desert, and we usually don't get that heavy of snow, but not that winter. That winter it came a snow storm that like to never quit. It snowed and snowed and snowed, so much so that I worried my roof might just cave in under all that snow.

The whole town pretty much shut down since there was nowhere to go and no way to get there. Why, my little sulky was worthless. There was no way it would go through that deep heavy snow, no matter how hard my Ginger might try. Valentine's string was in the same shape; the snow was impassable.

Why, even the trains quit running for a time. The mountains between here and California were snowed up way beyond anyone's reckoning, and the Ruby Mountains over by Elko were the same. Days were short there in the dead of winter, but seemed to drag on forever. Once I realized that we were pure snowed in, I started saving on lamp oil and food. It was a little scary. It just seemed like winter might never end.

Each day the snow stacked up a little more. In some ways, that helped the house stay warmer, I think. It felt like we were in a cave. Though the snow didn't cover all the windows, it covered some, so the house was dark and gloomy. James did pretty good trying to keep the back door so it would open and we could get to the outhouse. The snow soon became crusted from the wind, so we would walk on top of it, way up high, with even the fences turned into lumps and waves in the yard. Then the next storm would come and cover our track again. It was not possible to get to the pump, so we scooped snow and brought it in to melt for our water. We had to be careful with that too, since hauling snow in let all our heat out.

I worried about Kenna and how she managed in that big house of hers. I wondered if Valentine was holed up in his little shack down by the river, if he starved, if he had wood, or if he perhaps was up the hill with Kenna.

Sometimes in the evening would come a howling wind so that the house shuddered in the storm, the windows rattling in their frames, sometimes even causing the flame in the lamp to sway back and forth and the curtains to stir; terrifying. If my little house didn't hold up, we all would be dead before sunrise.

We were in snow up to our eyebrows and we felt pretty somber at our house. Yes, we had food and a fire, but there just didn't seem to be any end in sight. James and Tom sat by the

stove, whittling scraps of wood before chucking them in the
stove, or carving their initials in an old piece of leather, becoming very fractious with each other. We all had cabin fever.

Each morning, I peeked out the top of the west-facing
kitchen window to get a look at the sky, taking stock of what we
might expect. Each time I saw the lowering clouds, my blood
turned cold, for I could see another storm bearing down on us,
and I just didn't see how we could stand much more.

"James, let's stock a bunch of wood in here. It's going to
storm again, for Pete's sake," I said. He gave a big groan, but did
what I told him. He dug his way out enough to open the door
and then he hauled in armloads of wood until it completely
lined one wall, I standing at the door, opening and closing it
quick as he came and went. He brought in a big bucket of coal,
too. I sure was thankful that Valentine and James had got us
all that wood, not to mention buying the coal. I felt better after
we prepared; battened down the hatches, as they say. We could
surely hold out against one more storm.

And storm it did, Miss. Came a storm like I've never seen,
howling wind and blowing snow. I wouldn't let James out at all,
even to go take care of Ginger.

"That mule is locked up in the lean-to," I told him. "She's
got some water. She'll be fine for a day or so until this storm lets
up. If you go out in this, you won't find your way back."

"I'm going to go feed and water. I can't let Valentine's mule
die out there, Ruby! I can't let that happen!" James was like
to cry, like a little boy again, and I realized that he would do
anything to avoid disappointing Valentine.

"Valentine will never forgive *me* if I let you die out there, mule or no mule. You're not going," I told him. It seemed like he understood that I couldn't disappoint Valentine either, so he stayed inside.

The wind howled for about three days. James would hardly talk at all, but read the walls over and over. Many a night I watched him lean in toward the wall, reading again the dusty newspaper glued there, his finger tracing every line. He squinted like an old man, and I wondered if he didn't need glasses.

Tom took to napping every day and looked about wrecked, his white hair standing on end all different directions. The babies fussed continuously, until I wanted to smack their butts. It was just such a long winter! I dreamed of my garden patch and the green cottonwoods shedding a snow of their own, dreamed of yellow hills dotted with juniper and sage and golden rabbit-brush, dreamed of bird song.

Then, the worst of it all, Miss, I came to the realization that we had missed Christmas! Christmas gone by without us even knowing it. I felt a panic then, and it seemed like the whole world had disappeared and just left us. I went over to James and whispered in his ear that we had missed Christmas. My heart about broke for him, for he got a very anguished look on his face.

"Christmas? Are you sure? We missed Christmas?" He looked like a little boy, younger than Tommy.

"I think so. I'm about sure of it, James. I'm about sure."

Now, we had never had much of a Christmas before, but at least we had a little something, a special dish or pie to eat, and sometimes we sang old Christmas songs, and once, when Frank was doing good, he even brought the boys each some hard candy and me a nice cast iron pot. Sometimes it's easier to forget those times with Frank; better to let that go. Anyhow, I felt bad for sure, since I was the grown-up and supposed to be taking care of everyone, and here I had gone and forgot Christmas! I was like to cry.

Then James said it again. "We forgot Christmas?"

"Yes, James, we forgot Christmas," I said, becoming very irritated with him. "For heaven's sake, we forgot!" I said, right sharp. He looked so forlorn I couldn't stand it. "Let's have Christmas now, tonight," I said, and right away I wondered what in the world I was thinking of doing since I was very low on food, and certainly had nothing for a special dish. Kenna and I had sewn our gifts, but all that was up at Kenna's. There was nothing for gifts in my little, icebox house.

"I'm going to make a pie crust and put some sugar on it and put it in the oven, and that will be our Christmas," I said to James. He looked at me like I was crazy, and maybe I was. It was the only thing I could think of. But then he got the idea of it, and he was game for it.

"I'm going to fix up the house. Tom and me will sweep up. We'll do something," James said, nudging Tom in the ribs.

So, they got going on the house, and I made us some supper and I made that pie crust and cut it into strips, sprinkling it with my precious sugar. I had some cinnamon too, but I didn't tell the boys, saving that for a surprise. By the time I had some dinner warmed up, the boys had swept the floor and rerolled the rugs for the door sill. James trimmed the lampwick too, and polished the glass chimney so the light glowed through.

We sat down to eat while the wind howled round the corners

of the house, frozen bits of snow making sharp, tapping sounds when it hit against the few inches of window not covered by snowdrifts. The corners of the house were right cold, and the boys' room for sure, but we were warm and together, sitting at that little kitchen table.

When we were done eating, I quick put the cinnamon crust in the oven for a few minutes to brown it up. It raised up, puffing here and sinking there, smelling heavenly when it was done, and all the young ones were right happy with their Christmas gift. We ate that pie crust when it was still so hot it practically burned our fingers, the sugar and cinnamon melted together, the pie tin burned black where the sugar melted entirely. If I close my eyes, Miss, I can hear them talking round the table, passing round that pie tin. I can almost smell that hot cinnamon and pie crust. You know how that smells, Miss; how it flooded the whole kitchen with that warm scent? Christmas would forever after be linked to the smell of hot cinnamon for me; hot cinnamon and pie crust.

They slipped away from me, Miss. Where have they gone? How did I let them get away? How did that happen? I can't forgive myself for what I did; I can't get past how I let them get away. I can't forgive myself for that.

CHAPTER 29

I guess that was about the best Christmas of my life. The five of us were together, figuring out how to make a go of it, living together and helping each other. It didn't seem to matter that we had Christmas on the wrong day. We didn't care at all, nor did it matter that we had no gifts. That Christmas was about something else besides gifts. It was about family.

Well, after that big storm we really were in a fix. James couldn't get the door open anymore at all. We were snowed in. It was pretty scary because the snow was way up the sides of the house, and stacked on the roof too. It felt like we were in a trap and no way out. I worried about the stove chimney and if it could get closed up by snow. I knew we needed air, even if it was miserable cold air. I spent a lot of time looking at the ceiling to see if it was swaying in, because I didn't see how it could hold out under all that snow and ice. Before, the howling wind had nearly driven me crazy, but once the snow got deep like that, there was no sound to be heard, and the silence was much more trying.

"We are all going to stay in the same room from now on. We're going to stay in the kitchen," I told the boys.

"What? Why we got to do that? Where we going to sleep?" James asked, scowling so that he looked like Frank.

"Just do what I say, James. Go get the straw ticks off the beds and drag them in here. We're sleeping in here."

I figured if the roof fell in, at least we would be together. I knew I couldn't dig someone out if they were far from me, so I made everybody bunch up. James minded what I said, but he wasn't very happy about it.

"At least it quit snowing for a minute," I said to no one in particular. "For a minute." I thought about Valentine and Kenna, worrying about them. I didn't know if Valentine was with her or what, since we were completely cut off from any sign of a living soul.

Long about the afternoon though, we heard a muffled voice calling to us from up on the roof it sounded like.

"Ruby! James! Can you hear me? Are you in there? Ruby!"

It was Valentine! Valentine on the roof! Happiness flooded over me. We were saved, by Valentine, as usual.

"We're in here!" I yelled, trying hard not to sound too panicked. "We can't get the door open!"

"Hang on! I'll dig you out!" he said, scraping and digging round the front of the house.

"Stand by the door and yell at me!" Valentine called. "I can't tell where the door is!" Well, then we set up a ruckus to beat all, and Valentine dug and worked until we finally saw some light through the window.

"We see you! We see you!" James yelled, and I saw that he was scared to death but had been hiding it from the rest of us.

Pretty soon, Valentine wedged the door open far enough to squeeze through, and what a sight he was! He had his big sheepskin coat on and his freight gloves that he used for when he was mule skinning, and on his feet! Lord, Miss, he had snowshoes on his feet, but they were made of chair backs and they were tied to his feet with reins. Yes! Valentine had cut up his chairs and made snowshoes so he could get out and help us! It was almost funny. Lord, that man! Snowshoes out of chair backs! Not the entire chair back, Miss, just the middle part of the back where the bent wood part was. But it worked, I guess!

The air made a cloud when he talked, and we quick shut the door. I couldn't believe how very cold it was.

"Is the world over?" I asked, quite simple. "Is it over?"

"No. It's not over, Ruby. Just a real bad blizzard. The wind made it worse on your place. A big drift is all down your road."

Then I sat down hard at my kitchen table, and it come to me that I had been preparing to die alone with my children all those days. My ears buzzed, and I was like to faint.

"Ruby! You all right? James, get some water!" Valentine knelt in front of me, taking my hands in his giant ones, chafing my wrists. He made me take a sip of water, and that made my eyes clear and my ears quit ringing so.

"This has just been too much on your ma," he said to James, like I wasn't sitting right there. "This has been quite a strain. You take care of her after I leave. Haul all the wood and coal and do all the work around here. Do you understand? Don't wait to be told to do it. Figure out what needs done, what can be done, and then do it, night and day. Do you hear me, James?"

"Yes, sir," said James, and I couldn't believe my ears. Valentine had a way of making a person feel special; he was a gentleman. He also had a way of making James respect his words; James snapped to.

Valentine sat and visited with us for a time, but not long. James got bundled up and they went out to feed and water together, and to dig us out a little better. I put on a pot of coffee for them. It was bitter cold, and coffee would be good when they got back to the house.

They finally came back in, both nearly frozen. The mule was all right, but surely in need of water, so it was a good thing Valentine got there when he did. They had to dig the stable out a bit, and it was hard work.

"I'm heading up the hill. I have to go see if Kenna is all right," Valentine told us finally, looking very concerned. "I hope she's all right. I haven't been able to get up there. I've been snowed in." He sounded desperate, like he was apt to run out in the snow any second.

"Kenna's a smart gal," I told him. "She's all right. She's got lots of wood and coal and a strong roof. I'm sure she's all right."

"Well, I'm heading up there to find out. It looks like another storm could be brewing up, so I've got to get going again. I'll try to check back in on you when I get a chance. I'm not sure when that will be."

"What about your string? Who will take care of them?" James asked.

"Ferris is living at the office for now. He was near homeless, so it is a good place for him. He's feeding and watering, and keeping a fire going."

"Oh," James said. "I guess he's a good hand."

"Not as good as you, James. You've still got a job when this is all over. Don't worry about that. Take care of your family."

Then Valentine tied his snowshoes on again, looking up in time to see James give him a funny look.

"I guess you know that the whole town is going to hear how you tied chairs on your feet," James said.

"I guess they won't know unless you tell them," Valentine smiled at James.

"Oh, I'm going to tell them, all right. I'm going to make sure everyone hears about this!" James said, laughing like anything.

"Don't forget, I'm your employer, boy. Don't forget that!" Valentine stuck one big foot out the door, then the other, and he was gone.

CHAPTER 30

How the days dragged by after that, each blending into the next until I lost track altogether. It finally quit snowing and blowing, and the sun even came out a little, but by then we were way snowed up. It was still too cold for the snow to melt, so there we were.

I wrote a little poem that winter. The only poem I ever wrote, and I only did it because we were trapped there, and I had nothing to do. I said it in my head a million times before I wrote it down. I prayed it over and over while I stared at the tiny, sputtering fire or fixed us a little something to eat. I almost believed that if I thought about Valentine hard enough, he would show up again. That's where the poem came from; my dreaming and conjuring.

It's this, Miss.

When the summer comes around

Or when the summer thinking comes around,

I will conjure your ghost.

I will bring you here.

When I sit in my garden
In the poetry of the evening
I will call your name.
I will remember slivers of time.

When I stand between moonlight and deep shadow
In the sultry midnight of summer
I will cast a spell of recollection.
Peace will elude you.

When it rains,
When the rain comes around,
I will listen to the sound,
And, as if by magic,
It will be your voice that I hear.

Each day we waited for Valentine. He didn't come back for
eight days, or at least I think it was eight days. For eight, long
days we worried and wondered if he even made it to Kenna's or
if he froze to death on the way. In my heart though, I knew he
made it up there. I knew they were snowed in together.

I could see them in my mind's eye. It was just like all the other
times when I watched them and they didn't know I was there.
It was just like that, except this time I was more like Watching
Ruby. I didn't conjure Valentine to come to me, but accidentally
conjured myself to go to him. That's how it seemed, and when I
went to the Hill House, my body sat without moving at all, the

babies clamoring around me without voice; I had no consciousness of my little house; I was gone.

I saw how he got to the house finally, his cheeks crimson with the cold and his feet numb, even though he still wore his snowshoes. The dooryard fence was under a drift, with only a dim shape of it visible. A great drift had blown up on the porch, blocking entrance there and forcing Valentine to head around the side of the house.

The kitchen door wasn't much better, but Valentine decided to dig it out.

"Kenna!" he called. "Kenna, can you hear me? Kenna! Answer me!"

There was no sign of life from the house, causing Valentine to dig furiously, stopping to shout at Kenna every little while. Once he had dug out the frozen and packed snow, he wrenched the door open a few inches, calling inside to his beloved.

"Kenna! Kenna, are you there? Kenna, I'm coming in! Answer me!"

Grabbing the side of the door with both hands and giving a mighty tug, he opened the door far enough to enter. He scrabbled through, calling all the while, frowning when he noticed there was no fire in the stove at all. Panic squeezed his heart as he tore off his snowshoes with shaking hands. He slammed the door shut and ran through the house, calling all the way. Seeing no sign of Kenna in the parlor or dining room, Valentine bounded up the stairs, taking two at a time.

Just as he reached the top, Kenna opened her bedroom door and peered out, her hair tousled from sleep. When she saw Valentine, she rushed to him, throwing her arms around his neck.

"You're here! You came to me! Oh, Valentine, you're here, finally!"

"I've been yelling my head off for you! Why didn't you answer? I thought you were dead!" Valentine said, holding her away from him for a minute and then gathering her close again. "I thought you were dead!" He shuddered.

"I'm sorry! I didn't hear you. I was asleep. I've been staying in my room and only building one fire. I'm trying to conserve my firewood."

"Well, God's sake, Kenna, keep an ear out for a fellow, will you?"

"Come in here by the fire and warm up. Don't be mad! I'm fine." With that she dragged him into her room and shut the door. A little fire blazed away there, her table by the window set with cup and saucer and a few jars of food from the larder.

"What are you eating up here with no stove? Bread and butter pickles?" Valentine asked, looking at Kenna as if she had lost her mind. "That's no way to survive a blizzard!"

"Well, it just worked out that way. The fire went out in the kitchen days ago, and I just stayed up here. It worked just fine."

"Let's go downstairs and get the stove going and have some hot food, and then you can tell me all about your adventures. Wrap up," he said, handing her the shawl that was draped across the back of the chair.

Down they went, Valentine leading the way. He straight away built a fire, adding kindling and a chunk of coal. He pulled a kitchen chair near the oven, and said, "Sit here and stay warm. I'm going to get this place organized. We need more firewood and coal. Stay right here."

Valentine spent the next thirty minutes improving on the situation. Sometimes when he came in with an armload of wood, Kenna hopped up and opened the door for him. Every once in a while, he added a bit more wood to the fire until he had a nice blaze going in the firebox. He poured the bucket of water into Kenna's reservoir on the stove to heat, filling the kettle as well. Kenna looked on, her arms clutching her shawl close around her.

When things were in better shape, Valentine finally pulled up a chair and sat close to Kenna, taking off his big gloves and holding his hands to the fire. They sat like that for a bit, quietly warming by the stove in Kenna's fine kitchen.

"Well, now," said Valentine, smiling crooked.

CHAPTER 31

"First thing we need to do is cook up some grub in this house. How's the larder? Empty yet?" Valentine asked.

"No, it's not bad," Kenna said. "Let's cook something up. I'm starving!"

"Well, no wonder," said Valentine. "Going without eating all these days!"

"I ate," said Kenna.

"Hmph," said Valentine.

So, they cooked up a supper there, the puny sun already sinking on the short, winter afternoon. They ate at the kitchen table, with the door to the rest of the house closed to conserve heat.

"We need to fix you a place to sleep down here, Kenna. That way you can stay warm and have a place to cook, too."

"Shall we move the settee in here? It won't be very comfortable."

"I'm going to drag your feather tick down here. You'll be warm as toast."

For Valentine, thinking was doing, so off he went to get the mattress. Kenna followed, gathering her sheets and blankets, a few books, and her nightgown from upstairs. They tromped up and down the stairs, moving Kenna into the kitchen, just as we slept in our kitchen down in the Ford. Kenna lit a lamp, and the two of them set about making the bed and moving the worktable to one side to accommodate it.

"It's already dark, Valentine. You better stay here for the night," Kenna said, smiling sweetly at him.

"Shall I drag in the *settee*?" Valentine asked.

"No, I don't think we need the *settee*," Kenna answered. They laughed then, and fell together, arms around each other.

Then they stopped laughing and looked at each other, very seriously, he with his head tilted down toward her, she with her head tilted back from him, her hair falling prettily from her pins here and there.

For eight days I pictured them like that, night and day, awake and asleep. I would find myself imagining them and try to stop, but my brain wouldn't let me. Next thing I know, I'm seeing them again. Even when I could fall asleep, I dreamed of them up there in that house. My heart and my brain didn't know it was a dream; my heart and my brain acted just the same as if I had been peeking in the window; it was real to me.

"Come to bed with me, Valentine," Kenna whispered. "Come to my bed."

Without a word, Valentine turned and blew out the lamp, cloaking them in darkness for a moment, and then he opened the door to the stove, allowing the firelight to spill out. The wind howled something fierce around the house, rattling the windows and door, causing the embers in the stove to burst into new flames.

Valentine turned back to Kenna and began unbuttoning her blouse with all its tiny mother-of-pearl buttons, his big fingers fumbling with every one.

"So many buttons!" he said.

"Tear them off, Valentine," Kenna laughed. "Just tear them all off!" She reached for her blouse as if she herself would get rid of the buttons.

He pushed her hands aside. "Are you insane? Ruby will kill you if you tear off all these buttons!"

They laughed together again, and then Valentine kissed Kenna fiercely, bending her head back and holding her waist like anything. I didn't want to watch this private moment, Miss, but I could not escape! I was trapped there!

They finally shed their clothes, Kenna's skirt in a puddle at her feet, she only wearing her chemise, and Valentine's shirt slung over the back of a chair. Valentine pulled back the blankets on their makeshift bed, lifted Kenna in his arms, and gently lay her down there, covering her with the thick quilts. He took off his big brogan boots and his jeans, and crawled in beside her.

I was sure they had already been lovers, but when I saw them there in the kitchen, I realized I was wrong! They had never been together like this before. Valentine made love to Kenna, there in the kitchen, whispering her name. When the covers slid off them, Valentine grabbed them back to keep her warm. Kenna's hair spread across the pillow like the sea, waves and curls and ringlets.

At last, they gave up on the covers, not needing them anymore. The huddling stove with its open door gave off lots of heat, the chimney ticking in the night. Firelight flickered across the tick, the rumpled blankets, and Kenna's forgotten chemise; the heat caressing Kenna's bare legs and Valentine's lean flank and flat belly. Valentine rose up over Kenna, moving purposely above her. The lovers locked eyes like they always did, Kenna crying out in pleasure.

"Hot damn," whispered Valentine.

Hours on end, I pictured them in my head. I tormented myself all those days. I saw how Valentine helped Kenna out of her clothes every night, how he hung them over the kitchen chair and quick wrapped her in a blanket, their eyes on fire for each other. The more the terrible winter wind shook that house, the better they liked it. They never wanted the world to come back; they wanted snowed in forever.

During the day, I watched them there in the kitchen, eating together, talking, and sometimes working on something, and sometimes they played cards for hours and hours. They played cribbage with Kenna's old board; most times Kenna won, but sometimes Valentine won, and when he did, he leaned across the table and kissed Kenna's frowning forehead.

I saw how starving hungry they found themselves, for they forgot to eat for a whole day, so deep in loving each other were they. They quick dressed and built up the fire so they could fix some food. They cooked together and set the table together; they fed each other at the table, Valentine sharing his food with Kenna. He buttered his bread, and then put it on Kenna's plate without a word, but very sweet.

Kenna left her hair down, night and day. It hung round her face and down her back in glowing curls. Valentine loved it like that, and stared at it while Kenna figured what cards to put in the crib and what all. When they lay together, it spread all across the pillow. They held hands when Valentine made love to Kenna, clinging together for dear life. When it was over, Valentine turned onto his back and pulled her close, wrapping her in his arms and stroking her hair; he whispering her name and she whispering his name back to him.

"Valentine."

CHAPTER 32

Jealousy is a terrible emotion to have, Miss. I was so jealous it was eating me alive; the pain of it was almost more than I could bear. It was out of my hands too; I couldn't stop it; I couldn't rein it in. It was a sickness that came upon me and would not be cured. When I found myself conjuring them like that, I would say to myself, "Stop! Stop thinking like that!" But next couple minutes, there I was again, dreaming of them!

That's what I was doing when Valentine finally showed up again. I was sitting at the kitchen table, conjuring Valentine and Kenna in the Hill House.

"Hello the house!" his voice boomed across the snow.

"It's Valentine! It's Valentine!" both boys yelled together, and then the babies started yelling it too. "Valentine! Valentine!"

James opened the door, and there he stood, his black hair curled around the nape of his neck and the collar of his big coat.

"Valentine, come in!" James called, and held the door open for him. Valentine still wore his snowshoes, as the snow was still a mess. He stepped in and sat down in a chair to take them off.

"Hello all! How are you doing here? How is everyone? I came to check on you all. Where are my beauties? Babies! Come here!" and he held his arms so the babies could swarm him.

"How is the traveling up to the house?" James asked, and Valentine allowed as how it was pretty slow.

"You have to watch out for walking over big sagebrush. The snow caves in and down you go!" Valentine told us. "It's pretty deep, and the drifts are unbelievable! Eight feet deep in spots, I would say."

"How's your string?" James asked. "How they doing in this weather?"

"I don't know. I've been up at Kenna's this whole time," and Valentine looked at me quick. "Ferris said he would help me out with them, so I guess they're fine."

I made some coffee for him then, and he sat and visited with us. He looked very happy, like he loved being alive. My little house suddenly felt very full and cheerful, voices layering one on top of another, everyone trying to talk at once.

"Here's some coffee for you, Valentine," and I put a cup before him.

He picked it up, holding it close to his face. "Smells wonderful, Ruby. Thank you!"

I watched while he drank and visited, but I couldn't say much. I felt like he knew I had been dreaming of him and Kenna up there; felt like he caught me spying. When he finished his coffee, him and James went out to do some chores round there, check the roof and what not. I sat down heavy when they went out, wanting to scream, for when he went out the door, the light went out of the house at the same time, and I knew I would never get over Valentine DeRoo. I saw that I was saddled with this stupid heartache for life, and I was so disappointed and tired out, grieving and wearying for that man.

CHAPTER 33

Valentine pretty much just started living up at the Hill House then. The snow sunk down some finally, and folks could get around a little. The trains started running again, thank the Lord, but the first time we heard that whistle blow, we all about jumped out of our skins. When we heard it every day, we never paid it much mind, but when it had been gone all that time and then came back, it startled us plenty.

Of course, everyone in town was plumb shocked that Valentine would stay up there like that, with the whole town watching. No one said much to me about it since they knew Kenna was my friend, but they were talking. Every day, Valentine walked down to the Ford to take care of his mules and do a little work. There was no freight moving anywhere, so I don't really know what he worked on, but he did some work.

Finally, when things straightened out enough for wagons to pass, Valentine went back to using his wagon to go up and down the hill. One day, he stopped in to see us and invite us up the hill for Christmas.

"I guess we all missed Christmas," he said, "but Kenna and I were thinking we could celebrate now. Kenna wants to invite you all up to the house for dinner. How does that sound? I have to go feed the string, but I can pick you up and haul you up there in a couple of hours. Kenna says you could all spend the night so the babies won't have to go out in the cold tonight. She's already fixing supper, so you can't say no. What do you say, Ruby?"

"Sounds real nice," I said. "We'll be ready when you come back around."

"Fine. See you later."

"Can I go with you, Valentine? I'll help out!" James offered, and Valentine took him up on it, so James was back to work.

It seemed like years since I had seen Kenna. I sat there waiting for Valentine to come back and haul us up the hill. Part of me was so anxious to get up there, and part of me was scared to see the kitchen and know that I had dreamed it just right. I wanted to see Kenna, but then again, I worried she would take one look at me and know Watching Ruby had been to her house. I was in a big mess, just like always.

I quick got the babies and Tommy cleaned up and ready. Then I got the recipe book out, wrapping it in a flour sack and tying it shut with kitchen twine. The book wasn't quite done, but I figured we could add to it as we went. I knew Kenna would love that recipe book! I hoped that when I saw her, we would be like old friends again, but I didn't know for sure how it would be. I guess my jealous mind had built up a whole world and had fenced me inside it.

We were all bundled to the gills and loaded in the wagon by the middle of the morning. It was still plenty cold, and I was glad we were spending the night so the babies wouldn't have to be outside again that day. Up we went through the deep ruts, and slow going it was, but finally, there we were at the Hill House. It looked none the worse for wear after all that cold and snow.

Kenna came running out the door, yelling and screaming for us to get out that wagon and get in the house. She wore her nice apron over a pretty calico dress, her hair pinned up like a Gibson Girl. Her face glowed, she was so happy to see us.

Valentine walked round the wagon and gathered a baby in each arm and tromped through the dooryard with them.

"Look what I found, Kenna! Look at these girls here! Here's your Christmas present!" and the babies squealed like anything.

"Give them to me! Here, give them to me!" and Kenna was like to cry. Then I could see how very much she had missed us.

When I got up to the porch, she put the girls down and gave me a big hug.

"Ruby! Ruby! I've missed you so!" and she leaned back to look at me and then hugged me again.

"Kenna," I said, "it's so good to see you. I was thinking I would never see you again! I thought the winter would never let us out again!" I hugged her hard, too.

"Come in, come in!" she said, hugging first one child and then another, pulling them all to her several times before Valentine finally said for her to quit.

As usual, the house smelled heavenly, a mixture of furniture polish and books and good food cooking in the kitchen. A fire burned in every fireplace, making everything so cheery and warm. There were paper parcels tied with string in the parlor, and each had a name written on it in Kenna's pretty hand. I added Kenna's recipe book to the stack.

Well, it was hustle and bustle after that, with cooking and visiting and Valentine letting the little girls take turns playing "This is how the lady rides" on his big work boot. Surprise of all, I could see no clue of a tick having been in there on the floor, no cribbage board on the kitchen table, nothing of all my dreams I tortured myself with. Just Kenna's pretty little kitchen with everything put just where it belonged, as neat as a pin.

We set the dinner table real pretty with Kenna's fancy dishes. The daylight was short, so we lit the lamps and set them around too. Then it was time to get the pumpkin pie out the oven and sit down to eat. It was like old times with all of us sitting round that table. Valentine visited with the boys like they were grown men, and it was plain to see that the babies were in love with Valentine. One sat at each side of him while we ate. They ate like big girls too, with nice manners; they were growing up before my eyes.

When dinner finally ended, we ate some of Kenna's delicious pie, dished right out of her fancy scalloped pie plate. Then we all trooped to the kitchen to clean up, boys and all. When the dishes were done and put away, Kenna allowed as how we should all go to the parlor for Christmas. We each found a place to sit, the babies on the rug in front of the fireplace, and the rest of us perched all around on Kenna's fancy furniture.

"Valentine, you should hand out the gifts," Kenna said, and so he did.

I get a lump in my throat when I think about those children

that night. They were so excited, even James, who was almost grown. Their eyes shone as they watched each other, the fire snapping and the wind battering against the house. We were safe and warm and together, and I felt glad that we had missed Christmas.

Tom and James opened their shirts and exclaimed over them, thanking us nicely. Valentine liked his shirt, too. The babies didn't care much about their pinafores, but Kenna gave them each a new dolly from the merc, and they were taken with those.

"Valentine, what about those cases behind you there?" Kenna asked.

"Well, I don't know. Let me see," Valentine said, squinting at the name tag on the cases. "This says, 'To Tom', and this one says, 'To the scoundrel, James,'" he said. "Here you go, boys."

We were all about floored, for Kenna and Valentine gave Tom and James each a gleaming mandolin that they had ordered from the mail order. They weren't wrapped with the other gifts, but just leaning in their cases against the wall there, in the parlor. James sat stunned, touching the velvet lining of the case.

"Why, Miss Kenna," he said. "Thank you very kindly! I can't believe it! Look at this, Ruby! Can you believe it?" James was the happiest I had ever seen him. His face beamed for a bit, but then he dropped his eyes and said, "But I can't play at all. I never touched a mandolin before."

"We'll see if we can't talk Wade into teaching you boys how to play a little," Valentine said. The boys allowed as how that would be a good idea, and James' joy was restored.

Then Kenna gave me a package, so I said, "Well, here's one for you, too." I handed her the flour sack parcel.

"You open yours first," she said. "It's from Valentine and me." I could see plain that she was very happy to give me a gift, and I felt happy too. We were still the best of friends, no matter what else happened, or how many times I spied on her. Kenna was my friend.

You see that brush and hand mirror set there, Miss? That's what Kenna gave me. I had never owned such a thing. Bring it here, Miss. Look close at this. These stones are called rhinestones, just like diamonds, they are, but blue! It has more pieces in the trunk, a comb and a powder jar, hairpins and hair forks. The combs matched my suit, don't you know. When I opened the paper, I could not breathe! I could not believe my eyes! I was like to cry.

"Kenna!" I said. "Kenna, this is so…" and I could not find words.

"Do you like them?" and she picked up a comb. "Aren't they pretty? Do you like them?" she asked, her eyes shining.

"Oh, yes, I like them!" I said, when I could talk. "I can't believe it. It's for me?"

Kenna laughed and said, "Of course it's for you, Ruby! Let's try a comb right now." She came to me and put one of the combs in my hair. "It's perfect with your hair, Ruby! Perfect!" and she hugged me again.

"Thank you, Kenna. Thank you, Valentine."

Then I told Kenna to open her present, so she did.

"What can it be?" she said while she was untying the string. "What on Earth?" and then she opened the little book, flipping through the pages. "Our recipes! All our recipes! Oh, Ruby, this is so wonderful! Oh, look, it's your pickled beets! And pickles!

Stewed tomatoes! My Winter Bread!" She went on and on, naming off each recipe like each was a gift on its own. "And look at this, Valentine! Some of the recipes have the dearest little drawings!"

"I'm so glad you like it, Kenna!" I felt happy inside to have a friend like Kenna, a friend who appreciated a simple gift.

"There's still one more package!" Tom piped. "Look, more! Who's it for?"

"Well," said Valentine, "this one says, 'To Kenna, from Valentine'. What do you think, boys? Shall we let her open it?"

"Open, open!" squealed the babies. "Open your present, Kenna!"

Kenna's hands shook as she took the square box from Valentine. "What the deuce? What have you done?" she asked, blushing like an angel.

"Open and see," said Valentine, his face glowing too.

Kenna took the paper off the box, and I could see that the box itself was covered with the most beautiful and rich burgundy velvet, and it had tiny golden hinges on one side and a tiny golden clasp on the other. Kenna opened the clasp and lifted the lid, and then she sucked in her air. She looked quick at Valentine, and then quick in the box again. Nestled there, in more velvet, was a garnet necklace like nothing you have ever seen. It seemed like hundreds of garnets set in gold, some round and some teardrops, some tiny as a mustard seed and some as big as a navy bean. When the firelight caught them just right, they glistened deep red, but then the next minute they shone the color of strong coffee, and then the next, purple as our beets.

It's in the trunk, Miss. Get it out of the trunk and bring it here. Look at this. Can you believe this?

Kenna lifted this necklace out of the velvet and she could not say a word; she just held it in front of her, dumbstruck. Valentine seemed like he felt sorry for her then, and he got up and took it from her. Even with his big hands, he gently opened the delicate, little clasp and moved behind Kenna to place the necklace around her throat, and then clasp it for her. It lay at the base of her throat, like it had been made special for her. The very front here, where the garnets are clumped up like a flower? That just lay at her throat, so pretty, so delicate! I thought how the necklace perfectly matched Kenna's garnet hair. Kenna touched the garnets with her fingers and gazed at Valentine like he hung the moon. I guess he did. I guess he did.

CHAPTER 34

After all the gifts were open, we remained in the parlor, lost in companionable silence. The fire crackled softly, as the boys strummed a little note now and then on their new mandolins. Each had a music book included in the case, and they were pouring over those, too.

"I don't know a thing about reading music, Valentine. Does Wade read music? Can he teach me that, too?" James asked, hope written all over his face.

"I don't know if he does or not, but I bet if he does, he'll teach you. You can learn to play either way, but we'll see what he says," Valentine said.

"What's these sticks for?" asked Tom, picking up a vase filled with brown twigs. "Is this for Christmas?"

"Put that down, Tom! Stop touching everything!" James said, reaching for the vase. "Give me that! What's wrong with you?"

"It's all right, James," said Kenna. "Those are my rowan branches. They're not for Christmas, but just something I like.

They are magic, from my father's home."

"*Oh boy,*" I thought. "*Here we go with another Kenna wild idea. She's going to teach the boys to be heathens.*"

Sure enough, Kenna commenced to telling the boys all about the magical rowan tree from her far lands.

"The rowan tree is beautiful, boys; beautiful and sacred. It is connected to many legends and stories. It often grows near streams or rivers, and grows best high in the mountains. In spring it grows full, white blossoms and in fall, red berries in great clumps. Rowans turn red in the fall, more beautiful than any other tree. When I was a girl my father used to say I had rowan hair. My hair was brighter when I was a girl, just the color of a rowan in the fall."

Both the boys stared at Kenna as if hypnotized, and even the babies stopped their dolly game to listen to their beloved Kenna.

"All down the centuries, people have told stories of the rowan tree and its powers," she went on. "For you see, the rowan is a witch tree. Well, really a tree that offers defense against witches. It can protect you from witches and dark arts."

"What's a dark artist?" Tom asked, his eyes as big as dinner plates.

"Dark arts," Kenna said. "Witchcraft!" She leaned forward, making claws of her hands. I thought Tom was going to die on the spot.

"Lord, Kenna, don't scare him to death," Valentine said, thinking the same thoughts as me. "She's just pulling your leg, Tom. No such thing as witches."

Kenna just kept going with her story as if she hadn't heard a word Valentine said. "And the song, 'The Rowan Tree', tells the story of mothers and fathers with their children underneath the rowan tree. The rowan tree belongs to all women; to all mothers, and it offers protection for our children."

"Perhaps the best part of all is the flying rowan. For if a seed from a rowan is blown away and lands just right on any other tree, in the fork of the branches, it will take root there and grow a new rowan tree right out! So, it transfers its gifts all around, and shares with all while partaking of all. It is a great gift. It is a great fortune to find a flying rowan growing on your lands, for it foretells good safety for children and protection from witches."

"You got a rowan tree, Kenna?" Tom asked. "You got a rowan in your yard?"

Kenna looked at Tom with wide eyes. "No," she said. "No rowans here."

"Well, how you stay safe from witches then? Can't Valentine get you one up on the Summit? He'll get you one, Kenna. Did you ask him?"

"Valentine can't fix everything, Tom," Kenna answered. "Besides, rowans don't grow on the Summit. They grow across the ocean."

"Well, that don't seem fair. Not fair at all," Tommy said. I could see he was quite concerned for all our safety.

Finally, Valentine said, "That's about enough on witches, don't you think? I think we need less witches and more pumpkin pie!" That set the babies to squealing for Kenna's pie, so off we all went to the kitchen.

So anyhow, that's how Kenna was with her stories, Miss, only it wasn't a story to her. It was real; she believed all of it, even the part about witches.

CHAPTER 35

Well, that was a real nice time, and the next day, too. When it came time to go home, it just didn't seem right to go, so we stayed an extra day, but finally we did get bundled up and Valentine hauled us down the hill. Then he and James went on to the freight office to work.

I put my gifts from Kenna and Valentine on my crate and every little while I would go in there and look at them; pick them up and turn them this way and that way in the light. I've kept them here all these years, though now I have a highboy instead of a crate. I have treasured them all these years.

The rest of that winter was pretty quiet. It took a long time for the snow to go, and when it did, if we didn't have a muddy mess round here; mud and more mud. It wasn't worth going outside, so we had to wait that out. We had used up most of our food, the venison being all eaten, the vegetables very scant, the squash long gone; we needed spring to get there for sure.

And finally, it did. I started going up to the Hill House

every day then, taking my little sulky. James went to talk to Mrs. Ricker and bought it off her, so I didn't have to borrow it anymore, so that was good. He bought little Ginger off Valentine too, plus a little horse for Tom named Boy, so we were rich. That James was turning into a fine young man, thanks to Valentine, and not near so skinny as he had been the year before. Valentine taught him how to take care of other people and not just worry about himself; taught him to be a man and provide for others.

I helped Kenna get her garden planted that spring. We made a sister garden again, planting all the same things as the year before. We hauled manure and straw to the garden patch as the soil was needing some help. The soil here is like a sand dune once you get it uncovered, Miss, like easy digging in sand, but it wears out quick. After we got the sister garden all planted, we drew pictures of it in the recipe book, showing all what we done and how we planned it out.

Kenna gave me a few chickens to take down to my house. The chickens started laying eggs again right soon after, so I had eggs again. This time I got water glass too, and a crock and started in to saving eggs for the winter.

We did all kinds of jobs then. Some days we polished the wood in her house and some days we washed the windows. Sometimes we sorted through our cloth and worked on a quilt. Lots of times we did cooking together, and baking and what all, and at the end of the day I would take some of the food down the hill to my house. Then, I still had work to do at my house, and sometimes I was pretty worn out, but my work at Kenna's was keeping us alive, so I didn't complain, but just kept on going like folks do.

One time, we were just working up at Kenna's house in the kitchen there. Valentine and James were gone to Golconda, hauling something to the folks who lived out there. Tom was off to the Ford, raising Cain no doubt; the girls played in the door-yard, the birds twittered and flitted about, and Kenna's bees buzzed and circled; just a perfect day.

Then, out of the blue, Kenna said, "Ruby, Valentine and I are going to marry. We're going to marry soon, and I am going to make a wedding dress. Will you help me? Will you help me make my wedding dress, Ruby?" She looked at me like she was real scared, and I had never seen Kenna scared before.

I tried to hide my big breaking heart and said, "Of course I will help you!" I stopped work to give her a hug. "Of course! What is wrong with you? Of course! What will your dress be, Kenna? What you going to do?" for I knew she had something in mind.

"I ordered a pattern and some dress goods. It's all upstairs. I want it to be just right, Ruby. I want it to be perfect, and I want to wear my tartan somehow. We have to figure it all out. I have to go down to the Ford and talk to the preacher so we can get the church. I want to invite the folks from the Ford and then I want to have a big gathering up here to beat any gathering we have ever had." She talked on and on about her plans, so very happy and excited was she.

"What we doing standing around, kneading bread? Let's get after that dress! Show me the pattern!" Up the stairs we clattered, laughing like schoolgirls.

The pattern was beautiful indeed, Kenna saying it was the newest fashion from Boston. The picture on the pattern envelope showed a beautiful lady with a tiny waist, wearing a beautiful silk gown that had rows of ruffles looped all around the full skirt, and each ruffle was edged with gossamer roses and lacy leaves. It had only tiny sleeves so the lady's arms showed, and the neckline was revealing as well. Down the back looped more ribbon, starting at the waist and cascading to the floor. Valentine would be floored for sure when he saw his bride in that.

Kenna showed me the ivory silk that was to be the dress. She had yards and yards of it, and matching silk piping to boot, boxes of roses made from the same ivory silk wrapped in tissue paper. She had silk leaves too, the color of the junipers right after a nice rain.

"Look at these shoes," she said, lifting the lid of another box. There were the daintiest, white, half-boots I have ever seen, with pearl buttons all up the side and a pretty heel and pointed toe. They were wrapped in tissue paper as well, and looked way too pretty to wear.

"Well, Kenna!" was about all I could say. Everything I saw was way past beautiful. "Oh, Kenna!"

"What do you think, Ruby? And here are the gloves." She showed me the tiny, kid gloves she would wear, and they were white too. Then she looked at the pattern again, and she said, "Now, you see this wide ribbon going down the back of the dress? I was thinking of using my tartan for that. What do you think? Do you like it?"

"Well, let's see. Where is the tartan? Let's try it out." I acted like I knew a hill of beans about patterns and fabrics and what looks good with what; it felt as if it wasn't even me talking, but someone else.

Kenna went quick to get it from her room; Kenna's tartan. I showed a piece of it to you before. You remember, Miss? It was her family tartan from their far lands. Her family had been here a long time, but they kept with their traditions, and I guess they loved that tartan. Kenna brought it from her room, and it was very long and wide, of good fabric; a plaid pattern of squares, and each square was edged in garnet red, of all things. Some of the squares were a deep blue color and some of them a deep green, like Kenna's eyes. It was right beautiful and felt very rich, and hardy, you might say.

"How you going to make that go down your back?" I asked, trying to solve another sewing problem I could never solve.

"Well, I won't use the whole thing. I'll have to cut it, Ruby. I'll make a narrow strip from the side. There's plenty here." Kenna eyed the lovely tartan, her brain racing with sewing ideas.

"You going to trust me to help with the handwork on this dress? I don't know about that. I'm leery of that," I told her, hiding my rough hands behind my back. I was right nervous about the whole thing.

"We'll do it together. But we better get started soon! Today!" she said, blushing prettily.

"When you planning to marry, Kenna?"

"Very soon. As soon as we can get everything ready. Oh, Ruby! I'm so happy! I want to marry Valentine tomorrow!"

I snorted at her then. "Well, that isn't going to happen. We best get to work! Let me go scrub my hands before I touch anything to do with this dress." It seemed like if I acted very busy, I could keep my face from giving me away; from letting

Kenna know that I was sick inside, but not surprised, for I knew this day would come.

We quick finished the bread and got it to proofing, then back upstairs to start work on Kenna's wedding dress. I was just there to find pins and what all for Kenna. She jumped right into the sewing job, cutting out pieces of the dress before you know it.

It took us days to make that dress. I got good at sewing ivory roses to the edges of this piece and that, and adding in a leaf here and there. I sewed the piping round the edges of every ruffle until I was like to scream. The sewing machine sang its own music, Kenna's head bent over it and her feet running the treadle like anything. Bit by bit, the dress came together. It was beautiful and put every other piece of clothing we had ever made to shame; it was perfect.

Came the day the dress was about done and Kenna said she need to go down to the Ford and talk to the preacher. There was only one church in town in those days; a pretty little, white church perched between bunches of cottonwoods. It had a pointed steeple with a bell and all. The preacher was big and round, and came from the East somewhere. I never really talked to him, but I had seen him round the Ford a couple times. Anyway, Kenna headed down the trail while I stayed at the house to work and keep the babies out of trouble.

I had a peaceful couple of hours then, for the babies took a nap and I worked around there, doing my jobs to help Kenna out. I made a pot of coffee and sipped some while I worked in the kitchen. I could see out the window to the back yard, and Kenna's place looked right beautiful; all her little trees were growing and budding out, and her baby plants from the

Summit were waking up and seemed to be surviving. I loved Kenna's place.

All at once, here came Kenna, blasting in the front door, and she was fit to be tied, screeching and yelling and saying all kinds of curse words. I ran into the front of the house to see what all the carrying on was about. Her face was crimson red, her hair falling down and flying everywhere. She was right furious, and for a minute I was scared to ask her what the trouble was; I soon found out though, as she went on with her cussing, and she was cussing that preacher.

"That no-good, son of a bitch," she said, and I was shocked once again by Kenna and her swear words. It didn't seem like such ugly words could come out of such a pretty head. "That low-down, bastard!" she hissed.

She cussed him for good and all, so that I worried about her eternal soul and what not, but I didn't dare interfere out of fear for my own life. Kenna was a hot head when she got fired up, and she was putting on quite a show, throwing off her wrap and flinging her gloves into the parlor.

When I could see she was winding down some, I said, "What is going on, Kenna? What's the matter?" But she still wouldn't answer me.

"For heaven's sake, Kenna, whatever is wrong? What's got you going like this? Tell me!" I said, taking her arm to lead her into the parlor to sit down. "What's going on? Tell me right now or I'll do some cussing of my own!" I felt a little peeved with her for carrying on and on, but not answering me.

Finally, she got it out, though, and I was floored. "The God damned preacher won't marry us in the church! He says we are living in sin and he won't 'sanctify our unclean union'! I could have killed him! What does he know about my life? How dare he judge me, the bastard!" She commenced to cursing again and calling the round, little preacher all manner of names whilst commenting on his girth.

"That pompous, fat bastard! Bible-thumping piece of shit!"

I just sat and waited for her to finish, but when she stopped cursing, she was like to cry, and Kenna never cried back then. It was heartbreaking to see her so.

"Well, why you even need a preacher? I didn't get married by no preacher. Me and Frank just went to the judge down home, and he married us right out, and he didn't spend any time wondering about our 'union'," I said to her. "I don't like the looks of that preacher anyhow, and his fancy little church and all. I say let that one go by, Kenna. Get the judge from over at Unionville to marry you two, and you can marry right here in your house. Why you need a church? That's what I'd do. Why, I'd marry right here in the parlor, and you can walk down the stairs in your pretty dress. What you think of that idea? And then we can have the gathering right here at the same time. Folks will already be here for the wedding."

I couldn't believe how much talking I was doing, how much I was fixing up Valentine's wedding day, but I was. At first Kenna just sat there steaming, but the more I talked, the more she started to see the reason of my talk. Then she allowed as how she would talk to Valentine and see what he thought about the judge.

Now, Miss, but a while later that church burned to the ground, and the round, little preacher burned up with it. I didn't see Kenna do any praying or fire dance, but I will say this. It didn't pay to get that little gal riled up.

CHAPTER 36

Came their wedding day, and when the sun came up, first thing I did was bust out crying in my pillow. I hid my face from my young ones and completely threw a fit into that pillow. When I was done, my eyes were almost swelled shut, and I looked a fright I am sure. But Miss, that was a hard day, for I could not stop my heart from loving Valentine. There was no way out of it, and it seemed like I couldn't quit fighting my fate.

When I came out in the kitchen, James looked at me funny, and he was getting grown up enough to figure things out, so I quick cooked some food and then went outside to look at my baby garden. It was real bad, because the more I looked at those tiny plants, the worse I felt. I wished there was some way I could stay clear of that wedding. There was no way out though, since I was to be a witness; I was to stand up for Kenna. I was divided between my dear friend and the fact that she was marrying the only man I would ever love. It was terrible, Miss.

The day crawled by so long. Finally, came time to get ready, so I got the babies dressed in their little dresses and pretty, white aprons, and the boys scrubbed and combed all on their own. Then I tied up my hair with my blue combs and put on my clean shirtwaist and skirt Kenna made for me. So, up the hill we all trooped.

Once we got there, the boys busied themselves with sweeping the porch and all. Valentine was nowhere to be seen, but Kenna was upstairs getting ready for her wedding. I went upstairs to help her button her dress and pin her curls, and we put one of the silk roses in her hair. I don't think we talked at all; I don't remember talking. When she was all ready and it was close to time to go downstairs, Kenna gave me a hug and said, "Thank you, Ruby. Thank you." Then I walked down the stairs to join the folks gathered in the parlor.

I guess about the whole Ford was there. Maybe a few of the preacher's best churchgoers were missing, but most the folks were there. I shot a quick look at Valentine; a glance, and then looked away. Then Wade struck up a pretty little tune on his fiddle for Kenna's wedding song, but it wasn't that black hair song. It was some other song, but sounded like Kenna's mountain music. Real pretty it was, but it had a mournful sound underneath, and my throat pure closed up and I was fighting hard not to cry. I had never been to a wedding before except my own, and I didn't know that lots of folks cry at weddings, so I kept my feelings to myself.

Seemed like that wedding day was the beginning of the end, for all would be changed before that summer was over; nothing would ever be the same. Sometimes I think about that day and what would have happened if I had put on my traveling suit and just walked onto the train, leaving the babies and the boys and Kenna and Valentine behind me. What if I had a done that? Would that have changed things?

Funny thing about life; we turn left when we should turn right, ending up in perdition, not even knowing it until it's too late, and the whole time we're turning, we aren't scared or worried, or what all. We just blindly walk into ruin, and then marvel at ourselves for doing it, or blame someone else when it's us that did the turning. I look at you and your young face, and I feel sorry for you. You got lots of turns to make yet, and no way of knowing if you're going the right way.

But that day, Valentine and Kenna were making a turn of their own. I don't know how I made it through the day, how I kept from screaming at the sky or throwing a fit in front of the whole Ford, but somehow, I did it. I hid my secret heart and my secret heartbreak.

Kenna was a beauty, Miss, and when she came sweeping down those stairs, we all sucked in our air. Her hair shined, pinned so pretty round her face, and her eyes sparkled bright. She wore her beautiful wedding gown with all the silk roses and leaves, and at her throat lay her garnet necklace. She pinched her skirt and held it up off the stairs, just an inch, like I had seen her do before. The sun was just about to set, and the light shone through the stained glass on her as she made the turn in the stairs. I could see the violet and green colors reflected in the folds of her gown.

Valentine stood in the parlor and looked up at Kenna, and

it was clear that he loved her terrible. He wore a new, white wedding shirt that Kenna had made for him. It had a fancy yoke across his broad shoulders and stiff cuffs with pearl snaps. Valentine put his hand to his heart when he saw Kenna; put his hand to his heart and watched her walk to him with her skirts swishing with every step.

I don't remember the words they said, nor the judge talking or what all. I don't remember it at all; don't remember if Valentine took her hand and held it to his heart; don't remember if Kenna blushed; don't remember if he said his vows with his rumbling voice. Did he put a ring on her finger? I guess he must have. Just all at once, it was over and we were walking out the front door and heading round the house to the back for the gathering.

Later on, though, I got ahold of the papers from the wedding. I have their wedding license and the poem Kenna said to Valentine at the wedding. First time I read it, I could hear her voice saying it that day, but I guess I just locked it out of my memory. The papers are in the trunk there, but I can tell you the poem. Only Kenna didn't talk like normal when she said it, but she said it the way folks from her far lands talk, with their Scotch accent. It was this, Miss.

The way that you set face and foot
Is the way that I will go,
And brave I'll be, abreast of ye,
The saints and angels know.
With loyal hand in loyal hand,
And one heart made of two,
Through summer's gold and winter's cold,
It's I will walk with you.

I loved it when Kenna talked her far lands' talk like that, and she knew lots of poetry by heart. She said her mother taught it to her when she was little, how they would sit around and tell poems to each other for entertainment. She had one brother, and she said how he knew lots of poems, too. But I didn't remember the wedding poem until I read the papers, Miss. I have tried to remember that part, but it won't come to me. I bet that Valentine was plumb swept away when she recited that poem.

Anyhow, after the wedding was over, we all trooped out to the barn for the gathering. It looked like people had worked on the barn to fix it up for the gathering, the lanterns all polished and glowing in the fading daylight. There were streamers of paper hanging down from some of the rafters, and the boys had hung chairs and Valentine's snowshoes on the wall for a joke on Valentine. I guess James kept his word and made sure folks knew about the chair-shoes.

The boys struck up the music right away and Kenna and Valentine had the first dance. The boys played a real pretty waltz with lots of wailing fiddle in it, and those two swayed around the floor in the lantern light. Valentine placed his big, old hand on the small of Kenna's back, and she tilted her head back to look up at him, her garnets catching the light from the lamps, and sometimes throwing out light of their own. Her Fletcher tartan flowed down the back of her dress; her pretty tartan with garnet and green and blue.

After that waltz, Valentine handed Kenna a package wrapped in plain, brown paper and tied with kitchen twine.

"What the deuce?" she asked, and then blushed when everyone chided her for her language.

"It's your wedding present, Kenna. Mrs. DeRoo." Valentine said.

Kenna unwrapped the paper and let it fall to the dance floor. There, carved from rich, burnished wood was a butter paddle, perfect for making fresh butter.

"For butter!" said Kenna, looking at Valentine like he was a god. "Thank you! It's for butter!" she repeated.

Valentine gave her a quick kiss, and the music started up again, just in time for them to sweep on around the floor, Kenna clutching her butter paddle like anything. Leave it to Valentine to give Kenna a dance floor for her birthday and jewels for Christmas, but then come up with a plain, old hand-carved butter paddle for a wedding present, and Kenna just as pleased as punch.

That gathering didn't last quite so long as other ones had. Guess we all wanted to leave the newlyweds to themselves. Not too late, and we all wandered down the hill and back to the Ford. James took Tom and the babies in the sulky, but I walked down the road alone since it was getting to be a good trail with all the back-and-forth wagons. It looked like two, skinny ribbons laying in the desert that night; two, skinny ribbons side by side showing me how to get home the easy way. So, I took it.

I didn't sneak back up there either, Miss. No need to anymore since I could conjure them up all on my own. I spent a terrible night, dreaming of them in their big tall bed, man and wife. Now she was Kenna DeRoo, and that didn't sound right to me. But think of Ruby DeRoo? Stupid; pure stupid sounding, and never to be.

CHAPTER 37

I didn't go back up there for days; I didn't want to. I didn't want to see them for a long time. But then Valentine came by and got James to go on a freight haul to some mine in the Sonomas, somewhere. He rode his nice horse to the house bright and early and gathered James up. I saw him coming down the road a ways off, so I made sure to go out back the house to the garden and act busy. I sat in the dirt and picked some weeds, and all they did was yell to me that they were leaving and would be back in a few days. I waved back like I didn't have a care, and so off they went. But I went around front after a minute and watched them go. Valentine rode and James hurried alongside as they headed down to the freight office.

I went up to the Hill House then, for I couldn't act like I was staying away because of the newlyweds anymore. So up I went, and it was starting to get hot then. The windy road up there was still two, narrow ribbons, but there was getting that real fine dust that we have here at the Ford; dust as fine as face powder, laying in the wagon wheel ruts. A little bit of grass grew in between the ruts, and the sage was plenty healthy and smelled good. The babies and Tommy sat in the cart, talking nice in the sunshine.

Kenna was working in the kitchen when I got there, so I called to her. "Whoo-hoo?"

That's what we said when we got to one of our houses. "Whoo-hoo?" and the other person would answer, "Whoo-hoo? Who goes?" That is how we always greeted each other, but when Kenna called back to me, I got stinging eyes real bad, so bad that Kenna said, "What's wrong, Ruby? Are you feeling all right?"

"Oh, it's this durn dust we got here," I lied. And that's what I thought of myself too; I was just a big liar, and my whole life was a big lie. I hated myself.

But Kenna gave me a hug and said, "I've missed you so much! I'm so glad to see you!"

"I missed you too, Kenna. How are you? Are you happy?"

"Oh, Ruby, I'm so very happy. I didn't know a person could be this happy!" she beamed at me.

"Well, I'm right happy for you, Kenna, for both of you," I lied some more.

"What shall we do today? Do you feel like putting up some peas? I think a bunch of the peas are ready. Also, some of my herbs and roots can be taken care of today, as an early batch. We can make some tinctures and maybe some infusions," Kenna said, as she led us back to the kitchen again.

"Well, I don't know much about any of that, Kenna. I don't even know what a tincture is!" I said.

"It's part of my healing medicines, Ruby. Remember when

you were hurt? Some of the medicines I used for you? Those were from Boston, so it's time to make new. I don't have the same plants, but I can figure it out. We'll need medicines for fever and digestives. There are so many things to make!"

"How do you know what to use? Who taught you?" I asked.

"I knew a healing woman back home. She showed me what to do for the basics. Since then, I've been teaching myself, and testing on myself, too. I'm really anxious to try out some of the plants Valentine brought down from the Summit, especially the sarviceberry. I know that is going to be something wonderful," she said.

"That doesn't sound like a good idea to me, Kenna. Sounds like a good way to poison yourself or somebody else. You shouldn't mess with that, Kenna, unless you really know what you're doing," I said, for I felt very uneasy about making potions with Kenna.

"Oh, Ruby, you are such a worrywart! It will be fine, and the next time one of the babies has a fever, you'll be singing a different tune."

"Kenna," I said, for I could see there was no arguing with her. "Let me go unhitch the sulky. Will you watch the babies for a minute?" and I quick went outside to get some air. My heart beat like fury, and I didn't want Kenna to see my face right then, for I didn't like her wild ideas and witchcraft potions. Besides, every time she told me something I had conjured during the winter, I turned red as a beet and felt like a sneak thief; like she knew I spied on her. Kenna had the sight, Miss, and it was near impossible to hide things from her.

Once we got going on the work, it seemed like we were more

back to our old selves, and I could keep my eyes hidden from Kenna by looking down at the work. The babies helped us pick the peas and then we sat in the kitchen to shell them. They were sweet and good and it was a right good crop. We got a nice batch of jars, and still had time to work on potions.

Kenna took leaves, bark, and roots from the sarviceberry bush to start with and then moving to the rest of her herb garden, choosing each sample as if her life depended on it. She hummed while she worked, gathering bits of plants in her apron, stopping to smell different leaves, even tasting a couple bits of different herbs. Once she had a good collection, we headed back into the house where she could wash and steep her treasures. She saved each concoction in a jar, sealed and labeled before she stowed them away in the larder.

"Which do you want for your share, Ruby? You want some of this yarrow or feverfew? Maybe some mint?" she asked, all innocence.

"No thanks, Kenna. You best keep those here. I have no idea how to use any of that," I answered.

"All right," she said. "It will be here when you need it." Kenna smiled, acting like she didn't see my disapproval, but I know she did.

By late afternoon, Kenna and I decided to sit down and have a cup of tea, like we always did. It seemed like I was getting better and better at hiding my eyes, and seemed like Kenna was too happy to notice. We talked about the garden and surveyed what would come ready next, and then we talked about our quilt. We went upstairs and looked at scraps a while.

I walked over to the window and looked down into the

dooryard. My mind went back to that day I watched out the window and saw Valentine ask Kenna to marry. It seemed like I could see them there again, and I saw Valentine walk off and hold his hand back for Kenna; saw how he wiggled his fingers at her like, "Come on, come on," and Kenna running to catch up to him, saw him take her hand as they walked off round the corner of the house; saw the whole thing again just like it was real again, and it burned into my head.

"What are you thinking about, Ruby? You look so far away, and you haven't heard a word I said. Ruby?" she asked after me.

"Oh, I don't even know! Just looking at the grass and your little trees. Your place is looking real good, Kenna."

Kenna just looked at me funny, knowing I was lying, but she let it go by. Guess if I didn't want to tell, Kenna didn't want to know. She was free like that; you didn't have to tell her everything. She knew how to give a person room to live, she gave me room, and didn't ask again. She let it go by.

CHAPTER 38

Well, just as we headed down the stairs, who should bust in the front door but Valentine. His face was white as ashes and he was fit to be tied. It scared us both real bad right when we laid eyes on him, and we both shouted out, "What's wrong? What's wrong?"

"James is hurt. James is hurt." And I swear, Valentine was wringing his hands. Like to scared me to death. I flew down those stairs and got to Valentine right quick.

"Where is he? Where he at? Valentine!" I asked, grabbing his arms to shake him. "Where is James?" and in my mind I pictured James hurrying along beside Valentine's horse as they were leaving that morning, his hair too long, flopping in the breeze as he looked up at Valentine, talking and gesturing in a very lively way. My heart almost stopped beating, thinking of that picture of James and thinking of him hurt somehow at the same time.

"He's at Dr. Brock's. He's at the doctor's house. I got him to the doctor." Valentine was not himself.

"Is he awake? Is he awake, Valentine?" I asked with my heart in my throat. I was thinking James was hurt on his head for some reason, and I was scared that if he wasn't awake, he might never wake up again.

"He's awake, but his leg is hurt real bad. It's broken. He broke his leg!" Valentine liked to be sick. "I shouldn't have let him come along. Oh, God, I shouldn't have asked him to do the work of a man. He's just a boy!"

"Let's get to him right now. Let's go. I'm going." I was out the door and hotfooting it to the Ford. I didn't think about the babies or Tom or what all, but just headed down the road. Valentine finally got going again and jumped back on the wagon; a wagon and team I had never seen before. He turned the wagon round and headed down, and when he caught up with me, he stopped and I climbed on. Then we went on down to the Ford right quick.

There was James, laying on a cot at Dr. Brock's place, writhing in pain, his face as white as the sheets he clutched. I liked to died right then, and I realized that James was a son to me, same as my own babies; he was my son and he was in a bad way.

I ran right to his side and kneeled down by the cot. "James, James! I'm right here, Sweet Boy. I'm right here. Oh, my Sweet Boy."

He came to himself a little then and looked at me. "Ruby! Ruby!" he said through gritted teeth. "Ruby, it's bad. It hurts real bad!"

"The doctor will help us. Just hang on a minute. Hang on, James. Try to breathe."

"Am I dying? Am I dying, Ruby?" he asked, and he was filled with anguish. My heart broke for him. "I'm sorry for being bad to you. I'm sorry, Ruby. Forgive me." He squirmed around some more.

"Stop that, James. Stop that right now. You are my son. Sons apt to say the wrong thing sometimes to their mama. And you aren't going to die. The doctor is here and he's going to help you."

Then the doctor was there, and he made James take a couple swigs of some medicine, and I knew that would fix James up just like it fixed me up that time. Soon I got him to hold my hand and stop squirming quite so much.

"Look at my eyes, James. Look here for one second. Look, Sweet Boy." James came to himself for a second and looked at me. Then pretty soon the medicine started helping with the pain, and he stopped squirming altogether.

Then the doctor allowed as how I should go to the other room and he would put James into a sleep so he could set his leg.

"Don't go! Don't leave!" James said, slurring his words.

"I'm right in the next room. I'm waiting right there until the doctor says I can come back. Try to sleep for a minute." James closed his eyes. Then the tears came on me right fierce, and I was like to die. I sort of slumped over and hid my face and Dr. Brock led me out of there to the next room where Valentine waited, and he was a mess too. His big paws shook as he ran them through his hair.

"You two stay here. This won't take long. I'm going to set his leg and brace it. It's a bad break and we will have to watch James closely, but I think he will recover. Just wait here," and off he went.

I finally came to myself enough to look at Valentine, and that scared me too. He didn't look right.

"Valentine, you best sit down a bit. You don't look so good."

"James could lose his leg. I know what that is. You know how many boys I've seen missing a leg or arm? You know what it's like to live with no leg? You know how terrible that is? How it ruins your life? Oh my God! Oh my God!" Valentine covered his face with his hands and sunk down on a chair. I had never seen a man take on so, and I didn't quite know what to make of it, but I walked to him and put my hand on his back and tried to soothe him.

"Valentine, we'll take good care of James. He will be all right again. I know it. Stop taking on so. Come on, now." I rubbed his back, but seemed like Valentine was far gone to some other place; he would not be consoled, so I just stood there like that, and he hung his head like that, and we were a pair.

"Can you tell me what happened, Valentine? How did James get hurt?"

"It's my fault, dragging him around the countryside, working him like a man. I should have left him to you, Ruby. I should have left him alone." I could see that Valentine suffered terrible.

"That's nonsense," I said to him. "You hiring James on kept us warm and fed this whole year. James needed that job. If he didn't work for you, he would have had to find something else. Just tell me what happened though. I need to know."

"We were heading up to Unionville with a load of goods. There's a pretty steep place up there, and the team stalled. James jumped off the wagon to walk up to the lead mules to help get them going. But I guess he misjudged his jump, because he landed wrong and ended up rolling down into the gully there. I guess he rolled about thirty feet down the siding, and by the time he got stopped, his leg was broken. I didn't see it because I was sitting on the other side of the wagon seat. Just heard it," and Valentine clutched his head again. "I heard him falling and I knew it was bad. Oh God, Ruby, I can't get the sound out of my head! I just keep hearing it over and over. I couldn't get around that wagon fast enough. Just crawled under real quick, even though I knew that was stupid; crawled under and looked over the edge, and there's James, laying down the wash with his leg twisted the wrong way." Valentine was like to cry.

"Oh, Lord," I said. "How'd you get him up?" I pictured the whole thing in my head, wondering what I would have done, feeling grateful I wasn't there to see it all.

"I scrambled down there as fast as I could. James wasn't really conscious at first, but moaning. I could see it was real bad. I just picked him up and carried him down the wash a ways to a place where it wasn't so steep, then up to the road and laid him in the shade of the freight wagon."

"We were about halfway between the Ford and Unionville, and the team wasn't going anywhere, so I unhitched a mule and lifted James up on him. Then, I headed back down toward Hasting's place, and he loaned me his wagon and team so I could get back here faster. Of course, you know Hastings; nothing but bad news ever comes out of his mouth. He made sure to tell me that James was going to lose his leg, if not his life." Valentine's face turned even whiter than it had been before.

"That isn't going to happen, Valentine. You'll see. James will mend. Just you wait and see." I said like that every little while, but I don't think Valentine believed me. We stopped talking for a while, but sat quietly side by side, Valentine clasping my hand in his great paw. I studied our hands together, seeing how our brown hands matched in roughness, his with big veins across the back, and mine with dirt under my nails from digging in the garden. I loved holding his hand like that, and I have thought back on it many a time, for it seemed like we were together, and James our son while we waited for the outcome of this horrible accident; a family.

Finally, Dr. Brock came out and Valentine and I both stood together, still holding on to each other.

"James is sleeping," said Dr. Brock. "I was able to set the bone and stitch up the wound on his leg where the bone tore through."

Then I sat down quick, my ears buzzing and my sight going dark, like to faint, because I didn't know the bone came out. Valentine sat beside me, his arm around my shoulders. We shuddered together.

Good God, it was terrible, Miss.

CHAPTER 39

Those were some long days. I stayed by James all I could, only running home to sleep a little or get cleaned up or what all. Valentine was there a lot too, bringing me food from Kenna. Kenna kept Tom and the babies so I didn't have to worry about them. And slowly, very gradually, James began to mend.

Came the day Dr. Brock said James could go home, and he allowed as how Valentine should bring a wagon to fetch him.

"He can't ride in a wagon. I'll carry him home," Valentine said, beside himself with guilt. He had lost his sideways smile and jaunty step. Poor Valentine, he made it his job to take care of everyone and suffered for it many a time. Well, anyhow, Valentine went in there to get James, and James liked to have a fit when Valentine said he was going to carry him through the Ford to our house.

"Just bring the wagon. I can ride in the wagon," James fumed.

"Wagon's too bumpy. It'll hurt your leg. We aren't taking any chances."

"Good God, Ruby! Help me!" James yelled at me.

"Far be it from me to tell Valentine DeRoo what to do. You're on your own, James." I walked out to the front porch of the doc's place. Pretty soon, here comes Valentine, carrying James like a baby wrapped in a blanket with his splinted leg sticking out. James had his arms round Valentine's neck, his face purple with rage and embarrassment. Down Railroad Street they went and over to my house.

Valentine carried James through the kitchen and into my room, putting him on my bed. I had already made the bed all ready for James; all the pillows we had were on there, and a couple quilts rolled up too. Then Valentine and I helped get James situated on the bed with his leg propped a little and pillows behind his back. James was in a fix for sure, and he was trying awful hard to maintain his dignity with no pants on and what all. Finally, James let out a string of cuss words.

"Who do you think you are? Kenna?" Valentine asked him. That just got us some more bad words. "James, I'm going to stay here and take care of you. I'm going to help you out until you are on your feet." Valentine looked quick at me since he forgot to ask me first, just making free with my house.

"Where will you fit? We're out of beds," I said before I thought to keep my big mouth shut. Here was a chance to spend time with Valentine, if I could just be quiet for a minute.

But it was too late, for Valentine said, "Well, what if you go stay up at the house and I stay here? Just for a week or so until James is stronger. Then we can get him up the hill and he can stay at our place. How does that sound? Would that work? I need to stay here to help him out."

So, there we went again with me moving up the hill and Valentine moving down. It seems like that's all I did. The babies, Tom, and me moved up there for a while and Valentine stayed in my house with James. Every day, we all came down the hill, though, to bring food and Kenna's poultices and teas for James, which I did not like. Her tinctures were black as tar sometimes and smelled like the devil, making James gag when he took a sip, but I did see how the sarviceberry tincture made him sleep like a baby, not moving at all and scarcely breathing at times. Kenna tried to make me give that tincture to James, but I refused, for I saw how very careful Kenna was with his dose, and I thought I could accidentally kill James as easy as look at him.

I got used to being around Kenna and Valentine as husband and wife. I was too busy worrying about James to worry about them. It's terrible to say, but James getting hurt helped me stop feeling so sorry for myself all the time; it made me start thinking of someone else for a change.

I've never seen anyone take up for someone the way Valentine did for James. He carried him around when he needed to move, helped him clean up, hauled him to the outhouse, asked him what he wanted to eat. Every day, Valentine looked close at James' leg, like he was looking for a flea. He made the doctor come over every few days and check James out. Of course, I helped out too, but Valentine did the real care and James was able to keep his privacy.

Next thing you know it's time for us to play musical houses again, so me and the young ones moved down and Valentine very slowly hauled James up the hill to the Hill House. They made James a place in the music parlor so he didn't have to worry about the stairs. I think Kenna decided that because she knew Valentine would pack James up and down all day if she let him.

As James got on the mend, Valentine made him a pair of crutches out of cottonwood, with hand grips crossing a fork in the branches he chose. It didn't take him long to do it, making me think Valentine might have done that job before, and I remembered what he said about boys with no legs. Valentine made nice crutches and he wrapped the tops in soft, tea towels to make it easy on James.

Seemed like that whole summer was spent on James' leg. Finally, came the time we told Valentine he best get back to work with his freight or lose the whole thing. James was getting to where he could get around some. In fact, he got pretty good with those crutches. So, that is how our days went. Valentine gone now and then on a job, James getting better and better at hobbling around, Tommy playing from dawn to dusk, and the babies growing like bad weeds.

I took the babies up to Kenna's about every day to do our work, and most times I hauled my vegetables up there, and we mixed our crops together and canned all day long. Kenna loved to use her little recipe book every day, even though we knew the recipes by heart. She would still get out her book and find the recipe we were doing, reading it over, pointing to the words while she did it. Then if we tried something new, she made little notes in there, or if we tried a new recipe, she would add that on one of the empty pages.

Sometimes I would just go stand out in the sister garden and hide in the tall corn. I liked to study how the plants were hanging onto each other; how the beans and squash grew little green strings that curled up like the babies' ringlets and then wrapped all around whatever they could find. It got to where the garden was a big tangle, and the greens so pretty and bright that it liked to break your heart; how stickery the leaves on the squash were and how rippled the edges of the corn leaves were, like Kenna was gathering them into a ruffle. Even in our hot, desert summer, the ground stayed wet and soft because of those wide squash leaves making shade for everything. I loved Kenna's sister garden.

One day as I was getting ready to head up the hill with the babies and a batch of green beans, I saw Valentine's wagon coming down the trail, and here he comes with James sitting beside him. James was growing up fast, and looked like a man sitting there beside Valentine.

"Good morning," I said to them. "What's going on?"

"Well, James has decided it's time for him to move home. He's pretty stubborn. Won't stay with us anymore," Valentine said as he looked at James.

"I'm fine. It's time for me to live here again, time to be home," James said, his face one big scowl. "But I thank you for helping me out, Valentine. I surely do."

"Sit still and let me get you down," Valentine said, jumping out of the wagon and running around to get James. He lifted him down, leaving James leaning on the wagon. Then he grabbed the crutches out the back of the wagon and handed them to James, one at a time. James put one under each armpit, and then James held out his hand to Valentine and they shook hands. I knew James was a man; he was a grown man.

"As soon as you are a little better, you can come back to

work doing little jobs around the office. I'll check in on you," Valentine said.

"All right, that sounds fine," James said, crutching himself into the house. Valentine tipped his hat to me, climbed up on his wagon, and slapped his reins. The wagon jerked and then he headed down the street.

CHAPTER 40

A couple of things happened toward the end of that summer; things I didn't pay mind to at the time, but later when I looked back, I realized that they were important. First thing that happened is the church burned up. No one knows what started the fire, but it was gone pretty fast; went up like a tinderbox; poof, and the preacher gone too. None of us went to his funeral, since we were too busy.

Second thing happened was the coyotes showed up at Kenna's. Kenna and I were working in the kitchen, making pickles and canning pieplant and all, just like every other day. We washed things up a bit, standing side by side by at the white, enamel dish pans. Kenna washed and I dried and put things away, making sure everything was in its place, for Kenna liked a tidy kitchen. We were having a nice day, the babies down for a nap on my old bed.

Then here came the coyotes, wandering into the backyard in the broad daylight like they owned the place, the three of them.

They walked here and there, sniffing and trotting back and forth with their noses to the ground and their tails held high. Then the biggest one lifted his leg and peed on the clothesline post. Kenna and I stood there as still as statues, watching them from the window, my hand still in the jar I had been drying.

Kenna whispered, "That's not good."

I whispered back, "I'll say."

We stood there, transfixed. The coyotes sniffed around some more, paying special attention to Kenna's little henhouse. Not a sound from in there, and the coyotes didn't try to get in. They surveyed the whole place, looking around but not acting hungry; only taking stock. Then the big one sat down on his rump and looked right at us, showing us his big, coyote grin. He looked right in my eyes, Miss. It was frightening, I don't mind telling you; he stared right in my eyes, laughing at me.

"It'll be a cold day in hell before I put up with something like this," stormed Kenna. She grabbed a dish towel, and out the door she went, screaming like a banshee and waving her tea towel. I did not follow her, but stood stupid, looking out the window. Kenna was outraged.

Laughing Boy didn't run off straight away, but continued grinning until Kenna was just a few steps away. Then it seemed the spell was broken, and all three of the scoundrels took off, running like anything, their haunches bunched down low to the ground, sharp claws digging into the dirt for purchase and kicking up clouds of dust. They ran out past the garden, cleared the back fence, and raced into the hills. They were gone; we saw them no more.

Kenna came back inside, and she wasn't scared or mad; she

was insulted. She muttered to herself about lowdown coyotes coming into her dooryard and peeing on her laundry. She forgot I was even there, and for once, I kept my mouth shut, and for some reason, we didn't say a word about it that day or the next.

On the third day, though, Kenna said, "You know, the old Scots believed an animal only showed itself to you if it wanted to, that it was never an accident, and they thought that different animals brought different messages. Many Indian tribes think the same thing."

"Do tell," says I, thinking, *"Oh, boy, here we go. Kenna and her wild ideas."* But I kept my face serious and looked at her like I wanted to hear the rest, and I'm thinking, *"Coyotes, Paiutes, and Scotch. Great."*

"That's right. My ancestors called them allies, viewing animal appearances as omens, either for good or bad; allies if you keep your eyes open and pay attention."

"I'm guessing a coyote is bad," I said.

"It depends on how you look at it. They say the coyote represents the trickster, so I guess we should be on guard a little, maybe on guard times three."

"So, not a happy trick?" I asked.

"I don't think so. You haven't seen Frank, have you?"

"His animal is a skunk!" I said, snorting a laugh, but Kenna didn't laugh, but only looked at me like I was a dimwitted child. "No, I haven't seen Frank. I think he moved on."

"I hope so," Kenna said, looking out at the Sonomas from her kitchen window. "I hope so. Be careful, Ruby. Will you? Promise me. Be careful."

"Lord, Kenna, you beat all I ever saw. Yes, I'll be careful. You be careful."

"Yes, I'll be careful. I'll be careful."

We went back to our work. I loved those days working with Kenna, having something to show for our efforts; not like laundry or cooking supper. When you were done canning, you had something that would last for months and months. It was like catching summer and putting it in a jar.

Our summer evenings then! The boys were learning to play their mandolins, and we liked to sit outside and listen to them. Many times, we took the kitchen chairs outside to the dooryard so we could listen while they played. There was James, with his bum leg sticking out. I loved to sit on the step with a baby on each leg and listen to those boys. When they played, it looked so clear that they were alike—close brothers, their hands the same, only different sizes, their wrists and arms, even the way they bent their heads over their mandolins. They were brothers, my good boys.

Who invented a mandolin? That's what I want to know. Who knew how to make something that would make that high, sweet sound? For a mandolin has a tiny sound, Miss, a high sound that says a lot. It soothes my soul to hear it. And the size of a mandolin is pleasing to me, just the right size with a pretty shape and interesting to look at. I love to look at the strings and the frets and all, how the strings come in pairs. Isn't that funny? How I miss hearing those boys play. I miss it. I miss it a lot. Do you play, Miss? You don't play, do you?

We didn't have many gatherings after that. Valentine was gone too much and James was hurt. Kenna didn't want a gathering with the town; she just wanted all of us together. She got a look about her then; a married woman look; a satisfied look. Life was turning out real good for Kenna DeRoo.

It seemed I was doing better, too. My life was busy and full. I was happy with my children, happy with my house. Frank had disappeared, and I hoped he had got chopped up in a sawmill or some such accident. Life was good.

Well, we were going on like that. I was up at the Hill House working with Kenna. We were about worn out after a long day of work. We always liked to leave everything nice and clean before we quit though, and that's what we were doing when Tom showed up. We were just about ready to call it a day, and here he comes, sneaking in the kitchen door.

"Hey, Ruby, what you doing?" he asked me, like he's gone crazy.

"What you mean, 'What am I doing?' Why, I'm getting ready for the grand ball. Can't you see?" I curtsied for him; I was mean like that.

"Can you come outside? For a minute?" he asked, his hands shoved into the pockets of his filthy overalls. His face was covered in grime and his bare feet were black with mud and dust.

"What have you done, Tom? Just tell me straight out. I don't have time to track you down."

"Nothing. Just come outside for a minute." He looked right stubborn.

"Scoot out of here, Tom. We're busy. I'll be down to the house in a bit to fix some supper. Go haul some water and wood, why don't you?" But he just stood there. "Tom, I said scoot!"

He acted like it was about to kill him, but he slumped out the door, his head down as he mumbled something, and I went on with my work. Next thing I know, I hear Tom yelling at me from the dooryard. "Ruby! Ruby, come outside! Come out!" He sounded a little desperate.

"Well, what in the world? I'm going to get that boy!" I said, throwing my towel on the table and stomping out the door to see what was going on. There was Tom by the front gate, looking frantic.

"Tom!" I yelled at him. "What is the matter with you? I told you to get down to the house. Mind me, now. I mean it!"

"Ruby, listen to me! Please!" and he was like to cry.

So that stopped me short. "What is it, Tom? What have you done?"

"Nothing, Ruby. James sent me to get you! James said to tell you that there's trouble. James says for you to hurry home right away and don't bring the babies. James came clear down to the river on his crutches to find me. He made me run all the way up here. He said he's going to break a crutch on my head unless I mind him! He was fit to be tied, Ruby! Said for you to get there quick!" And then little Tommy did start crying; big, hot tears sliding down his freckle cheeks, leaving a trail through the dirt on his face. Sweet, little Tom!

"Don't tell Kenna! James said for sure, don't tell Kenna. Just come down to the house."

"Do you know what this is about, Tom?" I asked, feeling sick inside.

"No, I don't know! I don't know. Only please come down!"

"All right, all right! Let me go make up a story for Kenna. Head down and go straight home! I'll be there as soon as I can!"

Little Tom took off running through the sage, his arms pumping all the way. He was gone like a shot; that Tom was a runner. I never seen anyone who could outrun my Tom. I walked back in the house, and lies began flowing out my mouth.

"Kenna, will you watch the babies tonight? Tom has broke a window down in the Ford and is in the soup. I need to go take care of it. Will you keep the babies? And I think I'll just leave the cart here and ride the mule down. I'm about worn out." The more I talked, the sicker I felt inside, for I knew something was very wrong; very wrong indeed.

Of course, Kenna was happy to help with the babies. She loved having those babies around. She would have made a real good mama. So, I quick kissed the babies goodbye and got down to the Ford as fast as I could.

CHAPTER 41

At first, I just beelined it down to the Ford, but then it dawned on me that Frank could be watching me coming, just waiting for the right minute to pounce, so I stopped the mule up short and took a good look around, but I saw nary a soul. Just the same, I turned off the road and wandered toward the Ford through the tallest brush I could find. The whole way I was cooking up in my head what must be going on for James to take on this way.

I decided it might be best to come up on the house sideways, so I didn't head down Railroad Street straight to my street, Miss, but went a little farther on to Coffey Street, then round back of Mrs. Ricker's house and I tied the mule up to her fence and climbed through. I was being right sneaky. I figured Frank would have his horse in the stable, so I quick peeked in there; no horse.

But that Frank was tricky, so I didn't give up my sneaky ways. I hopped on the path to the outhouse, and very quietly walked up to the back of the house, peeking in first one window and then another, but no sign of life. I finally went around to the front and peeked into the kitchen window through a crack in the raggedy curtains. There were James and Tommy, sitting at the kitchen table, James' face as white as milk and his scrawny shoulders hunched around his ears; Tommy's face streaked with tear dirt and his towhead hair stuck down to his sweaty scalp.

I tapped on the window so they would see it was me and then I quick jumped in the house and shut the door. First thing I did was close the crack in the kitchen curtains.

"What in the world is going on?" I whispered, even though the house was empty. "What is this all about? This better not be some kind of game you boys are playing!"

"It's no game, Ruby. We got trouble. Real bad trouble," said James, blinking his eyes fast to hold back the tears.

"What is going on? Is it Frank? Where is he? Did he come here?"

"No, he's not here, but he sent someone here. A fellow came here and showed up at the door. Said he was looking for you and that he knows Pa, and that Pa sent him here. Said he needs to talk to you real soon. Said he'll be back here in a bit to find you. He said if he doesn't get to talk to you, it will be worse for all of us."

"What will be worse? Who is this fellow?" I asked, my heart beating out of my chest.

"Said his name is Jake Moffat. He's come here looking for outlaws. He's a bounty hunter, Ruby, and he's here to get Valentine. He left you this card." Poor James, he couldn't fight off the tears anymore; they filled up his eyes and spilled down his cheeks.

"What! That's crazy. That don't make sense. Valentine is no outlaw. Good heavens!"

"He showed me the wanted poster. It sure looks like Valentine, and it tells about his bullet scar. Valentine is a wanted man, and there's a $1000 reward, dead or alive. This Moffat fellow said it's going to be up to you how it goes. Said to tell you it's a present from Pa."

James laid his head on the table and put up a terrible fuss, his shoulders heaving and what all. That set Tom off, and they both threw a terrible fit. I sat down quick at the table and I wanted to set up crying too, but I didn't have time to cry, Miss I had to think quick and figure out what to do.

"James, shut up!" I said. "Shut up right now! Now!"

James shut up then, but that really got Tom tuned up, so then I told him to shut up quick, or else.

"We've got to figure out what to do here. Where is Valentine? Do you know?" I asked James.

James wiped his sleeve across his face. "He's on his way back from Andorno. I thought he could get back yesterday. He's bound to show up any minute, and if that Moffat fellow spots him, he'll kill him. I know it. He's a bad man, Ruby. I looked in his eyes, and it made my blood run cold. He shows a big smile, but his eyes don't smile. He's bad news."

I could see that James loved Valentine the way a boy loves his pa, and not just like a family friend. Valentine helped James turn into somebody, and James could see no wrong in anything Valentine did. He didn't care a whit if Valentine was an outlaw, and at that moment, neither did I.

"When this is over, I'm going to go find my pa and I'm

going to kill him." I looked quick at James, for his voice scared me. His voice sounded more like a man and less like a boy, and deadly to boot. I believed him when he said he was going to kill his pa. All he needed was one little chance, and Frank would be a goner.

I got a picture in my head of Valentine coming down the dusty road from Andorno; how the Ford would come into sight as he moved along with the jingling harness chains and sweaty mules; his hat pushed up on his forehead and his feet perched on the footrest; his giant, rawhide gloves holding the reins. He would look out to the Ford and whistle at the wheel mules to hurry them home. He would not be wary or careful at all, but instead roll right into a deathtrap.

All at once I got to be like a banshee myself, and I was like to cry for my beloved Valentine. I could not stand the idea of him laying in the ground, nor of him drug off somewhere to be hanged. Miss, it was not in my power to stop myself, and it seemed like it wasn't even me who started talking and telling those boys what to do. It felt like I had the plan in my head my whole life, just waiting to let it fly, and fly it did.

"Tom, wash your face. Stop bawling right now, or I'm going to give you something to bawl about. Get cleaned up a little. James, get your crutches and get out of here. Go hide out back of Mrs. Ricker's place. I want you nowhere around here, and don't let her see you either. Don't let anyone see you at all. Take that chunk of bread and leftover deer meat with you. Stay put until I come get you, but if I don't come get you in three days, why then you can come out, but not for three days. You hear me? Now get." My voice sounded dead in my ears; poisonous.

Tom quick wiped some of the dirt off his face, but his chest was still jumping up and down from carrying on.

"Listen to me, Tommy, and do just what I say," I whispered, grabbing Tom's arms and giving him a little shake for good measure. "Do you hear me? You do just what I say."

"I will, Ruby. I will!" he wailed, so I shook him again.

"Sneak up to the Hill House and don't let anyone see you. Sneak in the brush like a Paiute, Tommy. When you get up there, peek around a little and see if you can spot Kenna. When you figure out she's in the back of the house, sneak in the front door, but don't let her see you. You hear? Don't let her know you are there at all! Tom! You hear!"

"Yes! I hear you!" Tom sang out like a squalling cat.

"Sneak upstairs to Kenna's room. You have to get Valentine's old pistol. Bullets too. It's in the top drawer of that big chest. You will have to stand on a chair to get it. Climb up and get it and then put the chair back. Don't forget the chair. Tom, if you forget the chair, I'll beat you within an inch of your life. You mind me now!"

Poor Tom only nodded his towhead.

"Then you hotfoot it back to the house. Run like the wind, Tommy, only don't let anyone see you. Bring the pistol and the bullets here right quick, but sneak back. Watch all the way and stay away from folks. Get here. And when you get here, come in the back way in case your pa or this other fellow is here. Now go!" Tommy was gone in a flash. That boy was right fast when he wanted to be.

"What are you going to do, Ruby? That Moffat fellow will kill you as soon as look at you. You don't know what I saw in his eyes. He's real scary, Ruby. He's going to kill Valentine. I know it!"

"James, hush. That ain't helping. Hush up and get out to the back and hide right now. I don't want that fellow to see you again, ever. Get."

Well, James did what I said, but he wasn't happy about it. I guess he was too scared to figure out anything else to do, so out the back he went. Then I quick cleaned myself up a bit, pinning my hair better and pinching my cheeks for color. I put on my clean shirtwaist, my hands shaking so bad I could barely button it. I conjured a picture of Valentine riding into town without any idea of what awaited him.

Next thing you know, here came my little sneak thief, Valentine's old pistol weighing gigantic in his hands, Miss, too heavy for little Tom to hold almost, but he had it, and one pocket bulged with bullets.

"Did you do what I said, Tom? Did anyone see you? Did you get past Kenna?"

"No one saw me, Ruby," Tom puffed, for he was out of air. "No one saw me. I did just what you said."

"Did you put the chair back? Did you close the drawer?" I asked him, picturing his every move in my head.

"Yes. I made double sure. When I was leaving their room, I turned around to check and see if it looked right. You couldn't tell anything was gone at all. I was real sneaky, Ruby!"

"Good boy, Tommy. Now you go out back and hide with James. He's hiding in Mrs. Ricker's horse stall or somewheres. Don't you come back in here until I come get you. Even if it's all night, you stay put. Do you hear me? Do you hear me, Tom?" I asked, glaring at him fiercely.

Big tears slid down his cheeks again. He looked brave too though, and he said, "Don't worry about me, Ruby. I'm good at hiding. I been hiding my whole life." He grabbed me quick round the waist and hugged me tight, hiding his eyes against my skirt. I hugged him back as hard as I could, as if he were my own boy, thinking what an odd thing for a little boy to say.

"Be a good boy, Tom. No matter what happens, you be a good boy," I said, pushing his white hair a little out of his face. "Now, scoot. Out you go." Then he was gone, and I began the waiting.

CHAPTER 42

I was not afraid, Miss. The more I conjured Valentine in my head, the more brave my heart became. I was ready to kill Jake Moffat before I had even laid eyes on him, and I was not too worried about what would happen after that. For one time in my life, I was the one saying what would be and what would not be. It was up to me, and I was determined to see that things turned out right, but not afraid; no, ma'am, not afraid at all.

I loaded the pistol first thing.

It's the pistol I showed you, Miss, from the trunk. It's a Dance Brothers .36 from Texas. It was already pretty beat up, even back then, with scuff marks on the barrel and a good nick in the cylinder. It looked like Valentine had used it plenty, but up until that day, I had never questioned how or why. I had looked it over carefully once, Miss, when I was snooping around in their room. I'm ashamed to say it, but it's true. Sometimes I needed to see into their lives.

I had not done much shooting, but I knew enough, so I

loaded every chamber with a killer bullet. Then I hid the pistol on the shelf behind my precious canned goods; there it lay between my beets and green beans, and I laid it careful so I could grab it quick if I needed it. Then I sat down and plotted out the rest of my murder scheme. Finally, came the time I heard a horse out front of my house, and I knew that bounty hunter was back, just like he said he would be. I jumped up and began clattering around in the kitchen, like I was fixing to cook some supper. Here he came, and knocked sharp on the door.

I don't know what I thought I would see when I opened that door, but when I did, I beheld the most beautiful man I have ever seen. He was very handsome, Miss, with striking, blue eyes beneath thick, black brows. His skin was brown as a berry, smooth and nicely shaved except for his big mustache. His chin was square and strong, his teeth white and shining. He was tall and lean, taller than Valentine, and he wore a cleanly brushed, black, frock coat.

Right when I opened the door, he swept off his bowler hat and introduced himself.

"Miss Ruby? I'm Jake Moffat. I'm an acquaintance of your husband."

Then I started acting like a nice lady; like Kenna. I said, "How do you do, Mr. Moffat? James told me you would be coming by. What's this all about?"

"I'm here to apprehend a criminal, a man who is a thief and a murderer. Let me show you." Then he reached in his coat, pulling out a frayed wanted poster, unfolding it as slow as molasses. There is Valentine DeRoo staring back at me from the poster drawing, and it says how he is a bad outlaw wanted for War

Crimes, that he was a raider with Quantrill, Miss.

I reached out and took that paper from Moffat, reading the whole thing close. It told all about Valentine; how tall, how old, and that he came from Missouri. It even included how he got a "distinguishing star-shaped scar on his right shoulder" from a bullet wound.

It didn't name him Valentine DeRoo, but William Hulse, claiming that he was in Lawrence, Miss; Lawrence, Kansas, and that he killed lots of innocent men and boys. It said the United States of America wanted him, dead or alive, with a reward in gold coin either way. The paper said lots of outlaws from the war were pardoned by Lincoln, but the worst could not be pardoned, and had to fall under the hand of justice. It said that even after what was left of Quantrill's raiders were pardoned, even after the war ended, they traveled the country, robbing banks and laying waste to the countryside. The paper said Valentine was to be tried in Kentucky, if he lived that long.

By the time I was done reading that, my head was swimming. Lawrence, Kansas, Miss. Why, I'm from Lawrence, Kansas, and I knew exactly what killing the poster told about. All my menfolk were killed by Quantrill's men. All of them, Miss. My papa and my brothers, all the boys I knew, just about every man in town was killed during that raid by Quantrill; blood running in the streets by the time it was over, with 300 widows left wailing.

Something came over me then. I raised up above myself and floated in the air over the top of my house, and when I looked down, I saw the top of my own head bent down reading the poster and the top of Jake Moffat's head standing there beside me, his hair parted perfectly down the middle of his head.

I watched as I handed the poster back and said straight out, "I'm from Lawrence. You know that? Did Frank tell you that?"

"Why, yes ma'am, Frank told me that. He thought you would want to know in particular that this outlaw, Hulse, was at Lawrence. Said you would be very interested to hear that. That's why I came here first, ma'am, instead of talking around town. Since Frank set me onto this outlaw and sent me here to the Ford to find him, I'm giving him a fee once I collect the bounty. Of course, that's if this man turns out to be Hulse."

It was funny, because I could hear my voice clearly, and Moffat's voice too, even though I hovered in the air. I hung there, watching to see what would happen next. My brain worked lightning fast though, and I quick checked to see if I hated Valentine, and I thought over that day of the raid from minute to minute, but it only took a couple seconds to see the whole raid. I quick looked for Valentine in the killers, but I couldn't find him. There were plenty of them though, Miss, so that just meant I didn't know he was there. Then I slammed back down into my body, and wobbled on the step there.

"Oh, Miss Ruby, you look peaked. Let me help you sit down." Jake Moffat took my elbow and helped me back inside to the kitchen table, and we sat down. Jake put the poster on my table where Valentine had eaten before, and he sat in my chair, where Valentine had sat before, and he looked at me like he knew what I would say next. I sat down too, and smoothed out the folded paper. Then I read it all again and then again, another time, and that Jake Moffat just sat there quiet and let me read.

Finally, I said, "Yes, I know this man. He lives here in the Ford, but he's not here right now. He'll be in tonight. He's on a freight run but he'll be back tonight, late. I can take you to him."

Moffat looked surprised, raising his black eyebrows. "All right. I must say, I'm surprised. Frank said you might try to protect this miscreant."

"Did you hear me say I'm from Lawrence, Mr. Moffat? All my menfolk dead and gone. And you know what? If my papa had lived, I doubt he would have allowed Frank Holt to come near me. I doubt I ever would have married Frank at all, and my whole life would be different. So, you see, Mr. Moffat, that raid ruined my life. You understand that, Mr. Moffat?" I asked him, and I looked at him sharp. "Isn't it funny that we would both end up here in the Ford? Life is funny. And isn't it funny you would meet up with Frank and he would send you here? Very funny."

"Please, Miss Ruby, I'm so sorry I have caused you new pain," he said to me, very sweetly. I noticed he looked closely at me and my womanly form and all. I looked at him again, seeing that he was a handsome man and he had some money too, but I also saw that he was truly a bad person, just like James said. I could see in his eyes that he was no good at all.

"It's all right. It's nothing new for me. But I will ask one thing of you. I will show you where to find this outlaw, but I need your help after that. I need to leave this place. I need to get out of here, for good. If I help you get this fellow, will you help me leave? Will you take me with you?" Then I turned into Kenna for all I was worth, and I tipped my head just so, pulling at a little curl behind my ear. I gave him a nice smile and leaned forward toward him a little.

"Will you help me, Mr. Moffat? Just for a night or two?" I asked, like a hussy. He saw my meaning right away, and it looked like Jake Moffat decided to help me for sure.

Then I let myself shed a little tear, and I picked up my apron and dabbed at my tears, just like I had seen Kenna do, saying how sorry I was to carry on this way, and I cried in my apron a little more.

"There, there, Miss Ruby. I'll help you out. We can leave straight away after I take care of this fellow."

"Well, how we going to do that? Will you take him along with us? What will you do? I expect he will turn deadly once he finds out who you are," I said.

"No, I won't take him anywhere. I can have the judge sign an affidavit showing he is dead. Then I just take the affidavit in to collect my reward." Mr. Moffat talked about killing Valentine the way Kenna and I talked about sewing up a shirt; just the day's work to him.

"Where are you to meet up with Frank then? He'll be wanting his share, I guess."

"He's supposed to be on his way here, ma'am. We were to meet here."

"Oh, well, that changes things. I guess I can't help you. I don't want to see that Frank. He's no good for me. So, I guess you can just go on now. Goodbye, Mr. Moffat," I said, standing up but putting my hand on the table, like I needed to lean on something; near to faint but being brave. I thought of Kenna again, pretending to be her.

"Well, hold on now. Let's don't get carried away here. Maybe we can avoid Frank altogether," said Jake.

"Well, I don't see the sense of giving any money to Frank Holt. He hasn't done any work to earn it. You'd just be throwing it away, if you ask me." I dabbed my eyes some more.

Jake's plans were just as clear to me as if he told me straight out. I knew he planned on robbing Frank of his share anyway, and that he was going to kill me before he left the Ford, whether I carried on with him or not. His card said he was a Pinkerton agent, but that didn't matter either. Pinkerton or not, I saw that he'd take all the money, no matter what. But I wasn't done with him yet, and he thought I was simple.

"What do you say to this idea? You help me corner this outlaw, Hulse, and I'll skip giving any money to Frank. Instead, I'll give it to you. Then you can leave town whenever you want," he said, speaking to me slowly, like I was a dimwit.

"You'd do that? You give me a share so I can leave? How much would you see clear to give me? Because I'll tell you what, if I help you catch this fellow, folks here in the Ford won't want anything to do with me. I'll have to have a way to get out of here."

"I promise I'll help you leave the Ford, Ruby," Jake said, and he meant it, only he wasn't going to help me buy a train ticket. Right then, I didn't know if Jake and I would be together that night or not; I didn't know what was going to happen between us.

"Why don't you come back here around dark? I'll take you to Hulse then. If we wait until after dark, it'll be easier to surprise him. He's pretty cagey. After dark will be better, I think," I said.

"That's not necessary. Just point me in the right direction and I'll take care of Hulse on my own. Then I'll come back here to see you." Jake obviously thought I was as stupid as a rock; no doubt Frank had been talking about me.

"Oh, no. Meet me here or forget my help. As I said, I need my share." Jake looked at me again and he must have thought that maybe I wasn't so stupid after all.

"Very well. I'll be back in a few hours." Then he stood up and left the house.

"Mr. Moffat," I said as he was leaving. "You best bring a wagon with you when you come back. I'm not walking."

He bowed then, turned, and left. I liked to faint.

CHAPTER 43

After that, all I could do was sit at the table and hold my head in my hands, for Valentine was a raider. I could not believe it! I knew he had a shady past, but I never dreamed he was with Quantrill! I jumped back in time then, and there I was in Lawrence. I could hear my mama scream as she stood over my daddy, who lay in a puddle of blood. My mama tipped her head back and wailed like anything. I didn't though; I just looked, growing hatred in my heart.

I knew about those boys from Missouri and our boys from Kansas, and how they played at war with each other, raiding back and forth across the state line and pretending that it was real. Why, sometimes our boys would catch a Reb and make him promise to quit fighting, and then let him go so he could break his promise and start up fighting again the next day. The Rebs did the same thing with our boys. Sometimes our folks went to the Burnt District and stole all the things from the houses and farms that had been laid waste.

But came the day Quantrill's boys quit playing at war and started fighting for serious, and they came to our town and killed all the men and lots of boys, too. Then it came clear that Quantrill and his raiders were too good at fighting, and needed wiped out. The fight was on.

Those were terrible, dark days, Miss; horrible and bloody. The war came home, and it wasn't a boys' game anymore. I have always felt that if they let us women do the fighting, things would be different, for yes, we grieve our lost boys and we grieve for all the mothers who lose their beloved boys and lay them in the dirt; grieve for every mother, be she enemy or one of our own; and yes, women folk have a way of truly understanding the heavy cost of war, but just the same, we women could do some terrible fighting, if given the chance. I will tell you; women would not play at war. It would be deadly serious, with no quarter given. I would have killed every Reb I came across, no questions asked. I would have been a fierce fighter, Miss, and so would any other woman. Even you, Miss—even you.

Do you think it is easy for me to know this about myself? Don't you think I want to be a nice, little lady, baking bread? But I am way past that, Miss. I know myself for all and good, and I understand war and killing. When I think of all those boys laying in the dirt, when I really understand what it means for them to be gone, my heart breaks. And the worst is there's no undoing, no changing any of it. They are gone and laid in the dirt, and folks keep on living, not even thinking about it at all anymore. They have all forgotten, but not me. I know of the bones mouldering in the ground. Those poor boys! One day this country will be mended and folks will think of the war as something that happened to someone else, long time ago. That's how it always is. War gets far enough away that it doesn't' seem that bad; seems like something that needs to happen. That's how it's always been, Miss, with war, and how it will always be.

No, folks forget, but there are some of us, Miss, who don't forget. Some of us carry the sadness around forever, and some of us can't forgive; some of us don't want to forgive. I carry it, Miss, but not for one side or the other. I carry it for all the mothers who weep in the night for their boys, for all the mothers who can't bear to see the light of day, or the taste of good food, or the voice of a boy from down the street. I carry it, Miss, for the whole world, and I'm right tired of the job, and I think it's killing me.

But that day I just sat at my table, thinking about Valentine and how he was a killer, how he had played at war too, and how he had come to the Ford to hide, and all that he was running from. I thought about how he suffered over James getting hurt, and I couldn't make it make sense, for he must have hurt lots of people. How could my Valentine have done these crimes? I could understand me doing evil, but not the Valentine I knew. I didn't want to believe it, but in my secret heart, I knew it was true. Valentine DeRoo was a killer.

I don't remember really deciding what to do exactly, but seemed like I started doing things. I gathered my few belongings and put them in my satchel, adding Valentine's pistol in there too, just in case. I began talking to myself, allowing how Ruby Holt would not be done in; said as how lots of folks would have some talking to do before I was done. I felt poisonous and deadly; I became the judge, the jury, and the hangman.

I changed into my travel suit, fixing my blue combs in my hair. I got a little scrap of paper and I wrote, "I shall not be moved," slipping it in my corset, next to my heart. I gathered all my magic around me. Yes, I put on my pretty dress.

CHAPTER 44

It seemed like I didn't have to wait that long. Come evening and the sun sank down, the sunset making a pretty picture, for flimsy clouds streaked across the sky, and all the colors streamed across from one end of the horizon to the other; pink and lavender up high and orange down by Frenchman's Mountain. I could hear the quail out in the yard; mamas clucking at their babies, keeping them from harm. The way the Ford smelled on a summer evening, Miss, with dust and cottonwoods and sage from far off. I loved my Ford then! I loved my place there, wishing I could just let all this go past me, but that was not to be.

The boys stayed good and hid, and that made me glad. They were minding me, seemed like. I sure didn't want my boys tangled up with Jake Moffat.

Finally, here he came, like a coyote sniffing around the henhouse, and I acting like a hen inside, quiet as can be. I watched him come, seeing how deadly this man was; seeing that his beauty was part of his lethal nature, and wondering why

God would do such a thing; making a snake look like an eagle.

He rapped on my kitchen door, and I went to answer. His eyes got big when he first saw me in my finery, too, and I wondered for a minute just which one of us was the snake and which the eagle.

He quick took off his hat and bowed a little, saying, "Evening, Mrs. Holt. You look absolutely beautiful this evening!" He ran his eyes up and down me.

"Why, thank you, Mr. Moffat," I said, very sweetly, blushing a bit. "I decided to be ready to travel before we meet up with Hulse instead of after."

"But where are your children?" he asked, trying to see around the door.

"Off to the neighbor lady down at the Ford," I lied, as easy as you please. "I'm thinking it's better for them if I just leave without saying goodbye. They won't know the difference anyhow."

"I see," said Moffat, but he didn't really see at all. He was becoming a little confused. "Well, shall we go meet this Hulse? Which way?"

"I'll show you." Then Moffat took my satchel from me, helping me climb in the little carriage he had procured from the livery. He handed my satchel back to me, and I put it on my lap. Then I floated up above the carriage for just a minute, so that all I could see was the top of it, my delphinium skirt sticking out a little to the side. Moffat's saddle horse was tied to the back of the buggy, still saddled. I watched Moffat walk round the back of the buggy, rubbing his hand along the flank of his horse, then climbing in to sit beside me. Then, bump, I'm back down.

I told him to drive down Coffey Street and to the Ford.

There stood Valentine's old shack, no one living there since the bad blizzard. It was a pretty sad sight too, with dank weeds growing up all round the sides of the adobe and the wood pile, the door to the shack still hanging crooked, the step still there in the front. It made me think of the night I had wandered down there to get Valentine to run away with me. A little smile came round my lips.

"You look very deep in thought, Mrs. Holt, but not unhappy," Moffat said.

"Well, remember, I'm from Lawrence."

"I remember," he said. "I guess vengeance truly is sweet."

"I guess it is, Mr. Moffat. I guess it is." And I smiled at him nice. Then I said, "It doesn't look like anyone is home. You best take the buggy somewhere else so Hulse won't get scared off. I'll wait inside." He helped me down, and then off he went to hide the buggy and his saddle horse over behind the Gables. That is a guest house, Miss. Maybe you have seen it? Down by the river?

I yanked the door to the shack open and a cloud of dust rose up. I stepped inside, and what did I see, but a pile of cut-up chairs and reins. It looked like Valentine left everything in that shack except for his spare shirt. It was just like he left it during the blizzard so long ago, not a chair left for sitting, Miss, and I could tell Valentine had been in a state the day he got out of there with his chairs tied to his feet. He must have been near panic, I guess. He left and never looked back.

I quick looked around to see if there was any sign of a killer living there, hiding in plain sight, but I saw no sign. It just looked like lanky old Valentine's place, minus Valentine, and it was getting dark fast. Then here came Moffat back on foot, stepping in the crooked door.

"What a mess! This can't be where the man lives!" he said, curling his lip.

"Just bunks here once in a while, but he always stops off here before going anywhere else. I think he has money buried in the floor here or something. He always stops here." I said, surprised at myself for turning into such a liar with no work at all.

That made Moffat look around good, hoping to see if he could find Valentine's stash of money. I stepped this way and that to let him look around. He looked close at the dirt floor for signs of digging, close at the walls for a nitch, but the light was fading so fast he was working pretty hard to see.

"Just wait till he gets here and make him show you where the money is," I said. "It can't be much longer now."

"All right," said Moffat. "I guess we wait then."

"I guess so," I said. I saw him looking at me sideways, and I didn't know if he was going to kiss me or shoot me. I felt pretty jumpy then, and for a minute it seemed like Valentine really would be there any minute; it seemed like my brain made up a story to keep me from running off into the night. I dreamed of Valentine's pistol too, wishing it was in my hand and pointed at Moffat, but it wasn't. It was in my satchel, setting yonder on the floor. It looked like deadly Ruby Holt is in a bit of trouble, with each passing minute causing Moffat to look at me with more suspicion.

He moved to either kiss me or kill me, I don't know which, but he kissed me very sweetly, bending my head back and all. He smelled good; clean, and he was good at kissing. I almost lost my will for a minute.

He kissed on me for a while, but then his hands encircled my neck, squeezing all around to kill me. I tried to get away, but he was very serious about killing me. He stopped kissing and just concentrated on killing, and here I was in another fight with a man. It seemed like he was getting taller every second, but maybe he was on his toes or I was sinking down. I remember thinking that my travel suit was going to get dirty on that floor.

I was seeing spots before my eyes and thinking all my worries soon be over, when here comes James from behind Moffat, giving him a good one over the head with a crutch. Down Moffat goes, and I see it's his clothes going to get the worst of it. He was down but not out, and almost right away, groaning while trying to get up, his hand grasping the back of his bloody head. James was fit to be tied, and he reared up to hit Moffat again, but I stopped him.

"That's enough, James. Stop now." I don't know why I stopped him. My thoughts were all stirred in a mix. I was trying to get to breathing again, and my neck felt squished. Then it came to me that we had gone too far to stop now. Moffat would kill us both if he got up.

"Get out of here, James. Go home." Right then I see that this could destroy James' life. I didn't want him packing a box of rocks around the way I was. I wanted him free of this mess we were in. "Go home and look after Tom. Right now."

"Stop telling me what to do!" James hissed at me, for he was trying to be quiet still but furious, too. "I'm going to kill him and you won't stop me. Get out of the way." James was in a state, holding up his crutch and ready to go at Moffat some more, and the whole time Moffat was getting better and better.

I knew I didn't have time to argue with James. Then I saw Watching Ruby at the door, looking calm and quiet, and she made me calm and quiet, too. I slow walked over and picked up my satchel. I opened it, and dug around for Valentine's pistol. It seemed like it took me a long time to find it. That's what I remember, Miss, digging around in there, trying to find that durn pistol. Funny too, because I had put it in there so carefully so I could get it quick. By the time I found it, my hands were shaking like anything.

Of course, James had no idea what I was doing. When I put a bullet in Jake Moffat, James about jumped out of his skin. But I just shot Jake Moffat in the back of his head, and he quit trying to get up. In fact, the life was thrown out of him so fast it surprised me; he just lay flat on the dirt and didn't move anymore. So, his troubles were over, but somewhere Jake Moffat had a mama who would wail for him, and I felt sick for killing him. I hated myself for this terrible sin I had committed, and right in front of James, too. He stared at me with his mouth hanging open. Watching Ruby nodded her head at me and walked out the crooked door.

It seemed like James came to himself, for he said, "Good God, Ruby! The whole town will be down here now! God!" He reached and took the pistol out of my hand. I guess James didn't trust me at that moment.

"No, they won't. Nobody thinks anything of a shot. Maybe I was shooting at a coyote, for all they know." I don't know how I knew no one would come, but I was right sure that we had nothing to worry about on that account.

I don't think James had ever seen a dead man, for then he sat down hard on the floor, his broken leg sticking out. He stared at that Jake Moffat, who was right then meeting his maker. James never said a word. There was so much blood draining out of Jake Moffat and staining the dirt floor of Valentine's shack. It sunk into the desert dirt in a widening circle around his head, and I was transported back to Lawrence and the vision of my own father dying in the dirt.

I allowed as how we needed to do something about Jake. We started digging a grave for him, there in the floor of the shack; dug a good long ditch but not very deep, used the pieces from the chairs for digging and used our hands, too. It took us a good, long time to get the job done, for Valentine and the years had packed that dirt down solid. It was pure dark in that shack by the time we got done. We did no talking, but we both cried some; quiet crying, James crying for the last time as a child, me crying for Jake's mama; very serious crying it was.

James couldn't even help drag Jake into his grave, but I got it done. My dress was a ruin, streaked with dirt, my hair sticking to my sweating scalp, but I got it done. When Jake lay in the ditch, one arm lay crossed over his body and the other was sort of tucked under him. I took one last good look at what I had done and started pushing dirt in on him. Then I remembered the wanted poster, so I had to dig out a little and get that out of his pocket. I don't know what else was in Jake Moffat's pockets, for I did not look. I'm not a thief, Miss; only a murderess.

Do you think bad of me, Miss? Are you scared of me now? You cannot judge me harder than I have judged myself all these years. You cannot hate me more than I hate myself, and you cannot fear me more than I fear myself. I may be low and uneducated, but I studied myself, and I know all about me.

I wonder if telling you this truth helps me at all. I can't get forgiveness no matter what I do, Miss. I can't give it and I can't get it. It is easier to tell you than I thought it would be, as if saying it out loud after all these years makes it smaller instead of bigger. I killed Jake Moffat; shot him in the back of his handsome head. Lord. Well, no matter now, I guess. I'm going to die and see what happens next.

That night I buried Jake Moffat in the floor of Valentine's shack while James sat and watched me like he was walking in his sleep; buried him good, scraped the blood-dirt in on Jake's chest, smoothed out the floor, put chair pieces back on top. Then I got Valentine's tinderbox and some weeds and some wood and some chair parts and built a fire right on top of Jake Moffat; built a fire and fed it for a bit until it got going good, fed it some more until it was right hot in there. My mind raced, thinking of all the problems I had, for all of a sudden, I see that I have a hundred jobs to do so no one ever finds Jake Moffat. I kept working on the fire and thinking about what all I needed to do.

"James, can you sit a horse at all?" I asked him.

"No," he snorted at me. "I can't bend my leg at all, Ruby." I could see he was disgusted with my question. He thought I was stupid, but I was not stupid, Miss.

"Well, we got to figure out a way to get rid of Moffat's horse. It's tied to the buggy over at the Gables. We got to get rid of it before daylight."

James seemed to realize that maybe I am not so stupid after

all, so he said, "Well, I can't sit a horse, but I can stand in one stirrup. I could sneak it home, standing up."

"That's good, James. That's what you got to do. Go to the Gables real quiet and get that horse and take it to the house. Leave the buggy there. Hide the horse in Ginger's stall. Don't worry about unsaddling it or anything. Just get it out of sight. I'm going to stay here and watch this fire for a bit."

James hobbled off on his crutches, blended into the night and was gone. My poor James.

You know, that adobe shack turned into a regular oven. Once it got going good, I helped the fire quick gobble up the roof, and it fell in and burned bright in the night. I got my satchel and got the Sam Hill out of there, once I knew it was good. I just walked on down to the Ford where it was nice and dark; where I could watch; stood there in the dark chill of the river, my sweaty scalp cooling in the night breeze, listening to the river in back of me and the fire in front of me.

It didn't take too long for a few folks to come down to the shack to watch the fire, but no one tried to put it out. It was just an old shack, too far gone to worry about. It burned up good with just parts of the walls left standing.

When all the folks wandered home, I came sneaking out of the shadows and looked close at the mess. It would take a deal of work to discover what was hiding under there. Once I felt satisfied that Jake couldn't be found, I snuck home, quietly, in the shadows of the cottonwoods. I thought about Valentine disappearing in the blackness of my backyard, and I tried to be like him; walking quiet while watching for other people.

James had hidden Jake's horse in the stall, just like I told him to. He was a good boy; minded me good through that whole time. I took saddle and bridle off the horse and hid it up in the stall rafters. I was too dog-tired to take care of that horse that night.

When I got in the house, I saw Tom asleep in his bed with his white hair ruffled across his forehead, James sitting at the kitchen table. He was still in a state, and we said not a word to each other, only sat and stared at the dry planks of my table.

The next day I sent Tom and James down there, to the adobe shack, I mean. James acted like he's only looking at the burned-up shack, but he got Tom and some other boys to push the walls down into the middle of the ruin, and they only thought they were playing. Silas Jacoby, who ran the livery, found his horse and buggy at the Gables that day, but no sign of the fellow that rented it. He allowed as how the fellow just up and left, without bringing the goods back; not very friendly of him, for the horse stood there all night and half the next day with no water.

I was as nervous as a cat all the next day. I couldn't eat at all, spending plenty of time in the outhouse with my nervous stomach. Finally came nightfall, and when it got late into the night, I went out back and tied a rope round that horse's neck. I led him out by the Shoshone camp, quiet as I could. I turned him loose out there. I figured the Shoshone would spot him the next morning and hide that horse for me. As far as I know, that's what they did.

My dress was a ruin, so on the third day, I easy washed it in the tub and got the dirt out as best I could, but the color never was the same. When Kenna saw it weeks later, she gave me a withering look like she was finally seeing the savage living in her midst, but she never said a word. I snuck Valentine's pistol back up to the house and put it in his drawer. And that was that. And I guess it don't pay to cross deadly Ruby Holt.

CHAPTER 45

The days of guilt after that! Every day when I woke up, I pictured Jake Moffat in my mind, his eyes staring out at nothing, his lifeblood draining out of his head. Sometimes in the middle of the night, I sat right up in bed, listening for his footfalls, for seemed like his ghost would come back to my house to seek his own revenge. I spent all my waking day reviewing every detail, checking to see if I had forgotten something that would land me in the hangman's noose, and all the while acting normal and like my old self, when my old self was long gone.

Valentine finally showed up the next afternoon, just as cool as a cucumber. Here he came, jingling into town with his team and tall wagon, his hat pushed back on his head and his feet up on the footrest, just like I had conjured him. He came driving right by the house when he got to town. He was on his way up to the Hill House, but stopped for a minute to check in on us. It just so happened that the young ones and I were out front of the house, the babies playing and shrieking in the sun, but the boys and me just sitting and looking around.

"Well, hello Ruby, boys" he said, like nothing had changed, because he had no way of knowing that I had learned about his war days and war ways. "How's everything going around here?"

"Not so good right now. Not good at all," I answered him. Tom got a scared look to his face and ran off around the house. James looked scared too, but stayed put.

"What's wrong? Is Kenna all right? Is it Kenna?" Valentine asked, his face turning white. "What's happened?"

"No, it ain't Kenna," James told him. "Maybe you better come in the house for a minute. Come in and let's have a talk." I quick looked at James, for he spoke so calmly, and I knew he was anything but.

"All right," Valentine said, jumping down from the wagon. He was pretty spry and made the jumping look easy.

We all walked in the kitchen, but I went in last. I took a good look around to see who was seeing us. Really, I was looking for Frank. Jake had already told me Frank would be showing up, and I figured it could be any minute.

We sat down at the table, but seemed like neither James nor me could say a word. Finally, I went in my room and got the wanted poster out from under my tick, laying it on the table for Valentine to see. First, he looked puzzled but then the situation dawned on him and he rubbed his face and groaned.

"Where's the marshal? Is he coming back to get me?"

"It wasn't a marshal," I told him. "It was a Pinkerton. Frank sent him here to get you."

"Frank! What the hell?"

"Yes, Frank met up with this fellow, Jake Moffat. When he

saw the poster, he sent him here to the Ford to get you; sent him here to this house so I could find out about you and what you have done." It seemed like saying it out loud made me so sorry; made me feel that it would be best to just die. Then the tears came so hard, I couldn't even see Valentine's face across the table.

"What I did was fight a war. Long time ago too. And after the war I was granted a pardon. Not that I had committed any crimes, anyway. This has to be some kind of mistake. I was pardoned along with the rest of the boys. We were all pardoned in Kentucky after Quantrill was shot and killed. This doesn't make any sense at all." I saw that Valentine was trying to swim to the top for some air; trying to make sense of this big surprise.

"So, you did ride with Quantrill though? That part's true?" I asked, feeling deadly again, hearing the screaming ringing in my head. "You rode with Quantrill and you were at Lawrence? Tell me the truth, right now."

Then Valentine looked at me funny and allowed as how, yes, he was there and took part in the fighting. "James, would you mind leaving Ruby and me alone for a bit? I think we better have a private talk."

"All right," James says, but he shot me a fierce look, and then he crutched out the door.

"Ruby, what is going on? What is wrong with you? Are you all right?" Valentine asked me, reaching across the table and taking both my hands in his big paws. "Why are you carrying on like this?"

"If I say out loud what I'm thinking, nothing will ever be right again. Why did this happen to me? What am I supposed to do with this?" I asked, but I wasn't asking Valentine. I was asking the good Lord. When Valentine took my hands, I knew I still loved him terrible, even if he was a raider. No matter what he had done, I still loved him terrible.

Now, Miss, I don't know about you, but I believe that each person has to have bad times in their life. How else would you recognize a good time? How would you know the difference? But there I was, a young woman, with another mess on my hands, and it just didn't seem right; didn't seem right at all.

I looked close at Valentine, stared right in his eyes, and said, "Sweet Valentine, I am from Lawrence. My people are from Lawrence. My daddy died at Lawrence. Don't that just beat all? Don't that just hang the cat?" I squeezed his hands, hot tears sliding down my face. I shook so hard that my curls wobbled on my head.

Valentine stared at me like he didn't understand English; like he had lost his mind. So, there we sat, holding hands and staring at each other, deciding if we love each other or hate each other, or if we're going to kill each other or save each other. Valentine ducked his head, trying to hide from me, but I could see he was crying. He wiped his eyes with the cuff of his shirt, and closed his lips in a grimace. And Miss, I will tell you, it was a very strange moment; maybe the most peculiar in my life, for we were on the edge of something, and it didn't look like it was going to turn out good.

"You better say something to me, Valentine DeRoo, and you got a short time to say it. You better help me see that you are not the biggest liar I ever met. You better help me see that you are you, Valentine, and not a killing monster."

Miss, I was swept away by the greatest sadness of my life, not like any other time with Frank or when my daddy died or what all. I was swept away with a terrible pain in my heart for losing the Valentine I loved. I threw a terrible fuss then, crying and sobbing like to die. Then I said to my poor Valentine, "Can't you fix this? Can't you undo it? Please, I'm begging you to undo this. Right now, Valentine, undo what you have done," and I said like that for a while.

Of course, poor Valentine could not undo what had already been done. None of us can do that, Miss, no matter how much we try or how much we want. That's outside our power, isn't it, Miss? So, he just held my hands in his and looked at me like he was like to die too.

"Ruby, can I tell you what happened? Will that make any difference to you? I had reasons for going to Lawrence with Quantrill. Let me tell you about what happened."

"I'm sure you had plenty of reasons for what you did. Didn't all you boys have your reasons? Didn't you all just? Blood lust. That's what you got. All you all."

"You said you wanted me to talk, Ruby. You want to hear or not?" and I could not deny that he was reasonable on that. I did tell him to get talking, so then I allowed as how I would try to listen.

Then came the story of Valentine and his life before the Ford. He said, "I was born and raised in Missouri. My family settled there long ago, long before the war, and at one time we were well off. But times changed for my family. My old man lost the farm, and we ended up with a few scant acres is all. Parcels of land next to each other, but we could eke out a living. Just a bit of cropland, an old house, a barn."

Valentine told me the story of how he had a little wife with shining yellow hair and a pretty smile, how she was real tiny like Kenna, and how he loved her terrible.

"We were so young, Ruby, with no understanding of how hard life could get. Seemed like we only saw the good things to come. We started off our new life together, but soon the talk turned to war. I can't believe it, but I was so swept up! Everyone was signing up to fight, and so did I."

So, Valentine said how he went to play at war with William Quantrill and they rode around and gave the Federals the Dickens every chance they got.

Valentine said, "I would get to go home from time to time to see my Onika and steal away a happy moment in the middle of all that heartache. But at the same time, it weighed on me to see our little place falling apart. When I was out riding with Quantrill and the boys, I missed her fiercely, and I dreamed of her every night." When he said this, Valentine got a very wistful look to his eye, and he swallowed hard.

"Yes, I dreamed of seeing her all the time—night and day. And I worried for her and prayed she would be safe. Things were getting very dangerous in our county, for the Jay Hawkers were constantly coming after us, and they didn't care if they were fighting men or women or children or what. They were just on the fight."

"Came the day I made it home to see Onika and she told me she was going to have a baby and we were so happy. By then, I had seen plenty of killing and I knew how very bad things could get. I wanted to take her away, maybe to Mexico, just to get away from all that blood. But I was no deserter, and I couldn't protect her. I couldn't protect her," he repeated. "So, what I did do was take her to our neighbor's farm—to Captain Anderson's farm. Anderson was a crony of Quantrill. A group of six wives ended up there together." And here, Valentine scoured at his eyes. "Ruby, I rode off with those boys and left her waving from the veranda. She had on her pretty dress and her yellow hair was tied up with a ribbon. She waved and blew me a kiss, and I rode out of there, hellbent for leather."

When he talked about that little wife, he got a real painful look in his eye. Then I knew Valentine wasn't running from any lawman when he came to the Ford. No, he was running from a broken heart.

The whole time he told me the story, I cried like anything. Sometimes I right out squalled, knowing no good was going to come out this story, for that little gal was nowhere to be seen; not living in the Ford nor nowhere else. But I listened on.

Valentine said, "I kept her at Anderson's farm and rode off with the boys. Rode off to play at war and while I was gone, the Federals came and took all those women. Took them all off to Kansas City and locked them in prison for helping us raiders. Chained them to big iron balls and locked them all together, plus a few other women the Federals had captured. And Onika was one of them."

"I don't know everything that happened to her, but I am tortured every day, thinking about what it was like for her. I know she was waiting for me to come save her. I know it. She was looking out for me, and I never got there. I never got there, Ruby. Oh God, I never got there."

That made me squall all the more, and I carried on like a mashed cat, for the idea of that little gal looking out the bars for Valentine made me weep. The torture! The regret! For, of all things, Miss, the Federals dug out around the bottom of the walls so that the prison collapsed and they left all those gals in there to die. And they all did die. Even Valentine's little wife and a babe growing inside; died with chains on her feet.

Then I thought of all the times I waited for Valentine to laugh or look happy, and I was ashamed of myself. I was wanting something that could never be—never go all the way to his heart.

No one ever heard of such a thing as this prison collapse. It didn't seem like that could have happened, but Valentine swore it did. Valentine got a fierce look about him when he told how she died, how his little baby died inside her. Right then, I saw that Valentine must have gone crazy after that, and I guess he did become a killer, and no wonder.

When he got done telling that story, he hung his head and cried on my kitchen table, Miss, cried and held my hands.

I had never seen a grown man cry, and it's not something you want to see. It broke my already broken heart, and I put up a terrible wail then. I don't know why Mrs. Ricker didn't come running, for she surely could have heard us.

Then Valentine became quiet and said in a deadly voice, "Ruby, I went to Lawrence to kill every man I came across, and I did. I killed plenty that day. I was mad with grief; mad with hatred. I don't know if I killed your people. I hope I didn't, but

I may have. I killed many men that day. I killed so many men that day. I had reason to kill. I killed them for my sweet wife and little baby."

Then I was torn two ways, for I could see how Valentine would have gone so fierce like that to seek vengeance on those Feds who harmed his wife. That made sense to me, but then I thought of all the men and all the times they all had some reason or other to spill blood. Yes, Valentine was justified, but then the boys from Kansas that went after Quantrill and his men were justified after Lawrence. Then more killing circled on more killing, until the fields all turned red with blood, Miss, and all the boys were gone and laid in the dirt.

I said that to Valentine, too. I said, "Well, when does it ever end, Valentine? For now, they are coming back for you and want to kill you. Then James will go after them for your sake. There's always a reason. Everybody always has a reason, so when does it ever end?"

"It's over now, Ruby," he said, and I'll never forget, he said. "The war's over, Ruby. It's over now."

"No, it's not," I said to him. "It's never over. Not as long as men are walking on this Earth. It's burning in your blood and in the blood of every man. There will always be war. War after war after war, and folks will always have a reason."

I think he really listened to me, for he got a strange look on his face like he could see the future of us all, and all the boys laid in the dirt, and he knew I was right. He looked sorry then, and I thought he was worrying for James and Tom. And Miss, so was I. So was I.

CHAPTER 46

Do you have any single idea how hard this is on me, Miss? Any idea? Yet here you come, every day, looking for a story. Don't seem right. Don't seem right at all, digging into my business, making me remember what it all was like. I was just a young girl, Miss. Just young and not deserving all that trouble, but there I was, blood on my hands, loving a man that I had no business loving.

And you know what? Even after I found out all about Valentine, I still loved him. Then I knew what it was to really love a man; to love someone who had done something so terrible, but to still love him. When Valentine saw that I kept loving him no matter what, he came to love me too, in a different way; in a humble way, from far away, for he was never unfaithful to his wife. No, he never broke his vows, but sometimes I saw him look at me and I knew that he loved me, or when we stood side by side, I felt his silent love. And Miss, that is far worse than not being loved at all.

Well, anyhow, you should know that I am old on the outside, but still that young girl on the inside. I am looking out of this face, *these eyes, but it's like the real me is here, behind the faded hair and wrinkled face, behind the eyes. The real me is still that young girl. I don't feel any different, no different at all, but only look different.*

Isn't that funny, Miss? Don't that just make you wonder what this is all about? Why we get old and die, or die young? Why do we even die at all? What a puzzle life is.

I don't want you to think I was never happy or never had a good time, for I surely did. As years went by, I was able to find my own kind of happiness. Happiness in everyday things, like the way the dirt in the garden feels on bare feet or how the desert smells after a thunderstorm; how the Sonomas look in spring with a light coat of green on their slopes; how I enjoyed the smell of my tomato plants of a morning, and them all dusted and powdered like ladies dressed for a fancy party. I found joy, Miss.

But for all my days did this murder hang over me. Ne'er a day goes by that I don't think about Jake Moffat and how I laid him in the ground. It doesn't matter that he was a bad man. I killed him dead. Nobody knows me, Miss. Why, I might jump up out this bed and kill you right now. Nobody knows me. Nobody knows you either. Truth is, Miss, don't nobody know nobody.

We sat there in my kitchen that day and seemed like we bared our very souls to each other, but he still didn't know me; how terrible I could be; how fierce.

I remember him saying, finally, "Well, I have to try to straighten this out somehow. I can't have this bounty hunter showing up and trying to haul me off to Kentucky. I'm going straight to Unionville to see the judge. I'm going to get this cleared up, once and for all."

"How are you going to do that?" I asked him, thinking how simple men can be. "You changed your name, Valentine. You going to tell Kenna that her married name isn't her married name? That she married someone she doesn't even know? You going to tell the judge all that?"

"I'm ready to," Valentine said, and I could see he was very serious. "I can't spend the rest of my life looking over my shoulder. I've done that too long already. I'm going to clear my name, and end this nightmare."

"Just like that, huh?" I asked him. "Now that you're a fine, upstanding citizen, all you have to do is go talk to the judge and he's going to somehow make this all go away? I guess he'll just write a letter to the president and tell him that Mr. Lincoln was wrong about you. Why did you change your name? Don't you have plenty to hide?"

"I truly believe that I did not commit any crime. It was a war. How do you think people would view Lawrence if the Confederacy had won the war? Do you think I'd be wanted then?"

"Well, I guess that doesn't matter a whit because the South didn't win, in case you didn't notice. You didn't win, and now folks are trying to kill you, and the war is supposed to be over!" I yelled.

"You best listen to me now, Valentine DeRoo. You best listen. You can't go to the judge. You can't go back to your other name. You can't undo anything that has been done. The only thing you can do is try to forget this ever happened and keep pretending to be Valentine. I'm telling you now. There is nothing to do." I was hoping like anything that Valentine would listen to me. I just knew that if he went to the judge, why, the whole Jake Moffat catastrophe would come to light. I couldn't let that happen, so I tried my best to steer Valentine.

"Ruby, you aren't making any sense. I can't just do nothing! Moffat is still here somewhere. He's still looking for the reward. Did he tell you where he's staying or how to find him?"

"Ha. Why would he do that? No, he didn't tell me nothing. I don't know where he is. I haven't seen him since that day he came here."

"That doesn't make any sense at all. I'm going to go find him and take care of this."

"Have you listened to anything I said?" I asked him with a big hammering heart. "He will kill you on sight. He's gunning for you. Best thing for you to do is get out of town and stay out for a while until he gets on to some other outlaw."

"I'm no outlaw. Don't say that about me, Ruby. I'm no outlaw."

"Well, you might say that, but seems like other folks have a different picture of you. You best listen to me now. Go see Kenna for a minute and then get the Sam Hill out of here. If Moffat shows up again, I'll try to send him somewhere. I'll tell him a story. I'll tell him you ran off to California. And I hope Frank don't show up at all. James is like to kill him."

"Ruby, do you know where Moffat went? Is there more to this story than you're telling me?" Valentine looked at me suspiciously. He could see that things weren't adding up quite right.

"How would I know where Moffat went? I have no idea where he went. I'm trying to keep my boys in line and keep the babies safe, and here you are asking me questions about some bounty hunter I never should have laid eyes on. You've got a lot of nerve, asking me anything. I am not responsible for your troubles, Valentine. I'm not your wife, to sit and worry about you and your shady past."

That shut him up, Miss, just like I knew it would. I had not told one lie to Valentine, for I did not know where Jake went, after he died; none of my business either. 'Judge not lest ye be judged,' and what not. I knew from long ago that the best lies are those that are closest to the truth, so I lied very gently.

Valentine's big shoulders kind of slumped down, and he held his head in his hands. He stared down at his work boots and didn't say a word for a long time. Finally, I had to start talking again.

"Valentine, I'm real sorry this all happened. It's all Frank's fault, really. He sent Moffat here. I swear, I hate him."

Valentine said, "My whole life, I tried to take care of my people; my folks, my sister, my wife. I never could seem to get the job done, and it weighs on me, Ruby. I feel so guilty for leaving Onika unprotected, sometimes I can't breathe."

"I want to take care of all my people here in the Ford, too. Kenna, the young ones, and you, too, Ruby. I just want to make sure everyone is all right, and now I've brought ruin to all of you."

I felt sorry for him, for I could see he was telling me the truth. It was his job in life to take care of his people, and when he couldn't do that, it was right hard on Valentine.

When he quit talking, I said, "Well, you do take care of all of us. We take care of each other. That's how it's supposed to be. Things will settle down again. You'll see. We just got to wait this out and keep an eye out for Frank." Again, I was not lying.

"I need time to think this out. I need to figure out what to do," said Valentine, staggered by his troubles.

"Well, you best get up the hill and see how Kenna is doing, then figure out how to get out of town for a while. Then let's just sit tight and see what happens." But I felt sick to my stomach, thinking about Frank and how he knew all about my Valentine.

I tried to keep my lies to Valentine down to a minimum, but Kenna I lied to with every breath. It wasn't fair to her either. There she was, going about her business, thinking she knew all about her own life, when she didn't know much of anything; she was innocent of all the secrets and lies. Poor Kenna. And if she ever had found out, look out! She would have had a fit for sure. I told myself that I was keeping her safe and happy, but it was wrong. It was worse than if I had stolen Valentine away from her and run off with him to San Francisco or somewhere. It was wrong, and it has plagued me all these years.

Miss, can you get me outdoors. I need out of this old house. Just a bit of sunshine and air would do me good. Can you help me? I want to sit in the front yard by the steps, like I used to do with my young ones; like I used to do before Jake Moffat came to my door and turned me into a killer.

CHAPTER 47

It was down in the summer—August, and Kenna's birthday had come and gone with no gathering at all, but just a nice supper with all of us together. I made a spice cake for my spicey friend; she loved that too.

But then, when all the trouble brewed up and Valentine was in the soup for sure, here he came with an idea to solve all our troubles. The next day, the day after our terrible talk, here came Valentine on his buckboard, and Kenna was with him. Her eyes shone when she came busting in the kitchen door, yelling for the babies. They came screaming, and jumped on Kenna like they hadn't seen her in a year. While Kenna was busy with the babies, I shot Valentine a quick look and we locked eyes. It was unsettling, Miss, for now we held more secrets from Kenna.

Anyhow, when Kenna finally finished kissing on the babies, she said, "Ruby, we are going to the Summit to get this year's wood. I'm going along. Come with us! Won't it be fun to sleep in a tent! We can cook for the men while they work on the firewood. We can bathe in the creek! Come with us! Will you?" Kenna asked, giving me a hug, like she always did.

"Well, I can't just run off and leave my garden. I'm counting on that garden this fall," I said.

"Ferris' boys are watering for us. They will water for you, too," Valentine allowed.

Now here's what I know, and I knew it then too. Sleeping in a tent and cooking outside and washing in the creek is anything but fun. It's terrible, Miss; it's awful. A person cannot stay clean, no matter what. And the babies up there? It made me shudder to think of it, but I looked at Kenna, and she was so excited! I looked at Valentine and thought about my advice for him to get out of town, and I see that I am going on the wood gathering.

Then Valentine said, "Come on and go with us, Ruby. Someone's got to teach Kenna how to get by without her fancy tub." Valentine winked at Kenna and smiled his crooked smile. "Plus," he said, looking at me again, "We all need to get out of town for a while. It will do us all good."

That made Kenna give him a big hug, and that made the babies hug him, too. Valentine scooped them up, even though they were getting so big. I stood there, looking at him holding my babies; Minnie resting her little hand on his shoulder, and Elsie hugging one arm around his neck; both talking to him at once. Then Minnie grabbed Valentine by the chin and turned his head to her, so he had to listen to her. Valentine made big flirting eyes at her, and Minnie made eyes back at him. Then we all laughed at little Minnie, and for just a minute it seemed like times were good.

"We'll leave early in the morning, so get packed up,"

Valentine said. "We only have one tent, so that will be for you ladies," and he made eyes at the babies again, "and we gents will sleep under the stars."

"How long you thinking of staying up there, Valentine?" I asked, still thinking about living filthy in a tent.

"I would imagine about like last year, a few weeks," he said.

"I'm thinking I'll take my sulky up there. That way if the babies wear me out, why, we can come back down without troubling the whole bunch," I told them. "We might need the sulky anyway, to haul wood around or what all."

"Why, that's a good idea," Valentine allowed. "Good idea, Ruby." My heart skittered when he said my name.

I spent the rest of that day getting ready, packing a grub box with some of my dried corn and beans and such. I got some flour and sugar and coffee and threw that in there. I was out of meat, but I figured we'd hunt up there anyhow. I still had lots of squash though, and those were easy to haul, so I put some of those in the stack. I figured we could make stew with those precious squash. I gathered bedding and pans and skillets; just everything I could think of to keep us going up there. There would be no milk for the babies, and that was hard, but they had gone without before, and were still growing all right. I started in baking bread, cookies, and gingerbread crackers to save trouble up on the summit.

Of course, Tom was a big help. He got some grain for Ginger and he helped me load up the sulky. It didn't hold that much, especially since we had to leave room for the babies, so we made a stack by the road of things we would add to Valentine's wagon. James did what he could with his crutches, and he kept an eye on the babies.

Next morning, we were ready, bright and early. The babies were so excited, asking for Valentine and Kenna every minute. I can hear their voices ringing in my head even now. "Where Kenna, Mama? Where Kenna?" Then finally I heard Valentine's big wagon rattling down the road. The babies heard too, and they shrieked and ran in circles.

How pretty Kenna looked, sitting up high on that wagon, her hair braided and tied up good, wearing one of her old dresses, smiling like anything.

As soon as we finished loading up, James climbed in the sulky to ride with me, but the babies yelled to ride with Kenna and Valentine, and that was fine with Kenna. I allowed as how we would take turns with them. Little Tom rode Boy, and did he look proud on that horse! Of course, Valentine had his big freight wagon and a pretty good string of mules.

The sun was up good by the time we finally pulled away from the house. Down my street and to the Ford we went, with Valentine in the lead. The river was pretty low that late in the summer, but it was still disconcerting to drive off into the water. I watched Valentine go first, and after his wagon was clear up the other side, I slapped the reins to get Ginger going, and thus we forded the river.

Kenna climbed down to watch us cross, and then she came up to me, her face beaming, and said, "Here we go, Ruby! Off to the Summit!"

CHAPTER 48

*O*h, Miss, I was dreaming! I was standing in my room at Kenna's with the window open, the breeze blowing the curtains. I could smell the rain from out of the Sonomas, and the air was so sweet! When I looked out the window, I was up so high, and all of Kenna's trees were way tall; much taller than now so I could look right into them! From the window, I could see them a whole different way—the way a bird must see a tree. I looked round the room, and there was not a speck of dust. Not anywhere! I could hear Kenna down in the kitchen, clattering around, and I could hear the babies, Miss! I could hear their little baby voices! Oh, Miss! It was so real! I thought it was real! It was Kenna's heaven I saw!

It's a puzzle to me how I could dream of that, but it helps me remember our times together so clear; those days I thought were so dark, when really my biggest problems were broken ribs and a wandering eye; not like now at all, nor like the days after I killed Jake.

We made it up to the Summit. Of course! I stayed pretty far back from Valentine's wagon all the way because of the terrible dust. It was as fine as face powder and just coated everything! There was no way out of it, but I stayed back just the same.

So, we headed straight north that morning, staying pretty close to the river for miles. There we were, in the flat bottom of the valley with the mountains rising up on either side, in the hot desert with lots of sagebrush and rabbitbrush and tumbleweeds. Finally, the river turned off east, but we kept going north toward the little town of Paradise, so we left the river.

On we went through that desert bottom, and durn if we didn't come to sand dunes just like the ones from the Bible stories; like the sands of Egypt for sure. It was good there was a worn track there, or we would have sunk into the sand for sure. Just when I thought we were out of the dunes, I looked close at a hill and see that it's still a dune, but has a few weeds and brush growing on it.

Tommy was having a big time, riding back and forth between our wagons. A couple other wagons were coming along behind us too, Wade and them. So, Tom rode back to check on them too, a regular ramrod. A couple times he would get one of the babies from Kenna and bring her to me to ride in the sulky. Then he would trade them around back and forth, so that made the trip easier for the babies, and pretty soon they were worn out and fell asleep under the shade cloth on Valentine's big wagon.

By late down in the afternoon we come around a huge hill and there loomed the Summit. I had never seen it up that close, and it was beautiful. A great mountain it is, and the top of it has no trees or plants at all, but only steep, gray rock cliffs and peaks and all; but below that it is covered with little sections of darkest green forests and glades. Beautiful! And each one looks like the best place to go. I was in a hurry to get up there then, and seemed like Ginger was too, for she picked up her step.

At the foot of the mountain, we came to Paradise. It's a pleasant, little town with friendly folk. The trees there are gigantic, Miss, they must be so old! A pretty little creek runs right through the town; Cottonwood Creek, they call it, and the air on that creek was a gift; cool and green on that creek, and crowded with downed trees and cattails and all.

That's where we camped that first night, out behind the saloon and beside the creek. Didn't anyone mind. So, then it was time for Kenna's first night out under the stars, and I thought this would be a good show, but no, here came a nice lady from town, offering Kenna and me and the babies a bed in her house.

Her name was Ann, and she had the prettiest little house there on the creek. Spanking new, it was, with gingerbread round the porch and giant cottonwoods in the yard. It had pretty siding on it too that looked like bricks but when you look closely you see it's tarpaper, but still real pretty.

So, we stayed there that first night. It was a pleasure to clean up in her little kitchen. She had a hand pump right in her kitchen so we didn't have to carry water; very fancy it was. Mrs. Wolicki allowed as how we could cook on her stove for the men, and that's what we did. We invited her to eat with us, and then after supper and dishes washed, we had a grand gathering under her cottonwoods with music and a campfire.

The boys played their mandolins, and Wade was there too, with his fiddle. The creek made her own music, and the bugs weren't bad at all. We had a fine time! That James was getting to be very good on his mandolin. I guess his broken leg gave him plenty of time to practice.

Well, everyone was pretty tired, so we didn't stay up late. We knew we had a big day coming. Valentine kissed Kenna on her forehead and ambled off with the boys. Then Kenna and I went into Ann's pretty little house and fell in bed.

Next morning, we continued heading north, only now we could follow Cottonwood Creek, for it came right off the Summit and would lead us where we needed to go. It was still plenty dry out there, but the mountain hung over us, and once in a while a little breeze floated by. We started a steady climb up the foot of that mountain. It didn't seem such a climb until I turned around once, looking down on Paradise way below us. Then I understood how very massive the Summit is. James rode with Valentine and Kenna that day, and they had the babies too most of the way, so it was just Ginger and me. That was all right by me; I liked being by myself sometimes.

Finally, it got to where the road twisted back on itself in a very sharp curve, twisting around a steep gully. That made me a little nervous, so I kept Ginger way over to the mountain edge of the road. I didn't even want to think about how it would be to bring the sulky down off there, and the idea of a wagon full of wood trying to get down was even worse. I didn't much like this wood gathering.

My eyes were pretty much glued to Ginger's rear-end, as we curved very tight this way and that, but then, for some reason, I looked up and realized we were in a big rock bowl of sorts; tall cliffs and rocks bigger than Kenna's house all round; patches of sweet, green grass in between. In some places, the rocks made fortress walls with great, tall rock columns standing side by side, and the dark green places I had seen from Paradise turned out to be peaceful groves of quakies, with tiny, waving leaves everywhere and shadowed paths underneath. Then, surprise of all, growing right by the road was the prettiest sarviceberry tree I have ever seen, covered in berries too; all pink and lavender and some deep purple.

All of a sudden, I saw it all at once, Miss; saw the whole world, and when I truly saw it, my throat closed up and my eyes took to stinging, for I saw creation as if God's hand had just left off a minute ago. I saw how very small I was, how small we all are, and it made me feel better; it made my sins seem less heavy. I looked close all around and, even with all my troubles, I thanked God for the sight. I thanked God for all that beauty up there. Then I slapped the reins at Ginger, and on we went.

I was getting used to sharp turns this way and that when I saw up ahead that Valentine had turned off our windy road, so it looked like we were getting close to the wood camp. He turned into a hidden little gulch that was pure full of quakies and grasses and wild flowers growing all around, so pretty! And that's what we named the place, Hidden Gulch, for we didn't know if it already had a name of its own. We still followed the creek, and I thought I could take up living there in Hidden Gulch.

CHAPTER 49

We set up our camp right by the creek. It was a good place, pretty flat, and we had lots of shade from the quakies. The creek made a soothing noise, but it wasn't so noisy you couldn't hear yourself think, just nice and cooling. That creek we ended up naming Bear Creek. It seemed like we thought we owned the place, I guess, since we kept on naming everything like we were the first people there, and I am sure we were not.

The boys got to work right away, setting up the tent and hobbling the team so they could graze nearby. There was already a fire pit built there, and I could see this was where the boys had camped last year. There was even a bit of firewood left there from the year before, so we were home.

The first thing Kenna wanted to do was to get a better look at the creek with the babies, so that's what we did. It sure was pretty down there. The babies were hot and tired, so in the creek they went. Poor little babies, their faces turned into running trails of dirt when they got in that water before Kenna and I washed them off. I could see I was right about being filthy the whole time we were up there; it was a trial.

It was getting toward suppertime, so we got back to the fire circle and got to work. James had built a fire while we were at the creek, so that was a help. We had dried corn and beans and deer meat, and we got that right to boiling for supper. That was just the first of many meals we made up there. We didn't have much variety, but we did our best and scoured the countryside during the day for plants to add in.

You ever eat a cattail, Miss? Or dandelion green? Or wild carrots? We had all those and more up on the Summit, and down in town too, for that matter. You can boil cattail roots like you do a potato, and they are very tasty. Dandelion greens with vinegar, so good in the summertime!

Of course, we gathered every berry that was fit to eat; gathered and ate them up there and gathered a bunch to take home too, for jelly; sarvisberries and currants, thimbleberries and gooseberries. The babies even helped us get berries, and all the while all the men were just a bit higher up the gulch, felling pines and dragging them down to the clearing near the camp. So, we all worked plenty hard.

I did get to see Kenna find a way to live in a tent, and sometimes it was very entertaining, for she could not stand being dirty, just as I knew before we ever went on that trip. By the third day, she whispered to me that she would never try this again, and she peppered her promise with some of her choice curse words while she was at it. I nodded at her and agreed that from now on, we would stay home to quilt and can and drink tea. But we were stuck there then, and so we made the best of it.

Kenna had a flower press that she brought to the Summit with her. Whoever heard of a special machine to press flowers? Why, we always just used books and such, but no, Kenna had a fancy store-bought press made out of smooth boards and it had clamps that squeezed it shut. So, as soon as we got settled into our daily routine and had the food going and the babies in hand and what all, we took to gathering flowers to put in the press. Kenna allowed as how we would study them and find their names in books and we could use some of them for medicines or cooking.

Each afternoon, after the babies fell asleep on a blanket under the quakies and we were so dirty we were fit to be tied, Kenna and I would strip down to our chemises and take a dip in the creek. It wasn't very deep, so it was hard to really get very clean, but at least we rinsed off some of the dust. It helped cool us off, too.

We even took to napping under the trees in our chemises, Kenna's white shoulders shining in the dappled sunlight, ropes of her coffee, garnet hair tumbling down around her like a cloak. We hung our dresses on the trees near the creek, and that meant no men to come around there. In fact, we went wild, running around in our underthings half the day. Kenna said we were turning into water fairies. I wasn't sure what that meant, but I got the idea. She said we were just disguised as women, but really, we were selkies with the power to bewitch any man we came across. I swear, her mind took her far and wide, Miss, without much effort.

Most every day we read together, with mostly Kenna reading to me, but sometimes I read to her, too. We read "The Lady of the Lake" up there, Miss. Have you read that poem? That is one long poem, Miss, but we enjoyed it a lot and we read it out loud and drew little lines in the book to show the parts we loved the best. That was my favorite when the babies napped under the quakies while Kenna read to me, flies buzzing lazy in the sun. I lay there on my quilt, looking up at the sky through the silver aspen leaves, picturing the story in my head. From the first minute I met Kenna, she taught me things. She educated me, Miss, through poetry. She taught me how to speak and reason and wonder, all the while speaking to me in rhyme from her favorite poets. What a gift that was, Miss! To see inside Kenna's mind, and learn from her; she completely changed my existence, molding me from an ignorant farmgirl into someone who can think and ponder on the ways of the world.

Doesn't that sound fine, Miss? Don't you want to see the Summit? You would have a hard time up there at first, but I bet you would figure it out. I bet you would do all right. Of course, that's if you manage to avoid the bears. Yes, Miss, I said bears. Well, why you think we named it Bear Creek?

Kenna and I, we had our routine down pretty good. We had been up there for a couple weeks. It was a cloudy afternoon, and we decided to go gather some berries instead of napping by the creek, so we got us a couple little buckets that Kenna had brought, and we gathered the babies and Tom, and off we went to find some berries. There were lots of berry patches around there, but on that day, we went further up the gulch to a narrow little canyon way up the way. The creek was little and skinny up there, with plenty of willows growing all up and down the little gully. The farther we walked, the skinnier it got, until we were pretty much hemmed in on both sides by willows and quakies and brush and what all.

We came to a funny place then, where the creek flattened out into a little swamp. It was sloppy to walk through, so Kenna and me each packed a baby across it, and Tom made his own way without any trouble. Then, not far past the little swamp, we come upon a nice bunch of sarviceberry. The bushes were so thick you couldn't walk through them hardly, and they were loaded with ripe, fat sarviceberries.

We commenced to picking, the babies sitting in the dirt at the edge of the patch, playing in the tall grass. Kenna and I visited, having a good time, and Tom talking to us, too. It was easy picking, so I didn't plan to be there for long.

We were just working away when the strangest feeling came over me, and all the hair on my arms stood straight up and my skin crawled. I told Tom to hush. I felt awful, and I stood up to take a look around.

"What's wrong, Ruby?" Tommy asked. "What's got you going?"

"Hush up, Tom. Hush!" I said sharp to him, trying to look everywhere at once.

"What's the matter, Ruby?" Kenna asked, continuing to pick berries.

"I don't know. Something doesn't feel right. I feel funny," I told her, still looking around. "I think we have enough berries."

"What?" Kenna said, like I was crazy. "We don't have near enough! I want lots of these! And I want to get some leaves too, to dry. These will be perfect for drying, since they grow right here close to the water. They are glorious!" I could see that Kenna wasn't listening to me, but dreaming of her stock of dried herbs back home.

"I don't know much about this place, but I've got a feeling we need to get out of here," I said. "Let's go right now. I mean it, Kenna. We've got to go," and I moved to get the babies.

Right then, a little bear came ambling along. She wasn't a tiny bear, but maybe a yearling bear, maybe last year's baby. I know now she was of the black bear variety, but she wasn't black; more of a cinnamon color, real pretty, and she had a white blaze on her chest. She was fat and healthy looking, and seemed happy to be living way at the top of Hidden Gulch, it looked like. So, here she came, very friendly and wondering what we doing in her sarviceberries. Now, Miss, if you see a baby bear, you got a mama bear seeing you. You can pretty much count on that. I may be from the flatlands, but even I know that.

Tom loved that little bear on sight. "Well, looky here! A bear! A little bear, Ruby!"

"Tom, help me get the babies and start walking very easy down to camp. We don't want nothing to do with a bear. Go on, right now. Just walk easy with the babies. We're coming right behind you."

Kenna did not have a peep to say then. All of a sudden, she was agreeing with me about having enough berries. Little Bear just sat down and started eating berries like he did that with folks every day.

"Kenna, start down the trail. Walk easy, but we need to get the Sam Hill out of here." We all headed down the trail as best we could. Now, we had a distance to go, and we had to cross the swampy place and all, so I felt very scared; terrified really; and I knew that mama bear watched me while she decided if she was going to get us or not.

Right then, I heard Tom yell, "Mama bear! Mama bear! We got a mama bear!"

Now, the willows were pretty thick and tall, so right at that second, I had lost sight of Tom and the babies, to boot. I could only hear the deep fear in Tom's voice; he was terrified. Miss, I picked up my skirts and I took to running toward my children, moving pretty fast, and the whole time I thought, *"Lord, I'm running toward a mad mama bear!"* But I kept on running! I know I didn't have to run far to get to Tom and the babies, but it sure seemed like it took a long time. I was so afraid for my children.

I came busting out of the willows at the edge of the swamp, and there stood Tommy and the babies, but no mama bear to be seen. Kenna came out right behind me.

"Where is she, Tom? Where is she?" I asked, breathing hard, my whole body shaking. I scanned the willows sharp, but I could see no bear; I couldn't see anything, and if that bear was there, she was *right* there, just a few feet away, and she must have been hiding *right there*!

"She was right there, hunkered down, looking at us, and she sniffed at me," Tom whispered, his voice shaking as he pointed to the willows. "Then she stood up on her hind legs, and she was a giant! Ruby, she looked just like Mrs. Ricker's cat looks right before it pounces on a mouse!" Tom said, his chin quivering.

I tell you, Miss, I have never been so scared in my life. I was so frightened for my young ones, for I thought that mama would come get them for sure. I trembled from head to toe, my eyes looking everywhere. I picked up a rotten stick and held it in my hand, ready to give that mama a pop on the nose if she showed herself. Can you imagine? A scrawny, rotten tree branch up against a furious, mama bear? But at the time, it seemed like a good idea. I had to do something, Miss.

Funny thing, I got a picture of a tiny chipmunk in my head right then, standing up on his hind legs looking all around very sharp. It come to me then, Miss. If you see a little animal doing that, it isn't looking for its pine nuts. No, it's looking to see who's hiding yonder in the scrub. So, I felt like a quarry then, and I was pure terrified. I had to get my babies out of there.

"Scooch together," I sort of yelled. I figured it would be better for Mama Bear to hear me talking big. "Clump up!" And that's what we did. I picked up little Elsie and Kenna picked up Minnie, and we got Tom between us, and we crossed that swampy place, then on through the willows, Tom pulling on our skirts all the way. Next thing you know, we heard a bunch of ruckus on the *other* side of the trail, not the Mama Bear side! It was another bear, Miss. I swear, I could hear it breathing, snorting around in the willows.

I lifted up my rotten branch in one hand, clutching Elsie with the other and said, "Keep going. Let's go!" And on down we went to the mouth of that little canyon.

We lost our berries and our buckets, and we never went back to get them, but the young ones were safe, and we had a good story to tell that night around the campfire. We all told our parts more than once, and every now and then, Tom would jump up and act it all out for us, even pretending to be me with my big stick.

CHAPTER 50

Well, that was about the end of my fun up at the Summit. When I thought about us laying around, sleeping in bear country, it made my blood run cold; the days little Tom ran wild up there and I didn't even know where he was; the babies sleeping defenseless under the trees while I took a dip in the creek. I shuddered with dark visions of bears and wolves and mountain lions and I don't what all.

So, that very next day I allowed as how I was going to take the young ones on down off the Summit and back home. Right away, Kenna said she wanted to head home too, so we began readying ourselves for a long ride. Valentine seemed fine with us leaving. I don't think he had thought about bears and lions and all when he took us up there.

Bright and early the next morning, we headed down the twisty road toward Paradise. We loaded the sulky with berries and the flower press and the babies. Tom threw a terrible fit when I told him he had to come home with me, so I ended up leaving him there with James, and James promised he would keep a good eye on little Tom.

How beautiful the trip down off of there was! I was pretty nervous about coming off of there in the sulky, but my good Ginger kept us going slow all the way down. We stopped quite a few times and let the babies wander a minute, and we stopped again at the first sarviceberry bush we had seen on the way up there, but this time, I marveled with Kenna, and we both allowed that it was a blessing to have eyes in our heads. Then we picked that bush pretty clean so we had berries and leaves and a little bit of root, in spite of that mama bear.

We got back to Paradise late in the day. In fact, it was near about dark. We went straight to Ann's house since she had already invited us to come back. That was a nice night too, because we got real baths with soap and hot water. The babies splashed and played in the tub for a long time there in Ann's kitchen while we told Ann all about our adventures up on the Summit.

Next morning, we were off again, bright and early. It was hard to leave the coolness of that great, looming mountain and go once again into the hot desert, but we knew we had our good houses waiting for us. Both Kenna and I were anxious to get back to our summer work and ways, in spite of my worries about Jake Moffat.

We did visit all the way though, talking about plans for quilts, and Kenna read to me some. We were still reading "The Lady of the Lake". The whole time I was waiting for Kenna to tell me her crazy ally stories since we had our run-in with a bear. Finally, I could wait no longer, so I straight asked her.

"Kenna, aren't you going to tell me about our powerful bear

ally? I been waiting to hear your story."

"I will if you like, Ruby. I don't think you take me seriously."

"I'll take you seriously, Kenna. I'll listen this time."

"All right. Well, the bear ally is very powerful, just as you said. You already know this truth, Ruby. The bear defends us from our enemies. She also guides our principles. She helps us do what's right, you could say."

"Helps us do what's right?" I asked. "Helps in the future or for what we've already done?"

"You know," She said. She was a puzzle.

"I know?" I asked. "I don't know."

"Think about it for a while. It will come to you. That's how allies work," Kenna said, patting my leg as we bumped along.

I sat there stunned, for it seemed as if Kenna knew every step I had taken as far as Jake was concerned. Did she know, Miss? Did she see me kill Jake? Maybe there was a Watching Kenna, too!

"You're pretty quiet, Ruby."

"I'm thinking," I said, hoping Kenna wouldn't ask me too many questions about how good the bear matched me. "What else, Kenna?"

"She helps us remember where we come from, and even shows us our destiny if we look closely. It may be frightening to meet an ally, but our reaction isn't important. It's fine to be scared. The important thing is to pay attention to the message, afraid or not."

We rode on in silence for a while, and the whole time I was thinking about this bear ally. Since I escaped the bear, did that mean I would escape the hangman? I took that message to heart,

Miss, praying I would get out of this terrible scrape.

"Listening to your stories is right scary, Kenna. I don't like thinking about all that. Too scary for me."

"Take it or leave it, Ruby. It's up to you. You decide."

That Kenna! She knew exactly how to shut me down.

It seemed like my time at the Summit had been a good escape for a while, and spinning a tale about my bear ally saving me helped, but the closer I got to the Ford, the more worried I got.

I expected Frank to be waiting for me at my house, Miss, with balled-up fists and the law. It was very terrible to ride those last miles, and when the Ford came into sight, it was all I could do to keep from busting out crying.

We crossed the river, easy as could be. The babies loved driving across the river, and I stopped Ginger right in the middle so she could get a good, long drink. I sat there in my sulky looking toward the Ford, the muddy, river water swishing by the wheels of my sulky. I wondered how long I could hold out before I got caught and hauled off to jail. I took a good look at the shack ruins, and it didn't look like anybody had been digging around there, so that was good.

We went straight up the hill to Kenna's house, unloaded her things, and packed the babies into the house. We took the berries and flowers inside her cool house; hers always cooler than mine in the summer and warmer than mine in the winter. I put Ginger in Kenna's barn for the night, feeding her and hanging up the harness. I was dog tired by then for sure. Even so, we still had to get the babies cleaned up and wash on the berries some and what all.

Then Kenna fixed us a cold supper from the garden and

the larder. It was soon on the table: some apple sauce, a sliced tomato, a cucumber with vinegar and salt, and some soda crackers; tea, of course.

While we ate, Kenna asked, "Why don't you stay here tonight, Ruby? No need for you to hurry down to that empty house. Stay here and then we'll go down there together tomorrow to put things together for you."

I was so tired, and the idea of sleeping in my old room upstairs was hard to refuse.

"That sounds good to me!" I said. "That sounds real good!"

"Let's heat up some water and get cleaned up. Then we can sit and listen to the crickets out on the porch."

Well, that's what we did. We didn't want hot baths, so it was easy to just heat a little water and haul the rest from the well. First, Kenna had a bath and then more water for my bath. How soothing that was, for Kenna put in some fragrant oils from her secret wares. I breathed in the sweet air there in her dressing room, feeling like the Queen of Sheba. Kenna loaned me one of her downy, soft gowns and if that wasn't wonderful, Miss, for it was still crisp from drying in the sun, but it had a softness too, and smelled clean and sweet.

After we emptied the tub again, we put the babies down for the night. Then we braided each other's hair, like schoolgirls. That's a lucky thing about being a woman, Miss. We are so blessed to have our dear, sister-friends to share clothes, to braid our hair, to help with house chores. That's how Kenna and I were; dear friends, and that's how we ended that night; dear friends in our gowns with our braids hanging down our backs, listening to the night sounds on the front porch, remembering what it was like to live in a real house again.

"Beautiful evening, summer is upon us," Kenna said.

"Is that a poem?" I asked.

"No," she answered. "Just words spinning around in my head."

CHAPTER 51

How I loved waking up in that pretty room up there in the Hill House, the curtains billowing out and the birds singing outside in Kenna's dooryard. That sweet, summer air floated in on me, and for a minute, I laid there without thinking about what was coming to me that day; what might happen when I got down to my funny, little house in the Ford, for I was sure Frank must be sitting there, waiting on me.

I finally rousted out when the babies came screaming into my room, trying to clamor up on my bed. I got up, washed my face and teeth, and dressed for the day.

When I got downstairs, I could tell Kenna had been up for a while. She had breakfast of corn mush waiting for me (what Kenna endearingly called breakfast food) and some steaming coffee. She was about as excited as the babies to be home from the Summit and more than ready to start our garden work.

"Let's go down to your place and get all your vegetables and bring them back up here," she said. "Then we can put them up together just like we did last summer. Do you remember how it was last summer, Ruby, with our jars lined up and ready for winter? Do you remember? Let's do that again!" Kenna was so happy that morning, looking forward to our work and happy in her life. I looked at her hard, because I wanted to remember her like that. I wanted to memorize the happy Kenna, for I feared that before too long, the happy Kenna might be a thing of the past. So, I looked at her close, engraving her to my heart.

"Yes, let's do it just like that," I said. "Let's get after it! I'll go hitch Ginger to the sulky while you clean up here, and down to the Ford we'll go!"

Pretty Kenna smiled at me broad, and out the kitchen door I went. Inside I was in a turmoil, feeling much like I did when I felt that mama bear looking at me. I felt the danger, Miss, and I was right; everything was about to change.

We got down to the Ford as easy as you please, and at first everything looked like it always did. We didn't run into any people, so we had no way of knowing that there was quite so much trouble. No, we didn't know for sure, but when we got to my house, the truth came crashing down.

I jumped down from the sulky and hauled out first one baby and then the other. Kenna got out on her side. Instead of going straight in the house, we went around the side to the garden to see how things looked, to see what we would put up first. The garden was a big tangle just like always, the squash big and fat. The corn stood tall on skinny legs, but it was ready to go; plump, bright, green ears lining the stalks. The tomatoes were about half ripe, but there were enough beans to feed an army.

Well, we stood there, talking about the garden and how it

looked, when I heard Frank behind us, saying, "Well, look who finally come home!" Kenna and I both spun around like tops to see what he's up to. He grinned wide; happy, and with Frank that was not a good sign. His bloodshot eyes told us that he'd been drinking, and the sour whiskey smell coming out of his skin proved it; peppery.

"You're not welcome here, Frank. Get on out of here. This isn't your place anymore," I said, shaking inside, for I knew Frank was not that easy to get rid of.

"This is my house and not yours, Ruby," he snarled back at me. "I have papers from the judge in Reno saying I own this property and I own it solely." He repeated the judge's words to me, and right happy with himself he was. "Far as that goes, you are standing in my garden. Get out before I go after the marshal."

I was fit to be tied then, for I knew Frank was right. It was his house after all, and just because he left for a long time didn't make it mine. I felt sick inside, but ready to walk away anyhow. I didn't want Frank and Kenna anywhere near each other.

"All right," I said, my voice trembling. "Let me get my clothes and the babies' clothes. Then we'll be gone for good." I moved toward the house.

"No," Frank said, looking very red around the gills. "You get nothing. Nothing here belongs to you. You too low to own anything. I'll let you take the babies for one year more, but after that, I'm taking them, too. You will have nothing. As soon as James and Tom get here, they are coming with me."

That whole time Kenna stood there and said nary a word, but then she said, "We'll see about that. We'll see. But for now, let's go, Ruby. You can stay at my house as long as you like.

When Valentine gets home, he will help you figure all this out."

"Oh, I wouldn't count on that if I were you," Frank hissed at Kenna. "No, I wouldn't count on much at all from your Valentine. As soon as he gets down off the mountain, he's going straight to jail and most likely the gallows right after that. And I'll be a rich man."

"What? Didn't Ruby tell you about your husband? Didn't she tell you who he is?" Frank asked, pretending to be surprised. "Why, Ruby, you didn't tell Kenna that her husband is a wanted man? That he's a criminal? I can't believe you would keep such important information from your best friend!" Frank was having a very good time.

"Let's go Kenna. Come on." I took Kenna's arm, trying to leave. "Don't listen to him. He's nothing but an old drunk."

Kenna pulled away from me, her blood getting up to a boil. "What are you talking about? You are despicable. You are a waste of skin!" Then Kenna began stringing her curse words together, hurling them at Frank. "You cowardly bastard! You go behind Valentine's back like this, you chicken shit! He'll kill you for this!"

He didn't listen long, though. He said, "I don't think so. Here's the wanted poster." He pulled a poster out of his hip pocket and unfolded it for Kenna to see. It was the same poster Jake Moffat had showed to me. "Take a look at this, Mrs. DeRoo!"

My face turned beet red, Miss, and my heart pounded like anything. I knew this would be the ruin of Kenna and me; the ruin of Kenna and Valentine; maybe the ruin of everything.

Kenna took the poster and read it, her shaking hands rattling the paper. I tried to take it from her, but she quick turned away from me so she could keep reading. I talked to her as fast as I could, saying how it wasn't important anyhow, and Valentine is still Valentine, and let's get up the hill now.

When she finished reading, Kenna looked at me and asked, "You knew about this? How did you know about this? Why didn't you tell me? Why did you hide this from me?" Kenna started up crying.

"She hid plenty more than that from you, lady. She's a big liar and don't care a whit for anyone but herself. She and your husband got feelings for each other behind your back and have had for a long time, and she knows who he is and what he done. She lies to you every day. Ever since she laid eyes on you, she done nothing but lie."

"Not only that. The fella who gave me that poster come here looking for Valentine, and now he's nowhere to be seen. I think Valentine killed him. I'm going to prove it. Then they'll hang him twice!"

Kenna stared at Frank like she didn't understand English; like she can't figure it out at all, shaking from head to toe, her face a deathly white.

"That's right, fancy lady," Frank sneered at Kenna. "Your husband ain't who he says he is. I doubt your marriage is even legal, since his name is Hulse and not DeRoo. Why, turns out DeRoo was his first wife's name. Oh, I guess you didn't know about his other wife, did you? Guess he didn't mention that. Well, I think Ruby knows about her, don't you Ruby. Didn't Valentine tell you all about her?"

"Shut up, Frank," I said, poison in my heart. I had never

hated him so much as I did at that moment. "Shut up. I'm going to kill you one of these days. I'm going to hire it done. You are over." I was shaking too, and scared so bad. My whole life was falling apart in front of my eyes. I was losing my only friend in my whole, sorry life. That damn Frank, how I hated him, Miss, and it burned in my veins.

Then I took Kenna's arm again and said, "Come on Kenna. Let's go. Let's leave this place." But she pulled away from me again, and this time she pulled away sharp. She looked at me with such hurt and sadness that it made me sick. I had seen Kenna mad plenty of times, but I never seen her look like this before; wounded.

"Leave me alone," is all she said to me. But to Frank, she held up her cupped hand at him and laid a curse on him. In a low and hollow voice, she said, "Nothing good will ever come to you, Frank Holt. You are going to die in the mud, where you belong." Then she walked out of the yard and left. She didn't look back. She didn't cry or rub her head or what all. She simply walked away.

"Well, looks like your best friend ain't your best friend anymore," Frank said, laughing and slapping his leg, purely happy. "What you going to do now, Miss High and Mighty? Where you going to keep Minnie and Elsie now, and how you going to feed them?"

I turned to look for the babies, thinking I needed to grab them and get out of there. I wanted to get away from that man, but he followed me around the side of the house, the whole way saying how I couldn't take care of myself and how I was no damn good. When the babies heard all that, they got tuned up good, squalling like anything, for they were scared of all the ruckus.

"Leave me alone, Frank," I said, and I started crying real bad. That made me so mad at myself, for I didn't want Frank to know that he had hit his mark.

"Where you going, No Good? Who going to help you now?" and he was so very happy. I could not believe how happy he was! He kicked my butt, causing me to fall to my hands and knees, right there in broad daylight. Anyone going by would have seen me. He talked real mean to me, grabbing my arm and jerking me to my feet. He shook me like a ragdoll, and then he said, "I'll tell you what. I'll give you one chance. Get in the house and clean the place up. Shut those brats up. Keep your mouth shut and get in there. We're going back to how we were, and if you don't behave, I'll make sure Valentine hangs all the faster. I've already told the whole town about him; showed the poster all around. All these fine folks are plumb shocked that one of their own is an outlaw. Yes, times have changed for Valentine, and now they're changing for you, too. Get in the house, woman. If you do what I say, maybe I'll let your outlaw live another day."

Then he backhanded me good so that I landed in the dirt of the dooryard again; fell down in the dirt, Miss, and wanted to die. My poor babies latched on to each other and squalled the more, so Frank slapped them each a good one on the head.

"Run out back, Babies," I said to them. "Go play in the back of the house. Mama will come get you in a bit. Go on, now. Mind me now," I said, dragging myself up off the ground. My beauty babies held on to each other and ran round the side of the house. That about broke my heart to see them taking care of each other. It was terrible, Miss.

Frank gave me a good shove in the door, and into hell I went.

"Get this place cleaned up," he said, "and fix me something to eat. I'm starving. We are back to husband and wife, and you better straighten out right now or I'll give you something to bawl about. Right now, Ruby." He talked to me like I was his dog; like he owned me. I guess he did.

Pretty soon I said, "I'm going down to the merc to get some supplies," surprising myself by how easy it was to talk to him like life was normal. "I'll be right back."

That made Frank laugh. "You ain't going nowhere. You stay put. I'll go get what we need. What we need? Some flour?"

"Yes, and sugar. And I need some milk. I need some milk for the babies."

"Give me your money. I know you have some money around here," he said, looking around the room. I quick got down the baking soda can where I hid my money, and gave it all to him; gave it all and gladly, for I wanted him to leave the house.

Frank grabbed me by my hair, twisting my head to the side. "I'll be right back, and don't you move. I'll kill you the next time I have to go looking for you." Then he threw me away from him, and out the door he went.

CHAPTER 52

Well, no, Miss, I'm not afraid of dying, not afraid at all. I do know this, though. I'm not going to no Christian heaven. I know exactly where I'm going. I'm going right up that hill; I'm going to the Hill House, back to my old room. It's going be just like that dream. I'll be upstairs, curtains blowing in the breeze. I'm going to be happy.

No need for you to be afraid either. Nothing bad going to happen to you, no matter what you believe, what God you listen to. You'll be just fine, Miss.

Of course, I'm sure. I've seen enough to know that you will be fine. I seen proof, Miss.

It seemed like every time I tried to do the right thing, it all just fell apart. I tried to help Valentine and Kenna, tried to protect them, and all I accomplished was framing Valentine for murder and betraying Kenna. Kenna, the only person who cared about me with no questions asked, who took care of me, who shared her whole life with me, and I let her down. It makes me squirm to remember that.

I didn't say prayers anymore; not for Valentine to love me or be safe, not for Kenna to forgive me, not for Frank to disappear into a deep hole somewhere. No, I left off of praying. I'll tell you what I did do, though. I made it real in my head, like I did that time of the big blizzard. I conjured it all, like it had already happened. I saw Valentine safe and happy; I saw Kenna as my friend again; I saw Frank, deader than a doornail. Why, right when he left the house that first day, I waited a bit and then I went out on the step and I looked down Coffey Street. I wasn't looking for Frank. No, I was looking for Ferris or somebody to come tell me that Frank was dead. I didn't pretend to see someone. I just looked and waited, because I knew that any minute, someone would show up to tell me that all my dreams had come true.

That first day, no one came to tell me that Frank was dead. Frank was gone a long time, and when he did come home, he was drunk as a skunk, toting a half-empty bottle. I guess he spent all my money on whiskey instead of milk for the babies. I was glad, though. I had to believe that everything he did was just right, that each minute was one minute closer to the time Ferris would come to tell me Frank had died. So, drunk was a good thing.

I fried up some squash for him and poured more whiskey to go with it. I made durn sure he had plenty. I put the babies to bed early and told them to stay real quiet. They minded me good, for they were afraid of their daddy, and they were right to be afraid, too.

I'm sorry to tell you this part, Miss, but I promised to tell you the whole story, so I will. I will tell it all.

So, came bedtime and here came Frank. He pushed me into our room and allowed as how I best get in bed. So, I did. I did, Miss. Watching Ruby came then, standing at the foot of the bed. She watched Frank climb on top of me and have his way. Watching Ruby stood there and watched Frank try to kiss me, and when I turned my face away, she watched Frank go near crazy. She watched him rear up and whale away on me, saying all manner of hurtful things about my face and my body.

Watching Ruby talked to me then. She usually didn't talk to me, but that night she did. She said, "Every minute, Ruby. Every minute going by." Then she faded away. I closed my eyes and waited for Frank to finish. It didn't take long. He cursed me and went into the kitchen. I lay like a stone, not crying. I just pictured Ferris coming down the road to tell me Frank was dead.

That's when I started building my wall in my mind. Every time my thoughts strayed away from my visions of Frank lying dead, I put them behind my adobe wall. I made it brick by brick; each day, each night. Some stretches of my wall looked smooth and strong; a wall that would withstand anything, but other sections leaned crooked with broken bricks stuck in all directions, and yet other sections were scarcely a wall at all and more like a pile of crumbling adobe. It didn't matter. I knew I could count on that wall. I put lots of memories and ideas back there too; thoughts of Kenna and Valentine, and sometimes even thoughts of my babies. My wall was my refuge.

Next morning, Frank was not to be wakened with the

Second Coming. I got out a paper and my quill and I wrote a letter to Kenna. I said how I was sorry for not telling her the truth about everything. I said how Valentine stayed true to her. I said how I wanted her to take my babies and raise them as her own, and I wrote down their names to make it legal. I wrote how I couldn't give them any kind of life, and I wanted something better for them. I asked Kenna to do this last favor for me. Then I thanked her kindly for all she had done for me all those times. I folded the letter shut and dripped a little candle wax on it to seal it.

I quick dressed the babies, even taking the time to put ringlets in their hair, wrapping little wisps of their wet hair around my finger, and there you go. Pretty ringlets. I got out their little pinafores Kenna had made for them. Those girls were shining like new dimes. Then I walked my babies up the hill, straight to the Hill House.

I walked up the hill so I could have time with my babies, so I could memorize them to my heart and my head; how their tiny, baby feet kicked up fine dust into the air, their curls bouncing in the sunshine and their voices piping on the air as I held their hands. I was going to give them away, to let go of those baby hands, Miss, and it broke my heart to do it, but I couldn't keep them anymore. I worried Frank would end up killing me before I could put the killing on him, and I didn't want to leave the babies to him. I couldn't stand the thought of it. I knew Kenna would take them; would keep them safe. I held their little baby hands and took them up the hill.

When we got to the dooryard, there was not a sign of life on the place, but I knew Kenna was in there somewhere. I closed the gate behind me and turned to the big house with its glowing glass. I easy walked up to the porch and laid the letter there, and then I called her name. "Kenna! Kenna, come out here! Kenna!" Still no sign of life.

"Babies, call to Kenna for Mama and ask her to come out," I said to my beauties. I started up crying, but not that loud squalling I usually did, but very sad crying to where I could feel my heart roll in my chest. The babies sang out to their beloved Kenna, saying, "Kenna, come out! Come out to us, Kenna. Mama wants you! Kenna! Kenna!" and like that for a while. Then sure as the world, here she came.

She was a sight, for her hair was down and tousled round her head and her eyes were wild; she looked about crazy. She stared at me and I stared at her, and then I bent down and kissed my babies goodbye.

"Go on, Babies. Go to Kenna," I said, and I gave them each a little scoot on the behind. "Go on, Babies. Go on. Mama loves you terrible."

Kenna took up a wail then, giving me a look I'll never forget, hating me and loving me, too, just as I hated and loved her. She went down to her knees there on the porch and the babies swarmed her. They didn't know what was going on; they didn't know to say goodbye to me. They clutched onto her, and she went to fussing over them and their pretty curls and white aprons.

"Come in the house, darlings," she said to my babies. "Come in and have some bread and butter. What do you say to that?" She took them through the door and closed it behind her.

And off they went. I waited in the dooryard for a while; waited for Kenna to bring them back, but she never did. I had walked up the hill to give my babies away, but when she took them, I was filled with rage. I couldn't believe she would do it! I fell in the dirt and wept, climbed the porch steps and banged on her door. Finally, I walked out the gate and found my way back down to the Ford. I had gone and give away my babies like extra squash out of my garden. "Here, you can have these two." I didn't mean to; I didn't mean it, but I did it.

Don't feel sorry for me, Miss. I was the one who did all these horrible things. It wasn't anyone else made me do it. Not my daddy dying or me marrying Frank or me chasing after Valentine. I did it, and I have to carry that around. I can't blame life or bad luck, or what all. I did it. Every decision I made was mine alone, but if you see a woman give her babies away, you ought to look close, for it is a terrible thing to do. It's against nature, Miss, to say goodbye to a baby like that.

Don't take on so, Miss. What the deuce? You act like it was you was given away. Here, Miss, come here. Good Lord. Hush then. Hush. You going to make me cry again! Well, yes, I will tell you. It was this:

From the wreck of the past, which hath perished,
This much I at least may recall;
It hath taught me that which I most cherished
Deserved to be dearest of all.
In the desert a fountain is springing,
In the wide waste there still is a tree,
And a bird in the solitude singing,
Which speaks to my spirit of *thee.*

You feeling better now, Miss? You doing all right? Let me dab off your face a little. There. Now, come help me out of here. Let's go down to the kitchen. How about I teach you how to cook something? How about that? Help me, Miss.

CHAPTER 53

Well, life went on after I gave the babies to Kenna. I didn't want it to, but it did. Every day the sun came up. I went on home to my little house, this very house here, Miss, and I went about my business. And you know, when Frank woke up, he didn't even ask after the babies. No. He didn't ask for about three days. When he finally did ask, I told him I sent them to Mrs. Ricker, and he seemed fine with that. He didn't care a whit about those babies.

Every time he woke up, I poured him some whiskey. I tried to keep him in whiskey night and day. I went down to the merc and bought more when I ran low, putting it on my tab, just like I had done long ago when Frank left me the first time. Folks around the Ford didn't have much to say to me. I don't know if they felt sorry for me, or hated me, or what. I didn't care. I didn't care about them anymore.

Most nights Frank would take me in his bed, that is if he wasn't too drunk. I tried to keep him drunk enough that he just fell in bed once he got home. When he did come after me, I just dreamed about him being dead, and sometimes I laid hands on his back like a saving preacher, only I was putting a killing on him instead of a saving.

Pretty soon, Frank started staying gone more and more. Sometimes he was gone all night, and I dreamed of him dying just as hard as I could dream, seeing his dead eyes staring at the sky. Sometimes I thought about that time Kenna cut my dress off me and put a curse on Frank, or the day she cursed him in the yard, and that made me happy, too. It gave me power to dream and have a dream come true.

You know, it didn't take that long, maybe a week or ten days after I gave the babies to Kenna. It was late in the afternoon as I sat in my kitchen conjuring Frank's death, when I heard a boot step in my dooryard. You know, it was Ferris. As I live and breathe, here came Ferris, looking very grave. I was surprised, yet not surprised at all. It was very strange, Miss.

"Ruby, are you home?" he called, tapping on my door frame.

"Hello, Ferris," I said, as calm as you please, but I was not calm on the inside. "What's going on?" I wiped my hands on a kitchen rag. "What's wrong?" I asked, for I could see by his face that there was trouble.

"Well, I'm sorry, Ruby, but I come to tell you that Frank has been killed. I'm sorry, Ruby," Ferris said, taking off his hat and looking at the floor.

Believe me, my head was swimming and it seemed like I must not have heard Ferris right. All his words were all jumbled together.

"What did you say? What's that?" I asked him.

"Please sit down, Ruby. Frank was in a bad accident today. He's dead."

I did sit down then, and laid one arm across the table, my vision going dark and my ears buzzing like anything.

"What happened? What happened to him? Where is he?" I asked poor, old Ferris.

"I hate to even tell you, Ruby. It's so awful. It's awful, and half the town saw it happen."

"What? What happened, Ferris?" I asked, conjuring Frank's dead eyes staring at the sky some more.

"Well, Frank came wandering out of the Lafayette, and he was pretty drunk. For some reason no one can figure out, he wandered out on the train tracks, even though the durn train was in sight; just staggered around out there, yelling and shaking his fist at the train. Before we could get him, the train hit him. I'm sorry. Believe me, there are plenty of upset folks round the Ford today. It was a bad sight."

"Lord God," I said, wiping my face with my towel, trying to hide it in case it gave me away. "Lord God. Where is he? Where's his body?"

"Ruby, let's don't worry about that right now. The boys just thought I should come let you know what happened. I best get going."

"No, tell me, where is he? Where's his body?"

"It's down at the undertaker's, he's at Cipriano's, what's left of him. Ruby, it was a bad accident!"

"Are you saying he's all cut up? Is Frank all cut up by the train?"

"What difference does it make? Let's go get Kenna to help

you." I could see that Ferris was very nervous to tell me about the state of Frank's body.

"No. Take me to the undertaker, Ferris. Help me get down there."

It was not far to walk down my street and around the corner to Railroad Street. It was right handy that Frank died nearby. Lots of folks milled about the street, talking very excited about how Frank got killed by the afternoon train, but when we came walking by, they clammed up. When we got to Cipriano's, Ferris took off quick as he could.

The undertaker fellow wouldn't let me see Frank, saying there was no need to put a picture like that in my head; allowed as how he would make me a special deal on the funeral and all. Cipriano didn't know I already had the picture in my head, Miss.

"Will you just tell me what happened to Frank? Why can't I see him?"

Cipriano was a little on the scary side, though he tried to be nice, too. He finally said, "Mrs. Holt, your husband's body was dismembered by the train."

"Dis-what?" I asked. It took me a second to understand what he was saying, but then it come to me, like my mind was having a hard time understanding English. But when I did understand, again I saw all those dress pieces laying on the floor of Kenna's bedroom; a sleeve here, a collar there, all chopped in pieces, and Kenna saying her bad words, and me saying, "Kenna, are you putting a spell on Frank? Because if you are, I feel right sorry for him."

CHAPTER 54

That's right Miss. Just stir it together real easy like. Not like that, Miss. Good Lord, you making shoe leather. The more you touch the pie crust, the tougher it's going be. You don't want to mess with it very much. You have to be easy. That's better.

Well, so Frank was dead, thank the Lord. I was so relieved! I tried not to act too heathenish for the folks around town; tried to be somber and all; but inside, I was so happy to be free, and I knew I would never marry again. I would never again give a man power over me and my kitchen.

Now, roll it out flat enough for your tin, but same thing. Don't beat it to death. Easy! More flour. Good! Time to put it in the pan. Here, let me show you. Hand me the rolling pin. Like this…just curl it around the pin and then unroll it over the tin. There you go. Now you push it down into the pan.

I wandered home from Cipriano's in a daze, trying to figure out how I would get this funeral over and done with. The boys were still up on the Summit, but that didn't really matter. They didn't want to see their daddy buried anyhow, as far as I knew. I just wanted it over and done with and behind me, for now I was a widow and could start a new life for myself.

How wonderful to be free of Frank! Even though I had long dreamed of it, the real feeling of it was like nothing I had known; I was a grown woman and free to be my own person!

Now pour in your pieplant. Yes, all of it. Scoop of butter on top. That's enough. Now lay your top crust on. Easy! I never seen the like. Have you ever baked at all before? Pinch it shut round the edge. Well, give it here and I'll show you. Just with your fingers, like this. And trim off the edge with a knife. Now, cut a few holes in the top. There you go, Miss. Your first real pie! In the oven with it! Well done! You might amount to something after all.

I guess Cipriano gave me a fair deal on the funeral. I bought the cheapest pine box he had, and a blank spot in the graveyard. Have you seen the graveyard, Miss? It's just across the Ford by the river there. I don't know why on Earth folks put the graveyard on the other side of the river, since that made every coffin have to cross over! Maybe it was meant to be a symbol, like in one of Kenna's poems. Nonsense, but that's what they did; they put it across the river.

As soon as I got home from Cipriano's, I washed my sheets and rough blankets, knowing that they probably wouldn't be dry by bed time. I didn't care; I wanted a new, clean bed to crawl into. My own bed, with no man to trouble me! Curling into myself in a clean bed with sheets smelling of sunshine and sagebrush was the second-best thing that happened to me that day.

Well, the next morning they laid Frank in the ground over there. Cipriano had a fancy wagon to haul the coffin. I didn't bother going. Everyone knew I was done with Frank and I didn't see a reason to pretend something else. I heard that no one else showed up either. I don't know if they knew about it, or not.

I sat at my little kitchen table that morning and did nothing for the longest time, thinking about how things had turned out, about Frank all chopped up, and how I had wished that on him; for I surely wished it on him; dreamed it on him, conjured it on him; laid hands on him, with killing in my brain. I'm sure it was me, Miss, that killed him. True, I didn't shoot Frank like I had done to Moffat, but I killed him all the same. Conjured it all on him, on my own husband, so that his blood is on my hands just the same as Jake's is.

Valentine and the boys were gone for ages, seemed like; way longer than they needed to be. How convenient they were always gone when there was trouble, only coming home long enough to make you miss them terrible when they leave. Foolish men.

I heard nothing from Kenna. I don't know if she heard about Frank's death. I never saw hide nor hair of her or the babies all those days. It was hotter than Hades, the hills burned brown all around the Ford, and the river was lower than I had ever seen it. Cottonwoods didn't look right either, all their leaves faded and sere. Some of the life had gone out of the very Ford itself.

I finally roused myself enough to put up the garden as best I could. I still had jars and what all, so I canned all I could.

I had some squash and corn and beans. I dried what I could. It was sad though, remembering how happy Kenna and I had been the summer before when we did all our canning together; how we used to visit and laugh together or just be quiet, side by side. Without her, all the joy was gone out of it; the smells didn't mean anything to me, and once the jars were lined up, they looked like supper fixings to me instead of those magical rows of soldiers.

Sometimes I would conjure Kenna and the babies in my head though, even though I knew it was dangerous. It was easy to get caught up in that and never get away, but sometimes I couldn't help it, I had to dream of my babies and Kenna up in the house. I saw how she sewed them up new clothes, taught them to say little rhymes, fixed them their food and they ate together at the big table like nice girls, talked like big girls; how they were growing up. I saw all that. How Kenna would take a bite of food and then look from one girl to the other while she chewed, and how the girls looked at her, all of them quiet, and then Kenna would make a funny face at the babies, and they would try to make it back at her.

I never conjured them missing me or asking after me. That's how I treated myself, Miss. I was hard on myself. When I think of it now, they must have asked about me, don't you think? They must have missed me. Back then, I never saw that; I only saw them going away from me, farther and farther, every day. It was terrible.

So those days, before the men got home from the Summit, were long ones. I was glad to be free of Frank, but very sorry to have lost my girls and Kenna. I didn't know Frank would go so fast, Miss; didn't know how powerful those bad thoughts could be; didn't know I could do that.

You know, Miss, I was born with a caul on my face. You know about a caul, Miss? You heard of that? Well, it's when a baby is born, but her face or head is wrapped in a thin covering that you can see through. Some folks call it being born behind the veil, for the caul is like a veil. My mama used to tell me the story of when I was born and how I had a caul on my face. She always said how the doctor said a curse word, how he said, "Well, I'll be damned. This baby has a caul on her face." Not many folks born behind the veil, Miss; not many babies at all. It's pure rare, in fact, purely unusual.

My mama allowed as how being born with a caul is a lucky sign. It means you going to have a good life, but she also said it can mean you are a bit fey. She allowed that I might know things I'm not supposed to know, or I might see things that other folks can't see. Well, I guess you can see that the luck part didn't really turn out. But the other part, Miss, well it came true, for I saw plenty. Watching Ruby who used to come around and see what was what, why, she knew lots of things. She could see far into the future or far back, either way, and she guided me sometimes or comforted me just by being there. When she came around, I knew to get quiet and try to pay attention.

I saw other things too, Miss, spirits, or shadows left over. I'm not sure. Sometimes I have heard things too, Miss. Far off echoes of someone's words or wailing. Or when I lift up out of my body and look down on myself, that's not normal, Miss. And sometimes, I have dreams that come true. Sometimes I dream something that I know is a powerful dream so I write it down. Then when it happens, I know I'm not fooling myself and that I really did dream it all before.

Now that pie is smelling good! Isn't it funny how something you smell can make you remember everything from a certain time or day? When I smell rhubarb pie, I about get tears in my eyes, remembering my grandma making a pie for me, or when Kenna took a pie out the oven, and little Tommy appeared out of nowhere, grinning for all he was worth, his white hair laying across his forehead.

No, it isn't ready yet.

Well, those boys finally came lumbering home from the Summit, wagons loaded down with good firewood for the winter. James and Tom looked beautiful behind their dirty faces and raggedy hair, healthy and strong. James' splint was gone, so he limped around pretty good, looking like he would be all right eventually. Of course, Valentine looked grand, skinny of belly and broad of shoulder, just like always. How my heart jumped to see him! I didn't want to love him, but I did. I loved him terrible.

"Well, hello Ruby!" he bellered at me, jumping down off the wagon. "Hello! Where are the girls? Girls! Where are you? Come give me a hug! Don't you miss me anymore? Girls!"

"Where are the girls, Ruby? Are they up at the house? Are they with Kenna?"

"Yes, they are up the hill," I said. "They are with Kenna." My face turned scarlet. "They are with Kenna," I said again, for I didn't know what else to say. "Looks like you boys got a good haul of wood."

"We did real good. There's more coming, too. Wade and the boys got more and we got some venison again too, so we will have another good winter I would wager. Tom and James did real good and helped out a lot. Seems like James' leg is getting better, too," Valentine said, smiling at the boys. "Looks like he's going to heal up all right." Then Valentine gave a great big stretch and allowed as how he was plenty ready to be home for a while and sleep in a real bed.

"Mama, we're going to get cleaned up out at the pump," James said, just as sweet as you please.

"All right boys," I said, "but don't go nowhere. I got to have a talk with you."

"We won't. Just got to get some of this dust off me," James said, limping around the side of the house with Tom walking along beside.

As soon as they were out of earshot, I said, "Come in the house. Valentine, I hate to tell you, but there has been some trouble while you were up at the Summit, just like always. Frank came home and caused quite a bit of trouble; told Kenna all about your wanted poster and all. She didn't take it too well either. And you should know too that he talked all round the Ford about you and your history, and the whole town knows you are wanted." I talked fast as I could to get the whole story out before Valentine could stop me to ask his questions. I didn't want to answer questions. I didn't want to tell him how Kenna hated me, and for sure I didn't want to admit that I gave away my babies; I was deeply ashamed of that.

"Oh, God," Valentine said a few times while I talked. He sat down at the table, taking deep breaths every now and then, gazing off across the house like he watched something far off and different from what I could see; remembering, I guess.

"Well, it was bound to happen. I should have told her the truth before she came down from the Summit. That was stupid of me. What the hell was I thinking?" I could see that Valentine felt very terrible. "I guess I better get up the hill and see if Kenna will still have me," he said, standing up but seeming not as tall as he had been a minute before; like he was cut down.

"Valentine, I got more to tell you though. I better tell you the rest," I said, even though I didn't want to tell him about Frank dying.

"God, Ruby! What more can there be? Can't a man just live his life in peace and build a fire for the winter? What else?" Valentine's eyes blazed, and he looked gorgeous. He was a beautiful man, Miss, even when he was in trouble or feeling a lot of worry. "What else?"

"Frank moved back in here, and then he got to be a worse drunk than ever, and then he got run over by the 2:17 train. He's buried over across the river and I am shut of him forever now, but he did his damage before the train made a mess out of him. I don't know who else will come after you now, but the folks around here are looking at me sideways and won't say much, so I don't think they are feeling all that good about you." I felt both sad and scared right then, for it seemed like everything was unwinding, and it didn't look good for any of us. Not to mention, I felt that I had killed Frank right out, and even though I hated him, it was bad to cause him to get all chopped up like that.

Valentine said, "I don't care about these folks here if they judge me for what I did in the war. I was fighting a war, Ruby, and I know you don't hold that in any regard, but I was fighting for my land and my people; for my wife. I will stand up to any man who questions me. And you won't talk me out of taking this to the judge this time. If I die trying, so be it. Good God! I want this to be over!"

I still loved Valentine just like always, but I didn't want him to bring the law in on this whole deal, so I tried to sway him out of it. "That won't do any good, and will only make things worse. You best just lay low. Maybe folks will let you go by."

"No, Ruby. I'm determined to set things right. I can't keep lying about who I am. I can't keep this part of myself hidden from Kenna, of all people. I hope she will still have me!" It was all Valentine could do to keep from running straight up the hill.

"Well, before you go up there, you better know that Frank told her that you and I have feelings for each other and have always had feelings for each other. He told her that you and I knew about Jake Moffat, and we lied to her. She was fit to be tied when she left here. I don't know if she will have you back or not, but she for sure doesn't want anything to do with me, anymore. I betrayed her, and she knows it. Kenna is too proud to put up with such goings on. Women know that men do stupid things, and we often forgive them, but for one woman to betray another is unforgivable, and she is done with me." Then I about burst out bawling.

Valentine frowned, trying to figure out why the babies were up the hill if Kenna was mad at me, but then his mind went on to something else and he never got around to asking me about the babies.

"I'm heading up there right now. I'll come back to check on the boys; see how they are doing after they find out about

Frank. It might be real hard on the boys, even if they know he was no good. I'll be back." Then my Valentine stood up and left my house, walked out this very kitchen here, Miss, and climbed back on his wagon. I heard his team jingling on up the hill to Kenna.

Douglas County Pie Crust

ONE CRUST PIE

- 1½ cups flour
- ½ teaspoon salt
- 5 tablespoons lard
- 6 tablespoons cold water

TWO CRUST PIE

- 2 cups flour
- 1 teaspoon salt
- ¾ cup lard
- 8 tablespoons cold water

Mix flour and salt. Cut in lard. Add cold water and combine gently Do not overwork dough. After sealing pie, brush crust with egg white. Bake until done and well-browned.

CHAPTER 55

What you go and bring him here for? I don't want no doctor, and I mean it. And you got no right butting into my business, Miss. Don't sulk up like that, either. You think that coming here very day gives you the passage to bring someone in here when I say no? That what you think? I got news for you, Miss. Get him out of here, and get yourself out of here too. Get!

Don't you walk out of here like that. Take him with you! Hey! I mean it now.

Don't come near me or you'll be sorry, Sawbones. Get!

CHAPTER 56

*Y*ou see that box of junk? See that? I want you to take it and leave here and don't ever come back. I'm way past a time in my life when I care about people, and I durn sure don't need you caring about me. What that be good for, Miss? Why would we do that? Take it and leave.

You don't need to dig through it right now. Just go. Well, yes, I'm giving you my combs. Just get them out of my sight. And yes, the garnets, for I care not a whit about them. I can see you could wear that necklace some, and I am tired of worrying that some thief going to come in here and steal it while I nap. Take it and leave me in peace.

Setting up such a fuss isn't going to change my mind, so clam up. I don't want to tell stories to you no more, and I don't want you clambering around in my head, or my kitchen. I was fine before you got here. Go on, now. I swear, you are worse than a stray pup. Gather up and get out!

You can sit there and squall all you want. I won't feel sorry for *you. I just want you to leave me be.*

Yes, the doctor listened to my heart, and yes, Miss, I am not long for this Earth. Are you satisfied? Is that what you wanted to know? I guess I can save you the trouble of waiting for me to die and just give you this old trash now. Is the recipe book in there too? Is it there, Miss? Take it.

What? Oh, those are Kenna's rowan sticks. Kenna and her witchcraft! She insisted on keeping them in the house, tying them this way and that with red thread every now and then, and when I asked her about it, she said, "My rowan boughs came all the way from home. They protect me, they give me energy; they keep me from giving up."

Yes, Miss, rowan sticks. What the deuce? Settle down!

Are you trying to kill me? I am a frail, old woman. Ask the doctor. I don't want you here. I don't want to tell you how the story ends. Leave me be!

Lord God. You are stubborn. Lord God.

What you mean, what do I want? I can't have what I want, Miss, for what I want is another go at it. I want to try this all again and do better at living.

No, there's nothing. Nothing at all.

What! No, I don't want the girls or Tom or James. The girls are both in Colorado and it's too hard for them to come home. It's not good when they come home, anyway. Too much water under the bridge, Miss. Too much time gone by. I don't even know where James is, and Tom is clear over in Reno. I don't want you going after any of them and trying to get them here. What good would that do? What would that help? They are fine without me. And once I'm gone, they can figure out what to do with the houses and all.

I mean it. Don't you go after finding them. Leave them alone. If you think I was mad when you brought the doctor, wait and see what I will do if you go after my children. I mean it, Miss. Leave them alone.

In fact, get out of here. I don't want you around. I don't trust you.

Is that right? I owe you? I owe you? Get out of my house.

Are you crazy? Are you pure crazy? No, I'm not going to tell you the rest. Did you ever think of someone else, ever once in your life? Did you ever think that it is hard on me to tell you this story? Does that matter to you at all?

The poem? Again? You beat all I ever saw. All right, all right. Write it down this time, so you can tell it yourself. This the last time I'm saying it to you. It's this, Miss. Here, come sit here by my bed. Sit down, for heaven's sake. You are a case.

From the wreck of the past, which hath perished,
This much I at least may recall;
It hath taught me that which I most cherished
Deserved to be dearest of all.
In the desert a fountain is springing,
In the wide waste there still is a tree,
And a bird in the solitude singing,
Which speaks to my spirit of *thee*.

You may have had your hard times and what all, but I'll say this. You are a spoiled brat, and whoever did this to you ought to be horsewhipped. You need to straighten out. How do you expect to make your way, acting like this?

Yes, Kenna, Valentine, and the story. All right. No, I'm not taking the medicine. I don't want it. I said no, Miss.

CHAPTER 57

Well, Valentine ran up the hill to Kenna and I don't know what all was said or how they worked things out or how long Kenna stayed mad. I never heard a word about it. Valentine didn't come back down to the house, and I didn't see him move down to his office or what all, so I guessed they patched things up.

I brought the boys in from the yard that first day, though, and told them how their daddy was dead. Tommy put up quite a fuss and cried in my lap; he was a big boy, but a little boy at the same time. I felt so very sorry for him, and I was worried for him, too. It's not good to lose your daddy when you are young, even if your daddy is no good. It was too hard on those boys.

James kept quiet when he got the news, not showing sadness like Tommy; just very quiet, and then he allowed as how his old man got what was coming to him, and how he was only sorry he wasn't there to see it happen.

"James!" I said to him, right sharp. "Don't say that! Tom is listening to every word you say. Is that what you want him to remember about his big brother?"

"I want him to remember how our old man was no good and how he come to no good. That's what I want him to remember. I'm glad he's dead! I wanted him dead!"

"That's enough out of you, James. That's enough! Not another word, and I mean it," I said. "Let's get you boys some supper and then off you go to bed. This has been a bad day, and more talking won't help anything. There's no fixing what has happened, and no point going on about it more tonight." Then I set Tom from me and got to cooking.

"Well, I will stop talking, but that won't change what I think. I said what I think, and that's that. But thank you, Ruby, for taking care of us all these times my pa was mean to you, and we were mean to you, too," James said, and I like to fell over, he sounded so nice.

"You're welcome, James. I'm glad to have you boys home."

"When are the babies coming down from Kenna's?" Tom asked. "They coming home tomorrow?"

I knew that I might as well tell the boys the truth and get it over with. It was hard to do, and I saw them both harden toward me after I did.

"Boys, when Frank showed up, I took the babies up the hill and gave them to Kenna. I didn't want them around him, and I didn't see any end in sight. Looked like Frank was going to be here forever, so I gave them to Kenna." I kept my eyes on my cooking, trying to sound like what I said made sense, even though it didn't make any sense at all.

James became angry right then, and said, "What are you talking about? You can't give away babies! You don't just give away your family! It's not like giving away a puppy, Ruby! What are you talking about?"

"It's over and done with, James. I sent them away. I'm sorry. I just couldn't do it anymore."

"You going to give me away too?" Tom asked, and that just broke my heart. "You going to give me to Kenna? I'll be good, Ruby, and I'll help with the chores. I'll go to school and work hard. You won't have to worry about me! I promise!" Tommy wailed.

"She's not giving you away, you simpleton. She can't give you away because you ain't hers to give! You got no one! No pa. No ma. You are nothing, and you got nothing! And neither do I!"

"James, stop it! You stop it right now! You and Tom could take care of yourselves around your pa. The babies couldn't, and I couldn't keep them safe! I was afraid for them! I had to get them out of here!"

"Well, go get them back! Get them back! What is wrong with you? Kenna will give them back! What will the babies think when they grow up and see that you gave them away? You can't do that to them, Ruby! I'm going to go get them right now!"

"Kenna is real mad at me right now. She doesn't want to talk to me. She's real mad about Jake Moffat and Frank and Valentine. She's hating me because I lied to her. I can't get them back right now! I wrote a paper giving them to her! I wrote it down! I can't get them back right now!"

"You are stupid. You are the most stupid person I know! I hate you. Valentine will fix this. Valentine will bring them back, and then he's going to see how stupid you are." Then James walked out. Out he went.

CHAPTER 58

It came a rain; a good, hard rain like we never have; water running everywhere, mud everywhere, lightning flashing and thunder rolling across the valley. I loved it! It seemed like the storm was a mirror of my heart. I was in a state. All night the storm crashed around my little house, and all night long my heart hammered in my chest.

I felt such a rage that night, Miss, experiencing all the stabbing pain I had been saving up my whole life. I hated my daddy for getting in the way of a rebel sword, hated my mama for crying about it, hated Frank and James, and even little Tommy. But the hatred that burned the best was my hatred for Valentine; it burned like the devil himself had climbed into my heart. I could not stop thinking about how he turned me away, how he only half loved me, how he treated me like a sister when he knew I loved him. He should not have been my friend. If he had any feelings for me at all, he should have not been my friend. You see what I'm saying, Miss? You see? It was wrong of him to befriend me when he knew I loved him so terrible.

All night, the rage in my heart burned for Valentine. All night long, and when the lightning crashed cross my little valley, I sent it rolling up the hill to the Hill House; sent it up there and hoped it would break out all the tall windows. I paced the floor and wrung my hands and wailed, Miss, and it was terrible. It was a very long night, to say the least, and I was glad when I saw the dawn breaking. I felt freed then, from the terrible spell that had held me all night, and I saw in the light of day how very evil and wrong my thoughts had been. I realized that I should not throw lightning up the hill and think hard on people. I got that sick feeling inside, knowing I had done something I should not have done, and I wished I hadn't done it, and I even promised myself that I would never be moved with such a rage ever again. I promised myself. I settled down then, but the damage was done.

That morning, it stopped raining, leaving all the heat washed out of the air. How sweet that air smelled, all the dust knocked down, and the sky just as blue as it could be; all the cottonwoods washed clean of dirt, their leaves as fresh as the day they sprouted. The sand in the road was drying on the edges a bit, but outlines of raindrops covered the road, and mud puddles were spaced all along the way; a nice day there in my Ford.

James had not come home. I wasn't too worried about him since he had gone to Valentine. I figured he stayed up there for the night, so he could calm down. I figured that was Valentine's idea to help James get his mind straight. I spent my morning working around the kitchen, holding brighter thoughts in my mind, but my stomach turned over every time I thought of my rage from the night before. I mixed up some sourdough bread and got that in the oven, washed up the boys' spare shirts and hung them out to dry; just going about my business, trying to see clear to the next thing coming.

I can remember how I was that day; normal for me. Heartbroke but busy, and pure tired out from my night of raging, trying not to think too much about my troubles, trying to keep the house going, and though I felt plenty bad about Kenna and the babies, part of me thought I would get it all figured out. Part of me thought there was still lots of time to fix everything. We would be back to our days of working together; being dear friends.

Next thing I know, Ferris came tearing up to my house, jumping off his horse before it could slide to a stop. That set me off, knowing Ferris would never act like that unless there was something very wrong, and something was very wrong, Miss.

You sure you want to hear about this? You sure, Miss? We could end the story here and you can go get back on your train. How does that sound? Want to stop here?

Well, don't say I never warned you.

Ferris could barely talk, but he finally did get out one word. "Valentine!"

Lord God, Miss, I took his reins out of his hand and jumped on that horse. I don't really remember doing it, but I found myself on a high lope up that hill, leaning down low over that horse's neck and giving him hell to get up there. I was seeing and not seeing, hearing and not hearing, breathing and not breathing. But I was on the move, and good thing, for the sight I saw when I got to the house devastated me.

My beloved Valentine had gone and got himself crushed under the freight wagon, Miss, and it all weighed down with enough firewood for our two families. His legs stuck out the side of that huge wagon box, and it leaned at a terrible angle, and he was not moving, Miss, though I could see where his heels had dug in the damp dirt.

Lord God. My Valentine was gone; gone from me forever, and I didn't even get to say goodbye. I had been cheated out of telling him I really loved him, just like always; denied the chance to look close at his whiskered face and curling black hair. Gone from me, and my heart is never going to be over this. I am still pining after my beloved Valentine.

Kenna was sitting in the dirt between the wagon and the barn, keening after Valentine, her high screams floating up out of the yard like a fiddle in the dark; up and out over the brown Sonomas; floating up to the very heavens, and the angels must have cried to hear her pain. She sat in the dirt, keening like anything, and I thought, *"Well, that's the end of her. She's a goner,"* and my brain was working like that, like I was far away or up high over my body, but I wasn't. I was right there, Miss.

I quick jumped off Ferris' horse, and scrambled right under the wagon with Valentine. I didn't care who saw me. I crawled up to him, and it was hard because the wagon frame was fairly setting on his big, barrel chest; setting on him, and there was no breath; no breath stirring, and I could see he was gone. I laid my head in the dirt right next to his, and I wanted to be gone, too. I kissed him then on his stubbly cheek and again smelled his clean man smell; breathed it in.

Next, I hear a terrible wailing coming in my ears, like a banshee gone wild; a terrible wailing that made me so sad to hear, for it was heart-wrenching, Miss. It sounded like an old sound that been spinning around the Earth for centuries and finally found some ears to go in; found *my* ears to go in. And then it came to me that it was *me* doing the wailing. I scrubbed my face in the dirt and wailed the more.

Someone came and tried to pull me out of there; tried to talk to me and say, "Come out of there, Miss Ruby. Let me help you out of there. It's not safe, Ruby." Then, they tried to climb under there and get me. You ever seen a cornered badger, Miss? How it spits and turns so fierce? That's what I did. I took to spitting and kicking at whoever it was. They backed out.

I don't know how long I laid under there. I laid there a long time. I begged Valentine to come back to me. I begged Watching Ruby to come help me.

You know, Valentine wasn't that old. He still had so much life ahead of him, but there he was, dead and gone. It seemed like it must have been a mistake; like the world had stopped spinning for a moment, and when it started back up, things were wrong; things had changed, and it was a mistake.

It was my James brought me back to the world. James crawled under there and said, "Mama, come out now. Come on, Mama." James never called me Mama, but he did then. So, I let him help me out, but I was blind with grief, and I remember getting up and holding onto his arm to walk away from there; a bent, old woman grasping onto my son.

Well, surprise of all, the place is awash with people, milling around like we were at a gathering, seeing my Valentine like that, and it made me furious. I took to screaming at them all, allowing as how they were mighty low to gape around there like that.

Again, James saved me, saying, "No, Ruby. They come to help us. We have to get the wagon off Valentine and get him in the house. We're taking him in the house, Ruby. Come sit over here by Kenna. Come on now."

So, that's what I did. She had left off keening for a minute, but she was all covered with dirt, and it came to me that she been scrubbing around in the dirt, too. I took her hand in mine and sat down at her side. She looked in my eyes, but the Kenna I knew was not there; this was an empty Kenna, looking at me. Yes, she was a goner from the very beginning.

Well, the men commenced to unloading wood and throwing it here and there. They were working hard to get Valentine out of there, even though he was long gone; throwing wood and talking about how they could jack up the wagon. Very somber they were, for lots of folks liked Valentine and his crooked smile. But they worked on.

Kenna put her arm around my waist, and I put mine around hers, and we took to keening like anything, even though folks were looking at us sideways. I could smell Kenna's lavender-smelling hair, feel her tiny waist and her ribs and her breathing—short, little breaths that scared me a little. I was right worried about her.

James came to us once the wagon was propped up and asked real nice if we would go in the house for a minute. I guess he didn't want us to see them drag Valentine out from under there, but here came Kenna's voice very serious, and all she said was, "We stay."

"All right," says James, ambling off again. He looked like a grown man there, and I knew he was devastated but holding together. James loved Valentine. More than that though, he respected Valentine for the man he was, for the way he treated James like a real person and not some old piece of trash. I could not look at James at all then.

I spotted the hated Cipriano, lurking around in his ill-fitting suit, and murder came into my heart, though he had nothing to do with Valentine dying. I just hated him anyway; him and his ways of sneaking a corpse off across the Ford and burying it in the dirt whilst no one is looking. I hated him. I leaned to Kenna and said, "Don't let him take Valentine away, Kenna. We can take care of this ourselves. Please don't let him take Valentine away." Kenna only stared with blank eyes, continuing her puffy, little breaths. "You hear me, Kenna? Don't let him have Valentine. Please. I'm begging you." I thought I would take to screaming then, for she did not answer me.

Soon enough, here came Cipriano again, allowing as how he had his wagon there and he would take Valentine down to the Ford and "prepare him" for his burying. That whole time, Kenna and me just sat in the dirt. I didn't care at all; I didn't want to move ever again. But here came Cipriano, trying to talk business to Kenna, and Kenna just kept on staring with those empty eyes of hers. She gazed at nothing at all, but when Cipriano was done saying he could meet with her the next day to choose a coffin, Kenna quietly said, "Touch my husband, and that will be your last act on this Earth, Mr. Cipriano." Then back to her puffy breathing; back to staring and acting like she couldn't see what was going on around her.

That set me off weeping; not squalling like before, but slow, hot tears rolling down my face and dripping off my chin. I was furious, too; furious that Valentine could die like that; just up and die, and it didn't make no sense at all. No sense at all, Miss. Why did that have to happen?

James came back then and led Cipriono off to talk quietly, away from us. Next thing you know, the undertaker disappeared. I was so proud of James. I didn't know at the time what he said, but he got that fellow to leave, so he did it right.

CHAPTER 59

They put my Valentine in the parlor; laid him out in a nice coffin that Cipriano hauled up the hill, like James told him to do; covered him with a quilt—our sunshine and shadows. They took off his worn boots, leaving them to lay crooked at the foot of the stairs. It killed me to see his boots like that; his old, work boots that I had seen so many times, scuffed and worn at the toe and heel, left behind by my Valentine. My beloved Valentine.

I got his wedding shirt out of his dresser, and we put that on him, James and me. We dressed him nice, with clean suspenders and all. James did most of the work, moving Valentine this way and that to dress him. It was so hard to see how Valentine's limp arms dropped when James moved him around; to see his giant paw-hands that didn't move at all.

After we got Valentine dressed, we laid him out in the coffin again. I washed his head, washed his hair, combed it a bit; his "Black is the Color" hair, with the dear curls right near his collar. I combed it nice across his forehead, making it look nice. I sent James to the kitchen for the camphor and some rags, so we could wash his face and hands; washed him with camphor all afternoon, all evening, and all night. We sat by him and washed with strong-smelling camphor every little while, Miss. That kept his face from turning dark, kept him looking like the Valentine we knew.

It was an honor to do that, Miss, to care for him that way. My mama taught me to care for the dead; showed me how to do it when we laid my papa and brothers in the ground. We sat with them all night in just the same way, and we cared for our own, waiting for the grave wagon to come to carry them to the brand-new graveyard in Lawrence.

It gave me time to come to see him as dead, too; allowed me to remember all the times I talked to Valentine or all the times I admired him; let me look at that young girl who tried to steal away with him that night down by the Ford. It gave me time to forgive myself a little for throwing lightning up the hill at Valentine, and to forgive him a little for not choosing me.

Don't you think it's funny, Miss, that he would up and die like that, right after I had killed to keep him safe? After I have ruined my soul so that he could keep his life with Kenna? Isn't that funny, Miss, how life turns out? For it looked like Valentine was bound to die that fall, no matter what I did. I could not save him.

I think Kenna chose to slip away. She chose to let her mind go. She took her time to do it, but she started slipping away the second she heard that wagon crash down. She let go.

No, Miss, I didn't go crazy. Crazy is for rich folks; I couldn't afford it. Someone had to be brave, so I decided it was to be me. What else could I do? I had to keep going. I had to take care of the babies and the boys and the house and the freight company. But it was terrible. It was hell.

So, I sat up all night with Valentine and washed his face and neck and hands with camphor and kept him pleasing to the eye, as much as I could. I was so tired then, it seemed like I couldn't think straight. As James dozed, I saw things and heard things I didn't understand, and as the night wore on, I tried to figure out what was real and what was from my head; the quick steps across the porch and the sharp rap on the door, but no one there; or seeing someone walking down the stairs, but again, no one there. Shadows from my tired brain, for I was wrung out. No more crying or what all, but just tending Valentine while Kenna lay up in her tall bed.

Come morning and James fixed me a cup of coffee and brought it into the parlor. "Cipriano is coming pretty soon. We'll take Valentine down to the graveyard and bury him today, Ruby," he said.

"Yes, James. That's fine, if you say. I'm just staying here until it's time. I'll stay right here."

"Well, can I bring you something to eat at least?" he asked me, so sweetly.

"No, Sweet Boy. I'm not hungry. Maybe later. Maybe later." And I washed on.

Next thing you know, here came Cipriano, looking like he's going to meet his maker. He whispered to James, pointing this way and that, using his hands to talk, like he did. Then, James came to me and allowed as how the folks down at the Ford didn't want Valentine buried in the graveyard on account of his shady past and outlaw ways; those scoundrels that knew him all those years and liked his ways and came to his gatherings and wedding; even came to see him laying dead by the barn, and now they won't let him in their fancy graveyard. Have you ever heard such? If I could have reached a butcher knife right then, I would have carved Cipriano's liver for him, but the knives were clear back in the kitchen.

I hate undertakers, Miss. Don't give me to one, will you? Don't let them have me. You can manage to hide me away somewhere, can't you? Promise me, Miss. Will you promise? I wish I could have been buried next to Valentine. I never laid with him in life, wanted to lay by him in death. But that was not to be either. Anyhow, I guess it doesn't matter where you put me away, Miss, only keep the undertaker away. Will you help me? Can I count on you, Miss? I guess you could put me in the graveyard, down by the river. That would be all right, Miss, though Valentine was not allowed there.

Anyhow, Kenna lay up in her tall bed, as still as a stone. I snuck up there and said, "Kenna, I need to talk to you about Valentine's funeral. We need to figure out where to bury him. They won't have him down at the Ford."

She never even blinked an eye, but just said, "We will bury him over the hill behind the house, here. Just down the hill a little way where you can see the Summit; just over the hill here, Ruby. The Ford can burn in hell, for all I care. I will lay my Valentine over the hill." Then she gave up talking again.

When it was time to take that box over the hill and put my Valentine away from me, Kenna staggered down the stairs, carrying her tartan; her beautiful tartan from her far lands. She said, "Ruby, let's cut this in half and wrap Valentine in half of it and save the other half for me. What do you think of that?" She spoke to me like we are choosing what old apron to cut up for quilt scraps.

"That's a fine idea, Kenna," I said, taking the tartan out of her hands. "That's a grand idea. Valentine would like that. He loved your tartan."

"You cut it," she said, sitting down on the settee by Valentine's coffin.

So, I did. I got her scissors and I cut what was left straight in half out on the dining room table. I brought the pieces back to her and handed them easy to dear Kenna. Then surprise of all, she pulled them both over her head and hid her face and set to keening again. I let her have at it for a while, and then I sat next to her and took those pieces of tartan off her head.

"You better stop for a while, Kenna. Let's get this work done, and then we will have days and days to cry."

"Yes, all right, Ruby. All right." She shut off her keening for a while.

"Help me, Kenna. Help me put this on Valentine. James, help us. We got to lift him up some." So, James and Cipriano helped get Valentine's body to sitting up, and Cipriano held Valentine's head up, and Kenna and I wrapped the tartan around Valentine's broad shoulders and then we lay him down as gentle as we could and we got ready to put him in the dirt. Lord God, Miss, we got ready to put him away forever. Only Kenna said she wanted Valentine to be buried with his old pistol, so we put that in there too. So, Valentine would go away with his tartan and his sidearm, like the true warrior clansman that he was.

Cipriano, the bastard, closed the box and the boys hauled it out. James gave directions to Cipriano and he drove out over the desert with that box bumping all the way. Most of the dirt had dried up, but you could still see the spots where the raindrops had landed and made tiny footprints. They crumbled when we walked across them.

The babies were with Mrs. Ricker by then, but Tommy held my hand and James took my other arm, and we walked out into the sunny day and out into the desert there, at the foot of the Sonomas. Not many folks were with us; not many folks from town; only Ferris and Wade and Bragintons. James and Ferris each carried a shovel over their shoulders, and when Kenna said stop, we all did.

Kenna looked straight out to the north toward the Summit, and said, "This is the place. This is where we will lay Valentine." She did not cry, but only stood tall in her little body, the wind pushing her skirts back against her legs. Some of her curls came loose and waved about her face.

So, the boys commenced to digging and Cipriano brought the wagon closer. I could smell the good, desert earth and pungent sagebrush. When they got a good hole dug, they lifted out the coffin and eased it down into the damp ground. Kenna and I stood watching, neither of us crying. We just watched and waited, holding each other by the waist; holding each other up.

Then surprise of all, Kenna took a shovel and buried up her husband; covered him with that desert dirt. When James tried to help, I thought she was going to hit him with that shovel. It didn't take her long to get the dirt back in there. We all began gathering rocks then, and made a big stack of stones on top of Valentine's resting place; made a cairn is what Kenna called it. It's still there today, Miss. Valentine's cairn is still standing out in the desert.

Wade grabbed his fiddle out of Ciprano's wagon then, and played a pretty tune for Valentine; a sad tune that put me in mind of the war. It sounded like a song from Missouri or somewhere South like that, and I thought that was right nice of Wade to play a Dixie song for Valentine. Sort of showed that Wade didn't care if Valentine was a raider or not. It was right nice of him.

Then Kenna said a poem for Valentine, her voice hardly quavering at all, but instead ringing out across the desert. When she was done, her voice kind of hung on the air, very strange like. Oh, it was this, Miss.

If you were coming in the fall,
I'd brush the summer by
With half a smile and half a spurn,
As housewives do a fly.

If I could see you in a year,
I'd wind the months in balls,
And put them each in separate drawers,
Until their time befalls.

If only centuries delayed,
I'd count them on my hand,

Subtracting till my fingers dropped
Into Van Diemens land.

If certain, when this life was out,
That yours and mine should be,
I'd toss it yonder like a rind,
And taste eternity.

When that was all done, Kenna said everyone was to leave except for me. "I want to thank you all for coming here today. Thank you for standing by me during this terrible time. I will not forget who came here today, but if you don't mind, could just Ruby and I stay here alone? We'll be along directly."

Then those few folks wandered off toward the Hill House, and before long we lost sight of them as they went over the rise and disappeared; Cipriano's wagon, too. Then it was just Kenna and me standing by the cairn. We were quiet for a while, the wind breezing by us with nary a cloud in the sky.

Finally, Kenna whispered, "I know you loved my husband. I know you loved Valentine, and I'm sorry for you to lose him, Ruby."

"Kenna," I said, and I was right quiet too, but I shook inside. "Kenna, I loved him terrible." And we were mended. All was forgiven. We hugged each other tight and a desert wind came up for us; a little breeze on that warm, fall day, finally turning into a whirlwind. Then, as we stood there, I heard music coming to us from far off, from over the hill. We both turned to see who played, for it was a kind of music I had never heard; a strange music. And Miss, I tell you, as we stood there, we see a piper coming over the hill. First, we could only see the tops of his bagpipes as they swayed with his noble step. Then, we saw more and more of him. He wore a fine kilt, but it was not Kenna's tartan but some other tartan. He wore a clean, white shirt and thick, tall socks with a bit of fringe round the top.

When he cleared the top of the hill, he stopped there and played his mournful dirge for Valentine; played beautiful, and the notes came so high. I don't know why, Miss, but when I heard them, I saw the greenest mountains in my head, and I knew for sure exactly how Kenna's land looked. I wanted it then, so very bad! Like I belonged there but had lost my way.

"The Rowan Tree," said Kenna. "He's playing The Rowan Tree."

He played on and on, that piper, and a mournful sound it was. We stood and watched and when he was near done, he turned around and went back the way he had come, disappearing over the hill, the tune floating back to us for a while and finally fading away. Just as when he came, when he left, the last thing we saw was the top of his pipes with the tassels swinging with his step. And he was gone.

Arm in arm then, we followed him. We went back to the Hill House without much talk, walking along, dodging sagebrush and greasewood, winding our way. Kenna was with me then. She only said to me, "Wear your grief, Ruby, like fancy gloves. Don't hide it. Don't hide it from me. I don't want you to hide."

For once I was the one who did not answer. I stayed quiet.

CHAPTER 60

First thing I did was conjure how my Valentine died; conjured it over and over until I saw it all; every second of that morning.

All of it, Miss.

Except I still don't know why he crawled under that wagon; never could see that. Only that under there he was, looking up at the axle or something before it crashed down on him. It made a terrible noise when it fell—first, a loud pop of the axle breaking and then the wagon dropped, the load of wood in the box jumped up once and then down. Down on my Valentine.

Poor James was standing there, and first he tried to help. It took him a minute to understand what had actually happened to Valentine, but when he looked under the wagon, his eyes got big as saucers and he took to screaming for Kenna, his boy-to-man voice cracking high on the air. Kenna was already on the run, for she heard the terrible noise from the kitchen. Valentine's feet and legs stuck out of the side, his heels scratching in the dirt in a very panicky way, making deep grooves in the dirt there.

Kenna ran out there to him, her skirts held high, screaming to beat all.

"Get it off of him! Get it off!" Then they tried to lift the wagon, tried to throw firewood off, but it was no good. It was all too heavy for them.

Kenna crawled under the wagon then, seeing Valentine still there, still living. He couldn't breathe though, but he turned his head and looked at her; looked her right in the eye as she scrambled to him. She bent up her knees to push the underside of the wagon up off him with her feet, but it didn't budge. She tried everything, but it all came to no good.

Then she stopped, for Valentine grabbed her arm so she turned to him, kissed him, begged him to wait. "Just wait one more minute, and I will get you out!"

But Valentine shook his head no, and with his hand he motioned her to come closer to him; motioned like he always did as he walked away from Kenna.

"Come on. Come on," he said with his hand.

Kenna kissed him again, full on the mouth. Valentine waged one last battle of kicking his legs, trying to get free. He didn't want to die; didn't want to leave. One, little moment of panic and then he shook his head no again, closed his eyes.

Did he know he died? Did he think he just went to sleep?

White foam came out his mouth then, his eyes opened, and he was forever gone, forever gone, forever gone. Gone from this land of desert and powder-dust; gone from music and laughter and babies clamoring for his bristly cheek; gone from anger and fear and regret; gone from our Ford and crossing one of his own.

That's when Kenna took up her keening and screaming and digging in the dirt with her fingers, trying to dig him out; make room for him to breathe, but it was too late. James sat down hard in the dirt, stinging tears rolling down his cheeks. He didn't know what to do with himself. And poor Tom stood and stared with nary a sound, but tears washing a dirt trail down his cheeks.

Finally, James said, "Tom, run get Ferris. Fast as you can. Go!" Tom was off like a shot; his bare feet barely touching the ground as he ran to the Ford.

That's what I conjured, Miss, day and night. Most times I saw how Valentine only had eyes for Kenna as he left this Earth, but sometimes I dreamed that he thought of me for a second. Just for a little second in time he thought of me, and he was mine, but mostly I didn't see it that way. Mostly I saw how he loved Kenna terrible and she loved him terrible and they were the best kind of lovers; true lovers. So, I tortured myself like that.

After the funeral that day, though, we just walked slow back to the Hill House, not saying much of anything at all. We came up to the house from the side, and that was all right, but as soon as we rounded the corner where we saw the front of the house and how cheery it was, what a *good* house it was with the trees taking hold and growing up, the flowers blooming in the dooryard, our hearts liked to break, for it was so beautiful and good, but hollow at the same time, and we took up keening again; keening loud enough to wake the dead. Only not. Not loud enough to wake Valentine. He was out of our reach. James came out then and gathered us like old sheets off the line; gathered us one on each side and led us up the steps and into the house. Though we were blind.

Up the stairs he took us to my old room, guiding Kenna to one side of the bed and me to the other. We were exhausted, for we lay there and cried for but a few minutes and then both fell into a deep sleep; a slumber that let us escape for a while from our new lives, for everything was changed. We were two old widows, forever after.

When I woke up it was deep into the evening, the light barely shining in through the lace at the window. I lay there for a minute in peace, before remembering all that had come to pass, before it crashed down on me. Like a wagonload of fire-wood, it crashed down so I couldn't breathe. I turned my head to look at Kenna there, she looking back at me, dry-eyed too, for the minute, but heartbreak written in every line of her face, every blink of her eye. Heartbreak.

"How did you get a piper to come here, Ruby?" she finally whispered. "How did you do that? Who was he? Where is he from?" she asked, trying to puzzle that all out.

"I didn't get the piper," I said. "Where am I going to get a piper? I thought you got a piper for Valentine, or Wade maybe got him."

"There's no piper here that I know of. No piper anywhere around here. Have you ever heard of one?"

"Well, no, but that doesn't mean much. There's plenty I don't know," I told her. She looked close at me then, and a little sideways, like she didn't believe me. "Kenna, I don't know nothing about it!" I said.

"But you saw him, didn't you? You heard him?"

"Of course, I saw him. We both saw him. Why, I could see the tassels on his pipes, clear as day. What are you playing at?"

"Well, where did he come from? That's what I want to know. Where did he come from, and where did he go? What tartan was that he wore? I'm going to find out. And the tune he played. Do you know it, Ruby? Have you heard it before?"

"No, of course not. I don't know much about that far lands' music. Only what you taught me."

"Well, that is a special tune he played. It's called The Rowan Tree, and it's very special to me."

"Well, what is it? Tell me Kenna. Tell me the story again." I just wanted to lay there and listen to her voice; wanted to slip away in my head and go somewhere else where I could breathe without a catch in my chest, to escape for a little while.

"All down the centuries, people have told stories of the rowan tree and its powers. The rowan is a tree that offers defense against witches. It can protect you from witches and dark arts. The rowan tree belongs to all women; it gives protection to our children," Kenna droned, using almost the same words she used when she told the story to the boys during our Christmas celebration.

Instead of floating away on Kenna's easy voice, though, I began to feel sick inside, for I was the witch, Miss, and I durn well knew it. I wanted no rowan around me! I feared it might make me disappear altogether.

That was about the last of our piper talk, or rowan talk for that matter, and we never did find out who played those pipes for Valentine. No one in the Ford saw him nor heard of him. He didn't go back to the Hill House after the funeral, like we thought. No one saw him at all, and that made me feel funny; we saw something not of this Earth; someone came there to call Valentine home.

I thought about how Valentine knew Kenna's far lands' dance and how he jumped so high; thought about how DeRoo wasn't his real name and wondered where his people came from. I conjured that the piper was one of Valentine's own people from Scotland, and Valentine was a Scot too, just like Kenna. That only made me the sadder, for their blood was connected down all the centuries, and there I was with who knows what blood running in me. Not their fine Highland blood. No, not me. Not me.

I thought too about Kenna's poem for Valentine, describing waiting for someone and throwing away time until they were together again. It made me feel they were somehow just waiting to be together again, and it seemed like they would be, for sure; not in Heaven, but right there in the Ford. Like Heaven *could be* the Ford for them, and they would live their happiest times, over and over again. Maybe Kenna would walk the bride walk down the stairs every day for eternity, with Valentine waiting in the parlor for her. He would take her hand to his heart every day, for eternity. They would be in their Heaven.

That's what I still think now, Miss. I think they are together up there in that house. And though it is old and filled with dust and mice, for them, the wood is gleaming. For them, the fire is snapping, the feather tick in the kitchen, the coffee is on the stove. For them. And they lay together every night. They love each other every day, and they are always young and beautiful and strong and happy; every day, for them.

Isn't it funny, Miss, to be jealous of dead people? Don't that just about hang the cat? For they are dead and dust, and I'm still wishing I was with them, wishing they were with me. Missing them and wanting what they have, and they are both long dead. Don't that beat all?

It's right painful, Miss, for there is no winning for me. I can't steal Valentine away now, no matter how many years go by. There is no way for me to win, at all. I lost. I lost out.

And when I die, can I go there? Can I watch them out the bedroom window? Can I hear them clattering around the kitchen, or hear Valentine's rumbling voice from another room? Can I catch a glimpse of his shoulders and bent head when he hunkers down to start the fire, or watch him smile crooked at something that has someone else really riled up? Can I see the curls at his collar? What will be for me, Miss? Shall I haunt the ghosts? Shall I, Miss?

CHAPTER 61

Well, there wasn't anything else to do then, but move back up to the Hill House to take care of Kenna, so the boys and I loaded up our household and moved up there for good and all. We closed this little house here, Miss, and shut it up tight; loaded up the sulky and moved up the hill. Kenna was glad to have us too, and she said so every day, over and over, and sometimes it seemed like she didn't know she had already said it a whole bunch of times. I knew Kenna was slipping away to somewhere else.

There I was, back in my beautiful room with a nice quilt on the bed and lace at the window. Each morning, I brought Kenna a cup of tea or sometimes coffee, while she sat at her table to watch the sun "wake up the Sonomas", as she used to say. But the joy was gone for her, so mostly she only sat and stared, and lots of mornings the cup went untouched and I had to haul it back downstairs.

Everything was mended between us, from the day of the

funeral on. She forgave me for pining after Valentine, and I didn't blame Kenna for taking my babies when she got the chance. She was starving for those babies. I remember when I took the babies up there that day, and Kenna came out and got those babies. She couldn't help herself, Miss. She had to take those babies, and she couldn't stop. She wasn't trying to take something from me. She just was starving, and when you're starving, you got to take what you can get. I don't blame Kenna at all.

Not long, but Tommy went back to school and the babies went back to playing dollies on the floor. James' leg healed, and he went back to running the freight line. Ferris helped him out; helped him fix that damnable wagon. James acted like a grown man all the time then, and I guess he was a grown man. He took care of the business for Kenna and gave her the money. He was a good boy, my James.

And me, Miss, I turned old overnight, and it got to where I couldn't remember how old I was, or care either. I took to leaving my hair down night and day, and looking like something the cat dragged in. So, some days I took care of Kenna and some days she took care of me, but mostly I took care of her. Either way, we both looked a fright. I wonder what the boys thought of that. I wonder if they worried about us.

I remember watching her sitting on the porch with the babies that fall, dandling them on her knee and what not, but the light never got to her eyes. She never lost her deep sadness, missing her husband.

The first time it came a cold evening, I went to build a fire in the parlor. Kenna threw a fit, screaming and falling on the floor and carrying on, like to die; screaming about firewood and hell and I don't know what all. That set the babies to bawling, and pretty soon the whole house was in an uproar. I didn't know which screamer to tend to first.

I picked Kenna up and helped her stand up, pulled her up the stairs to rest for a while. "Good Lord, Kenna, we got to have a fire. We can't go all winter without a fire."

"Not that fire! Not that fire!" she kept screaming. "Help me get it out of here! Help me, Ruby!" She jumped for the fireplace like she was going to grab the wood and throw it out the door. I had to stop her, and it wasn't easy. It was terrible, Miss, to see her crazy like that.

Lord God, Miss, I feel so bad for Kenna. Her life was ruined, and she never got it back. Never stopped it from ruining, over and over every day. And everything she saw taught her just to keep on doing just that.

You know, Miss, Kenna could make the best bread in the world. I tried to get her to make it that fall after Valentine was gone, but she would have none of it. When I tried it, she only looked at me with a puzzled expression on her face. How I longed for her bread, but like many things, Kenna withheld that gift for the rest of her life.

Let's make some tomorrow! I'll tell you what to do. You got to make a sponge today and we'll finish tomorrow. Get the recipe book out and let's take a look at it. Get down Kenna's bread bowl from the cupboard. Now look at this! How I loved that old bread bowl!

After that first winter and spring came on, we took to sitting outside of an afternoon, watching the babies play in the yard.

Once our work was done, it was a good way to recollect the day, and what work we had finished. That is until a snake showed up in the dooryard, and there we were, sitting on the porch in the afternoon sun, the babies playing in the dooryard there with little sticks and pebbles all lined in rows.

Kenna looked over and said, just as cool as a cucumber, "Is that a rattlesnake?"

I jumped up and looked over the porch railing, and there he lay, sunning too, just like us, and only a little way from the babies; just stretched out and resting, enjoying his afternoon nap. Well, Miss, my air jumped out of me! I was so terrified for my babies, for the snake was between my babies and me.

But Kenna says, "Ruby, watch that snake." Like I watch big, old rattlers every day. Surprise of all, I took to bellering like anything, and I said, "Kenna, are you going to kill him?"

"Well, hell yes, I'm going to kill him. Watch him." And off she went, into the house. So, there sat the babies with their little game in the dirt, and Mr. Snake didn't move at all, but only slumbered on, not knowing his days were numbered. I studied him close then, and I couldn't blink. His hide was beautiful and frightful at the same time, a fancy patchwork quilt of diamonds and lines and triangles, and he was fat in the belly; healthy. It looked like spring had been pretty good to him already, Miss, like he had been eating lots of mice and such.

I jumped down the porch steps and made a wide path around the snake so I could get to the babies. Then we all three stood there and watched the snake, just like Kenna told us to do.

Pretty soon, here came Kenna out the door, carrying the shovel from the garden. Now, I am not that afraid of snakes, but was only scared for my babies, but even so, I would not want to kill a rattler with a shovel, Miss. No, no thank you.

But Kenna picked up that shovel and held it over her head, and it came to me that the last time she touched it was to bury Valentine. That seemed tragic to me; that these everyday things we have laying around jump into our lives in strange ways from time to time, and the whole time you don't think about it or know. So, when Kenna bought that shovel down at the Ford and had Ferris haul it up the hill, she never dreamed it would be so important; would bury her husband or save the babies, never saw it. Just left it leaning here and there until the right moment, and then everything is everything, and you better wake up. Better grab the shovel or broom or whatever is going to save you; better grab a skillet and whang Frank over the head or a crutch for Jake Moffat. You never know. You best look sharp; look and see what you got, Miss, for you never know.

Well, Kenna didn't even hike her skirts. She just stomped down there and gave the snake a good one on his head. That snake coiled and was fit to be tied before you could blink an eye. I guess he was hurt, but still plenty able to hurt back. He coiled and spotted Kenna all at once, and he struck at her.

Like a beauty dancer, Kenna stepped to the side, just moved out of his deadly path, and the snake struck past her. She only turned to the side, so graceful, and it seemed like time slowed way down. I saw Kenna's skirts swish to the side, and I saw that snake stretch out his neck and open wide his jaws; saw him shoot past Kenna and fall back to the dirt, but he was still on the fight. Still coiled, and Kenna hit him again, only this time he was all circled up in his coil, and the shovel went down on his whole body. He was not done yet, and Kenna hit him a couple more times.

The babies had backed themselves up against the gate, clutching my skirts on each side, staring at Kenna with big eyes. I can still see the sticks clutched in their baby hands. I stood there and squalled, and I don't know who I was squalling for—Kenna or the snake. It seemed like this show playing out for me in the dooryard was much more than what it appeared; much more than a city gal killing a snake with a shovel. I knew we would never be the same, *again*.

Then Mr. Snake was done in, and only lay squirming on the dirt and turning upside down to show us his white belly.

"He'll do that until the sun goes down," Kenna said, sounding like an old cowboy who had killed many a rattler, instead of our little lady from Boston. "Let's get the babies in the house."

She walked over to us, her shovel in one hand. We each scooped up a baby and turned back to look at the snake. He was still trying to die. The babies didn't make a sound, but only stared, their rosebud mouths agape.

"Snake ally; that's my snake ally," Kenna said. "I'm going to be free soon. I'm going to change." She nodded her head, and she smiled at me like she just found a new Sunday bonnet; as crazy as a bedbug; happy. But then your mother took a fright, and she said, "Oh Ruby, will I get to him? Will I find Valentine? What if I can't find him?" She was deathly white, shaking like anything. "What if the time is wrong?"

I said, "Your ma took a fright," Miss. That's what I said. She was not afraid of that old snake, but she was terrified to go to the afterlife without her beloved Valentine.

CHAPTER 62

Yes, Miss, you can copy the recipe. Of course, but you'll never make bread like your mama could make.

It came to me in a dream, Miss. Your name came to me. It's Rowan. You are Rowan. I dreamed I was out back of Kenna's house, and I heard her calling to you. "Ro-wan! Ro-wan! Time to come in now." Her voice was very far away, even though I could see her at the kitchen door. It seemed I was seeing something that happened somewhere else, some other time, but right here in the Ford at the same time.

That's your name, isn't it Miss? You are Rowan. When Kenna gave you that name, she had no idea that you would be my rowan, too. My flying Rowan, come here to set me free from my witchery; come here to save my soul.

It was me, Miss, stopped the world from turning. Not Kenna; it was me. When I saw Valentine look on her like he did, I struck him blind. I forgave him though; gave him his sight back. And when Frank came back; came back to my house, I let him in; and I laid hands on him, and I killed him. I sent him to that train track just as sure as if I'd chased him there with a rotten stick. I thought about Kenna chopping up my dress, and I began to wondering what could I do to get Frank all chopped up. Then it came to me. I guess a locomotive will chop up a person. And so that's where I sent him. Frank went out of my life.

You believe all that, Miss? You think I'm telling you the truth? Do you think I could make it rain? Do you think I could? Do you think I killed Frank? You know I killed Jake. I called in the bees and coyotes and the snake, and all. I brought all green to Kenna's house. Why, I brought her water! You believe all that? Then ask yourself this question. Who gone and killed Valentine? Who killed Valentine? Lord God, I think it was me.

I think my secret heart was pining for him so long, and seeing how it never was going to be. Maybe I dreamed it. Maybe I dreamed him to die. I don't know, but I know I killed him. I know it, just as sure as the world.

Kenna's Winter Bread

SPONGE

4   cups store-bought flour
    Dash of baker's yeast

2   cups warm water
    Stir together, cover, and let set all night on the back of
    the stove.

BREAD SOAK

Tear two bread ends into crumbs. Soak in water overnight.

DOUGH

- 3 cups store-bought flour
- 1 cup milled wheat berries (scant cup of berries makes one cup of flour)
- 3 teaspoons salt
- ½ teaspoon baker's yeast
- ½ cup wheat germ
- ¼ cup dried sunflower seeds (or other seeds available)
- 1 cup water soak, squeezed of excess water
- 1 cup warm water

Mix dry ingredients in large bread bowl. Pour water and bread soak into sponge. Mix with ingredients in the bread bowl. Mix by hand until combined. Let sit 30 minutes.

Knead in the bowl for 2 minutes. Let set for 30 minutes.

Knead in the bowl for 2 more minutes. Cover and let raise on the back of the stove for 2 hours.

Split dough in half with a knife. Form round loaves and let them raise for one hour. Place loaves in Dutch ovens. Score loaves with a knife. Sprinkle each loaf with one teaspoon sunflower seeds. Cover with lids and bake in very hot oven for 20 minutes. Remove lids. Bake 20 more minutes, making sure to keep fire hot.

CHAPTER 63

Do you really think I can't see her in you? Your hair? Your smile? Your tiny waist? Isn't something to get so stirred up about. No need for all these secrets, Miss. Your mother was a great lady, the best friend of my life. I'm glad to know you.

It doesn't surprise me one bit that Kenna never told me about you. She was very private, that one. But you can be sure that there was a very good reason for her leaving you behind and coming out here. She came out here to hide out, I'm guessing; came West to get away from something or someone bad, and had no choice but to leave you. Why, maybe they took you away from her. Did you ever think of that?

I'll say this, though. I've never seen another woman, before or since, pine after babies the way Kenna did. It was written in every line of her face; the way she held the babies, the way she turned a phrase with them or made them something pretty; the way she looked at them when she didn't know I watched. Even right to the end, Kenna loved those babies like they her very own.

Don't be mad at your mama, Miss. You have to forgive her. You have to. It will only eat you up inside, the way my hatred has done for me. You want to be a used up, old lady before your time? Well, just keep on hating and see where it gets you. Listen to me now. And I'll tell you something else; it is your job in life to connect with people. It won't just happen; you got to make it happen, and once you do, you have to keep the connection going. Don't let your people go, the way I have. Keep them to you, Rowan.

No, Kenna stayed with us for a little over a year after Valentine died; stayed with us in body, but began slipping away in every way she could. No more music at all, and if James acted like he was thinking of picking up his mandolin, she would tear out of the house. No more singing; no more harp or drum. Worst of all, no more of her beloved poems. She wouldn't tell me a single line; only loved on the babies in a quiet way, a kiss on the head or watching from across the room only.

She started talking about leaving us, started saying, "Come here, Ruby. I want to show you where the garnets are, in case of my untimely demise," or, "Here's where I keep the rest of the good dishes Ruby, so you know where they are." She made me send for the judge from over at Unionville to make out her will.

"I'm leaving everything to you, Ruby, so you can take care of the children and not have to worry. I want the babies to go to school, a ladies' school or a Normal School or something. I want them to be educated. I want them to be able to care for themselves and not need to depend on a man. See to it, won't you, Ruby? Promise me?" She rounded her shoulders and stared at the floor then. That kind of talk made me miss the Kenna I knew; for the spicy, sassy Kenna was gone, Miss.

It was terrible when she made her funeral plans. She put her pretty day dress in a box and labeled it "Last Clean Shirt", showed it to me. It was the forest green dress with the wide waistband and braiding down the sleeves and a big, full skirt and a white, lace collar. Kenna did look beautiful in that dress, Miss, for her eyes matched it just so, and her color was perfect with that green. Kenna and her green—no one wore it like Kenna.

"Bury me in this dress, won't you Ruby? Valentine loved this dress. Put me right next to Valentine, all right Ruby? Put a cairn over my bones so I can rest by Valentine. All right Ruby? Promise me."

I tried not to answer her; avoided making that promise, for when I heard the words it stung like a blade. I did not want to put her up on the hill with Valentine. I did not want to, Miss, for I wanted to be there myself. But finally, I did make the promise. She would not stop until I did.

"All right." I said, "I promise."

"No, say it all, Ruby. Tell me the whole promise." I guess Kenna knew better than to trust me.

"I promise to lay you by Valentine when you die, Kenna. All right? Now, stop talking like this. You're going to live a long time yet. Now, let's have some tea and bread and butter. Come on," I said, leading her off to the kitchen.

It seemed like Kenna became a very old lady, moving slow, stooped at the shoulder. Lines came around her mouth and her eyes got a hooded look; old before her time. Death will do that to you, Miss, or maybe it's love that will do that. Either way, she was an old lady within a year.

When I think back on it, I guess that snake really did mean Kenna was changing; transforming, as she called it. It was that summer she started seeing her shadows and forms from the corner of her eye. First, I didn't think much of it. We would be sitting at the table say, and Kenna would look past me; look behind me enough to make me turn my head and see what she was looking at, but nothing there. Then she took to looking hard out the kitchen window; looking hard at the dooryard or the porch; staring hard at the barn.

I finally had enough, so I said, "What you looking at, Kenna? What is it?"

"It's Valentine, Ruby. He's here," she whispered.

"Lord, Kenna, don't go saying that in front of the babies. They are missing him bad enough without you teaching them something like that. Stop it now. This is not good for you anyway. Kenna, come on. Let's start us a quilt or something."

"Don't talk against this now, Ruby. Don't make Valentine feel he can't come in this house. We have to be careful. We have to make the way easy for him."

I felt my skin crawl then. I felt he *was* there, watching us. "This is not right. You have to leave off this crazy talk. Valentine is gone, and you know it," I said. "He's dead and gone and nothing is going to bring him back. Leave off of this now, Kenna."

Then Kenna gave me a little half smile and said for me not to worry; patted my hand like I was a simpleton, and wandered off to the kitchen, but she did not agree to leave off the ghost talk.

I guess it was a few weeks along, and lo and behold, it happened to me. I had been harping at James to help me fill the wood boxes, but he was not helping me out. For once, he was acting like a boy instead of a man. Then I saw him walk past the kitchen door and head toward the parlor; saw him out the corner of my eye, slinking off instead of getting the wood. I started off following him, fussing all the way.

"James, I said for you to fill the wood boxes, and I'm not telling you again. What has got into you? You come do this work right now. I mean it, James." By then I was at the parlor, but there was not a soul there; no one at all. Then it came to me that I had not seen James at all. But I saw a tall person, and it was a man, so I don't know who I saw. I sat down hard on the settee and looked around close.

"Valentine," I whispered. "Is it you? Are you here? Valentine?" I looked up at the corners of the room, for wouldn't that be where a ghost would hide? Up at the ceiling? But there was no one there. No Valentine.

After that I took to looking hard too, just like Kenna. I don't know which one of us was the most desperate to see our beloved Valentine. I lived for it, night and day. I wanted him back so bad; needed to see him one more time. I planned what I would say, how I would tell him straight out that I loved him and forgave him, and I would invite him to come to the house whenever he wanted, and stay there forever. That's what I dreamed of.

I did see him sometimes, too, out the corner of my eye, but only for an instant. Not long enough to talk to him, never long enough to talk to him. Sometimes I would feel him around me, watching me cook in the kitchen or sweep the porch. Once I could smell him, like he was leaning near to my face. I smelled his salty, man smell, and I missed him terrible then, and remembered how I had leaned into him when he carried me into the house that time; missed him so bad, Miss, that my eyes stung like anything. The little glimpses I did get of him did not help me feel any better about being away from him. It didn't comfort me at all, but only made me mournful all the more.

Well, then one afternoon, Kenna and the babies napped upstairs and the boys were gone somewhere. I sat alone, listening to the ticking of the clock. The house was so still. Then all of a sudden, I heard scraping noises coming from the kitchen, so I headed back there to see what was going on. It sounded like a big animal had gotten in the house to make that much noise, but no. I walked into the kitchen, and there sat Valentine with his back to me, working on a broken axe handle. First thing I did was scream like a mashed cat. All my invitation plans went out the window, and I screamed like anything until it hurt my throat. But Valentine never paused in his task. He just kept on working. I could hear a baby crying upstairs though, thanks to my yowling.

I finally got my wits about me. I thought he would either turn around or disappear, but he didn't do either, but carried on with his work.

"Valentine!" I was finally able to say. "Valentine!" and I took up crying right away. I had been missing him so bad, and now here he was. "Valentine, can you hear me? It's me! It's Ruby! Valentine, look at me!"

There he sat on, ignoring me like he had since the first day I met him. He never could see me.

I tried pleading with him, begging him to see me, but to no avail. I wanted him to turn around. He was as real as you and me, though, Miss. I could see the hair at his shirt collar and the tan of his arm. I could see him plain.

Little Minnie come bursting in the kitchen then, squalling at the top of her lungs, and Valentine popped out of existence. I looked down at her and then back up at him, but he was gone in the blink of an eye. I was devastated then, to lose him all over again. I scooped up Minnie and we cried together.

No, he doesn't come here, Miss, not to this house. This house belonged to another man, and Valentine has no hold here. He is at his own place, up the hill there.

Things went on like that for a long time, but I only saw him clear like that a couple times. When I told Kenna about it, she allowed as how she was looking awful hard for him. She knew he could come to us like that.

CHAPTER 64

Sometimes we saw lots of signs of Valentine, and sometimes we were left alone. Sometimes I would hear his big boots tromping across the porch, and when I'd open the door, not a sign of anyone. Or the door would swing open on its own accord.

You know what I think it was? I think Valentine just fell asleep under the wagon there and didn't understand that he was gone, at first. Then, when he did get the idea, he couldn't leave us. He had to stay to take care of us, like he always had done. He had to be the steadfast provider, just like he always was. There was no peace for Valentine; he wandered the desert, finding no rest. It doesn't seem right, Miss, for he was a good person and whatever he did with the war was of no fault to him. He was only fighting for his people, and we all did that, Miss. We all did the same durn kind of fighting.

Kenna and I were growing apart—growing different from the women we had been. We hardly talked at all; only silence in the kitchen when we did work together, which wasn't that often.

Mostly she sat in the parlor or the dining room, a shell of herself.

One day she came slinking into the kitchen, and she put a paper on the table; a single sheet of paper with a poem written on it.

"Listen to this, Ruby," she said. "Listen to what I have written." For Kenna was quite a good writer when she put her mind to it. Then she read the poem to me. It was this, Miss.

When the summer comes around,
Or when the summer thinking comes around,
I will conjure your presence.
I will bring you here.

When I sit on my porch
In the poetry of the evening
I will invoke your name.
I will remember slivers of time.

When I stand between moonlight and deep shadow
In the sultry midnight of summer,
I will cast a spell of recollection.
Peace will elude you.

When it rains,
When the rain comes around,
I will listen to the sound
And,
As if by magic,
It will be your voice that I hear.

Now Miss, by the time she finished the last line and looked up at me with those piercing eyes, my blood was boiling. Before I knew what I was saying, I lit into Kenna.

"You going to conjure something, Kenna? You going to bring Valentine here? You able to do that, Kenna? Are you?" I asked, my hands shaking like the palsy, I was so furious.

She laughed at me then, and that made me hate her. Yes, I hated her. She said, "Why, no, Ruby. I don't manifest apparitions. I don't do such things, but you do. I wrote the poem for you. It's you bringing him here."

"You are crazy, Kenna. You are plumb insane. Maybe you better go to bed. Get some sleep. Clear your mind. Give me that poem!" I grabbed my poem from her and tore it in half. I quick threw it in the stove, and it curled into black ash in an instant.

She laughed so hard then; shrieked with laughter like the time we had made such fun of Frank; cackled until she lost her breath, held her ribs.

So, I pushed her, shoved her right out of the kitchen.

"Get out of here, Kenna! Get out! I'm full up of your crazy talk! Get!"

"I'm going," she gasped. "I'm going. It's just that…" and she was trying to talk around her laughing. "It's just that…" and she grabbed my arm and leaned toward me. "It's just that I know the words to the poem. Burning it won't change that. I know it, you see." And she screamed with laughing.

So, I slapped her right across the face. Her head snapped to the side and her wild hair flew out like a mop, but she stopped laughing; stopped for a second with her hand on her face and her eyes wide, and then laughed even harder.

"Get out! Get away from me! I hate you! I hate everything about you!" I screamed, and I pushed her out of the kitchen. I heard her crossing the dining room and climbing the stairs, laughing all the way.

I thought about her claiming my poem. I could hear parts of it ringing in my head. I was so disgusted with her; so mad at her for saying this truth about me. I had been calling Kenna a witch since I met her, but it was me Miss, could conjure a ghost.

Things were not the same between Kenna and me after that day. We never spoke of it and never mended our fences. It was as if the tie between us had become unraveled. I did not care *about* her. I did not care *for* her. I let her wear her same filthy dress day after day. I kept the babies away from her. I did not call her to meals. I let Kenna go.

CHAPTER 65

Who told you I killed her? Who said that? You tell me.

Well, do you believe it? Do you think I killed your mother? You don't have any idea what happened around here. You have no notion of what your mother became; what Valentine's death did to her, so I'll tell you, but you won't like what you hear. It will be the end of you and me, Miss.

It seemed like Kenna changed overnight, but when I look back on it, it was a gradual thing. That first year after Valentine died, she grieved terrible, but she grieved with me. When we saw the snake, it seemed like a turning point, just like Kenna said it was. She got to be so angry and spiteful. She refused to take care of herself. She went crazy, Miss.

I hate to tell you this, Miss, for your mama did some terrible things there at the end, but I'm going to tell you the truth, and the reason is I want you to understand what can happen if you let your *mind go; if you stop fighting. You understand? You hear what I am saying? It's not to convince you that Ferris is lying to you.*

Your mama took to making tinctures at all times of the day and night. I never knew for sure what she was up to, and sometimes her concoctions smelled up the whole house. She hid them here and there in canning jars and what all. Whenever I spotted any, I gathered them up and spilled them out behind the garden, sometimes killing whatever grew there. James and Tom helped too, sometimes bringing me a jar they found in the cellar or even the barn. And Lord help us all when Kenna caught us getting rid of her medicines! She screamed in fury!

It all came to a head, finally. James was up to Navaro with a load of freight. It was late in the summer, and I was working like anything to get the garden put up. Kenna was scarcely any help at all. The only cooking she did was making those damn tinctures. I walked in the kitchen that morning, and there she was, concocting away.

"What are you making, Kenna?" I asked. "Are you making another remedy?"

"Yes," she cackled. "The best remedy yet! It will heal everything!"

I didn't think much of what she said since she had got to be so crazy anyway. I went on about my business, drying corn and pickling our beets. No joy there, though. I was back to hard work with no end in sight.

Really, the next thing I remember is James dragging me out of the house, my head swimming like anything! He practically carried me across the front porch and laid me down next to the babies, who lay in the grass, sleeping like angels. Next, he flung my Tom down next to me. I lifted my head to look at Tom, and even in my sleeping state, I saw the flush of his cheeks and the shallow way he breathed. I cried out for James.

"James! James, what is going on? Where are you? James, help me! Help Tom! Something is terrible wrong with him!"

James staggered down the porch steps, carrying Kenna like a ragdoll. It come to me what she had done; what she had tried to do to all of us, even her beloved babies. I turned on my side and retched into the scraggly grass.

"Get up, Ruby!" James said. "Get up and help me! Help me with the babies!" and he was like to cry.

I drug myself to my hands and knees and crawled to the babies. I shook first one and then the other; they moved not at all. James reappeared with a bucket of water and took to splashing them and Tom in the face. I tried to help, patting their faces and chafing their wrists the way I had seen my mama do once long ago.

"Wake up, Babies! Wake up now! Mama says for you to wake up!" I was near to screaming at them, crawling from them to Tom and back again, stopping to retch when I could no longer keep from it. It was terrible, Miss.

"I'm going to get the doctor. I'll be right back! Keep working on everybody!" James said as he ran to the barn.

I have never been so scared, Miss; not when I thought Frank was going to kill me; not even when the Raiders came to Lawrence; not ever like I was that day. My little ones were everything to me, even if I didn't always know it; even if I gave them away or wished I had less work to do. They were my all.

By the time James and Dr. Brock got there, the babies were soaked in water. It seemed like it helped if I poured it directly on their chests, for a couple times they each drew a big breath when I did that. Their faces were as flushed as Tom's.

First thing Dr. Brock did was stick his fingers down Tom's throat. That set Tom to retching, even though he wasn't completely awake.

"I'm afraid to make the babies throw up," he said. "I'm scared they'll choke."

"Do it right now," said James, his voice deadly calm.

"All right," said Dr. Brock, picking up Minnie and holding her upside down. He made her retch, and then did the same treatment on Elsie. "Hold her upside down," he said to James. Keep her puking down."

I have never been so sick, Miss. We were all sick for days, retching and suffering with terrible gut cramps. My poor babies! How they suffered! But they lived. They kept on living, Miss, thank God.

Dr. Brock had worked on Kenna last of all, but he saved her, too. She suffered along with the rest of us, but she survived. Your mama lived through that terrible time, and had to face what she had done.

Bless his heart, James took care of us. He cooked a venison stew for us, and we all started out by drinking the broth, but in a few days, we were all able to eat some solid food. My Elsie took the longest to recover, and in fact, her constitution was never the same again. It weakened her system, Miss. Poor Elsie!

When I finally got my wits about me and thought about what Kenna had done, I raged like a banshee. How I wanted revenge, Miss! I wanted to kill her myself, and was sorry that Dr. Brock had saved her. When Kenna came around, though, she showed not one shred of remorse. She only felt sad that we had all survived. She told me so, Miss.

"Too bad James came home! Too bad he found us! We could all be together with Valentine right now if he would have minded his own business!"

I didn't bother to answer her, but instead I jumped on her and took to pummeling her like anything. I must have been a sight, for I was wild with anger and hatred. James pulled me off.

"Lord God, Ruby! Stop! Stop!" he yelled at me. "Stop now before you kill her!"

"I want to kill her! I'm going to kill her!" I screamed.

"Well, so do I, but we don't have a good place to hide her body," James said. I looked at him sharp, for there he was, making a joke out of our murderous history, but it helped me settle down.

"We've got to do something with her, James. She'll do it again, first chance she gets. I know it. Who knows where else she has hidden her poisons! We've got to protect the babies and Tom."

"I know. I talked to Dr. Brock about it. He says we can send her to the California State Hospital in Stockton. They will lock her up. We can 'commit her' is how he said it. It's $80 a month, though. That's enough to break us for sure."

"$80! We can't afford that! What on Earth!"

"I know. So, I have an idea, Ruby, but you might think it's crazy. We're going to lock her up in the barn. We can take care of her and keep her away from us, and keep our $80, to boot."

I had never heard James speak so harsh like that, and I

looked at him sharp. I saw myself in him, Miss, for he was hard-edged, just like me.

"Yes, James, we'll lock her in the barn. Carry her tall bed out there today, and a chair and what all. Put it all on the dance floor. Out she goes."

CHAPTER 66

I *don't know where James is. I ran him off a long time ago. When he helped me fix up the house, we were together every day; it got to be too much for me. It seemed like we were fighting over money and the freight company and all, but really, it was just I couldn't stand looking in his eyes and him knowing I killed Jake. He is the one living person who knows what I did; the one person besides you who knows what I am capable of. It made me nervous, even though he was my own son. I ran him off, but good.*

It's not that, Miss. I just don't know what to say to him. Nothing to say—no need to write. He's not really expecting to hear from me. He knows I would never write.

Why is it that you nag me like this? How about you mind your own business and let me mind mine? How about that, Miss?

All right! All right! Only you do the writing and I'll tell you what to say.

Dear Tom,

   ...

CHAPTER 67

Death was different for Kenna. She didn't just slip off into the hereafter the way Valentine done. It was the sarviceberry tea, Miss. She concocted a poison tincture for herself and hid it away from all of us. She took fate into her own hands. She drank that tea, and it killed her. She was locked up tight in the barn, Miss, laying on her filthy bed with her spiders and cobwebs; her dust hanging in the air. I've often wondered if your uncle's ghost came to guide her across to the other side, for that's where he too took his own life, you know.

James and I took turns going out to check on her—to bring her food and water. When you went out there, you never knew what to expect. Sometimes Kenna was very calm and sensible, asking us to take her back in. Other times she sobbed and tore at her hair, begging for sunshine and air, and one time she hid behind the door and jumped on James, trying to strangle him with her bare hands.

We heard her moaning and screaming one morning, crying

out for Valentine, and that's when we knew she had poisoned herself again. It was frightful and painful, Miss, and I had no way to help her; no way to ease her trial, and I didn't send for Dr. Brock. The tea's what done it, Miss.

I truly did get rid of it every time I came across any. I know people here in the Ford think I killed your mama, but I didn't. I let her die though, and that's just as bad, I guess. Kenna made that tea, hid it, and drank it down. Do you believe me, Miss? I understand why you would doubt me. Lord God, I killed plenty myself, so why not your Mama, too?

You're saddled with this curse, this terrible family. Your people are fierce, Miss; untamed and willful. They divided themselves in hatred, and we don't know why. Some of them killed themselves, and your mama tried to kill us all. Well, all right. That's how it is; that's what they did. That doesn't mean you have to. Same with blaming me for Kenna's death. You can spend your life hating me if you want, but you don't have to. You choose how to live. It's up to you, Miss. No history can bind you if you don't let it; no blame can scar you if you say no.

Don't you wonder, Miss, what happens when we die? Don't you want to understand all that is going on, and why we are even here in the first place? Wasn't Valentine meant to be with Kenna? Wasn't he meant to have years with her, but there was a moment that something went wrong? Somehow things got mixed up and he died when he wasn't supposed to, and then they were set off-kilter. Your mama just wanted to join back with him, but she had no way to do it without harming everyone around her. Don't you wonder about that, Miss?

I put your mama up on the hill, next to her husband; locked them away from me forever; swathed her in her tartan, left her clutching her rifle, just like I promised. I wound her braid round her noble brow, told her a pretty poem, built a cairn. She was at rest then.

Sometimes when I remember how Kenna forgave me, my heart stings, Miss, for she did it so easy, and I can't do it no matter how hard I try. No matter if it kills me to hold forgiveness away from myself, or from Kenna either. I've gone and trapped myself. I built myself a prison.

Do you look up at that house, Miss, and wonder if they are there? How on Earth do you stay away? Don't you want to go see if she's there? I can see the house in my mind. I see it late at night with no light coming through the windows. No light or life, only dust laying everywhere and weeds growing in the dooryard, fence falling down, all the lace rotten.

That's what it is, Miss. If I could breathe, I would go up there.

CHAPTER 68

Well, no, I'm not going. I can't go up there. That would kill me for sure. It would break my heart, but you should go. You go see what you see. Go find something from your mama. Get the key from the key hook in the kitchen. Go see what you find, Miss, and then you come back and tell me a story.

Just let this turn out how it's turning out. You've done enough saving, Miss. You've done what you came here to do.

I don't care if you do have a motor carriage ready to go. I'm not going. You understand me, Miss? I said no.

EPILOGUE

Dateline: Humboldt Courier; October, 2019

Human Remains Discovered

Excavation at the Sonoma Heights Housing Subdivision worksite was temporarily halted Tuesday when workers discovered human remains while digging waterline trenches. An alert backhoe operator spotted what appeared to be human bones, bits of clothing, and an old rifle barrel. Work was halted and law enforcement responded to the scene. The remains have been transferred to Carson City for forensic study.

Humboldt County Sheriff, Heath Ferris, stated that he does not expect Carson City to come back with evidence of foul play. "I think those bodies have been there a long time. What was left of the recovered firearm appeared to be very old, I'd say over a hundred years. We also recovered what looks like rotten pine boards, so I'd say whoever it was, was buried in a pine box." Ferris also said that woolen plaid fabric was collected at the scene. All the artifacts were sent to Carson City along with the remains.

Ferris added, "Once the people in Carson finish with the investigation, the remains will most likely be returned here to Winnemucca and interred in Pioneer Cemetery, down by the old Ford. I doubt we will be able to identify the individuals."

Representatives of Grady Construction reported that work will resume today. The work stoppage is not expected to impact the subdivision building plan and timeline.

ACKNOWLEDGEMENTS:

I would like to take this opportunity to thank the people who helped me write Crossing the Ford.

First of all, to my husband, Bill, who listened to this story for ten years before I had written one word.

To my dear sisters, Sharon and Devona, who showed me what it is to be a strong woman. They spent countless hours helping with research, plot lines, and editing, not to mention defending Ruby.

To my children, Andrea and Kelly, who showed me how to be a mother.

To my father and mother, Paul and Rosemary Hertzog, who gave me words and voice and lessons on how to kill a rattler.

To my brother, Brian, who painted The Green Lady.

To my grandmother, Minnie Hertzog, who showed me the wonder of looking into the past.

To my brother, Gary, who said, "Too many pickles."

To my great, great-grandfather, Valentine Hulse, who haunts

my little house.

To Jacelyn Rye, my publishing manager and writing consultant extraordinaire.

To Debbie Briggs Cook, my lifelong friend. The tie between us abides.

To Pam and Bruce Braginton, my gallant and spirited friends, who listened and said, "Keep going."

To Ann Wolicki, my dear friend.

To Kris Mace, my guardian angel, who fought and did not lose.

To Rae Edwards, my writing partner and teacher, who said, "I need to know the exact cuss words."

To Jerry Hirsch, my photographer.

To Teddy Swecker, my illustrator.

To AnnElise Hatjakes, my editor, who liked Ruby right off.

To Vicky Shea at Ponderosa Pine Design, who made my vision a reality.

To Brad Borowski at Anchor Soul Design Co, my website and logo designer.

To Lorie DeWorken at Mind the Margins, ebook conversion.

BIBLIOGRAPHY

Poems:

Byron, George Gordon, Baron. Stanzas to Augusta. 1816.

Dickinson, Emily. If You were Coming in the Fall. 1890.

Black is the Colour. Traditional.

The Way that You Set Face and Foot. Author unknown.

References:

Barton, O. S. Three Years with Quantrell, A True Story Told by His Scout, John McCorkle. 1998. First published in 1914. Armstrong Herald Print. Armstrong, Missouri.

Copeland, Peter F. Civil War Uniforms Coloring Book. 1977. Dover Publications, Inc. New York.

Luchetti, Cathy. Home on the Range: A Culinary History of the American West. 1993. Villard Books. New York

McCutcheon, Marc. Everyday Life in the 1800's, A Guide for Writers, Students, and Historians. Writer's Digest Books, 1993. Cincinnati.

Newcomb, Lawrence. Newcomb's Wildflower Guide. 1977. Little Brown and Company. New York.

Roberts, Les. Recipes of the West. 1984. Sun-Shine Distributing. Vernal, Utah.

Sams, Jamie; Carson, David. Medicine Cards. 1999. St Martin's Press. New York.

Springmeyer, Fritz. Willow Bark and Rosehips: An Introduction to Common Edible and Useful Plants of North America. 1996. Falcon Press. Billings and Helena, Montana.

Stratton, Joanna. Pioneer Women: Voices from the Kansas Frontier. 1981. Simon and Schuster, New York.

Swell, Barbara. Log Cabin Cooking: Pioneer Recipes and Food Lore. 1996. Native Ground Music, Inc. Ashville, North Carolina.

Tierney, Tom. Victorian Fashions. 1997. Dover Publications, Inc. New York.

Periodicals:

Bengoa Ratliff. Early-Day Transportation. The Humboldt Historian. 1980. North Central Nevada Historical Society. Winnemucca, Nevada.

Silver Pinyon Journal. October 30, 2012, October 27, 2012. Holzel, Dee.

Websites:

Alter, Alexandra. (July 19, 2014) "How to Undress a Victorian Lady in Your Next Historical Romance". Retrieved January 26, 2014 from online.wsj.com/.../SB100014240527023049 1110457644387161554438.

Pennington, William. (1998) "Roster of Quantrill's, Anderson's, and Todd's Guerrillas and Other 'Missouri Jewels'". Retrieved on January 26, 2014 from www. penningtons.tripod.com/roster.htm

Tattersall, Kate. "Women's Underwear." Retrieved on January 26, 2014 from www.katetattersall.com/?p-1842

Made in the USA
Las Vegas, NV
24 November 2021

35184205R00247